STUDIES

IN

THE HISTORY OF MUSIC

2

STUDIES IN THE HISTORY OF MUSIC

Volume 2

MUSIC AND DRAMA

1988

BROUDE BROTHERS LIMITED

NEW YORK

ISBN 0-8450-7402-4
© Copyright 1988 by Broude Brothers Limited
International copyright secured. All rights reserved.

Publisher's Preface

In this, the second volume of *Studies in the History of Music*, we have gathered ten essays that deal with some of the relationships between music and drama. We have looked especially for contributions that show how composers have tried to express by musical means such elements of drama as language, character, and action, but the papers presented here show also how composers of dramatic music have responded to such considerations as politics, philosophy, music theory, and what, for want of a better term, we may tactfully call the exigencies of the opera house.

In selecting papers for *SHM 2*, we have sought a balance of period and nationality. The papers offered here present the music of England, France, Italy, Russia, and the Austro-Hungarian Empire; they deal with music from the seventeenth to the twentieth centuries, and with genres as diverse as the *tragédie lyrique* and the comic opera. We would have liked to be able to include papers about music and drama in the Middle Ages and about Humanist "pre-opera," but no papers on these topics were offered us. Among the submissions we did receive, Purcell and Mozart were especially popular subjects; we are printing two papers on each (indeed, we are printing two essays dealing with Purcell's *Dido and Aeneas*), and we read others that we could have printed had we been willing to devote this volume almost entirely to these two composers.

As we did for *SHM 1*, we have looked for contributions that are rhetorically sound—i.e., that deal intelligently with realistically defined subjects, that present and develop their arguments logically and convincingly, and that convey their authors' ideas with precision and clarity. We have followed this policy because we recognize that a published paper, merely by virtue of its having been accepted for publication, acquires a certain influence. Both impressionable young scholars and their more established colleagues derive not only their habits of thought but even their turns of phrase from the published papers they read. Equally important, they form from the work they see in print the standards of quality that will guide them in conducting and refining the research that they themselves will submit for publication. Accordingly, we have asked our contributors to give us papers that can stand as models of their kind, and in some cases this has involved extensive rewriting. In today's "writer's market," where journals compete with each other for essays to fill their pages, rewriting is often regarded as something above and beyond the call of duty. Writers who care about thinking their ideas through and polishing their prose are all too rare; they deserve both our respect and our thanks.

The second volume of *SHM* has taken us rather longer to produce than we—or our contributors—expected. For this we must apologize both to our contributors and to our readers who have, with more or less patience, awaited its publication. We hope that the next two numbers of *SHM* will move somewhat more quickly; *SHM* 3 will deal with the compositional process, and *SHM* 4 with problems of editorial methodology.

Contents

Opera and Neoclassical Dramatic Criticism in the Seventeenth Century*

Piero Weiss

> "I hope you have preserved the unities, sir?" said Mr. Curdle.
> "The original piece is a French one," said Nicholas. "There is abundance of incident, sprightly dialogue, strongly-marked characters—"
> "—All unavailing without a strict observance of the unities, sir," returned Mr. Curdle. "The unities of the drama, before everything."
>
> Dickens, *Nicholas Nickleby*, ch. 24

I

We all know that modern European drama grew up under the scowling, disapproving eye of a Higher Criticism that based itself confidently on what it took to be the rules laid down by Aristotle in the *Poetics* and, to a lesser degree, by Horace in the *Art of Poetry*. To what extent that criticism actually helped to shape European drama is virtually impossible to determine. It is fairly obvious, at any rate, that Spanish drama of the Golden Age and English Elizabethan drama flourished unimpeded by the prescriptive dramatic theories that were even then being imported from Italy and promulgated by Spanish and English writers. In France, on the other hand, those theories acquired quite a different importance; and although Corneille and Racine, each in his way, rebelled against the excessive tyranny of the theorists, their tragedies today stand as monuments of the neoclassical ideal, and their differences with the theorists seem like disagreements among votaries of the same sect. Obviously, the authority of the ancients had found a favorable climate in the France of Richelieu and, later, Louis XIV. Yet this "doctrine classique" was so utterly different from and foreign to Aristotle's thought that one could say the

*This article is a much altered and expanded version of a paper entitled "The Rules of Tragedy, the Vagaries of Opera: A Chapter in Baroque Aesthetics," which I read at the annual meeting of the American Musicological Society, New York, November 1979. Originally conceived as a broad introduction to the topic, that paper (and this article) provided a starting point for the more particular investigations mentioned in notes 48, 70, 74, and 75 below.

French refashioned Aristotle in their own image and would have invented him, had he never lived. One thing is certain: their need for "rules." And Boileau, the great friend of Racine, fulfilled that need by embedding them in faultless Alexandrines:

> Qu'en un lieu, qu'en un jour, un seul fait accompli
> Tienne jusqu'à la fin le théâtre rempli.[1]

Thus, the three "unities." But, the ancients knew nothing of the "unities." It follows, then, that the ancients, and more particularly Aristotle's *Poetics*, served as a more or less vague pretext for the erection of artistic standards which, in fact, reflected contemporary ideals and tastes.

Opera, too, came under the scrutiny of neoclassical criticism, and the impact of the latter on the former (which is the subject of this paper) was considerable. To begin our investigation, it will be well to retrace our steps to sixteenth-century Italy, where both originated.

Aristotle's *Poetics* became available to the West for the first time in 1498, in a Latin version printed at Venice. The first Greek edition appeared, also at Venice, ten years later; it was based on an inferior copy of the oldest extant codex, and it remained the basis for all subsequent editions and commentaries until the second half of the nineteenth century.[2] Even among the works of Aristotle, which are not notable for their stylistic limpidity, the *Poetics* represents one of the thorniest texts to reconstruct plausibly and to interpret convincingly. As one modern commentator has wittily put it, "Editors have made the discovery that, if much of the book is left out, the rest becomes easier to explain."[3] And yet it is fair to say that no other classical text, certainly no other of comparable brevity,[4] has provoked such extensive commentaries, polemics, and popular misconceptions. That this should be so is not surprising: Aristotle's *Poetics*, though ostensibly an investigation into the essence and techniques of all poetry, is in fact mainly concerned (at least to the extent that the work has come down to us) with tragedy; and modern drama was just then burgeoning, first in Italy, then in the other lands of Western Europe. Even without its astounding intuitions, which today still strike one as shafts of light penetrating the darkness, the *Poetics* would have enjoyed the greatest prestige, as a work of "il maestro di color che sanno." Small wonder,

---

[1] *L'Art poétique*, in Nicolas Boileau-Despréaux, *Œuvres complètes* (Paris, [1969]), vol. 2: chant III, ll.45–46. These, and the verses quoted at the end, must remain untranslated. All the prose translations in this article (except one: see n. 47) are my own.

[2] The oldest extant codex is Parisinus 1741, of the tenth or eleventh century. The Aldine *editio princeps* was apparently based on Par. 2038 or on an allied manuscript. For a convenient discussion of the transmission of the text of the *Poetics*, see W. D. Lucas' introduction to his edition of the *Poetics* (Oxford, 1968), pp. xxii–xxv. Subsequent citations for the *Poetics* are to this edition.

[3] Lucas, p. ix.

[4] In the cod. Par. 1741, it occupies fols. 184–99; it consists of about 10,600 words.

then, that the text was not only scrutinized and interpreted, down to the minutest Greek particle, by Robortello, Segni, Maggi, Vettori, Scaliger, Minturno, Castelvetro, and other Italian scholars of the sixteenth century; but that it was, almost unawares, turned into a legislative code of the theater, a source of "rules" to be invoked, interpreted, and reinterpreted endlessly in connection with all the varied manifestations of modern drama:

> How many laws were made by Aristotle concerning the qualitative and quantitative parts of tragedy? How many on the constitution and unity of the fable? How many on manners, on thought, on diction, on spectacle? How many on the prologue, the episode, the exode, the chorus, the dirge? How many on the unraveling, the peripety, the agnition, all of which demand to be obeyed and carried out by anyone wishing to make a sound and perfectly wrought tragedy. . . ?[5]

And so, before the French, the Italians had already turned Aristotle into a theatrical legislator, as we can see from the above passage, taken from an opinionated little pamphlet by a Jesuit client of the Barberinis in Rome. By the end of the Cinquecento all the main themes of neoclassical criticism had been cast up, debated, and made current. A theory of genres had become solidified, indeed rigid. And in this connection some important writers, for instance Guarini, were already refusing to submit to the unquestioned authority of the ancients, anticipating the French *querelle des anciens et des modernes* by a century.

In such vigilant critical surroundings, it is not surprising that the inventors of opera should have been careful to remind a wider public that their experiment was prompted by a desire to revive a neglected aspect of classical drama, its music. Wrote Peri:

> It pleased Messrs. Jacopo Corsi and Ottavio Rinuccini (as early as 1594) that I . . . should set to music the fable of Daphne composed by the said Signor Ottavio, in order to make a simple trial of what the singing of our age could accomplish. And so, seeing that it was a question of dramatic poetry, and that therefore it was necessary by means of song to imitate speech (and there is no doubt that no one ever spoke singing), I judged that the ancient Greeks and Romans (who, in the opinion of many, sang the tragedies in their entirety upon the stage) used a harmony which, transcending that of ordinary speech, was yet somewhat below the melody of song and took an intermediate form. And this is why we see the iambic occur in those poems, for it does not rise to the heights of the hexameter,

---

[5]Tarquinio Galluzzi, *Rinovazione dell'antica tragedia e difesa del Crispo* (Rome, 1633), p. 58: "Quante leggi Aristotele ha fatte intorno alle qualitative, e quantitative parti della Tragedia? quante della costitutione, e dell'unità della favola? quante del costume, della sentenza, dell'elocuzione, dell'apparato? quante del Prologo, dell'Episodio, dell'Esodo, del Choro, del Commo? quante dello scioglimento, della Peripetia, dell'Agnizione, che tutte vogliono esser ubbidite, & eseguite da chi vorrà fare buona, e perfetta fabrica di Tragedia . . . ?"

though it is said to go beyond the limits of familiar discourse. Whence, abandoning all other manners of singing heard till then, I gave myself over wholly to searching for the imitation which these poems require.[6]

To anyone conversant with the dramatic theory of those times, these opening sentences in Peri's declaration conveyed a great deal more than would appear on the surface. Let us try a line-by-line commentary in the style of the Renaissance "spositori" of classical texts; for this is, in its way, a classical text, opening as it does a new era in the history of music and of the theater. "*The fable of Daphne, composed by* [etc.]": "fable" (Lat. "fabula") was the standard equivalent of Aristotle's μῦθος, "plot" or "story"; and how stories should be "put together" if the poetry is to be good is one of the topics announced at the very opening of the *Poetics* (1447ª9–10) and fully discussed later. Signor Ottavio, then, put together the story of Daphne: he *composed* it (he did not, of course, *invent* it). "*What the singing of our age could accomplish*": an obvious allusion (even more in the Italian: "di quello, che *potesse* il canto") to the much-vaunted *powers* of the music of the ancients: almost a challenge, though not as brash as that uttered by Rinuccini's Tragedy in the Prologue of *L'Euridice*, three pages later on, in the score itself. "*Seeing that it was a question of Dramatic poetry*": i.e., not epic, not lyric. Since the habit of the age was to think in terms of genres, the present case was obviously within the jurisdiction of Aristotle's *Poetics*. "*By means of song to imitate speech*": here "song" has taken the place of "verse." "By means of song to imitate speech," with its automatic espousal of the traditional classical theory of art as imitation, has an aura of respectability about it, yet it is totally unconventional; whereas "by means of *verse* to imitate speech" would have pointed to Aristotle's (and Horace's—cf. the *Ars poetica*, ll. 80–82) characterization of iambic trimeter as the meter best suited for the dialogue in drama. Aristotle's remark was famous. After outlining the early history of tragedy (its choral beginnings, Aeschylus' introduction of a second actor and greater attention to the spoken parts, etc.), he writes:

> When dialogue came in, nature herself discovered the suitable meter: for the most speech-like of the meters is the iambic: and the proof of this is, that we most frequently speak in iambics when we converse with one

---

[6]Jacopo Peri, *Le musiche Sopra L'Euridice del Sig. Ottavio Rinuccini* (Florence, 1600), "A' lettori": "Piacque . . . a' Signori Iacopo Corsi, ed Ottavio Rinuccini (fin l'Anno 1594) che io . . . mettessi sotto le note la favola di Dafne, dal Signor Ottavio composta, per fare una semplice pruova di quello, che potesse il canto dell'età nostra. Onde veduto, che si trattava di poesia Dramatica, e che però si doveva imitar col canto chi parla (e senza dubbio non si parlò mai cantando) stimai, che gli antichi Greci, e Romani (i quali secondo l'opinione di molti cantavano su le Scene le Tragedie intere) usassero un'armonia, che avanzando quella del parlare ordinario, scendesse tanto dalla melodia del cantare, che pigliasse forma di cosa mezzana; E questa è la ragione, onde veggiamo in quelle Poesie, haver' havuto luogo il Iambo, che non s'innalza, come l'Esametro, ma pure è detto avanzarsi oltr'a confini de' ragionamenti familiari. E per ciò tralasciata qualunque altra maniera di canto udita fin quì, mi diedi tutto a ricercare l'imitazione, che si debbe a questi Poemi."

another, but rarely (and then only when we abandon the harmonies of speech) in hexameters.[7]

Immediately we recognize the source of Peri's later reference to iambic and hexameter; but more on that presently. *"There is no doubt that no one ever spoke singing"*: here Peri has hit upon the great objection that will be raised against opera again and again in the years to come.

But the same objection had already been moved against verse itself, when used in dramatic dialogue, and on the same grounds. That year, for example, there appeared a tract devoted entirely to the subject: poets who make their characters speak in verse, wrote Paolo Beni,

> do not follow Nature as their guide: they do not uphold decorum and verisimilitude: but they forsake Nature: they disturb decorum and veri- similitude. On the other hand, those who entrust the fable to unbound speech not only escape these perils but preserve and uphold the decorum and dignity of the poem most worthily.[8]

"Decorum" and "verisimilitude": two terms to conjure with. The first corre- sponds to τὸ ἁρμόττον in ch. 15 of the *Poetics*, to τὸ πρέπον in the *Rhetoric*, bk. 3, ch. 7: it refers to the appropriateness of a speech to the character uttering it. Horace devotes several notable passages to it in his *Art of Poetry* too (e.g., ll. 156 ff.). As for "verisimilitude," Aristotle's τὸ εἰκός, it was now (about 1600) beginning to float away from its original context in the *Poetics*, where, mostly paired with τὸ ἀναγκαῖον in the phrase "according to likeli- hood or necessity" (κατὰ τὸ εἰκὸς ἢ τὸ ἀναγκαῖον), it was applied to the persuasive development of plot and character. Now, instead, it was being equated with a peculiarly rational sort of realism, and as such was soon to become the very foundation of the French "doctrine classique."[9] Beni's poets,

---

[7] 1449[a]23–28: *"λέξεως δὲ γενομένης αὐτὴ ἡ φύσις τὸ οἰκεῖον μέτρον εὗρε· μάλιστα γὰρ λεκτικὸν τῶν μέτρων τὸ ἰαμβεῖόν ἐστιν· σημεῖον δὲ τούτου, πλεῖστα γὰρ ἰαμβεῖα λέγομεν ἐν τῇ διαλέκτῳ τῇ πρὸς ἀλλήλους, ἑξάμετρα δὲ ὀλιγάκις καὶ ἐκβαίνοντες τῆς λεκτικῆς ἁρμονίας."*

[8] Paolo Beni, *Disputatio in qua ostenditur praestare comoediam atque tragoediam metrorum vinculis solvere* . . . (Padua, 1600), fol. 2[v]: "Ut . . . non Naturam Ducem sequantur isti: non decorum ac verisimile tueantur: sed a Natura discedant: decorum perturbent ac verisimile. Contra verò qui solutae orationi commendant fabulam, scopulos istos non evadant modò, sed Poematis decorum ac dignitatem magna cum laude custodiant ac tueantur." On this passage, see Bernard Weinberg, *A History of Literary Criticism in the Italian Renaissance* (Chicago, 1961), vol. 2, p. 707.

[9] On decorum, see the comments on *Poetics* 1454[a]22 in Alfred Gudeman, ed., *Aristoteles, Περὶ ποιητικῆς* (Berlin, 1934), pp. 271–72, where there is a convenient summary of literature on the subject. Verisimilitude, despite its central importance in neoclassical criticism, has not, to my knowledge, been treated thoroughly, in isolation from the other technical terms; but see René Bray, *La Formation de la doctrine classique en France* (Paris, 1927), pp. 191–214, as well as my own discussion below, pp. 20–23. References to technical terms are scattered throughout the two volumes of Weinberg's *History of Literary Criticism*, the index of which, however, is of little help in finding those that matter. Convenient treatments of the terms, not confined to the early modern period, may be found in the *Princeton Encyclopedia of Poetry and Poetics*, ed. Alex Preminger (Princeton, 1974).

who insisted on putting verses in their characters' mouths, were clearly flying in the face of decorum and verisimilitude. Jacopo Peri, with his *singing* characters, could expect very little mercy from such critics.

"The ancient Greeks and Romans . . . , in the opinion of many, sang the Tragedies in their entirety upon the Stage": compare the opening words of Rinuccini's dedication of *L'Euridice* to Maria de' Medici:

> It has been the opinion of many, Most Christian Queen, that the ancient Greeks and Romans sang the tragedies in their entirety upon the stage; but that noble manner of reciting, far from being revived, had not even, to my knowledge, been attempted before now, owing, as I thought, to the deficiency of modern music, vastly inferior to that of the ancients. . . .[10]

The first, obvious question must be, "Who were the 'many' who held that opinion?" The answer is, "Few."[11] It was necessary, first, to overlook two very clear indications to the contrary in Aristotle's *Poetics*. The first we have already seen: it dealt with the advent of dialogue in tragedy, and with nature's own discovery of the "speech-like" (*not* song-like) iambics for the purpose. In this connection it is peculiarly significant to read what Pietro Vettori had to say about the passage, since he and his pupil Girolamo Mei (who helped him edit the *Poetics*) were extremely influential with the Camerata.[12] He explains Aristotle's use of "harmonies" ("when we abandon the harmonies of speech") as follows:

> ἁρμονίας in my opinion does not mean song, in this passage: for we do not sing in conversations and in ordinary speech: however, since all speech has a certain mode of voice and a sound, which mode can be varied: and the voice, indeed, is raised and lowered again; so he says it may happen that we fall into hexameter verses, when we move out of that mode of speaking which is suitable to everyday conversation: and we make use of a grander sound: then, indeed, that elevated speech brings with it its meter and forces us inadvertently and involuntarily to emit these verses in speaking.[13]

---

[10]Ottavio Rinuccini, *L'Euridice* (Florence, 1600), p. 1: "È stata opinione di molti, Christianiss. Regina, che gl'antichi Greci, e Romani cantassero su le scene le tragedie intere, ma sì nobil maniera di recitare non che rinnovata, ma ne pur che io sappia fin quì era stata tentata da alcuno, & ciò mi credev'io per difetto della musica moderna di gran lunga all'antica inferiore . . . ."

[11]See Barbara R. Hanning, "Apologia pro Ottavio Rinuccini," *Journal of the American Musicological Society* 26 (1973): 249–52.

[12]Girolami Mei, *Letters on Ancient and Modern Music to Vincenzo Galilei and Giovanni Bardi*, ed. Claude V. Palisca (n.p., 1960), pp. 44 ff. See also Palisca's "The Alterati of Florence, Pioneers in the Theory of Dramatic Music," in *New Looks at Italian Opera: Essays in Honor of Donald J. Grout*, ed. William W. Austin (Ithaca, N.Y., 1968), pp. 9–38.

[13]Pietro Vettori, *Commentarii in primum librum Aristotelis de Arte Poetarum . . .* (Florence, 1560), p. 46: "ἁρμονίας hoc loco non arbitror cantum significare: neque enim in colloquiis, sermonibusque

In the other passage, Aristotle was even more explicit—so explicit, in fact, that it became a stumbling block to many who might otherwise have been inclined to think that tragedies were sung throughout (the Stumbling Block, I shall henceforth call it). In expounding the meaning of his famous definition of tragedy in ch. 6 ("imitation of a weighty and complete action, having a certain magnitude, in tasteful language used differently in each of its parts"), Aristotle specified:

> Now by "tasteful language" I mean, that which has rhythm and harmony, i. e. *melos*, and by "differently in its parts" [I mean] that some are done through meters only, others again through *melos*.[14]

Once more, let us read Vettori's interpretation:

> And so he declares this to have the following meaning in his definition, and himself to have alleged it for the following reason: that certain parts of the tragedy are prepared and completed with meters only and with the addition of no further embellishment that might lend delight and sweetness to it: then again, that other parts are made only with song, which here he calls μέλος: while above, as I opine, he calls it ἁρμονίαν.[15]

On the other hand, this did *not* mean, as a great many people then and later thought, that the music of Greek tragedies was limited to the songs of the chorus. Even without leaving the *Poetics* one could find evidence for singing on the stage (the chorus, of course, operated below, in the orchestra—hence Peri's and Rinuccini's insistence that ancient tragedy was sung "upon the stage"): in ch. 12, after listing those sections that were to be found in all tragedies, Aristotle mentioned, as only occasionally found, τὰ ἀπὸ τῆς σκηνῆς, "[songs] from the stage," and κομμοί, *kommoi*, the latter defined as dirges shared by the chorus and the stage, i. e., the actors (1452[b]18, 24–25). Apart from this rather fugitive reference in the *Poetics*, which attracted no special notice at the time, there were two more in the musical portion

---

familiaribus canimus: sed tamen, quia modum quendam vocis, sonumque sermo omnis habet, qui modus variari potest: & intenditur enim vox & remittitur, tunc inquit accidere posse ut in hexametros versus incidamus, cum egredimur modum illum orationis, qui est aptus cotidianae locutioni: grandioreque sono utimur: tunc enim magniloquentia illa secum trahit numerum eum, cogitque nos imprudentes & invitos, in dicendo versus hos edere."

[14]1449[b]28–31: *"λέγω δὲ ἡδυσμένον μέν λόγον τὸν ἔχοντα ῥυθμὸν καὶ ἁρμονίαν καὶ μέλος, τὸ δὲ χωρὶς τοῖς εἴδεσι τὸ διὰ μέτρων ἔνια μόνον περαίνεσθαι καὶ πάλιν ἕτερα διὰ μέλους."* Editors from Vettori to this day have had some difficulty over *"ἁρμονίαν καὶ μέλος"*; Gudeman's interpretation, "harmony, i.e., *melos*," seems preferable to altering the text, which is unmistakably the same in the codices. *Melos* implies texted melody.

[15]Vettori, p. 57: "Declarat igitur id in definitione hanc vim habere: seque hac de causa id posuisse, quod partes quaedam tragoediae conficiuntur, absolvunturque tantum metris: nullo alio condimento, quod leporem ac suavitatem eo importet, adhibito: rursusque aliae partes conficuntur tantum concentu, quem concentum hic vocat μέλος: cum supra, ut opinor, ἁρμονίαν, illum vocarit."

(Book 19) of the *Problems*: nos. 30 and 48.[16] They speak of modes best suited to "those on the stage," and they received due attention.[17] Indeed, no. 48 was cited as prime evidence (which it is not) for the *continuous* singing of the actors upon the stage by Francesco Patrizi, who was close to the Camerata, and by Vincenzo Galilei.[18] Both found themselves confronted with the Stumbling Block. But Patrizi concluded that singing must have been continuous in the primitive days and that the actors spoke their lines only at a later period in history. Galilei merely observed that Aristotle, in the *Poetics*, seemed to differ from his earlier opinion in certain particulars; and he let it go at that.[19] *"And this is why we see the iambic occur in those poems,* [etc.]": if *everything* was sung, including the dialogue, then the iambic, "the most speech-like of the meters," must have been sung in a manner "intermediate" between actual conversation and song. And so the recitative was born.[20]

If Peri tackled questions of decorum and verisimilitude, Rinuccini meanwhile addressed himself to the sacrosanct unities. I have already quoted the opening sentence in his dedication of *L'Euridice*; here is the closing one, just before the salutation: "I have followed the authority of Sophocles in the *Ajax* in varying the scene, for otherwise Orpheus' prayers and lamentations could not have been shown."[21] He is, of course, apologizing for violating the unity of place—of the three unities, the one Aristotle never dreamt of.[22]

[16]That the authenticity of both ch. 12 of the *Poetics* and the whole of the *Problems* has been questioned in modern times has obviously nothing to do with their reception in the Renaissance, nor, ultimately, with their usefulness as historical documents. As for the modern historical view on the question, it is very satisfactorily summed up in A. E. Haigh, *The Attic Theatre* (3rd ed., rev. A. W. Pickard-Cambridge; Oxford, 1907), pp. 266–71. Recent literature is cited in Annemarie Jeannette Neubecker, *Altgriechische Musik: eine Einführung* (Darmstadt, 1977), passim. Cf. also W. Beare, *The Roman Stage . . .* (3rd ed., rev.; London, 1964), pp. 219–32. For a recent edition of the *Problems*, see the Loeb edition, edited by W. S. Hett (London, 1936–37).

[17]E.g., from Antonio Sebastiano Minturno, who paraphrased no. 48 in his *De poeta* (Venice, 1559), p. 250.

[18]Francesco Patrizi, *Della poetica: la deca istoriale* (Ferrara, 1586), ed. D. A. Barbagli (Florence, 1969), pp. 328–37; Vincenzo Galilei, *Dialogo della musica antica et della moderna* (Florence, 1581), p. 145.

[19]"Vero è che nella Poetica, quando viene alla diffinitione della Tragedia, pare che egli scordi [i.e., discordi] in alcuna cosa da quel primo parere" (p. 145).

[20]It would, at best, be flippant to suggest there were not other, more profound influences at work. Claude Palisca has been kind enough to communicate to me a paper entitled "Peri and the Theory of Recitative," which he read at a meeting of the New England chapter of the American Musicological Society on 9 February 1980; there he analyzes much of the remainder of Peri's preface, entering into details which, though beyond the scope of the present study, must be considered central to a complete understanding of the origin of recitative.

[21]Rinuccini, p. 3: "Ho seguito l'autorità di Sofocle in L'Aiace in far rivolger la scena non potendosi rappresentar altrimenti le preghiere, & i lamenti d'Orfeo."

[22]I resist the temptation to discuss the origins, and the theory, of the unities—"the Fatal Three, the Weird Sisters of dramatic criticism," in the words of George Saintsbury—and refer the reader to that author's *A History of Criticism . . .* , 3 vols., 2 (Edinburgh, 1902; 7th impression, 1961]): 83–84; or better

Thus, carefully protecting themselves from anticipated attacks, did the fathers of opera introduce what they hoped would be taken as, yes, an innovation, but one based on the study of classical models and faithful to the precepts of neoclassical criticism.

II

In the course of the seventeenth century, the neoclassical precepts tumbled like the walls of Jericho before the onslaught of opera. This is not the place to investigate the causes of that development. Spanish influence (accentuated by the Spanish presence in Italy) must have contributed a great deal to it. Less tangible influences—the currents that went to make up marinism[23] and *secentismo* generally—were obviously at work here also. All these were accelerated immensely by the establishment of commercial opera in Venice in 1637.

The attitudes of the poets (it will help a great deal not to fall into the anachronism of calling them "librettists") towards the neoclassical ideals present a curious spectacle: at times, especially in the earlier years, their prefaces read as if the precepts were still safe—only a slight liberty taken here and there. Soon, however, the disaster is too evident to be glossed over; and then it is each man for himself—one will adopt a scornful attitude towards his métier and the tastes of his public, another will make fun of the "rules." One thing is certain: the "rules," though violated in every imaginable respect, are never forgotten. They function as a conscience; and even the hardened criminal has a conscience, though he may never act on it. Let us inspect some cases, drawn from the years 1639–62.

Giulio Strozzi, in the preface to his "poema dramatico" *La Delia O Sia La Sera sposa del Sole* (music by Manelli; Venice, 1639), exemplifies the earlier attitude: a few liberties have been taken. He writes:

> I have divided the work rather methodically into three acts. A division common to all things: beginning, middle, and end. The ancients made five in theirs, because they interspersed them with singing [i.e., choruses]. This work, being wholly sung, has no need of so many courses.

> I have introduced here the hilarode of the Greeks in the person of the cheerful Hermaphroditus, a novel character, who, between the severity of the tragic and the facetiousness of the comic, stands out to advantage upon our stage.

---

yet, to J. E. Spingarn, *A History of Literary Criticism in the Renaissance* (2nd ed.; New York, 1908), pp. 89–101.

[23]On marinism, see Fernando Salsano and Tomas Guadiosi, *Marino e marinismo* (Rome, 1977).

I have taken a few hours' license: I know not whether Aristotle or Aristarchus will let me have them. If I have erred in naught else, so much the better for me. . . .[24]

The three-act division had come to Venice from Rome, where it was common.[25] Five was the statutory number of acts according to neoclassical theory, which made Greek drama conform to the Horatian rule with Procrustean methods. And five acts as against three became as it were a matter of pedigree by the end of the century, a signal that the poet subscribed to neoclassical dogma. Departure from "the severity of the tragic" and "facetiousness of the comic" is symbolized by a white-clad hilarode, who might also stand for a loosening of the rigid theory of genres; and indeed, so might Strozzi's subtitle, "Poema Dramatico." Finally, there is noted a mild infraction of the unity of time: a few hours more than Aristotle's famous, and baffling, "one revolution of the sun" (1449^b13).

Two years later, dedicating his "drama" La Finta Pazza (the music was by Sacrati) to a nobleman, Strozzi expresses fears that he himself might be afflicted not by feigned but by true madness "for submitting so willingly to the rigorous examination of the theaters, and of the printing press, not considering that nowadays 'tis the author that deserves to be bound, more than the book." He then informs the reader:

This is my eighth theatrical labor; five of which have already trod the stage several times, and in this one I have most happily succeeded in unraveling more than one knot without magic, and without resorting to supernatural or divine intervention.[26]

[24]Pp. 6–7: "Ho partita con qualche metodo l'opera in tre azzioni. Division comune di tutte le cose: principio, mezzo, e fine. Gli antichi ne formavano cinque, perchè vi frammettevano il canto. Questa ch'è tutta canto, non hà dibisogno di tante posate.

"Hò introdotto qui l'Hilaredo de' Greci, e questi sarà il giocoso Ermafrodito, personaggio nuovo che tra la severità del Tragico, e la facetia del Comico campeggia molto bene sù le nostre Scene.

"D'un paio d'hore mi son preso licenza: Non sò s'Aristotele, ò Aristarco me le farà buone. Quando non havessi errato in altro buon per mè. . . . "

The hilarode, described in one source as a "singer of wanton, delicate songs," wore a white garment and a crown of gold, and was accompanied by a player on a string instrument (cf. Pauly-Wissowa, Real-Encyclopädie der classischen Altertumswissenschaft [Stuttgart, 1894–1963], s.v. Σιμφδοί). Aristarchus was the Alexandrian grammarian and critic of the second century B.C. For the Venetian poet Strozzi (1583–1660), see Ellen Rosand, "Barbara Strozzi, virtuosissima cantatrice: The Composer's Voice," Journal of the American Musicological Society 31 (1978): 243 ff., and the entry in The New Grove.

[25]Cavalieri, in the preface to the Rappresentatione di anima, et di corpo (Rome, 1600), had already observed that "experience" taught that three were enough. What experience? Either the Rappresentatione itself or, as I believe, other dramatic presentations, possibly Spanish. (For the Cavalieri, cf. A. Solerti, Le origini del melodramma [Turin, 1903], p. 7.) Strozzi's threefold division, incidentally (beginning, middle, end), is an authentic Aristotelian precept found in the Poetics ($1450^b26–27$), though the neoclassical interpreters did not choose to apply it to acts.

[26]Strozzi, La finta pazza (Venice, 1641), pp. 3–4, 5: "Dono à V.S. Illustrissima la mia Finta Pazza, ma

Here Strozzi is congratulating himself for having followed the advice given by Aristotle in ch. 15 of the *Poetics*:

> Now it is clear that the unraveling of the fables must emerge from the fable itself, and not as in the *Medea*, from the machine [i.e., by divine intervention] or in the *Iliad* the story concerning the sailing home.[27]

Since the *Iliad* is an epic, commentators are in agreement that the "machine" frowned on by Aristotle in this passage stands metaphorically for divine intervention. Woe to Italian opera if it had been deprived of its *real* machines!

Niccolò Enea Bartolini, the author of a *Venere gelosa* set to music by Sacrati in 1643, displays in his preface an eccentric compulsion to cite authorities in every sentence—if indeed one may call "sentences" what is in fact an unpunctuated mass of words; for convenience sake, I will insert bracketed references to Aristotle's *Poetics* but will forbear to discuss them, since their only point here is their cumulative effect:

> The principal part of composition is the fable [1450ª38–39], and the novelty of this fable is capable of that orderly arrangement which with verisimilitude and the marvelous [1460ª17] gives pleasure and instructs our lives [Horace, *Ars poetica*, ll. 343–44].
>
> The subject which I have woven for you is quite new, contains a complex, not a simple, plot [1452ª12–18], whole [1450ᵇ24], not fragmented, neither so small as not to satisfy, nor so great as to weary you [1450ᵇ36–1451ª3]. . . . Here is thread, knot, involvement [1455ᵇ24 ff.], and everything else of the kind which the art requires, and this is the sentiment of Scaliger, Patrizi, Mazzoni, and Erozio [Erizzo?], founded upon the doctrine of Aristotle, who in all things was the greatest of all, and always worthy of himself. . . . There is so much knot and involvement in this Work written to be sung, that it need fear no competition from those which are merely recited.
>
> As for the manners, the number of the good characters is greater than that of the bad, as Aristotle ordains [1454ª16–17].[28]

---

dubito, che questa volta sarò io il pazzo vero, col sottopormi si vogliosamente al rigoroso esame de' Teatri, e della Stampa, non considerando, che hoggidì bene spesso merita più d'esser legato l'Autore, ch'il Libro."

"Questa è l'ottava fatica rapresentativa, che mi trovo haver fatta; cinque delle quali hanno di già più volte passeggiate le Scene, e'n questa m'è riuscito assai felicemente lo sciorre più d'un nodo di lei senza magìa, e senza ricorrere a gli aiuti sopranaturali, e divini."

[27] 1454ª37–1454ᵇ2: "φανερὸν οὖν ὅτι καὶ τὰς λύσεις τῶν μύθων ἐξ αὐτοῦ δεῖ τοῦ μύθου συμβαίνειν, καὶ μὴ ὥσπερ ἐν τῇ Μηδείᾳ ἀπὸ μηχανῆς καὶ ἐν τῇ Ἰλιάδι τὰ περὶ τὸν ἀπόπλουν."

[28] Niccolò Enea Bartolini, *Venere gelosa* (Padua, 1643), "Al lettore" (unpaginated): " . . . la parte prima de componimenti è la favola, e della favola è la novità capace dell'ordine, che col verisimile e'l maraviglioso diletta, e ammaestra la nostra vita.

"Il suggetto, che v'ho tessuto non è stato più sentito, contiene un azione composta, non semplice, intera, non tronca, ne così minuta che non appaghi, ne così grande che v'annoi. . . . Qui è 'l filo, il nodo

One might suspect the author of satirical intentions, if he were cleverer. The next year, however, there appeared an open attack on classical authority, from the pen of "l'Assicurato Academico Incognito," who identified himself as the poet of Monteverdi's *Ritorno d'Ulisse in patria*: Giacomo Badoaro. The fourteen-page epistle with which he prefaced his "opera musicale" *L'Ulisse errante* (music by Sacrati, scenery by Giacomo Torelli; Venice, 1644) amounted to a bold aesthetic credo—or better, "non credo." Here are a few excerpts from that lengthy essay:

> Unhappy century, if the footprints of those gone by were to confine our steps to an unalterable path; for then, well might our age be called that of the blind, who can do naught, but be led. . . . Several years ago I produced *Il ritorno d'Ulisse in Patria*, a drama wholly derived from Homer and deemed excellent by Aristotle in his *Poetics* [?], and even then I heard dogs barking, but I was not slow to respond with stones in my hands. Now I present *L'Ulisse Errante*, which consists, in substance, of twelve books of Homer's *Odyssey*: . . . nor do his many wanderings make several fables, but rather several parts of one fable, so that it is one whole action, and of fair size, as Aristotle prescribes. . . . If some wit should assert . . . that it is a subject fit for an epic, rather than for a tragedy, I will say, that whoever wishes to read it in an epic will go to Homer's *Odyssey*, and whoever wishes to hear it in a tragedy, will come to the Theater of the Most Illustrious Signor Giovanni Grimani, where in a short time, and with less labor, he may behold it in greater pomp upon the stage. I might add that the precepts of poetics are unlike mathematical propositions, which are certain and permanent; they are not certain, for in them the Ancients, too, did err, disagreeing amongst themselves. . . . The precepts of poetics are not permanent, besides, because the changes wrought by the centuries give rise to different ways of composing. . . . [In tragedies,] changes of place were once detested; and now, to satisfy the eye, what once was forbidden appears to be a precept, for every passing day brings a greater number of scene changes; we think nothing (to enhance the spectators' pleasure) of producing unlikely effects, provided they do not deform the action: whence, as we have seen, to allow more time for the scene changes, we have introduced music,[29] in which a lack of verisimili-

---

l'intrecciamento, e tutto quello che in simil materia è desiderata dall'arte, e tal sentimento, è dello Scaligero, del Patrizi, del Mazzoni e dell'Erozio, fondato nella dottrina d'Aristotile, che in tutte le cose è stato maggior di tutti, e sempre eguale a se stesso. . . . [V'è] tanto nodo, e intrecciamento in quest'Opera fatta per cantare, che non teme il concorso di quelle che solamente si recitano.

" . . . Quanto al costume è più il numero de buoni, che de cativi, così vuole Aristotile."

I have corrected the grosser misprints for the sake of clarity and left the others untouched (my policy throughout this study).

[29] A novel explanation of the origin of opera. However, in the case of *L'Ulisse errante*, with its five acts and many scene changes designed by Torelli, it is probably a pretty fair statement of the music's main function.

tude is inescapable, since men transact their most important affairs in song; furthermore, so that all sorts of music may be enjoyed in the theater, it is the custom to have consorts of two, three, and more [voices], which give rise to another unlikely effect, for, speaking all together as they do, they say the same things without premeditation. . . . Our only obligation towards the precepts of the Ancients is to know them. . . . The writers derived the precepts from the usage of the poets . . . ; had they composed differently, the *Poetics* would have appeared with different precepts. . . . Let this work, then, be seen; and should it have the good luck of being successful, let no one tax me with the rules; for the true rule is to satisfy the listener.[30]

A remarkable statement in many ways, though its boldness is undermined by Badoaro's repeated appeals to the authority of Aristotle in defense of his own two dramas. But that was a common enough symptom, shown by all who tried to rebel.[31] At least he had the courage to declare that his main concern was to please the public; in this, at any rate, he was more truly Aristotelian than the critics who mingled morality with their dramatic theory.

Pietro Paolo Bissari, author of *La Torilda* (music by Cavalli; Venice, 1648), chose instead to pretend that the "rules" were absolutely intact. His preface,

---

[30]Badoaro, *L'Ulisse errante* (Venice, 1644), pp. 5–16: "Infelice Secolo, se l'orme de' passati obligassero il nostro piede ad un'inalterabil camino; ben potrebbe chiamarsi questa l'Età de' ciechi, che non sanno se non essere guidati. . . . Feci già molti anni rappresentare il ritorno d'Ulisse in Patria, Dramma cavato di punto da Homero, e raccordato [*sic*] per ottimo da Aristotile nella sua Poetica, e pur'anco all'hora udii abbaiar qualche cane, ma io non fui però tardo à risentirmene co' sassi alle mani. Hora fò vedere l'Ulisse Errante, ch'è in sostanza dodici libri dell'Odissea d'Homero: . . . nè i molti errori fanno molte favole, ma molte parti di favola, che la costituiscono attione tutta una, e grande, come ricerca Aristotele. . . . Se vorrà affermar un bell'Ingegno, . . . che il soggetto è più da Epopeia, che da Tragedia, io le dico, che chi vorrà leggerlo in Epopeia anderà nell'Odissea d'Homero, e chi vorrà sentirlo in Tragedia, venirà nel Theatro dell'Illustrissimo Signor Giovanni Grimani, dove in poco tempo, e con minor fatica lo vedrà più pomposo comparire sopra le Scene. Potrei aggiugnere, che i Precetti della Poetica non sono come le Propositioni Matematiche, certi, e permanenti; non sono certi, perche hanno in essi vagato anco gli Antichi, non accordandosi trà di loro. . . . Non sono poi permanenti i Precetti della Poetica, perche le Mutationi de' Secoli fanno nascer le diversità del comporre. . . . Erano in queste detestate una volta le variationi di loco, & al presente per dare sodisfattione all'occhio, pare precetto ciò che all'hora era prohibito, inventandosi ogni giorno maggior numero di cambiamenti di Scene; niente si cura al presente per accrescer diletto agli Spettatori il dar luogo a qualche inverisimile, che non deturpi la Attione: onde vedemo, che per dar più tempo alle Mutationi delle Scene, habbiamo introdotta la musica, nella quale non possiamo fuggire un'inverisimile, che gli huomini trattino i loro più importanti negotii cantando; in oltre per godere ne' Theatri ogni sorte di Musica, si costumano concerti a due, tre, e più, dove nasce un'altro inverisimile, che essi favellando insieme possano impensatamente incontrarsi à dire le medesime cose. . . . Non [teniamo] noi altro obligo circa i precetti degli Antichi, che di saperli. . . . Gli Scrittori hanno cavati i precetti dall'uso de' Poeti . . . ; se questi havessero in altra maniera composto, con altri Precetti sarebbe uscita la Poetica. . . . Vedasi dunque l'Opera, e quando habbia fortuna ella di bene incontrare, non mi tassi altri con le regole; poiche la vera regola è di sodisfare a chi ascolta." Later in the same epistle, Badoaro eulogizes Monteverdi, who had died a few months earlier: see U. S. Library of Congress, *Catalogue of Opera Librettos Printed Before 1800*, ed. O. G. T. Sonneck (Washington, 1914), p. 1112.

[31]Even by Molière. Cf. his *Critique de l'École des femmes* (1663), sc. 7, in which he attacks the rules and at the same time asserts that his comedy observes them all.

couched in florid language and full of conceits, reads like a learned treatise, complete with marginal references to the authorities quoted in Latin and Greek in the text—this, in a libretto that was sold at the door of the opera house and read by candlelight inside! His thesis was that the operas then being produced in Venice were, all of them, faithful replicas of the ancient tragedies; and he found classical precedents for everything, including comic scenes, frequent changes of scenery, dances, and (of course) music. The synopsis of his plot, to be sure, gives us pause: it deals with the fortunes of a Norwegian princess and is filled with Grecian gods and satyrs.

Francesco Sbarra of Lucca delivered himself of a well-known pronouncement concerning a new phenomenon that was further to wreck verisimilitude in the mid-1600s: the aria, or (as it was called during the Baroque) the "arietta." As fate would have it, one of the singing characters in his "dramma musicale" was none other than Aristotle himself, billed as the preceptor ("governatore") of Alexander the Great's sister:

> I know that the ariettas sung by Alexander and Aristotle will be judged contrary to the decorum of such great characters; but I know, too, that it is improper to recite in music, since thus one does not imitate natural speech but deprives the dramatic composition of its soul, which must be nothing but an imitation of human actions, and yet this fault is not only tolerated by the current century, but received with applause; today this kind of poetry has no other end but to please, so that we must adapt ourselves to the customs of our times; if the *stile recitativo* were not interlaced with such trifles, it would cause more tedium than pleasure; and so forgive me that error, which I have only committed to lessen your weariness.[32]

Bontempi's famous preface of 1662 to his "opera musicale" (in German, "Gedicht zur Musica") *Il Paride*, of which he was also the composer, may serve as a fitting conclusion to this segment of our investigation: one could hardly wish for a wiser, wittier, more thoroughly learned and yet practical guide to the dominant taste in Italy at the time. For though his *Paride* represented a new departure from common practice, being probably the first in the series of splendid court operas produced north of the Alps, yet Bontempi himself was the product of Barberini Rome and of the Venice of Monteverdi

---

[32]Sbarra, *Alessandro vincitor di se stesso* (Venice, 1651), "L'Autore A gli Spettatori del Dramma" (unpaginated): "Sò che l'Ariette cantate da Alessandro, & Aristotile, si stimeranno contro il decoro di Personaggi si grandi; mà sò ancora, ch'è improprio il recitarsi in Musica, non imitandosi in questa maniera il discorso naturale, e togliendosi l'anima al componimento Drammatico, che non deve esser altro, che un'imitatione dell'attioni humane, e pur questo difetto non solo è tolerato dal Secolo corrente; ma ricevuto con applauso; questa specie di Poesia hoggi non hà altro fine che il dilettare, onde conviene accommodarsi all'uso de i Tempi; se lo stile recitativo non venisse intermezzato con simili scherzi, porterebbe più fastidio, che diletto; condonami però quell'errore, che solo hò commesso per meno tediarti." The composer of this opera was Cesti.

and Cavalli. How did this extraordinarily talented man stand with regard to the neoclassical precepts? Approximately as did Lope de Vega, who knew them all by heart—and locked them up whenever he wrote a play:[33]

> As I ponder the matter and the form of the work . . . and as I employ all the powers of my weak intellect to discover some difference, whether generic or specific, that might reduce it under a name consonant with the quality of its content: I fear my pen may have given birth to Horace's monster,[34] since after considering it, dividing it, subdividing it piece by piece, I am unable to reduce it to any genre or species.
>
> It is divided into five acts: but the first makes no beginning of the matter or the argument; the second does not set things in motion; the third offers no impediments; the fourth shows no signs of unraveling; the fifth unravels not with artifice.
>
> There is no prologue containing the usual oration to the audience. There is no protasis, to sum things up. There is no epitasis, to begin the complication of the plot. There is no catastasis, to show it at the height of its complication. Nor has it a catastrophe, to reduce it at last to an unhoped-for tranquillity.
>
> It is not a comedy; for the matter it contains was not derived from civic and private actions. It is not a tragedy; for it does not express, or conclude, fearful and pitiful happenings. It is not a tragicomedy; for it takes no share, either in comedy or tragedy. It ought to be a drama; but the quality of its subject and plot will not reasonably allow the bestowal of that name.
>
> I would call it EROTOPAIGNION MUSICUM (that is, a Game of Love, suitable for Music); but as that is an unusual name, though founded on reason, I know not (Reader) whether it will satisfy you.[35]

---

[33] *Arte nuevo de hacer comedias en este tiempo* (Madrid, 1609): "Y, quando he de escrivir una comedia, / Encierro los preceptos con seis llaves." The lines were to be taken up as a battle cry by Victor Hugo in his polemical preface to *Cromwell* (1827).

[34] The reference is to the opening lines of the *Ars poetica*, in which Horace conjures up the image of an incongruous monster (with a man's head, a horse's neck, etc.) to point out the dangers of incongruity in poetry.

[35] Giovanni Andrea Bontempi, *Il Paride* (Dresden, 1662), "A chi Legge" (unpaginated): "Rivolgendo nella mente la Materia, e la Forma di quest'Opera, . . . & impiegando tutta la forza del mio debole Intelletto, per trovar qualche differenza, o generica, o specifica, che la riduca sotto un nome, non dissentaneo dalla qualità che contiene: temo, non habbia la mia Penna partorito il Mostro d'Horatio, poiche, considerandola, dividendola, sottalternandola a parte, a parte, non so ridurla ne a Genere, ne a Specie alcuna.

"E divisa in cinque Atti: ma il Primo, non comincia, ne la Materia, ne l'Argomento, il Secondo, non riduce le cose in Atto, il Terzo, non porta gl'impedimenti, il Quarto, non mostra la via di risolvere, il Quinto, non risolve artificiosamente.

"Non v'ha Prologo, che faccia la solita Oratione a gli Spettatori. Non v'ha Protasi, che narri la somma delle cose. Non v'ha Epitasi, che cominci a confonder la Tessitura. Non v'ha Catastasi, che dimostri il colmo più confuso di quella. Ne v'ha Catastrofe, che finalmente la riduca in tranquillità non aspettata.

Reason, alas, seldom prevails; or we should have had a perfect (if unpro-
nounceable) name for all the operas of the Baroque, and several later ones, too.

III

Two events that occurred within a few weeks of each other signaled, if not
the beginning, then the intensification of two opposite trends in theatrical
history. One of these has already been mentioned: the establishment of
commercial opera in Venice, with the inauguration of the rebuilt Teatro Tron
di S. Cassiano in February 1637.[36] We have seen the long-range effects of the
public's participation, as a paying patron, in molding its favorite form of
entertainment: the abandonment of virtually all classical restraints. The other
event took place one or two months earlier, at the Théâtre du Marais in Paris:
Corneille's *Le Cid* took audiences by storm and ushered in not only the great
period of French drama, but a new concern for classical precedent and authority.[37] The attacks made upon *Le Cid* by Corneille's jealous colleagues and the
ripostes by Corneille and his admirers burgeoned into one of those *querelles*
that make French literary history so entertaining. The *querelle du Cid*,
however, was more than just entertaining: at the request of Scudéry (Corneille's chief rival), the then newly-formed Académie Française passed
judgment on the play. In *Les Sentimens de l'Academie-Françoise sur la
tragi-comedie du Cid*, Jean Chapelain, with the assistance of a few *confrères*,
analyzed that masterpiece, none too favorably, in terms exclusively of Aristotle's *Poetics*.[38] It was the first official publication of the Académie Française,
and it helped to enthrone the "rules" on the French stage.

"Non è Comedia; poiche la materia, che contiene, non è tratta da attioni civili, e private. Non è
Tragedia; poiche non esprime, ne conclude casi atroci, e miserabili. Non è Tragicomedia; poiche non
partecipia, ne della Comedia, ne della Tragedia. Dovrebb' esser Drama; ma la qualità del Soggetto, e della
Tessitura, non ammette ragionevolmente l'imposition di questo Nome.

"Sarei per nominarla, EROTOPEGNIO MUSICALE ('Ερωτοπαίγνιον *Musicum; quod est Ludus de
Amore, ad Musicam pertinens*) ma per esser nome inusitato, quantunque fondato su la Ragione; non so se
sia (Lettore) per sodisfarti."

[36] The libretto's dedication, dated 6 May, declares that the première took place two months earlier, or in
early March; but Nicola Mangini (*I teatri di Venezia* [Milan, 1974], p. 38) points out that Lent, that year,
began on 25 February.

[37] Traditionally, the event is said to have taken place in November 1636, for which there is no evidence at
all; on the other hand, a letter of Jean Chapelain dated 22 January 1637 informs his correspondent that the
public has been enjoying *Le Cid* "depuis quinze jours." Cf. *Lettres de Jean Chapelain, de l'Académie
Française*, ed. Ph. Tamizey de Larroque, Collection de documents inédits sur l'histoire de France, 2nd ser.,
vol. 9, no. 1 (Paris, 1880), p. 134.

[38] The original manuscript was collated with the printed version by Colbert Searles; see his edition of *Les
Sentimens de l'Académie*, University of Minnesota Studies in Language and Literature, no. 3 (Minne-
apolis, 1916). Here, too, are found the famous marginal notes supposedly in Richlieu's hand, which gave

Though enormously influential in shaping theoretical thought, Chapelain's work on this occasion (as on other occasions, too) was directed at a specific poem. Soon afterwards two treatises of wider scope were written at Richelieu's behest: Jules de la Mesnardière's *La Poëtique* (1639) and François Hédelin d'Aubignac's *La Pratique du théâtre* (c. 1640).[39] Both merit some notice here.

La Mesnardière, a physician by profession, turned to poetry and letters as a means to rise in elegant society, and he succeeded. His *Poëtique* had the advantage of being the first to introduce Aristotelian concepts to a wide readership in French.[40] It read easily, despite its many classical references and quotations, enjoyed a brief vogue as being the only one of its kind, and was then forgotten. If it is mentioned here at all, it is because of the unexpected prominence given in it to music, as one of the six "qualitative" parts of tragedy in Aristotle's scheme (plot, manners, thought, diction, spectacle, music):[41] the whole final chapter is devoted to the music of the theater, which is termed "the most marvelous of all," in ancient times. La Mesnardière evokes the memory of Sophocles himself singing and playing on the harp, of Aeschylus conducting with his hand, of Nero performing in the theater. After several pages of colorful descriptions of this kind, he enters into a discussion of the difference between the Greek terms "meter" and "rhythm": the former he defines as the arrangement of syllabic quantities into feet and lines, the latter as "the art of enouncing in music the quality of each thing expressed in the poetry." "And so," he continues, after some technical discussion, "if they had undertaken to fit their music and their theatrical attitudes to the words of a princess overcome by several misfortunes, they would have imitated the thoughts of our Camille as follows."[42] Whereupon the poet-physician breaks into song:

---

rise to the legend (still widespread today) that Richelieu "instigated" the *Sentimens de l'Académie* from variously imagined motives (including political), directed against *Le Cid*. I concur entirely with Searles's conclusions (p. 6), which are corroborated by Louis Batiffol in an illuminating study, *Richelieu et Corneille: La légende de la persécution de l'auteur du Cid* (Paris, 1936): namely, that the reports of Richelieu's involvement in the *querelle* are grossly exaggerated and were, themselves, politically motivated. The point matters, since it would have been tempting to ascribe the new authority of the dramatic "rules" to such a direct intervention. We must be content with less personal, though not less significant, conclusions regarding the rise of centralized political authority in France and the influence of the poetic legislators.

[39] La Mesnardière's work came out in 1640, Aubignac's only in 1657 (both in Paris).

[40] See Helen Reese Reese, *La Mesnardière's* Poëtique *(1639): Sources and Dramatic Theories*, The Johns Hopkins Studies in Romance Literatures and Languages, vol. 28 (Baltimore, 1937; the series was reprinted in 1973). The author lacked the preparation to deal with the musical references, which are discussed in musicological terms here for the first time, so far as I am aware.

[41] μῦθος, ἦθη, διάνοια, λέξις, ὄψιο, μελοποιία. They are discussed in ch. 6, shortly after the definition of tragedy (1449^{b}31–1450^{a}14).

[42] *La Poëtique*, pp. 426, 427–28: "L'Art d'énoncer en Musique la qualité de chaque chose exprimée dans la Poësie." "S'ils eussent donc entrepris d'accommoder leur Musique & leurs Postures theatralles, aux

Having thus delivered the sorrowful thoughts of that afflicted princess, here, more or less, is the melody with which they would have accompanied the expression of the promptness with which Hippolytus' love for her was declared, after he saw her atop a bastion, while besieging the city in which she was confined. A promptness which she enounces by means of the impetuous figure which the masters of rhetoric call *velocitatem*, and which we might call *quickness*.[43]

parolles d'une Princesse accablée de divers malheurs, ils auroient imité ainsi les pensées de nôtre Camille." The two songs that follow are on pp. 428–29 and 430. See H. R. Reese, pp. 213–17, where this chapter is summarized.

[43] "Ayans recité ainsi les sentimens douloureux de cette Princesse affligée, voici à peu prés les Chants dont ils eussent accompagné l'expression de la Prontitude avec laquelle fut menée l'amour qu'Hippolyte eut

As will be seen, La Mesnardière has in both instances given us three pairs of Alexandrines set to music in the free rhythmic style, and in the notation, of the *chanson de cour*.[44] What makes their placement here, in a treatise on poetics, so remarkable is that the author has unwittingly bridged the gap between the *vers mesurés à l'antique* and the *chanson de cour* on the one hand and the yet-to-be-created French opera on the other by suggesting the use of the former in *dramatic* recitation. With amazing foresight, he concludes by prophesying, and advocating, the advent of French opera:

> I learn that the Italian [stage] has chosen to adorn itself in the ancient fashion in the production of two poems which were recently sung; and that a Prince of the Church displayed his magnificence in the musical expression of the misfortunes of Saint Alexis.
>
> Although the harmony whose marvels we are seeking has not yet been wholly recovered, and only a rather confused notion of it survives amongst us; nonetheless it is very certain that it appeared miraculous in that noble Alexiad, according to those who heard it.
>
> They say they never experienced the like of those five evening hours which that tragedy lasted; and that the charming illusion of those delightful dreams we sometimes have when we sleep has nothing comparable to the graceful enchantments of that rare melody.
>
> We must not expect our own public spectacles to be thus enriched, for that would be above their means. It will be enough for now if the dramatic writers will attempt to suit the airs which separate their acts to the nature of the thoughts each one expresses. However, we may hope that the sovereign powers who hold verse in esteem will be so magnificent as to display in their theaters, at a happier season, all the things that must escort the majesty of a muse once so respected.[45]

---

pour elle, aprés l'avoir considerée sur le haut d'un bastion, tandis qu'il assiégeoit la ville où elle étoit enfermée. Prontitude qu'elle énonce par la Figure impetueuse que les Maîtres de Rhétorique appellent *Velocitatem*, & que l'on peut nommer *Vitesse*." La Mesnardière states in his preface that all French verses here are his own.

[44]Cf. the example by Antoine Boesset, "Plaignez la rigeur de mon sort," to words by La Mesnardière in André Verchaly (ed.), *Airs de cour pour voix et luth*, Publications de la Société Française de Musicologie, Ser. 1, Vol. 16 (Paris, 1961), pp. 198–99, reproduced from Boesset's *XVIe livre d'Airs de cour avec la tablature de luth* (Paris, 1643), fol. 24[v].

[45]Pp. 431–32: "J'apprens que [la Scéne] d'Italie s'est voulu parer à l'antique dans l'exposition de deux Poëmes qu'elle a chantez depuis n'agueres; & qu'un Prince de l'Eglise a fait voir sa magnificence dans l'expression musicale des malheurs de Saint Alexis.

"Encore que l'Harmonie dont nous recherchons les merveilles, n'ait pas toute été recouvrée, & qu'il n'en reste parmi nous qu'une idée assez confuse; cependant il est tres-certain qu'elle parut miraculeuse dans cette noble Alexiade, au rapport de ceux qui l'ouïrent.

We will note, of course, that La Mesnardière is here giving us a rare, hitherto unnoticed, report on the Barberini production of Landi's *S. Alessio* (Rome, 1632). In so doing, the pleasure-loving expounder of Aristotle prophetically bridges yet another gap: the forty-year gap separating the lavish productions of the Barberinis from those of the future Sun King. And while waiting for that "happier season" to arrive, La Mesnardière very sensibly recommends that the only music heard at French dramatic performances, namely the "airs" played by string ensembles between the acts, reflect at least the mood of each act.

D'Aubignac's treatise was much more influential than La Mesnardière's and, in its rigorism, more characteristic of the stance taken by the French theorists, from Chapelain to Rapin (1674) and Dacier (1692). I tend to agree with a recent commentator that it was d'Aubignac who at last wrenched the concept of verisimilitude from its original moorings and made of it the foundation of neoclassical criticism.[46] D'Aubignac writes:

> Here is the bottom and ground work of all Dramatick Poems; many talk of it, but few understand it; but this is the general touchstone, by which all that comes to pass in a Play is to be tryed and examin'd[; in a word, Verisimilitude is, so to speak,] the very Essence of the Poem, without which nothing rational can be done or said upon the Stage. . . . Now is it most certain that the least Actions, brought upon the stage, ought to be probable, or else they are entirely faulty, and should not appear there. There is no Action of Humane Life so perfectly simple, as not to be accompanied by many little Circumstances, which do make it up; as are the Time, the Place, the Person, the Dignity, the Means, and the Reasons of the Action; and since the Stage ought to be a perfect Image of the Action, it ought to represent it entire, [so] that [Verisimilitude] be observ'd in all its parts.[47]

"Ils disent n'avoir vescu que les cinq heures de la nuict que dura cette Tragédie; Et que la charmante illusion de ces songes délicieux qu'on fait quelquefois en dormant, n'a rien qui soit comparable aux gracieux enchantemens de cette rare melodie.

"Nous ne devons pas demander que les Spectacles publics ayent cét enrichissement, qui est au dessus de leurs forces. Il suffira pour cette heure que les Ecrivains Dramatiques taschent d'accommoder les Airs qui distingueront leurs Actes, à la nature des pensées que chacun d'eux exprimera. Mais nous pouvons esperer que les Puissances Souveraines qui sçauront estimer les Vers, seront assez magnifiques pour fair voir sur leur Théatres en des saisons plus heureuses, tout ce qui doit accompagner la majesté d'une Muse autrefois si respectée."

[46]Cf. Hans-Jörg Neuschäfer, "D'Aubignacs *Pratique du théâtre* und der Zusammenhang von *imitatio*, *vraisemblance* und *bienséance*," serving as preface to the facsimile of the 1715 ed., Theorie und Geschichte der Literatur und der schönen Künste: Texte und Abhandlungen, vol. 13 (Munich, 1971), p. xiii. My references will be to this edition.

[47]I thought the reader deserved, for once, to hear the music of authentic seventeenth-century English: it is from *The Whole Art of the Stage*, an anonymous translation of d'Aubignac's work (London, 1684), pp. 74, 76. The original (pp. 65, 67–68) reads: "Voici le fondement de toutes les Pieces du Theatre, chacun

Now, Chapelain and La Mesnardière had both adopted Castelvetro's interpretation of the word (though they did not credit him with it): "There are two
kinds of verisimilitude, one being the kind that represents realities which for
the most part take place in an established way, the other, realities which at
times stray from the usual way."[48] Chapelain had termed the two kinds of
verisimilitude "common" and "extraordinary," and had gone beyond Castelvetro in ranging under the extraordinary "all surprising accidents which are
ascribed to Fortune, provided they are brought about by a concatenation of
those things which happen in the ordinary course of events."[49] D'Aubignac
acknowledges rather perfunctorily the "common" and "extraordinary" kinds
of verisimilitude dealt with by his predecessors. He proceeds to ascribe to
"extraordinary" verisimilitude events brought about through divine intervention or magic: for him, it involves the marvelous, "le merveilleux."
Having said which, he scarcely mentions it again in the course of his long
treatise.[50] D'Aubignac, in other words, really accepts only "common verisimilitude"; and he pursues it rigorously to its ultimate conclusions in all
matters theatrical.

D'Aubignac's attitude towards the *stances* of French tragedy will demon-

---

en parle & peu de gens l'entendent ; voici le caractere general auquel il faut reconnoître tout ce qui s'y passe:
en un mot la Vraisemblance est, s'il le faut ainsi dire, l'essence du Poëme Dramatique, & sans laquelle il ne
se peut rien faire ni rien dire de raisonnable sur la Scéne. . . . Or l'on doit savoir que les moindres actions
representées au Theatre, doivent être vraisemblables, ou bien elles sont entierement defectueuses, & n'y
doivent point être. Il n'y a point d'action humaine tellement simple, qu'elle ne soit accompagnée de
plusieurs circonstances qui la composent, comme sont le temps, le lieu, la personne, la dignité, les desseins,
les moiens, & la raison d'agir. Et puis que le Theatre en doit être une image parfaite, il faut qu'il la
represente toute entiere, & que la Vraisemblance y soit observée en toutes ses parties."

[48]Lodovico Castelvetro, *Poetica d'Aristotele vulgarizzata et sposta* (2nd ed. ; Basel, 1576), p. 400 (Parte
terza, particella ventesima): "Sono due maniere di verisimili, l'una di quelli, che rappresentano le verità, le
quali avengono per lo piu secondo certo corso, et l'altra di quelli, che rappresentano le verità, che alcuna
volta traviano dall'usato corso." He is commenting on *Poetics* 1456ª24–25: "As Agathon says, it is
verisimilar that many things should happen contrary to verisimilitude" ("*ὥσπερ Ἀγάθων λέγει, εἰκὸς γὰρ
γίνεσθαι πολλὰ καὶ παρὰ τὸ εἰκός*"). I have dealt with this formulation more fully in "Baroque Opera and
the Two Verisimilitudes," a paper read at the annual meeting of the American Musicological Society,
Boston, 1981, and now published in *Music and Civilization: Essays Presented to Paul Henry Lang*, ed.
E. Strainchamps and M. R. Maniates (New York, 1983), pp. 117–26.

[49]*Sentimens de l'Académie*, ed. Colbert Searles, p. 27: "Par ce que nous pouvons juger des sentimens
d'Aristote sur la matiere du vray-semblable, il n'en reconnoist que de deux genres, le commun, et
l'extraordinaire. . . . Dans cet extraordinaire entrent tous les accidens qui surprennent et qu'on attribue à la
Fortune, pourveu qu'ils naissent de l'enchaisnement des choses qui arrivent d'ordinaire." It is one of the
exquisite pleasures of a researcher in this field to find that at this point in the original manuscript Richelieu
entered his first remark: "Il faut un Exemple" (see plate III in the source). And the Cardinal's difficulty over
Agathon's "unlikely likelihood" obliged Chapelain to insert an example from Euripides' *Hecuba*! (La
Mesnardière, in adopting Chapelain's distinction, cites the same example [pp. 40–41].)

[50]P. 67. On p. 322, apropos of machines, he deplores the recourse to miraculous interventions as
betraying poverty of invention and risking the public's mocking disbelief.

strate a significant consequence of that premise.[51] (Perhaps the most famous example of *stances* is Don Rodrigue's "Percé jusques au fond du cœur . . . ," in *Le Cid*; here it may be noted that d'Aubignac's feelings towards Corneille are decidedly mixed.) To him, the ordinary verse of French drama, i.e., the Alexandrine, stands in the same relationship to spoken conversation as did the ancient Greek iambics, and for the same reason (Aristotle, of course, is the authority here). Now, if Alexandrines represent spoken dialogue, any change in meter, such as occurs in *stances*, will immediately be noticed by the public and taken to represent poetry. Not just poetry, but lyrical poetry—that is to say, poetry meant to be sung, to an instrumental accompaniment. *Stances*, then, can only be made verisimilar if the character who is to deliver them is given enough time to go home and compose them, or have them composed for him, so that, later, he can come back and perform them for us. As for a certain young nobleman (i.e., Don Rodrigue in *Le Cid*), torn between love and duty in the most famous of all French tragedies, it was condemnable to have him improvise a song then and there, fine as it is: "better to have given him the leisure to compose that charming complaint."[52] It is the same argument used six years earlier by Sbarra against the operatic aria.

Unpromising as is his attitude on *stances*, d'Aubignac feels no great need to proceed from there and attack opera by logical refutation; after all, the few Italian operas presented in Paris before the publication of his treatise in 1657 had fallen of their own accord. He dismisses them on different grounds:

> There remains [to be discussed] the *manner of delivery*, which can only be varied by being mixed with music; but just as I could never approve of this Italian practice, believing (as I always did) that it would be tedious, so now I suppose that Paris has reached the same conclusion by experience which I had reached by my imagination. To be sure, the theater may well suffer music; but it ought to awaken the appetite, not satiate it; no pleasure can be enjoyed to excess without bringing disgust.[53]

However, the logical premise once stated, others, as we shall see, would draw the necessary conclusions.

Saint-Évremond's witty essay "Sur les Opera: à Monsieur le Duc de

---

[51]See the monograph by Marie-France Hilgar, *La Mode des stances dans le théâtre tragique français, 1610–1687* (Paris, 1974), pp. 9–25, for a history of the phenomenon and its critical reception.

[52]"Il eût fallu donner quelque loisir pour composer cette agréable plainte." The whole ingenious argument may be found on pp. 242–43.

[53]Pp. 103–4: "Il reste la *Maniere de reciter*, qui ne peut être variée que par le mélange de la Musique; mais comme je n'ai pu jamais approuver cette pratique des Italiens dans la creance que j'ai toujours euë que cela seroit ennuyeux, j'estime que Paris en est autant persuadé maintenant par l'experience, que je l'étois par mon imagination. Le Theatre peut bien sans doute souffrir la Musique, mais il faut que ce soit pour réveiller l'appetit, & non pas pour le saouler; il n'y a point de plaisir qui puisse rassasier sans dégoût." The passage is omitted in the English version of 1684.

Bouquinquant" is too well-known to require a lengthy exposition here. He, too, in his indictment adduces a surfeit of pleasurable sensations as the cause of ultimate boredom.[54] But, though he must by no means be counted among the neoclassical legislators,[55] he does bring up other arguments that are based on the conventional criticism, e.g., on decorum. Of particular interest is his exemption of arias from his general accusations, on the grounds that they correspond to the *stances* of French drama, of which he approves.[56]

We know enough now concerning "common" and "extraordinary" verisimilitude to understand why the *tragédie en musique*, when it finally came in the 1670s, naturally took to mythological subjects or, after *Amadis*, to subjects drawn from romance: only within the context of "le merveilleux" could the sung drama be verisimilar. The field was now equitably divided: "common" verisimilitude was the province of spoken tragedy, "extraordinary" that of opera—a solution that ought to have pleased everyone in that age of reason. Yet the last two important exponents of Aristotle's "rules" in France objected to the newcomer.

Father Rapin, writing a textbook *ad usum Delphini* in 1674, declared himself from the outset an orthodox follower of the Greek philosopher: "Indeed, his *Poetics* is, properly speaking, simply nature turned into method, and good sense reduced to principles: only through these rules can we attain to perfection: and we stray the moment we stop following them."[57] Perhaps it is not surprising that this strait-laced pedagogue should have seen French tragedy threatened by opera. Speaking of the French stage's past glories, he continued:

> And we have among us some happy geniuses who have already made their mark in the theater, and who promise to go on doing so: but the fancy for musical operas, which has turned the heads of the masses and even of solid citizens, will perhaps eventually succeed in discouraging good minds from [writing] tragedies, unless care is taken to stimulate them with [the

---

[54]Cf. Charles Lamb's "A Chapter on Ears," in *Essays of Elia*: "To pile honey upon sugar, and sugar upon honey, to an interminable tedious sweetness" partly describes his reaction to music—instrumental music, to be sure. And he had the good grace to admit he had "no ear."

[55]He was no friend of d'Aubignac's, and it is to him that we owe the story of the great Condé's reaction to a tragedy which the theorist had written according to all the rules: "I am much obliged to Monsieur d'Aubignac," said the Prince, "for paying such attention to Aristotle's rules; but I cannot excuse Aristotle's rules for making Monsieur d'Aubignac write such a bad Tragedy." ("De la Tragédie ancienne et moderne," in *Œuvres en prose*, ed. R. Ternois, 4 [Paris, 1969]: 170.)

[56]Ibid., 3 (Paris, 1966): 153.

[57]René Rapin, S. J., *Réflexions sur la poétique de ce temps et sur les ouvrages des poètes anciens et modernes*, ed. E. T. Dubois (Geneva, 1970), p. 9: "En effet, sa *Poétique* n'est à proprement parler, que la nature mise en méthode, et le bon sens réduit en principes: on ne va à la perfection que par ces règles: et on s'égare dès qu'on ne les suit pas."

prospect of] glory and compensation. It is for those who govern to think of it.[58]

Curiously enough, this passage was expunged from the second edition, which came out the following year. Perhaps the Dauphin's papa did not like being lumped with the "masses" and "solid citizens," for we know that he, too, had been seized with the "fancy for musical operas."

Far more thorough, though by now a solitary voice crying in the wilderness, was André Dacier, in his demolition of opera's insolent pretensions. He translated Aristotle's *Poetics* after a fashion and furnished it with a remarkably crabbed commentary.[59] His uncompromising attitude may be inferred from his rejection of the Alexandrine verse as a suitable medium for tragedy: it was not as natural as the Greeks' iambics and therefore ought to yield to prose (pp. 53–54). His interpretation of the passage in Aristotle which I called the Stumbling Block earlier is as arbitrary as it is simple: "Verse reigns alone in the course of the acts. Dance, music, and verse in one part of the chorus, and verse and music in the other."[60] Opera had little to hope for from such a commentator. And indeed, while commenting on a minor Aristotelian distinction ("By 'diction' I mean the composition of the verses, by 'melody' that whose meaning is perfectly clear"),[61] he unleashed his thunderbolt:

> If tragedy can subsist without verse, it can do so even better without music. We must indeed confess we do not understand too well how music can ever have been considered as being in any way a part of tragedy; for if there is anything in the world that seems foreign and even contrary to a tragic action, it is singing—with all due deference to the inventors of *tragédies en musique*, poems as ridiculous as they are new and which would not be suffered if there existed the smallest amount of taste for plays or if we had not been charmed and seduced by one of the greatest musicians who ever lived. For operas, if I may dare say so, are the *grotesques* of poetry, grotesques the more intolerable in that they are passed off for regular works.[62]

---

[58]Ibid., 113, n.: "Et nous avons parmy nous des génies heureux qui se sont déjà signalez sur le théâtre, et qui promettent encore de s'y signaler davantage: mais la fantaisie des opéra de musique, dont le peuple et mesme la pluspart des honnestes gens se sont laissez entester, sera peut-estre capable dans la suite de décourager les esprits pour la tragédie si l'on ne pense à les exciter par la gloire et par la récompense. C'est à ceux qui gouvernent à y penser."

[59]*La Poëtique d'Aristote traduite en François. Avec des remarques* (Paris, 1692). There exists an English edition: *Aristotle's Art of Poetry, Translated from the Original Greek, According to M. Theodore Goulston's Edition. Together with Mr. D'Acier's Notes Translated from the French* (London, 1705).

[60]P. 81: "Le vers regne seul dans le cours des Actes. La danse, la musique, & le vers dans une partie du chœur, & le vers & la musique dans l'autre."

[61]1449[b]34–36: "λέγω δὲ λέξιν μὲν αὐτὴν τὴν τῶν μέτρων σύνθεσιν, μελοποιίαν δὲ ὅ τὴν δύναμιν φανερὰν ἔχει πᾶσαν."

[62]P. 82: "Si la Tragedie peut subsister sans vers, elle le peut encore plus sans musique. Il faut même

He went on to wonder how music got mixed up with tragedy in the first place and concluded it was due to the invincible superstition of the Greeks, who insisted on dancing and singing when worshiping Bacchus. Their music, he added, was at any rate confined to the chorus. It was not essential, but a matter of *bienséance* and ornament.[63]

It will be noticed that it was Quinault who was insulted, not Lully. Both were dead by then, but Louis XIV was not, and Lully had been too close to the throne to be attacked without incurring displeasure. It was Quinault, too, who had taken the brunt of anti-operatic criticism in the 1670s and '80s. But after 1700, his reputation began to rise until it reached unparalleled new heights: Voltaire and his contemporaries adored him. The *tragédie lyrique* (as they now called the *tragédie en musique*) even began to exert an influence on the spoken tragedy, and the new treatises on poetics gave it a place of honor.[64]

IV

Opera came to France too late to interfere with the full unfolding of her greatest dramas. In Italy, the conditions for the development of the spoken theater were missing; for, if the experiences of Spain, England, and France are any indication, a centralized, focused sense of nationhood was a prerequisite. Instead, opera flourished in Italy with the abandon of an uncultivated vegetation, its constituent parts barely, if at all, held together. The music, its distinctive feature, thrived; the rest was in total disarray. Then, say the older books, came the reform, "la riforma del melodramma." First Zeno, then Metastasio made the opera "regular" (i.e., observant of the rules). Goldoni, in his *Mémoires* (Paris, 1787), wrote:

---

avoüer que nous ne comprenons pas bien, comment la musique a pû jamais être considerée, comme faisant en quelque sorte partie de la Tragedie, car s'il y a rien au monde qui paroisse étranger & contraire même à une action Tragique, c'est le chant. N'en déplaise aux Inventeurs des Tragedies en musique, Poëmes aussi ridicules que nouveaux, & qu'on ne pourroit souffrir, si l'on avoit le moindre goût pour les pieces de Theatre, ou que l'on n'eût pas été enchanté & seduit par un des plus grands Musiciens, qui ayent jamais été. Car les Opera sont, si je l'oze dire, *les grotesques* de la Poësie, & Grotesques d'autant plus insuportables, qu'on prétend les faire passer pour des ouvrages reguliers."

[63] Pp. 82–83. Twining, in his note on the same Aristotelian passage, cannot resist adding (nor can I resist quoting him): "Dacier is amusing here. He wonders what could induce the Greeks to make Music a part of their drama; and at last, '*aprés bien des recherches*,' he discovers one principal cause to have been this—that they had very musical ears; but he does not discover the cause of his own wonder, which, in all probability, was, that *he* had not." (Thomas Twining, *Aristotle's Treatise on Poetry*, 2 vols. [2nd ed.; London, 1812], 2:28.) Cf. Lamb, n. 54 above.

[64] On the influence of the *tragédie lyrique* on the spoken tragedy, see Jacques Truchet, *La Tragédie classique en France* (Paris, 1975), pp. 153–57. Examples of later treatises favorable to opera are *Réflexions critiques sur la poésie et sur la peinture* by the Abbé du Bos of the Académie Française (2 vols.; Paris, 1719) and Jean-François Marmontel's *Poëtique françoise* (2 vols.; Paris, 1763).

To these two illustrious authors, Italy owes the reform of the opera. Before their time, one saw nothing but deities, and devils, and machines, and marvels in those harmonious spectacles. *Zeno* was the first to believe that tragedy could be performed in lyrical verses without being degraded, and that it could be sung without being enfeebled. He carried out his project in a manner most satisfactory to the public, and most glorious to himself and his nation.

One sees, in his operas, heroes as they really were, or at least as the historians depict them for us; the characters vigorously sustained, his plots always well-executed; the episodes always subject to the unity of action: his style was virile, robust, and the words of his arias [were] well adapted to the music of his time.

Metastasio, who succeeded him, brought serious opera to the fullest degree of perfection it was capable of: his pure, elegant style; his flowing, harmonious lines; an admirable clarity in the sentiments; a seeming facility concealing the painstaking labor of precision; an affecting energy in the language of the emotions; his portrayals, his tableaux, his delightful descriptions, his gentle morality, his penetrating philosophy, his analyses of the human heart, his erudition frugally dispensed and applied with art; his incomparable arias, or better, madrigals, now Pindaric, now Anacreontic, have made him worthy of admiration, and have entitled him to the immortal wreath which the Italians have yielded him and which strangers do not begrudge him.

If I dared make comparisons, I might suggest that Metastasio imitated Racine in his style, and that Zeno imitated Corneille in his vigor.[65]

---

[65] Carlo Goldoni, *Opere complete*, ed. Gius. Ortolani et al., 36 (Venice, 1936): 207–8: "L'Italie doit à ces deux illustres Auteurs la réforme de l'Opéra. On ne voyoit, avant eux, dans ces Spectacles harmonieux, que des Dieux, et des diables, et des machines, et du merveilleux. *Zeno* crut le premier que la Tragédie pouvoit se représenter en vers lyriques sans la dégrader, et qu'on pouvoit la chanter sans l'affoiblir. Il exécuta son projet de la maniere la plus satisfaisante pour le public, et la plus glorieuse pour lui-même et pour sa nation.

"On voit, dans ses Opéras, les héros tels qu'ils étoient, du moins tels que les historiens nous les représentent; les caracteres vigoureusement soutenus, ses plans toujours bien conduits; les épisodes toujours liés à l'unité de l'action: son style étoit mâle, robuste, et les paroles de ses airs adaptées à la musique de son tems.

"*Métastase*, qui lui succéda, mit le comble à la perfection dont la Tragédie lyrique étoit susceptible: son style pur et élégant; ses vers coulans et harmonieux; une clarté admirable dans les sentimens; une facilité apparente qui cache le pénible travail de la précision; une énergie touchante dans le langage des passions, ses portraits, ses tableaux, ses descriptions riantes, sa douce morale, sa philosophie insinuante, ses analyses du cœur humain, ses connoissances répandues sans profusion, et appliquées avec art; ses airs, ou, pour mieux dire, ses madrigaux incomparables, tantôt dans le goût de Pindare, tantôt dans celui d'Anacréon, l'ont rendu digne d'admiration, et lui ont mérité la couronne immortelle que les Italiens lui ont déférée, et que les étrangers ne refusent pas de lui accorder.

"Si j'osois faire des comparaisons, je pourrois avancer que Métastase a imité Racine par son style, et que Zeno a imité Corneille par sa vigueur."

We know, of course, that neither of those poets accomplished such a feat as the "reform of opera" unaided, whatever their other qualities might have been.[66] The reform—and a reform did take place—was only the most visible result of that period of reassessment and self-criticism that marked Italy's emergence from her own very pronounced "barocchismo" into the rationalistic, cosmopolitan mainstream of modern Europe. It was the period of the Arcadia;[67] and one of the Arcadia's chief endeavors was its attempt to forge an Italian tragedy. We can appreciate the poignancy of those aspirations when we remember what share Italy had in the early history of European drama; and we know how hopeless they were, not only for the reason mentioned earlier, but also because all of Europe, and not just Italy, was entering upon an epoch favorable to prose, to journalism, to satire, to comedy, but deadly to tragedy. And so, despite ephemeral successes, all the efforts of the theorists and authors of Italian tragedy, of Lodovico Muratori, Scipione Maffei, Vincenzo Gravina, Pier Jacopo Martello, and the rest, were doomed to failure.[68] And the only form in which those efforts "took" was opera.

Opera, that is, was the beneficiary (direct and indirect) of the efforts of those theorists and authors: the direct beneficiary, in that they all addressed themselves to opera in their criticism;[69] the indirect, in that their attempts at tragedies, although never altogether successful with the public, nevertheless provided models that confirmed the poets of opera in their new path. And that new path, as Goldoni quite correctly described it, involved the *rejection* of "extraordinary verisimilitude," of divine interventions, of "le merveilleux," in favor of the rational, "common verisimilitude." Italian opera, in that sense, walked the same path as French tragedy, not French opera.

Why Italian opera chose that path, in striking contrast to the *tragédie en musique*'s preference for "le merveilleux," is a question that can be answered only with surmises. The central factor, surely, was that musical drama was a more natural art form to the Italians than to the French and so did not need the justification of a supernatural context. Then, as we have seen, opera fell heir to the missed opportunities of the Italian spoken drama—functioned, as it were, in its stead. And here, the enormous prestige of the French spoken tragedies,

---

[66]On Zeno, see Robert S. Freeman, *Opera without Drama: Currents of Change in Italian Opera, 1675–1725* (Ann Arbor, 1981); also the same author's "Apostolo Zeno's Reform of the Libretto, *Journal of the American Musicological Society* 21 (1968): 321–41.

[67]No one has captured the moment better than Benedetto Croce in "L'Arcadia e la poesia del Settecento," ch. 1 of his *La letteratura italiana del Settecento: note critiche* (Bari, 1949).

[68]See A. Galletti, *Le teorie drammatiche e la tragedia in Italia nel secolo XVIII* (Cremona, 1901).

[69]See Freeman, "Opera without Drama." See also my "Pier Jacopo Martello on Opera (1715): An Annotated Translation," *The Musical Quarterly* 67 (1980): 378–403.

which were translated and imitated widely in Italy, must be taken into account. The subjects of the new *opera seria*, when not taken outright from French tragedy (e.g., *Il Cid* by Alborghetti/Leo), often enough revealed their sources under a thin disguise: well-known cases are Metastasio's *La clemenza di Tito*, patterned after Corneille's *Cinna* (originally subtitled *La Clémence d'Auguste!*), and his oratorio *Gioas Re di Giuda*, after Racine's *Athalie*.[70]

At first glance, the differences between the best tragedies of the French classics and the best "drammi" of Metastasio seem greater than the similarities. The Frenchmen's Alexandrines, linked in rhyming couplets, enthrall the listener with their recurring, yet ever-changing cadence, rising to great climaxes, descending to delicately nuanced understatement. The messengers' descriptions open up visions of a world beyond the stage, where bloody events and natural catastrophes may take place; but the stage itself remains immutable, untouched by anything that might distract our attention from the all-consuming interplay of the protagonists' emotions. The unities (in the dramas after c. 1645) are strictly observed. There is decorum. There is verisimilitude. (Both Corneille and Racine were rapt students of Aristotle's *Poetics*, which they read in Greek.)[71]

Now let us take Metastasio's *Demofoonte* and attempt a comparison. The first discordant impression is produced by a description of the scenery for Act 1, scene 1 (hanging gardens), which, we know, will soon yield to other sets. And in fact, scene 5 presents us with a harbor view, complete with a practicable ship from which, "to the sound of various barbarous instruments," descend two princely characters with a numerous escort. Four more changes of scenery (two per act) are called for, and in Act 2, scene 9, there is a pitched battle, with "confusion and tumult everywhere"—enough to dispel all memory of the French classics. But wait. What happens after the barbarous instrumentalists have left the stage, together with the numerous escort? The two princely characters have an intimate dialogue, all alone in the enormous harbor, where they nearly, but not quite, declare their love for each other. And what happens after the pitched battle? The hero and heroine have an agitated dialogue, all

---

[70]See my "Teorie drammatiche e 'infranciosamento': motivi della 'riforma' melodrammatica nel primo Settecento," in *Antonio Vivaldi: teatro musicale, cultura e società*, ed. Lorenzo Bianconi and Giovanni Morelli (Florence, 1982), pp. 273–96, for a more detailed consideration of the forces behind the "reform" of opera in early eighteenth-century Italy.

[71]Aside from their prefaces, there is the direct evidence of Corneille's three *Discours* of 1660, best studied in *Œuvres*, ed. Ch. Marty-Laveaux, 1 (Paris, 1862): 13-122, and Racine's marginal notes to his copy of the *Poetics*, edited by E. Vinaver as *Principes de la tragédie en marge de la Poétique d'Aristote* (Paris, 1951). The standard work on the dramatic techniques of the French classics, which might well serve as a model for a similar approach to opera, is Jacques Schérer, *La Dramaturgie classique en France* (Paris, 1950).

alone in Apollo's temple, which a moment earlier had been the scene of so much confusion. Could it be that Metastasio has introduced the splendid stage settings to cater to the prevailing operatic conventions and expectations? It could be; in fact, with minimal alterations in the actors' lines, all of *Demofoonte* could play in a room, like a French tragedy.

When we next turn to the dialogue, we meet with a second discordant impression: the unrhymed hendecasyllables mixed with septenaries are as different from Alexandrines as is the Italian language from the French. Here there is a nervous realism, an agitation quite unlike the formal elegance of the other:

Dircea.   Credimi, o padre; il tuo soverchio affetto
                Un mal dubbioso ancora
                Rende sicuro. A domandar che solo
                Il mio nome non vegga
                L'urna fatale, altra ragion non hai
                Che il regio esempio.

Matusio.   E ti par poco? Io forse,
                Perchè suddito nacqui,
                Son men padre del re?

Now it happens that a manuscript in Vienna containing many unpublished fragments in Metastasio's hand became available to the editor of the most recent edition of his collected works; and among these was found a French version of this opening scene, cast in Alexandrines:

Dir.   Ah, croyèz-moi, seigneur: l'excès de votre amour
            En voulant me sauver, va me perdre en ce jour.
            Quel prétexte aurez-vous, quelle raison valable
            Pour refuser mon nom à l'urne redoutable?
            Nul droit vous autorise à cette extrémité
            Que l'exemple du roy.

Math.   N'est-ce pas donc assez?
            Qui peut contraindre en moi la nature à se taire?
            Faut-il donc être roy pour sentir qu'on est père?[72]

The illusion of French tragedy is perfect, down to the epigrammatic close of the last line. We can see how Metastasio's works, though written for music, came to be read so widely as tragedies in their own right by his contemporaries: their surface, their tone was that of the great French tragedies, and they embodied the same neoclassical ideals, at least externally. But what made

---

[72] Pietro Mestastasio, *Tutte le opere*, ed. Bruno Brunelli, 2 (2nd ed.; Milan, 1965): 1300. Whether, as Brunelli, thinks, Mestastasio was the actual translator or, as I think, merely the copier makes little difference here.

them especially palatable to that untragic age is that under the tragic surface (as De Sanctis noted over a hundred years ago) the core was comic.[73]

Metastasio translated and annotated Horace's *Ars poetica*. An even larger effort along those lines was his *Estratto dell'Arte poetica d'Aristotile e considerazioni su la medesima*, a chapter-by-chapter examination of Aristotle's Greek text, done with a considerable show of erudition and wit.[74] Here his chief antagonists are the crusty old commentators, especially Dacier; his heroes are Corneille and Racine. But his main objective is to prove that he, Metastasio, has written nothing but pure, Grecian tragedies; indeed, that Italian opera is the direct descendant of Greek tragedy, with this difference only (and a sensible one, too): that where the Greeks had choruses, the Italians now have arias. Thus did Aristotle make his final appearance in operatic history; then he bowed out, with an enigmatic smile and wearing a powdered wig.[75]

---

[73] Francesco De Sanctis, *Storia della letteratura italiana* (Naples, 1870–71), ed. Niccolò Gallo (Turin, 1958), p. 868.

[74] These works may be found in *Tutte le opere*, 2:1229–78 and 959–1117, respectively. I have analyzed the *Estratto* in "Metastasio, Aristotle, and the *Opera Seria*," *Journal of Musicology* 1 (1982): 385–94.

[75] Yet neoclassical modes of thought lingered on: my "Verdi and the Fusion of Genres," *Journal of the American Musicological Society* 35 (1982): 138–56, shows them being applied to *Rigoletto* in 1851!

Recitative and Aria in *Dido and Aeneas**

Ellen T. Harris

"All opera, even modern opera, may be divided into recitative and air . . . ,"
or so wrote Edward Dent in 1934.[1] However much we may wish to question
this statement in specific cases, we would certainly accept its validity in regard
to Purcell's *Dido and Aeneas*; thus the modern editions of this work, from
Alexander Macfarren's in 1841 for the Musical Antiquarian Society, to
Margaret Laurie's 1979 New Purcell Society Edition, are consistent in labeling
all the solo passages as either one or the other. This procedure, however, stems
from a concept of opera which was in Purcell's time foreign to England and
which depends on a preconceived, and usually French or Italian, idea of what
opera should be. When *Dido and Aeneas* is heralded as the only English
opera—that is, the only English opera to be through-composed in aria-
recitative alternation—the models adduced have been exclusively continental
and often anachronistic. It is my contention that Purcell did not write any
recitative in the contemporary—or continental—sense for *Dido and Aeneas*,
and that our perception that he did derives from a late eighteenth-century
conception of that work.

Because the definition of through-composed opera rests primarily on the
use of recitative, it is on this aspect of *Dido and Aeneas* that attention is
usually focused. Thus Edward Dent writes in *Foundations of English Opera*:

> It is naturally in the recitative that *Dido and Aeneas* is most remarkable,
> since being the only real opera which Purcell ever wrote, it furnished his
> only occasion for writing musical dialogue of a genuinely human and

*This paper is largely the same as one I read at the Annual Meeting of the American Musicological
Society, Denver, 1980. In its preparation I have incurred many debts. I am especially grateful to Ellen
Rosand for her critical attention to my initial draft, and to Curtis Price, my respondent in Denver, for his
helpful commentary and constructive criticisms. Among the many people who were kind enough to
respond to this paper at Denver and afterwards, I would like particularly to thank Murray Lefkowitz,
Margaret Murata, Catherine Rohrer, and Joshua Rifkin, all of whom will find their hands in this revision.
Finally I would like to thank my seminar students at Columbia University (1978), whose interest and
enthusiasm concerning seventeenth-century England played such a large role in this paper's inception.

[1] "The Translation of Operas," in *Selected Essays: Edward J. Dent*, ed. Hugh Taylor (Cambridge,
1979), p. 8; originally published in *Proceedings of the Musical Association* 61 (1934/35): 81–104.

dramatic character. Purcell's recitative is obviously derived from the Italian chamber cantatas.[2]

This derivation was not half so obvious to Joseph Kerman in *Opera and Drama*: Kerman states that *Dido* essentially follows the scheme of a Lullian opera, "its dramaturgy [being] basically determined by chorus, dance, and formalized recitative."[3] Moreover, unlike Dent, Kerman considers the recitative unsuccessful. He writes:

> With recitative [Purcell] was able to do less though like Lully he devoted a great deal of attention to it. It is very carefully written, and vigorously declaimed, but impersonal, courtly, and bombastic.[4]

More recently, Eugene Haun has reconsidered the question of Purcell's indebtedness to foreign models. In *But Hark! More Harmony* he writes:

> The recitative of Blow and Purcell is certainly different from the "dry" recitative of the Italians and the arid declamation of the French, but it is recitative nonetheless.[5]

Although this statement strikes at the issue, it fails to penetrate its core. In order to accomplish this, we must first strip away our preconceived notions about through-composed opera and ask whether these musical sections are really recitative. Only after this is answered satisfactorily can the questions of national influence be re-examined. The inquiry properly begins with an examination of *Dido's* seventeenth-century English antecedents.

Music had begun to play an increasingly important role in English dramatic productions during the Elizabethan era, and the songs from these works have attracted a substantial amount of critical attention. They are typically divided into two classes, as by John Cutts in his study of the music of Shakespeare's theatre: (1) the composed, or courtly, airs, and (2) the unaccompanied street or folk songs.[6] In general, it is the songs from the first class that survive in contemporary manuscripts, and these can be further divided into two clearly distinguishable musical sub-groups: the simple or tuneful air, also called the dance air, and the more sophisticated declamatory air.[7]

---

[2](Cambridge, 1928; reprint, New York, 1965), pp. 188–89.

[3](New York, 1956), p. 56.

[4]Ibid., p. 60.

[5](Ypsilanti, Michigan, 1971), p. 133.

[6]*La musique de scène de la troupe de Shakespeare: The King's Men sous le Règne de Jacques Ier* (Paris, 1959).

[7]These are modern terms not found in contemporary sources. For examples of their use, see John H. Long, *Shakespeare's Use of Music: A Study of the Music and its Performance in the Original Production of Seven Comedies* (Gainesville, Florida, 1955); and Edwin S. Lindsey, "The Music of the Songs in Fletcher's Plays," *Studies in Philology* 21 (1924): 325–55, and "The Music in Ben Jonson's Plays," *Modern Language Notes* 44 (1929): 86–92.

The first type can usually be identified by regularity of rhythmic accent and phrase structure, by genuine tunefulness, and often by structural repetitions in addition to strophic form. The meter is often, but not always, triple. The second type, on the other hand, is usually less regular in rhythmic and melodic shape, as these features are determined in great part by speech or word accent. Furthermore, because of the close association between word and tone, this type is also less often repetitive or strophic, and the meter is usually duple. Another special feature of this style is a tendency toward more florid ornamentation than is customary in the tuneful air.

It is noteworthy that these distinctions parallel those made by Caccini in the contemporary volume *Le Nuove Musiche* (1602), where the songs are called aria and madrigal respectively. It is well to remember the differences between these two types in this more familiar way, and to recall the strong Italian influence on English vocal music at this time. However, unlike the Italian musical traditions, which changed and developed, the English song traditions were maintained through the end of the seventeenth century. A few examples will help to illustrate this point.

Robert Johnson (c. 1582–1633), perhaps the best known of the musicians involved with Jacobean drama, made a clear distinction between his declamatory and his tuneful songs. For example, the style of "Come hither you that love," from the Beaumont and Fletcher play *The Captain* (1612), may easily be identified by its clear and regular accents, tuneful and easily singable melody, and strophic form. (See Example 1.) On the other hand, the well-known "Care-charming sleep" from Fletcher's *Valentinian* (c. 1612), is clearly declamatory in nature, and the florid ornamentation provided in two of the three manuscript sources is yet another indication of its type.[8] (See Example 2.) Some other songs include sections in both styles, typically beginning with declamatory writing and then blossoming forth into the tuneful style. This particular format also became the identifying feature of the dialogue, where two voices begin in declamatory alternation and end more tunefully in a simultaneous duet.[9]

These four styles—the declamatory air, the tuneful air, the bipartite air containing both styles, and the dialogue—form the basis of the English song tradition. All continued relatively unchanged into the middle of the century,

---

[8] The sources are London, British Library, MS Add. 11608, and Cambridge, Fitzwilliam Museum, MS 52.D. See Johnson, *Ayres, Songs, and Dialogues*, pp. 72 and 70.

[9] Examples by Johnson of both these types may be found in the above-mentioned edition. "Where the bee sucks" from Shakespeare's *Tempest* (1611) moves from declamatory to tuneful style; "Charon, oh Charon" provides an example of the dialogue.

Example 1. Robert Johnson, "Come hither you that love" (from Robert Johnson, *Ayres, Songs, and Dialogues*, ed. Ian Spink, *The English Lute-Songs*, 2nd ser., vol. 17 [London, 1961], pp. 30–31).

Example 2. Robert Johnson, "Care-charming sleep" (from Johnson, *Ayres, Songs, and Dialogues*, pp. 34–36).

Example 2, continued

as is illustrated by John Playford's *The Treasury of Musick* (London, 1669).[10]
Dialogues, for example, may here be found by both Nicholas Lanier (1588–
1666), who during the Jacobean and Caroline eras worked predominantly with
the court masque rather than the professional theatre, and Henry Lawes
(1596–1662), who composed mainly during the Commonwealth (see Plates 1
and 2). These two composers, however, received particular acclaim during
their lives for their declamatory writing. Lanier is now often credited with
introducing recitative into England, and the most famous example from his
pen, *Hero's Complaint to Leander*, appears in one of Playford's later volumes

[10]*The Treasury of Musick* contains three parts, each of which had been published previously as a
separate volume. Part I first appeared in 1659 as the third volume of a series entitled *Select Ayres and
Dialogues*; Parts II and III in 1655 and 1658 respectively as the second and third volumes of a collection of
songs by Henry Lawes, *Ayres and Dialogues*. The persistent popularity of these songs illustrates the
perseverance of the older styles.

Plate 1. Nicholas Lanier, "A Dialogue between Strephon and Phillis" (from Playford, *Treasury of Musick*, 1669).

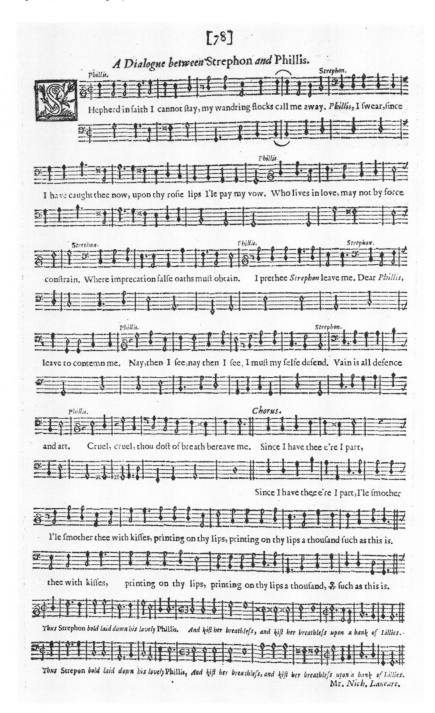

Plate 2. Henry Lawes, "A Dialogue: Shepherd and Nimph" (from Playford, *Treasury of Musick*, 1669).

(1683). It is a self-contained piece and, except for its length, it does not differ markedly from the declamatory air. However, Lanier is also said to have set two of Ben Jonson's masques (*Lovers Made Men* and *The Vision of Delight*) completely to music at least by the time of their publication in 1640, if not for their first performances in 1617. Unfortunately, these scores are not extant, but the implications for the use of recitative will need to be considered later. Lanier wrote in the tuneful style as well, and the example given here illustrates the growing interest in ground bass procedures even though the repetitions are not exact (see Plate 3, pp. 40–41).[11]

Like Lanier, Henry Lawes also composed a famous recitative scene (*Ariadne Deserted by Theseus*), which appears in one of Playford's earlier volumes (1653). His major claim to fame, however, rests on his collaborations with John Milton, who in 1646 wrote of him:

> *Harry*, whose tunefull and well-measur'd Song
> First taught our English Musick how to span
> Words with just note and accent, not to scan
> With *Midas* Ears, committing short and long;
> Thy worth and skill exempts thee from the throng,
> With praise enough for Envy to look wan;
> To after age thou shalt be writ the man,
> That with smooth aire couldst humor best our tongue.[12]

Not surprisingly, Lawes's songs for Milton's *Comus* (1634) are in the declamatory style. The declamatory air by Lawes given here from *The Treasury of Musick* illustrates that a harmonically rounded structure, however typical, was not considered a necessary element of song form (see Plate 4, p. 42).

Finally, in the works of John Blow (1648?–1708), teacher and colleague of Purcell, we can trace these patterns into the Restoration. In the published volume of his songs, *Amphion Anglicus* (1700), the tuneful airs are often distinguished by their composition over a ground, and the ornamentation in the declamatory airs is now written out. (See Examples 3 and 4.)

Of course, these examples are widely separated in time, but they are representative of a continuing tradition and illustrate particularly the importance of the declamatory style as well as the more tuneful air. These song types quickly became outmoded in Italy. The reason they were maintained over such a long period in England stems from the peculiar cultural and political milieu of seventeenth-century England.

---

[11]See the discussion of this piece in McDonald Emslie, "Nicholas Lanier's Innovations in English Song," *Music and Letters* 41 (1960): 25.

[12]"To Mr H. Lawes, *on his Aires*," ll. 1–8; Sonnet XIII in *The Works of John Milton*, Vol. 1, Part 1: *Minor Poems* (New York, 1931), p. 63.

Example 3. John Blow, tuneful air: "The sullen years are past" (from *Amphion Anglicus*, 1700: "A Song").

Example 4. John Blow, declamatory air: "What is't to us" (from *Amphion Anglicus*: "Solo, A Song").

Plate 3. Nicholas Lanier, "Loves Constancy" (from Playford, *Treasury of Musick*, 1669).

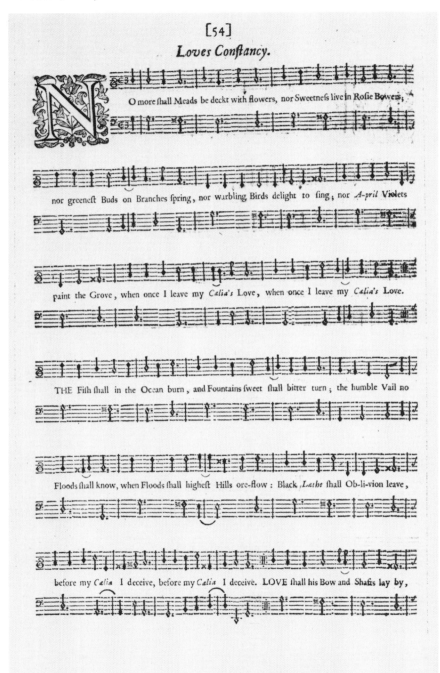

Plate 3, continued

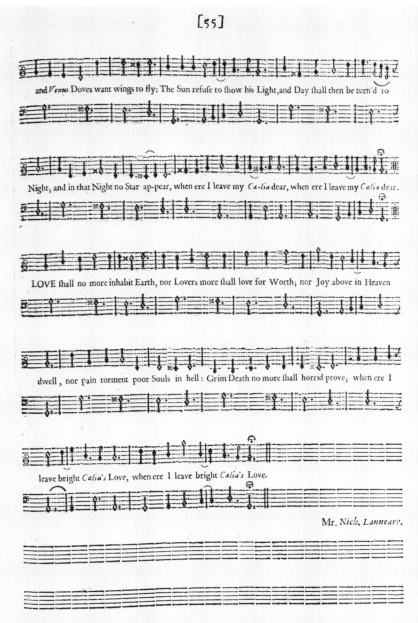

[55]

and *Venus* Doves want wings to fly: The Sun refuse to show his Light, and Day shall then be turn'd to

Night; and in that Night no Star ap-pear, when ere I leave my *Cæ-lia* dear, when ere I leave my *Cælia* dear.

LOVE shall no more inhabit Earth, nor Lovers more shall love for Worth; nor Joy above in Heaven

dwell, nor pain torment poor Souls in hell: Grim Death no more shall horrid prove; when ere I

leave bright *Cælia's* Love, when ere I leave bright *Cælia's* Love.

Mr. *Nich. Lanneare.*

P 2

Plate 4. Henry Lawes, "To a Lady Singing" (from Playford, *Treasury of Musick*, 1669).

Although, during the Caroline and Jacobean eras, the relationship between music and drama had been one of continuous development and increasing importance, the Commonwealth of 1642 instituted a totally different attitude, negative and moralistic, toward both of these arts. There is not the space here to discuss musical-dramatic developments during this period or to argue the intentions of William Davenant in his musical productions.[13] Suffice it to say that aside from Locke's music to *Cupid and Death*, which was probably not written until 1659, there is nothing of musical-dramatic interest to hold our attention during these years.

With the restoration of the monarchy in 1660 and the reopening of the theaters, a literal restoration of Elizabethan and Jacobean dramatic traditions took place. After twenty years of musical stagnation, with little or no music taught or performed, the Restoration brought with it an attempt to reach back and pick up traditions where they had left off. Thus, many of the plays produced with music were adaptations of earlier dramas—such as Shakespeare's *Macbeth* (1674) and *A Midsummer Night's Dream* (as *The Fairy Queen* [1692]), and Fletcher's *The Prophetess* (as *Dioclesian* [1695]),[14] *Bonduca* (1695), *The Island Princess* (1699), and *The Mad Lover* (1701). Moreover, the conventions for the use and insertion of music were borrowed quite clearly from the earlier traditions as well, even if the musical additions themselves were longer and more elaborate. The newly written dramas, such as Dryden's *King Arthur* (1691), and the French adaptations, such as Lully and Molière's *Psyché* (1671), also follow the same patterns.[15]

Dido and Aeneas (1689) differs from all these by being set throughout to music. This does not mean, however, that the musical traditions on which it was based were different, nor that it was any more indebted to French or Italian models. In fact, a close look at the *Dido* score reveals just three kinds of solo singing: tuneful air, declamatory air, and dialogue. The first category includes, of course, the three songs with ground bass—each clearly related to the dance and each including obvious repetitive patterns in the voice as well as the ostinato. "Ah, Belinda" begins in declamatory style (with the vocal part following the formal pattern AA) and moves into a tuneful air at "Peace and I are strangers grown" (BCB) where the voice takes up the theme of the ground bass.[16] "When I am laid in earth" follows the simple scheme AABB. "Oft she

---

[13] Extensive discussions of this period exist in the books by Dent and Haun mentioned above. In addition, I discuss musical developments in the Commonwealth in *Handel and the Pastoral Tradition* (London, 1980), pp.109 ff., where there are additional bibliographical references.

[14] *The Prophetess* was probably co-authored by Fletcher and Philip Massinger.

[15] See Curtis A. Price, *Music in the Restoration Theatre* (Cambridge, 1984) for a different view of this period. My view is described more fully in *Handel and the Pastoral Tradition*.

[16] I am indebted to Professor Curtis Price for sharing his analysis of this piece.

visits" is less regular, but after an exact repetition of the first line, each succeeding line is repeated with musical variation.

Some smaller songs also fall into the category of the tuneful air. "Shake the cloud from off your brow" and "Pursue thy conquest, love," for example, are both in ABA form. The one duet, "But ere we this perform," follows the scheme AABB, and the Sorceress' song, "Our next motion," is AAB. Finally, the solos that lead into choral repetitions, such as "Thanks to these lonesome vales" and "Come away, fellow sailors," also belong in this group.

All of these songs are too well known to be rehearsed here, and, further- more, their designations are unquestioned. What, however, of the so-called recitatives? Three of them are of particular interest: Dido's "Whence could so much virtue spring," Aeneas' "Jove's command shall be obey'd," and their dialogue "Your counsel all is urged in vain." As recitatives they are imme- diately striking for their tunefulness and harmonic closure despite their emphasis on declamation. Let me quote Dent once again (see Example 5):

> The recitative in Act I "Whence could so much virtue spring?" is a good example of [Purcell's] methods. The harmonies of Dido's first quatrain are as regularly disposed as the accent of the verse, simple in the extreme, yet always rhythmical; above them the declamation is forcible, the melody expressive, with a wide compass and rich variety of rhythm. To the modern reader perhaps the most striking features are the free alter- nation of·major and minor modes in the same key of C, the bold colora- tura, and the sudden burst of energy, heightened by its contrasting bass, in the concluding bar. Belinda answers in a gentler mood, moving through new keys—G minor, E-flat and A-flat, all untouched by Dido— and ending in suspense on the dominant; Dido leads the music back to the original tonality with a long ascending scale in broken rhythm that brings the whole movement to its emotional climax just before the end. The whole recitative is one continuous and logically constructed piece of music, beautiful and expressive even if no words were sung to it; yet the declamation is perfect, and every emotional point is seized with the most subtle delicacy and certainty.[17]

This is not the description one would expect of a recitative, and, of course, the piece in question is nothing of the sort; it is rather a declamatory air. The expressive, florid, and melismatic lines, harmonic stability, and closed form point clearly to this conclusion. The harmonic rhythm is also typical of the declamatory air; it begins in a very sustained manner and increases slowly to a more regular rate of change. Purcell's only concession to the dramatic position

---

[17]Dent, *Foundations*, p. 189.

Example 5. Henry Purcell, *Dido and Aeneas*, "Whence could so much virtue spring" (from my edition [Oxford, 1988], pp. 12–13).

of this song has been the use of three voices in alternation rather than one, but this makes little, if any, difference to the compositional method.[18]

A similar adjustment has been made in the dialogue at the end of the opera. Although basically between Dido and Aeneas, the dialogue also includes one response from Belinda, but again, this does not affect the underlying structure of the piece. The traditional dialogue form—beginning with the alternation of voices in declamatory style—remains clear, and the essentially melodic character of the declamation is illustrated by the importance of small-scale repetitions, such as the musical mirroring and harmonic intensification of Dido's thrice-repeated phrase "earth and heaven," and her ironic repetition later of Aeneas' pleading. Once again, there is also a tonally coherent and closed form. (See Example 6.) Although usually considered a recitative, this piece is obviously a rather straightforward dialogue in the traditional English manner. Indeed, Purcell used such a model deliberately: no obvious text existed for the concluding duet; one had to be created by extensive word repetition and the addition of a phrase not in the original libretto to Aeneas' part. The given text was thus adjusted according to the musical form Purcell desired.

There are few roles in the history of opera as maligned as Aeneas', and the complaints usually focus on the perception that he is given only recitative to sing. It is true that he is not given a ground-bass air, but this is appropriate to his position as catalyst in an opera that focuses on Dido's emotions rather than his. Still, the dramatic high point of the opera occurs in the dialogue that marks his departure and prepares Dido's lament; it is the only point in the opera when direct confrontation occurs. Similarly, the dramatic crisis of the opera occurs in Aeneas' only solo, the declamatory air that closes the second act.[19] (See Example 7, p. 50.) Its importance and effectiveness within the opera as a whole have long been underrated.

Aeneas sings that he will obey Jove's command and leave Dido though he could more easily die. He begins, "Jove's commands shall be obey'd / Tonight our anchor shall be weigh'd / But ah!" By extending this "ah" melismatically rather than setting it syllabically in the context of its line, "But ah! what language can I try," Purcell moves immediately into the realm of song. He is also, I think, trying to underscore the relationship between the action of Aeneas and Dido as implied by Tate's text. Aeneas says he could die more easily than leave Dido, but he leaves nonetheless. It is Dido who dies. And when she complains of her fate, as Aeneas has of his, she sings, "But ah! forget

---

[18]This expedient is already found in "Come away, Hecate!" from Middleton's *The Witch* (c. 1616) and "Get you hence, for I must go" from Shakespeare's *A Winter's Tale* (c. 1611), both perhaps by Johnson. Both may be found in Spink's edition cited above.

[19]For a discussion of the formal plan of *Dido*, see my *Handel and the Pastoral Tradition*, pp. 129–41, and my *Henry Purcell's Dido and Aeneas* (Oxford, 1988), ch. 6.

Example 6. Henry Purcell, *Dido and Aeneas*, "Your counsel all is urged in vain" (from my edition, pp. 71–76).

Example 6, continued

(13 measures of continuing dialogue)

Example 6, continued

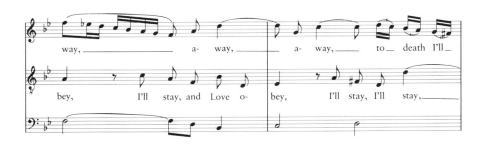

Example 7. Henry Purcell, *Dido and Aeneas*, "Jove's commands shall be obey'd" (from my edition, pp. 55–58).

my fate," and the second melisma on "ah!" is a direct mirror of Aeneas'
outburst. (See Example 8.) In the dialogue Purcell uses this same procedure—
contrasting the lovers' emotions by melodic reflection—at closer range.

Example 8. Henry Purcell, *Dido and Aeneas*, from "When I am laid in earth."

Aeneas' air is also harmonically coherent. The Spirit's message has been
delivered in A minor. Aeneas, too, begins in this key and confirms it with the
dominant, confirming as well his acceptance of the Spirit's commands. Then
with the words "What language can I try / My injur'd queen to pacify / No
sooner she resigns her heart / But from her arms I'm forc'd to part," Purcell
moves on each phrase from A minor to D to G to C, perhaps underscoring
Aeneas' own inconstancy. Aeneas goes on in E to blame the gods for his own
failure, and returns to A minor at the end. While these keys make perfect
sense within Aeneas' air, they also, like the melody, have greater referential
significance within the opera.

Aeneas' entrance occurs in another declamatory section in Act 1. Here the
key of Dido and Belinda had been C major/minor consistently for half an act,
but when Aeneas enters to ask if Dido will relent, she answers abruptly in A
minor that "Fate forbids what you pursue." Aeneas responds that Dido is his
only fate and he will defy destiny. The scene ends not in Dido's key of C,
however, but in E minor. This cadence makes an audible effect, for it is the
first movement away from C in the opera, and its use not only defies a tonic
resolution, but also implies that the final outcome will not be, so to speak, in
Dido's key.[20] This moment of harmonic tension is reflected in Aeneas' air.
Dido's A-minor reference to fate determines the key of the scene between
Aeneas and the Spirit. At the point when Aeneas thinks of Dido's feelings, he
moves into her key of C major for the first time; the only other time he does so
occurs in the dialogue when he offers to obey love, not fate. And when he
blames the gods for his fate he moves to E, as he had when telling Dido he
would ignore his destiny. Thus Aeneas' air is central to the workings of this
opera. His decision to follow his destiny brings on the denouement, and the

---

[20] Although this declamation is adapted to specific dramatic needs, a single song could also begin and end
in different keys, as seen in Plate 4.

setting musically harks back to his initial promise to do otherwise, while his expressions of grief look forward musically to Dido's more profound emotions.

All of these details illustrate a concern with heightened musical setting that is not characteristic of recitative. And, in fact, the opera as a whole contains very little true recitative. For example, the third act consists of a succession of closed forms which allow for the possibility of only two short passages of recitative, but even these are more apparent than real. The three-measure phrase at the end of the dialogue serves as a tag which helps adapt the song form to dramatic purpose. The eight measures preceding Dido's lament, however, may be seen as a declamatory section that forms an integral part of the air, such as happens in "Ah, Belinda" in Act 1. The chromatic descent in the voice from c' to c (circled notes in Example 9a) prepares for the chromatic ground (G to D, Example 9b), which is finally (and only) extended to the octave g' to g in the violin during the closing ritornello (Example 9c). Thus the declamatory and tuneful sections comprise a single air whose parts are once again balanced by the relationship of the voice to the accompaniment.[21]

The general lack of recitative in *Dido* is not unique to that work but exists as well, for example, in the masque entries that make up the musical portion of

Example 9. Henry Purcell, *Dido and Aeneas*, from "Thy hand, Belinda" and "When I am laid in earth."

a. Voice part

b. Ground

[21] For a more detailed analysis of the piece see my book *Henry Purcell's Dido and Aeneas*.

Example 9, continued
   c. Ritornello, violin part

Purcell's *The Fairy Queen*. In fact, the lyrical mode is precisely what distinguishes the masque from its contemporary operatic counterparts. Although Lully's recitative could indeed be harmonically closed, and although Stradella might make impressive use of the ground bass in his arias, only in the masque was the formalized succession of closed forms an integral element of the genre.

If we turn back to the Lanier-Jonson masque collaboration, for example, we find that *The Vision of Delight* has no dialogue whatsoever, but rather consists of a succession of short monologues. And although *Lovers Made Men* contains two sections of dialogue, these could easily have been treated within the declamatory air or dialogue form. In fact, behind the unresolved question of whether Lanier wrote his musical settings for the original productions in 1617 or in 1640 is the question of whether he wrote recitative, and it now seems highly unlikely that he did. The sections of pre-Commonwealth masques which are through-composed, such as those in *The Triumph of Peace* and *Brittania Triumphans* by William Lawes, always adhere to a succession of closed song-forms.[22] It is not surprising therefore that masques thought to have been entirely through-composed, including Lanier's and *The Triumphs of the Prince d'Amour* by William Lawes, allow for this type of composition throughout.[23] Recitative was not necessary in *Lovers Made Men* and would have been well-nigh impossible to compose for *The Triumphs of the Prince d'Amour* or *The Vision of Delight*.

This is not to say, however, that recitative, as a term or as a style, found no place in seventeenth-century England, although much depends, of course, on what was meant by the word. The version of *Lovers Made Men* in the 1640 folio of Jonson's works carries the information, "And the whole Masque was sung after the Italian manner, *stilo recitativo*, by Master *Nicholas Lanier*, who ordered and made both the Scene, and the Musicke."[24] This is the first use

[22]See Murray Lefkowitz, *Trois Masques à la Cour de Charles Ier d'Angleterre* (Paris, 1970). For example, the beginning of the musical sequence in *The Triumph of Peace* consists of: symphony, song (divided between two voices), trio, symphony, dialogue, chorus. See Songs I, II, and III, pp. 88–104.

[23]The extant portions of *The Triumphs of the Prince d'Amour* are included in Lefkowitz, *Trois Masques*.

[24]In *Ben Jonson*, ed. C. H. Herford and Percy and Evelyn Simpson, vol. 7, *Masques and Entertainments*, (Oxford, 1941), p. 454.

of the term "recitative" in England, but it cannot mean, as has often been assumed, that the entire masque was set to recitative music. Certainly, Lanier did not sing the entire masque, playing all the characters; and the one surviving song, Aurora's "I was not wearier," is not in recitative but in the heavily ornamented style of the declamatory air found already in Johnson's "Care-charming Sleep."[25] Rather, Jonson's statement simply makes the point that Lanier performed in this masque, as he had in Campion's *Masque for the Marriage of the Earle of Somerset* three years earlier in 1614,[26] and that he *also* composed the music and designed the sets. Although Jonson uses the term *stilo recitativo* again in *The Vision of Delight*, also from 1617 and first printed in the 1640 folio, there is no evidence that continental recitative was ever used in either of these Jonsonian masques. The term was undoubtedly a fashionable description of an already current style.

As late as 1654 Richard Flecknoe could still write of introducing Italianate recitative into England.[27] Although this plan apparently came to naught, William Davenant may have succeeded where his successor failed: in 1662 John Evelyn refers to Davenant's *Siege of Rhodes* as being in "Recitative Musique,"[28] and Dryden in 1670 does the same.[29] The music is not extant. It is interesting nevertheless to find such repeated efforts to set whole dramas to "recitative music" during the period 1640–60. After this time, the movement, if such it was, dies out. Its existence may at first have represented the direction in which England was moving before the Commonwealth, but during the Commonwealth it may simply have existed, as Dryden suggests, as a kind of subterfuge for having plays performed. Regardless, the restoration of the monarchy led England into an essentially retrospective musical period. Thus, the idea of opera as drama with movable scenery derives directly from Inigo Jones,[30] just as the Restoration idea of "recitative" derives from the Lawes

[25]This song has most recently been published in Emslie, "Innovations," pp. 23–24; *Four Hundred Songs and Dances from the Stuart Masque*, ed. Andrew Sabol (Providence, R. I., 1963), pp. 87–88; and *English Song: Dowland to Purcell*, ed. Ian Spink (London, 1974), pp. 47–48. Both Emslie and Spink describe the piece as a declamatory air.

[26]See the facsimile edition by David Greer (Menston, England, 1970), in *English Lute Songs*, gen. ed. F. W. Sternfeld, vol. 2, no. 7.

[27]See Haun, *But Hark! More Harmony*, pp. 36 ff.

[28]*The Diary of John Evelyn*, ed. E. S. DeBeer (Oxford, 1955), 3:309 (entry for 9 January 1662).

[29]"Of Heroic Plays," prefixed to *The Conquest of Granada* (1670); quoted from *Essays of John Dryden*, ed. W. P. Ker (Oxford, 1926), 1:149.

[30]Such non-musical definitions of Restoration opera are tentatively explored in Denis Arundell, *Critic at the Opera* (London, 1957; reprint, New York, 1980), pp. 54, 91, 100 ff., 122, 132; and in Hazelton Spencer, *Shakespeare Improved* (Cambridge, Mass., 1927), pp. 204 ff. See also my *Handel and the Pastoral Tradition*, pp. 112 ff.

brothers and their predecessors. Even continental influences during this period derive from older sources, and such had not always been the case.

At its inception the English song tradition was closely tied to Italian models. It has been noted that the declamatory and tuneful airs of Johnson relate directly to contemporary compositions of Caccini; the so-called "recitative" scenes of Lanier and W. Lawes and the through-composed masques of W. Lawes also reflect contemporary Italian trends. The music of Purcell, however, is closer in spirit to Cavalli and especially to Carissimi than to any foreign contemporary. Although these two composers were well known in Restoration England,[31] what is important about their influence is not that they were continental but that they were obsolete on the continent. Partly as a result of the Interregnum, the English song tradition had maintained these earlier styles, and they developed into a national idiom.[32]

For example, one important difference between Purcell's declamatory style and that of contemporary (or older) Italian counterparts lies in the verse forms of the texts.[33] The regular English use of metrical (tetrametric or pentametric) rhyming couplets in the declamatory sections effectively precludes a freer declamation and may itself lead away from recitative to song style. Always popular in English verse patterns, in the Restoration the rhyming couplet became the absolute standard of all heroic verse. As early as 1650, however, William Davenant had recognized the difficulties inherent in such a repetitive verse pattern. In the preface to his heroic poem *Gondibert*, which was never set to music, Davenant explains his choice of rhyme scheme, *abab*:

> I believ'd it would be more pleasant to the Reader, in a Work of length, to give this respite or pause, between every Stanza . . . than to run him out of breath with continued Couplets. Nor doth alternate Rime by any low-liness of Cadence make the sound less Heroick, but rather adapt it to a plain and stately composing of Musick; and the brevity of the Stanza renders it less subtle to the Composer, and more easie to the Singer, which in Stilo recitativo, when the Story is long, is chiefly requisite.[34]

In spite of Davenant's suggestions, however, the couplet retained its pre-eminence and consequent effect on English musical declamation.

---

[31] Cavalli's *Erismena* was translated into English and may well be the Italian opera Evelyn writes of seeing (5 January 1674); see Eric Walter White, "English Opera Research," *Theatre Notebook* 21 (1966): 34. Carissimi's music was particularly popular; in *The New Grove* (1980), Günther Massenkeil writes of the number of transcriptions of his music made during the Restoration as "astonishingly large" (3:788, s. v. "Carissimi").

[32] Similarly, the English madrigal school was indebted to Italian influence but became something quite different, special, and unique.

[33] I am extremely grateful to Professor Margaret Murata for suggesting this important distinction.

[34] Preface to *Gondibert*, ed. David F. Gladish (Oxford, 1971), p. 17.

As no examples of seventeenth-century English recitative survive, one cannot know exactly what Davenant meant by the term. It is nevertheless possible to define two distinct types; all recitative tends towards one or the other. The first, called *secco* or *semplice*, essentially represents common speech and is neither dramatic nor lyric. It is clear that this type was introduced to England only after Purcell's death. In his preface to the opera *Arsinoe* (London, 1705), Thomas Clayton wrote:

> The Musick being recitative, may not, at first meet with that general acceptation, as is to be hop'd for from the audience's being better acquainted with it: But if this attempt shall, by pleasing the nobility and gentry, be a means of bringing this manner of Musick to be us'd in my native country, I shall think all my study and pains very well employed.[35]

And in 1711 Joseph Addison wrote in *The Spectator*:

> There is nothing that has more startled our *English* Audience, than the *Italian* Recitativo at its first entrance upon the Stage. . . . Our countrymen could not forbear laughing when they heard a Lover chanting out a Billet-doux, and even the superscription of a Letter set to a tune.[36]

Purcell, of course, did not write in this style.

The other type of recitative, more sustained and highly dramatic, derives from the early years of the seventeenth century; perhaps it is best represented by the Messenger's scene in Monteverdi's *Orfeo*. But even with the development of the patter style, this type did not die out. One can still find such writing, reserved for highly-charged situations and often labelled "arioso," in eighteenth-century opera. Purcell, however, does not use this style either—the essential difference between his writing and both types of recitative is a heightened lyricism. Undoubtedly Kerman's indictment of the declamatory sections in *Dido and Aeneas* as "impersonal, courtly, and bombastic" derives from the assumption that Purcell attempted the sustained and dramatic style of recitative and failed. But Purcell made no attempt either to represent common speech or to treat the words in a highly affective manner. Although he had a great respect for speech rhythm and word meaning, he worked exclusively within the realm of heightened song. The dramatic power and emotional subtlety of his music can be witnessed equally in the tuneful airs (such as "When I am laid in earth") and in the declamatory sections.

Although the vocal music of Carissimi and Purcell can sometimes be likened in melodic idiom, Carissimi freely intermixes recitative, arioso, and aria, whereas Purcell maintains rather strict boundaries between successive song

---

[35] The passage is conveniently reproduced by Oscar Sonneck in U. S. Library of Congress, *Catalogue of Opera Librettos printed before 1800*, vol. 1: *Title Catalogue* (Washington, D. C., 1914; reprint, New York, 1968), p. 160.

[36] *The Spectator*, no. 29 (3 April 1711), vol. 1 (London, 1757), p. 155.

forms. The concessions he makes to dramatic style are those that had been used since the beginning of the century, such as the substitution of a number of singers as an alternative for a single soloist, or the use of open harmonic plans;[37] William Lawes, Matthew Locke, and John Blow had previously set complete dramas to music following such schemes.[38] Still, Purcell's ability to infuse a dramatic meaning into an essentially lyrical style, if not revolutionary, was of a special order, and it reveals something important about his particular genius. To look for continental models is to overlook this quality entirely.

The use of obsolete styles also helped create and solidify the English masque form. Thus contemporary Italianate recitative was introduced into English music little more than a decade after *Dido* by Purcell's immediate successor John Eccles. But at least thirty years after *Dido*, the old masque form— consisting of a succession of closed forms—is still apparent in Handel and Gay's *Acis and Galatea*. In all, *Acis* contains only 61 measures of secco recitative, 21 of which occur in one scene; many of the heightened pieces follow one another without any intervening recitative. On the other hand, Handel's *Radamisto*, written the next year, has 86 measures of recitative before the end of scene 3, and 273 measures in Act 1 alone. None of the arias directly follows another. Like *Dido*, then, *Acis* is operatic rather than opera itself, and, as in *Dido*, the general lack of recitative makes this clear. The masque is the musical tradition to which both works belong. After the Italian concept of through-composed opera conquered England, however, the masque form was reinterpreted as belonging to that genre. Not surprisingly, then, the idea that *Dido* is based on European operatic models and consists of aria-recitative alternation derives from a late eighteenth-century re-evaluation.

No musical score for *Dido* can be dated before 1750. A single libretto survives from the 1689 performance, but there are several playbooks from the 1700 performance of *Measure for Measure*, when *Dido* was broken up into pieces and placed out of order at the ends of acts. Neither score nor libretto exists for the documented performances in 1704 for which *Dido* was presumably reassembled and performed as a continuous whole. Then came half a century of apparent indifference, after which *Dido* suddenly reappeared. In fact, all six of the manuscript scores date from approximately 1775–1800.[39] During this time *Dido* was revived by the Academy of Ancient Music, and

[37] See above, note 18 and Plate 4.

[38] For a discussion of *Dido*'s musical heritage traced through the masque settings of these composers, and also for a stylistic comparison of the declamatory styles of Purcell, Carissimi, and Lully, see my book *Henry Purcell's Dido and Aeneas*.

[39] Tenbury, St. Michael's College, MS 1266 (c. 1775; now housed in Oxford, Bodleian Library); Tatton Park MS (copied by Philip Hayes, 1784–5; see Nigel Fortune, "A New Purcell Source," *The Music Review*

surviving librettos attest to two performances, in 1774 and 1787.[40] These librettos are identical in almost all details and reflect a newly revised version of the operatic text. Four of the manuscript scores contain this altered text; they also contain many musical changes based on eighteenth-century tastes. Among the most interesting aspects of this revision is the treatment of the declamatory sections, which are for the first time perceived and treated as recitative.

The 1774 libretto carefully prints all lyrical numbers in italic. These include, besides the choruses and tuneful airs, the duet ending only of the dialogue "Your counsel all is urged in vain." The idea of distinguishing between recitative and aria throughout the opera and even within the final dialogue itself clearly reflects eighteenth-century operatic practice, and this conception of *Dido* most seriously affects Aeneas' important soliloquy, which is cut and rewritten. (See Example 10.) The function of this piece as a declamatory air within the masque is ignored; in its badly mutilated form it behaves simply as a recitative bridge between the Spirit's command in A minor and the Sailor's farewell in B-flat.

Example 10. Henry Purcell, *Dido and Aeneas*, "Jove's commands shall be obey'd," eighteenth-century adaptation (London, British Library, Add. 31450 and 15979).

We cannot base our appreciation of a seventeenth-century work on eighteenth-century musical standards—nor need we demean the English seventeenth-century musical traditions by describing *Dido* in foreign terms. These attitudes first affected the eighteenth-century revisions, and the labelings of modern editions essentially continue to follow the 1774 libretto. For example, although we find that in 1979 Margaret Laurie labels the entire final dialogue "recitative" instead of dividing it into recitative and duet sections, she makes this very distinction in the preceding dialogue between the

25 [1964]: 109); London, British Library, Add. MS 31450 (copied by Thomas Norris and Mr. Hoblen, 1784); London, British Library, Add. MS 15979 (copied by Edward Woodley Smith, 1788?); Washington, D. C., Folger Shakespeare Library, MS cs 770 (late eighteenth century); and the Ohki MS (c. 1810; previously owned by William Cummings, now in Tokyo, Nanki Music Library).

[40] A copy of the 1774 libretto is in the New York Public Library, Performing Arts Division, Lincoln Center (Mus. Res. *MZ); a copy of the 1787 libretto is in the Royal College of Music, Portraits Gallery.

First Witch and the Sorceress, which in 1774 had been considered all recitative.[41] Any such interpretation, however, makes the different compositional styles of seventeenth-century English song function like eighteenth-century recitative and aria, and overlooks the very important roles played by the declamatory air and dialogue in seventeenth-century English music. Only when we can begin to appreciate such pieces as songs will we come any closer to understanding the true nature of the masque tradition and of that seventeenth-century English masterpiece *Dido and Aeneas*.

[41] Table of Contents to her New Purcell Society Edition of *Dido and Aeneas* (London, 1979), pp. vii–viii.

Purcell and Dido (and Aeneas)

Irving Godt

Dido had little joy of Pious Aeneas, but she gets a taste of revenge in Henry Purcell's opera.[1] Dido occupies center stage, while Virgil's hero shrinks to the stature of a bit player. Aeneas courts Dido, wins Dido, and jilts her, but he never gets an aria. And when injured Dido spurns his belated change of heart, the Founder of Empire has to slink off silently without so much as an exit line.[2] Poor Piety! Despite his fame as a pillar of antiquity, many seventeenth-century ladies would tolerate no defense of him; even a demigod might not escape their scorn for a faithless lover.[3]

Purcell's librettist, Nahum Tate (1652–1715; named poet laureate, 1692), was no more than a comfortable hack. Two years before his collaboration with Purcell, his Muse had produced a version of *King Lear* with a happy ending—including a marriage between Cordelia and Edgar. Tate did no better by Purcell, giving him only a slim outline of the classical story and populating it with stick figures who, for character and motivation, must rely upon an audience's familiarity with their circumstances.[4] The story of Dido was, of

---

[1] References to *Dido and Aeneas* (Z. 626) are to Margaret Laurie's edition, *The Works of Henry Purcell*, 3 (London, 1979), which includes a facsimile of the printed libretto with its prologue to the first performance. The revised edition of the vocal score prepared by Margaret Laurie and Thurston Dart (London, 1966) includes the editors' adaptation of that prologue to other music by Purcell. Z-numbers are references to Franklin B. Zimmerman, *Henry Purcell, 1659–1695: An Analytical Catalogue of His Music* (London, 1963).

[2] Curtis A. Price, *Henry Purcell and the London Stage* (Cambridge, 1984), p. 240, reports eighteenth-century attempts to remedy this defect.

[3] We learn as much from John Dryden—who would excuse Aeneas—in the dedication of his translation of Virgil (1697): *Essays of John Dryden*, ed. W. P. Ker (Oxford, 1900), 2 vols., 2:186.

[4] Tate patched this libretto from his earlier *Brutus of Alba, or The Enchanted Lovers* (1678), a thinly disguised version of Dido's story; see Price, *Henry Purcell and the London Stage*, pp. 226 ff.

Some critics hold more charitable views of Tate's works than I can muster. Imogen Holst, "Purcell's Librettist, Nahum Tate," in *Henry Purcell, 1659–1695: Essays on His Music*, ed. Imogen Holst (London, 1959), pp. 35–41, reads Tate with generosity. Eric Walter White, "A New Light on 'Dido and Aeneas'," in Holst, pp. 14–34, takes up those parts of Tate's libretto for which, if Purcell set them, the music is now lost. They do nothing to raise Tate's stature. Robert Etheridge Moore, *Henry Purcell and the Restoration*

course, no mystery to fashionable audiences in the London of 1689;[5] everybody knew it, and nobody expected—or wished—to meet any surprises in it. Tate gave them none. He retells the tale as one might for children, with embellishments (witches, jolly Jack Tars) that could appeal only to the most naive taste. His Aeneas is an utter nonentity—a practical expedient, perhaps, in an entertainment produced, presumably, by a cast made up largely of girls at Josiah Priest's School for Young Gentlewomen—but his Dido, too, is curiously neutral. She begins as a conventional, love-struck heroine whose secret must be coaxed from her by Belinda, the indispensable confidante of the seventeenth-century stage. Tate reports Dido's feelings—her response to Aeneas' suit, her painful choice between the claims of love and honor, and her anguish when Aeneas abandons her—in a dramatic shorthand so cryptic that it leaves us totally unprepared for (and perhaps unconvinced by) Dido's one high-souled moment: her indignant rejection in Act 3 of Aeneas' shamefaced offer to remain in Carthage in defiance of the gods. Dido will not endure a lover who had even for a moment entertained a thought of leaving her. Of course, this, too, is but another conventional posture from the French tragedy and the English heroic play of the era.

The rest of Tate's *dramatis personae* are also sketchily drawn. His witches, though direct descendants of the weird sisters in *Macbeth*, are supernatural yet impotent, omniscient yet small-minded; they are dramaturgical ciphers who—notwithstanding Purcell's wonderful music for them—serve only to justify some dances to please Mr. Priest, who just happens to have been a dancing-master.[6] As villainesses they contribute absolutely nothing to the movement or the tension of the narrative. It is true that they trick Aeneas into an early departure, but his reservations for the Italian tour had long been confirmed on Olympus. Their most malicious blow against Dido, whom they

---

Theatre (Cambridge, Mass., 1961), pp. 59–64, argues that the opera is as effective as it is because the libretto does not get in Purcell's way—that is, the opera is so good because Tate is so bad. There is, of course, an essential truth in Moore's observation; but the fact remains that Tate wrote not merely innocuous lines, but (as all agree) some insufferable lines, and that he patched situations together without motivation. Does not Moore's forbearance toward Tate present us with the contradiction that a better libretto would not have served Purcell better? Purcell's anthems do not seem to suffer where the quality of his texts improves. I cannot repress the feeling that those benevolent opinions of Tate spring from the critics' love for Purcell. It is never easy for us to accept the fact that a beloved genius (whether a Purcell or a Schubert) might on occasion consort with a literary lump.

[5] 1689 is the currently accepted date of the first performance. For a discussion of the date of *Dido*, see A. M. Laurie, "Purcell's Stage Works" (Ph. D. dissertation, University of Cambridge, 1962), fols. 51 ff., cited by Franklin B. Zimmerman, *Henry Purcell, 1659–1695: His Life and Times* (London, 1967), p. 179.

[6] Edward J. Dent, *Foundations of English Opera* (Cambridge, 1928; reprint, New York, 1965), p. 185, points out the material motivation for their presence. Tate's witches carry on a Restoration revival (cf. Davenant's *Macbeth*, mentioned by Price, *Henry Purcell and the London Stage*, pp. 231 ff.) of a tradition well established on the English stage before the closing of the theaters in 1642.

hate, is "to storm her lover on the ocean."[7] However, their storm arrives—if at all—after the curtain has fallen, and Dido dies without ever having heard a weather forecast.

If Tate's sailors serve any dramatic purpose, it is to echo the theme of loving-and-leaving. They provide a comic parallel to Aeneas' heroic posture.

Purcell succeeded in transforming this pedestrian libretto into a master-piece, not merely because he set it so beautifully, but because his music fleshes out character where Tate provided none. The Dido of the opera is Purcell's creation, not Tate's, and only partly Virgil's. His music conveyed to his listeners an affecting portrait of the heroine in terms they understood, and in musical symbols with which they were familiar. He drew her likeness, not only in the small-dimension madrigalisms and affective touches that abound throughout the opera, but in broader strokes that bespeak a reading of the story that is vastly richer than Tate's while remaining consistent with his thin libretto. Purcell might have done the same for Aeneas. He could have ex-panded a line or a couplet into an aria for the hero, just as he did for other characters—but he did no such thing. His opera is about Dido. With little help from Tate, he portrays the emotional crisis of a Queen who yields to in-fatuation and atones by taking her own life.

Considering the stuff he had to work with, it is small wonder that Purcell fixed upon Dido's *inner* conflicts as the center of his musical drama. His portrait of her rests on long-standing traditions of rhetoric and word painting well known to his musical contemporaries. Indeed, the opera as a whole is so rich in madrigalisms that it is often harder to find evidence of neglect than of concern for the text. Rather than list examples of such madrigalisms here, however, I have provided an appendix in which three numbers in the opera are analyzed in depth from the standpoint of text influences.[8]

While Purcell's madrigalisms reveal much about his responses to situation and character, they do so largely within local contexts circumscribed by the wording of the libretto. On the other hand, Purcell represents Dido's character most profoundly in the opera's three most important musical compositions: the overture (no. 1) and Dido's two arias, "Ah, Belinda" and "When I am Laid in Earth" (nos. 3 and 38 respectively). These three pieces cover a much broader psychological canvas, and they do so on a larger musical scale. From the first

---

[7] Their earlier storm, in Act 2, is no more than a minor irritant which interrupts the hunt and drives the royal party back to town. In Virgil, that storm (*Aeneid*, bk. 4, lines 161 ff.) drives the royal pair into the cave where they consummate their love (Josquin's "Fama malum" sets lines 174–77, which describe the ensuing rumors against the Queen's reputation). That episode could have seemed inappropriate for a production taking place in a girls' school.

[8] I expect to supply a more extended sample of the opera's madrigalisms in a book on word painting now nearing completion, tentatively titled *Music About Words*.

notes of the overture (the first of these famous pieces), Dido emerges a grander character than Tate's flimsy puppet beset by the malice of witches and the indifference of gods.

Purcell's overture is not Italian; that is, it is not a *sinfonia* designed to provide little more than a noise of music. Rather, it is an intensely expressive piece in two sections that follow the practice but not the spirit of the French *ouverture*: an adagio (unmarked by Purcell) in prominently dotted rhythm followed by a fugal allegro (Purcell marks it "Quick"). Unlike the model established by Lully, Purcell's slow section does not evoke the majestic style, and his quick fugato lacks a truly melodic subject. The divergences seem to stem from the distinct interpretative aims of his two sections. The opening adagio can be described only as unsettling. In ten of its twelve measures,[9] at least one chromaticism deflects the line, or at least one foreign note wrenches us toward a new goal. Chordal dissonances outnumber consonant triads beyond the normal alternation of stable and active beats,[10] while their resolutions may even arrive simultaneously with the onset of new dissonance or chromaticism (Example 1).

Example 1. Purcell, *Dido and Aeneas*, overture, mm. 1–6.

D = dissonance (passing tone, suspension, etc.)
C = chromaticism
H = diminished or augmented harmony

[9] There is an additional measure implied, since it ends on the downbeat of m. 13.

[10] The ratio is nearly 2:1. Double dissonance, C + D + E-flat, on the downbeat of the second measure foreshadows harmonic practice in the quick section.

During the course of the preceding hundred years, chromaticism had come to be identified with *pathopoeia*, the rhetorical term for an expression of pain, most often taken to mean the pains of love or of death.[11] Both meanings apply here. Theorists, of course, had always regarded dissonance as harsh and unpleasant to the ear. It is worth recalling here the wording of Tinctoris, writing towards the end of the fifteenth century: " . . . Just as the bitterness of enmity arises from the separation of two hearts from a mutual uniformity of sentiment, so the harshness of a discord is produced from two pitches not agreeing with each other."[12] The long, leaning dotted (or tied) notes that begin every measure (in at least one voice) suggest feelings of yearning—a reading supported by echoes of that rhythm in Dido's final song, in her longing utterances, "Remember me, remember me." The same quality of yearning attaches to some of the adagio's upward semitone motions, which exemplify the *passus duriusculus*, a difficult step requiring emotional or physical effort.[13] The best part of Purcell's audience, having foreknowledge of the story (and having made at least a passing acquaintance with the notions of rhetoric in the course of their education), would have had no difficulty in interpreting these traits of the adagio as conventional ways of expressing pain and longing—presumably Dido's. We may go a bit further and interpret its harmonic instability as a reflection of Dido's emotional instability. The seventeenth century applied many adjectives equally to music and to the emotions: words like fickle, shifting, and changeable just as easily described "changeable humours" as shifting harmonies.

The extraordinary allegro ("Quick") section portrays other aspects of Dido's feelings. An insistent *perpetuum mobile* in eighth-notes, it thrashes its way

[11] This musical usage had already acquired a long history in the Italian madrigal well before Joachim Burmeister listed the term in his *Musica poetica* (Rostock, 1606), pp. 61 f. Zarlino had associated semitone movements with *meste* (sad) subjects: *Istitutioni harmoniche* (Venice, 1573), pp. 319–20.

[12] Tinctoris was speaking, of course, of the proportions between discordant string lengths, but his diction expresses his attitude toward dissonance: *Liber de arte contrapuncti*, in Charles-Edmond-Henri de Coussemaker, *Scriptorum de musica medii aevi nova series* (Paris, 1864–76; reprint, Hildesheim, 1963), 4 vols., 4:120; translation from Albert Seay, *Johannes Tinctoris: The Art of Counterpoint*, Musicological Studies and Documents, 5 (American Institute of Musicology, 1961), p. 85. Morley voices the same sentiment in 1597: "You must then when you would express any word signifying hardness, cruelty, bitterness, and other such like make the harmony like unto it, that is somewhat harsh and hard, but yet so that it offend not": *A Plaine and Easy Introduction to Practical Music* ([London, 1597], p. 177), which was popular enough for long enough to receive a new edition as late as 1771. Modern edition by Alec Harman (2nd ed., London, 1963; reprint, New York, 1973), p. 290.

[13] Both of these usages, too, have a long madrigal history. The term *passus duriusculus* appears in Christoph Bernhard's *Tractatus compositionis augmentatis*, ch. 29, par. 2–5, but without any affective interpretation; see Joseph Maria Müller-Blattau, *Die Kompositionslehre Heinrich Schutzes in der Fassung seines Schulers Christoph Bernhard*, 2nd ed. (Kassel, 1963), pp. 77–78; for an English translation, see Walter Hilse, "The Treatises of Christoph Bernhard," *The Music Forum* 3 (1973): 103–4.

through 26 measures of quasi fugato.[14] The subject of the fugato (Example 2) is a crude alternation of triadic tones with stubbornly repeating pitches. The overall melodic texture of this quick section is markedly disjunct, rhythmically restless.

Example 2. Purcell, *Dido and Aeneas*, overture, mm. 13–15.

Although its harmonic rhythm strides along, changing harmonies with almost relentless regularity, usually every half measure, and while its chordal vocabulary seems at first less tortured than that of the adagio, it arrives eventually at a headstrong progression that would remain unrivalled in stridency for a century and a half (mm. 30–35; Example 3).

Example 3. Purcell, *Dido and Aeneas*, overture, mm. 30–35.

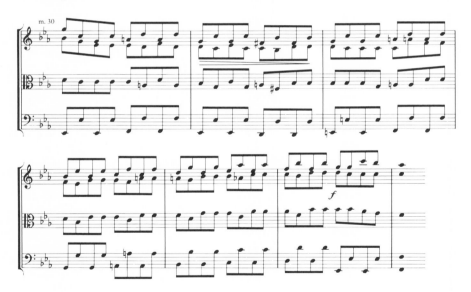

[14]There are two sets of irregular imitative entries. The first, beginning at m. 13, introduces its four voices in an order that we may describe as tonic/tonic/dominant/dominant. The second set, entering at m. 21, exposes only two voices, the first outlining the tonic chord, the bass answering a whole tone below (on B-flat). We hear some hints of the subject in the upper voices in the next few bars, but after this second entry, the saw-tooth subject of the fugato seems to have thrust the very idea of imitation aside.

Fundamentally, that passage consists of an obsessively long string of first-inversion triads (Example 4a) attacked by double dissonances (shown schematically in Example 4b) which resolve irregularly after the beat.[13]

Example 4. Purcell, *Dido and Aeneas*, overture, mm. 30–36, schematic reduction.

a.

b.

Those words "headstrong" and "stubborn" supply the key to this interpretation of the allegro. Purcell's listeners, having made a natural, obvious, and conventional association between the chromatic adagio and Dido's feelings, would just as naturally have carried that identification over into the quick section, which follows without interruption. There they would have met a less sympathetic description of Dido. They would have heard its stubborn pitch repetition, its obstinate rhythms, and its headstrong harmony (unusual even for Purcell) as open commentary on Dido's undisciplined emotions. Thus, the overture as a whole would have prepared them (as they must have expected) for a Dido ruled by passions she knew were forbidden to her. It was, after all, an age in which girls—like those in Mr. Priest's finishing school—were told whom they would marry; and duty—in tragedy as in life—dictated the marriages of queens.

To some, this reading may seem to impose its interpretation arbitrarily on a piece of Baroque instrumental music which might well have been heard as "abstract" music, but the context of the overture argues otherwise. From the rhetorical point of view, an overture is an *exordium*—the first part of a Classical oration, a beginning intended to prepare the audience to listen with

---

[15] The fact that the second half of m. 32 fails to conform to the prevailing pattern raises the question of a possible defect in the sources: whether an E-natural or an E-flat should stand in an inner voice at the gap left in the schematic reduction of Example 4b.

attention.[16] Indeed, it has been shown that instrumental pieces in more abstract contexts may have the function of an exordium.[17] Here, because of its position at the opening of a well-known tragic tale, the overture functions also in the character of a *narratio*—four generations before Beethoven and Weber began anticipating the dramatic and musical substance of their operas in their overtures. Seventeenth-century listeners sufficiently cultivated to recognize the context of Purcell's overture would have heard it as more than merely "generic" tragedy music. They would have interpreted what they heard in the Baroque terms that agreed with their musical experience. That experience was not operatic. Opera had not yet penetrated England to any great extent, and few in Purcell's audience could have been familiar with continental operatic conventions. The public music with which they were most familiar was the music they heard in church and at the playhouse. In church they heard solo and choral anthems which still employed the word-bound styles that had been evolving since the era of Josquin; in the theater they heard music of a more commercial character (overtures, entr'actes, dances, and solo songs), but this music too occasionally reflected the influence of its texts—a clear sign that audiences must have understood the conventions that had obtained in text setting for more than two hundred years. Theatrical composers, then as now, did not waste time on matters which their audiences did not understand. Whether or not an ordinary listener might have grasped all the implications proposed here for the overture, one point encourages the belief that Purcell himself may have interpreted it that way: Dido's arias seem to support the same reading of her character.

When we turn from the opera's overture to its vocal music, we no longer have to cope with the ambiguities of instrumental music; we have both text and context to guide us. Just as Purcell began to express the content of the story with the first notes of the overture, so he begins to deal in madrigalisms from the very first word of the libretto, Belinda's "Shake."[18] But the two arias

---

[16] For convenient discussions of the *exordium*, see Lee A. Sonnino, *A Handbook to Sixteenth-Century Rhetoric* (New York, 1968), p. 243; and Richard A. Lanham, *A Handlist of Rhetorical Terms* (Berkeley, 1969), p. 49.

[17] See Warren Kirkendale, "Ciceronians versus Aristotelians on the Ricercare as Exordium," *Journal of the American Musicological Society* 32 (1979): 1–44. The idea that instrumental music can express feelings despite its lack of words was expressed in England as early as 1515 in Book I of Thomas More's *Utopia* (Louvain, [1516]), Book II, "*Musica Utopiensium*" (unpaginated): "For all their musike bothe that they playe upon instrumentes, and that they singe with mannes voyce dothe so resemble and expresse the naturall affections, the sound and tune is so applied and made agreable to the thinge, that whether it bee a prayer, or els a dytty of gladnes, of patience, of trouble, of mournynge, or of anger: the fassion of the melodye dothe so represent the meaning of the thing, that it doth wonderfullye move, stirre, pearce, and enflame the hearers myndes." Translation by Raphe Robinsone, 1551: *"Utopia" with the "Dialogue of Comfort" by Sir Thomas More* (London, 1910; reprint, 1931).

[18] For a detailed discussion of madrigalisms in no. 2, see Appendix.

that mark the beginning and the end of Dido's tragedy, though not devoid of madrigalism,[19] search her mind more deeply than mere madrigalism would allow. The two arias share one vitally important characteristic: Purcell set both of them over grounds. Purcell adopted this peculiarly Baroque structural idiom (*ground bass, basso ostinato, ciaccona, passacaglia*, etc.) with particular enthusiasm and genius. In the probably no more than twenty years of creative life granted to him, he composed about 87 pieces that have been classed as grounds.[20] By Purcell's day, the ground had come to be classed as one of those repetitive devices subsumed under the rhetorical term *anaphora*.[21] The unremitting character of its repeating bass made the ground especially suitable for mournful or tragic affections. I do not mean that grounds implied only mournful associations. Their range extends from Monteverdi's predominantly cheerful *Zefiro torno* (*Scherzi musicali*, 1632), to Purcell's reverent *Evening Hymn on a Ground* (Z. 193), published a year before the performance of *Dido*.[22] Around the 1630s, ground bass became a favored medium for the operatic *lamento*, very often over a bass that outlined a descending tetrachord.[23] We shall see that both of Dido's grounds fit

[19] For example, in her first song: chromaticism and melisma on "languish"; in her last song: descending melisma on "laid in earth."

[20] On Purcell's use of grounds, see Hugh M. Miller, "Henry Purcell and the Ground Bass," *Music and Letters* 29 (1948): 341 ff. Miller includes in this tally pieces which treat the bass so freely that his figure may seem too high (see, for instance, his Example 12). However, he makes it clear that Purcell treats ground bass very freely, varying the principle from "near ostinato" to strictest ground bass. A clear formal classification of these procedures would be useful. See also Rosamond McGuinnesss, "The Ground-Bass in the English Court Ode," *Music and Letters* 51 (1970): 118 and 136 ff. McGuinness has doubted whether any common denominator applies to the texts of Purcell's vocal grounds, but the issue does not hinge on a common denominator; text-music influences have never been single-valued.

[21] Joachim Thuringus had made this association as early as 1624 in his *Opusculum bipartitum*, cited by Hans Heinrich Unger, *Die Beziehungen zwischen Musik und Rhetorik im 16.–18. Jahrhunderten* (Würzburg, 1941; reprint, Hildesheim, 1969), p. 69.

[22] I have the impression that grounds (instrumental and vocal) in minor keys tend to be more numerous than those in major—owing perhaps to the greater harmonic variety possible in minor. Richard Hudson lists early passacaglia and ciaccona formulae that seem to favor the minor keys: "Further Remarks on the Passacaglia and Ciaccona," *Journal of the American Musicological Society* 23 (1970): 312. An association between minor keys and the sad and serious affections appeared in Charles Masson's *Nouveau traité des regles pour la composition de la musique* (2nd ed., Paris, 1699; facsimile edited by Imogen Horsley, New York, 1967), p. 11. (A first edition of 1694—five years after the appearance of *Dido* and a year before Purcell's death—has not survived.) Masson was one of the first theorists to recognize just two modes, major and minor, but the approach seems to have been general for some time. English awareness of it became evident in revisions to the thirteenth edition of Playford's *An Introduction to the Skill of Music* (1697). See Franklin B. Zimmerman's appendix to the facsimile of the twelfth (1694) edition (New York, 1972), p. 198, where the anonymous reviser refers explicitly to a two-key system with "chearful" and "melancholy" associations. In his comments, Zimmerman (p. 13, n. 17) raises the possibility that Purcell himself may have had a hand in those revisions.

[23] See Ellen Rosand, "The Descending Tetrachord: An Emblem of Lament," *Musical Quarterly* 65 (1979): 346–59. Rosand calls attention to the possibility that Monteverdi's *Lamento della ninfa* (*Madrigali guerreri et amorosi*, 1638) may have contributed to the vogue for laments over a ground.

squarely into that emblematic *lamento* tradition. Because of their special qualities, it will be simpler to discuss Dido's final aria before turning to her first one.

That final aria, "When I Am Laid in Earth" is easily, as Donald Grout has said, "one of the most affecting expressions of tragic grief in all opera."[24] Tate evidently recognized the theatrical force of Dido's suicide; he makes her declare her intention three times during the preceding scene (her final breach with Aeneas), harping on the subject as if afraid the audience might not understand her. Tate never allows her to explain herself; he merely settles for the choral comment: "Great minds against themselves conspire" before Dido begins her last speeches:

No. 37   (1) Thy hand, Belinda; darkness shades me.
         (2) On thy bosom let me rest.
         (3) More I would, but death invades me;
         (4) Death is now a welcome guest.
No. 38   (5) When I am laid in earth may my wrongs create
         (6) No trouble in thy breast.
         (7) Remember me, but ah! forget my fate.

The rhyme rest-guest-breast suggests that Tate conceived the seven lines as a single unit; if he did, then Purcell must have recognized the greater pathos gained in reserving the first four lines for recitative and concentrating the aria into the last three. Purcell must have seen that the first part of the speech was too busy and that Dido's final moments deserved something more lyrical. Tate's repetitions assert her intentions, but only the closing lines characterize her feelings to any extent. Lines 5 and 6 express her resignation and her concern for the friend she leaves behind; line 7 expresses the paradox of her position: she wishes to be remembered by her friend, but since remembering will cause pain, she desires that Belinda forget her unhappy end. Dido's words and her well-known situation allow us to infer this despite Tate's telegraphic style.

Tate's last three lines, while they may be more lyrical, presented Purcell with a contradiction. The prevailing affection in Dido's speech is her feeling of regret; but an expression of regret, while it may sound an effective note of pathos, cannot supply much theatrical motivation for a character's suicide. Purcell required a solution that would preserve the first and generate the second. At least part of the expressive power of his solution resides in the manner in which he adapted the *lamento* tradition to his needs. His ground

---

[24]*A Short History of Opera*, 2nd ed. (New York, 1965), p. 144. In his textbook, *A History of Western Music*, 3rd ed. (New York, 1980), p. 350, Grout calls it without reservation "one of the greatest arias in all opera."

slides chromatically (and emblematically) down the distance of a tetrachord from G to D and elaborates the lower note functionally into a cadence (Example 5a).[25] The bass states the ground eleven times; statements 1, 10, and 11 are assigned to the orchestra, while the remaining eight (2–9) are reserved for Dido's accompaniment. Purcell, ordinarily a master at writing asymmetrical lines against an ostinato, here groups the first two lines of the song (lines 5–6 of the poem) into a single musical period, which he then repeats symmetrically. The sense of symmetry (and hence, of stability) is reinforced by the fact that the first line ("When I am laid in earth . . . ") and the second ("No trouble in thy breast") both enter against the pitch G in the ground, even though they enter at different points in the ground (notes 10 and 1 respectively). But this balance does not last. As Dido approaches her crisis, the repeated appeals, "Remember me," of the last line emphasize their urgency by becoming progressively more asymmetrical with respect to the ground: the first three appeals enter (reckoning by the accented syllable, "-mem-") against bass notes 10, 4, and 4; but when Dido repeats the entire section, they re-enter against notes 2, 6, and 4, creating thereby a whole new set of musical relationships, and a heightened emotional tension.

The instrumental postlude heard over the last two statements of the ground surely sounds the most touching moment in Purcell's score. Indeed, any sensitive dramatic composer would take pains to make it so, since it must accompany Dido's self-immolation. Purcell responded to the need with three imitative string entries that echo the downward chromaticism of the supporting ground, but the last entry (violin 1) extends the sequence until it has stretched over almost the whole twelve-note chromatic octave from g'' down to g' (omitting only the a-flat).[26] The mournfully sympathetic character of

[25] That chromatic fall had been used before Purcell (by Cavalli in 1643) and would be used again by Bach in his so-called B-Minor Mass (Crucifixus) and in the *Hauptchöre* of Cantatas 12 and 78. Compare Dido's ground with one from Cavalli's *Egisto* printed in J. A. Westrup, *Purcell* (London, 1947), p. 142. Rosand, "The Descending Tetrachord," p. 355, suggests that the emblematic tetrachord may also appear in inversion; however, that idea seems gratuitous in the light of an example given by Thomas Walker, "Ciaccona and Passacaglia: Remarks on Their Origin and Early History," *Journal of the American Musicological Society* 21 (1968): 300–320. Walker's Example 4b (pp. 311–12, from Monteverdi's *Poppea*, 1642) is not a lament, yet it is almost identical to Rosand's Example 1 (from Cavalli's *Hipermestra*, 1658). The histories of the ground and of the lament are obviously so closely intertwined that it seems unnecessary to resort to inversion in order to bring the inverted example into the tradition.

[26] The only earlier chromatic scale that covers an octave known to me occurs at the beginning of Marenzio's madrigal "Solo e pensoso," *Di Luca Marenzio il nono libro de' madrigali a cinque voci* (Venice, 1599), p. 12; modern editions: *L'arte musicale in Italia*, ed. Luigi Torchi (Milan, 1897–1908?), 2:228 ff.; *Geschichte der Musik in Beispielen*, ed. Arnold Schering (Leipzig, 1931), pp. 174 ff. (*prima parte* only); *The Oxford Book of Italian Madrigals*, ed. Alec Harman (London, 1983), pp. 282 ff. (transposed); and *The Comprehensive Study of Music*, ed. William Brandt et al., (New York, 1980), 1:266 ff. Marenzio uses all twelve notes in an upward and then a downward scale to symbolize a slow, painful progress. Here the chromatic descent represents a painful *katabasis* (see below).

Example 5. Purcell, *Dido and Aeneas*.

a. "When I Am Laid in Earth," ground.

b. "When I Am Laid in Earth," postlude, mm. 38–47.

c. "With Drooping Wings," soprano, mm. 1–3.

d. "With Drooping Wings," soprano, mm. 5–7.

that truly "dying fall" surpasses in expressiveness every other musical gesture of the opera (see Example 5b above).

Purcell makes use of a number of standard rhetorical devices in this aria. Chromaticism in the bass, just as in the overture, expresses *pathopoeia*, Dido's anguish. Its steady descent represents *katabasis*, a directional convention[27] often associated with some *locus topicus* such as sorrow, earth, burial, and here, death. But I take the very presence of the ground bass principle here to have an even more explicit intention. The "endless" repetitions of a strict ground make it consonant with a number of *topoi*: inevitability, destiny, eternity, eternal law, authority, endless flow, steadfastness, resolution—others are possible. It is not necessary to suppose that Purcell (or any other composer) had any one particular *topos* in mind *every* time he wrote over a *basso ostinato*, or even that he had to have any at all. That is beside the point. Here, in this context, that relentless bass becomes an eloquent symbol of Dido's fixed determination to die. Thus, against the prevailing affection of regret, the very structure of the song (the presence of a ground, the melodic shape and content of that ground, the relationships between it and the voice part) probes more deeply into Dido's anguish and her suicidal resolve.

Joseph Kerman has pointed out that "the lament does not end, but flows into the wonderful final chorus."[28] But something more than proximity connects the two numbers. The chorus, "With Drooping Wings," takes up the thread spun in the aria and turns it back upon itself. It converts dragging chromatics into firm diatonic steps and inverts the intervallic skeleton. Whereas the ground slides down a fourth by chromatic steps (G to D), delays on the dominant, then falls a fifth to the tonic (G), to fill an octave, in the chorus the soprano answers the ground's fourth with the complementary interval, the descending fifth (D to G), which it fills by diatonic steps, then falls the fourth (to D), to complete its octave (see Example 5c above). As if to emphasize its intent, the chorus replies also to the chromatic octave of the aria's instrumental postlude with complete diatonic scales down from the tonic (G to G) and from the dominant (D to D). The complementarity and the diatonicism of these choral parts create an antithesis that seems to seal the wound opened by the first bars of the overture (see Example 5d above).

On the basis of these readings of the overture and of Dido's final aria, we may now recognize the same remarkable coordination between structure and expressive content in Dido's first aria, "Ah, Belinda" (no. 3).

---

[27] What I call the directional convention refers to the association of upward or downward melodic lines or intervals with words implying those directions (such as heavenward and leaping, or falling and dying), and with affirmation or negation.

[28] *Opera as Drama* (New York, 1956), p. 60.

(1) Ah, Belinda, I am pressed
(2) With torment not to be confessed.
(3)   Peace and I are strangers grown.
(4)   I languish till my grief is known,
(5) Yet would not have it guessed.

In these lines we can see that Dido begins as she ends: in conflict with herself. The choice she makes in this first dilemma leads directly to her final conflict. It seems consistent of Purcell to have chosen to express both conflicts in arias built over grounds, but he does not treat them identically. In her final aria, Dido is resigned to death; in her first, she is tormented and irresolute. The two situations are different and call for different means of expression. Like the ground of "When I Am Laid in Earth," the ground of "Ah, Belinda" reflects Dido's feelings; but, as her situation at this point in the story is more complex, so are the means needed to convey it adequately. The bass states the ground 21 times, with the 9th, 16th, 19th, 20th, and 21st statements left as instrumental interludes. Unlike the ground of the final aria, which remains fixed in its original location, the ground of "Ah, Belinda" shifts to the dominant for two of its 21 statements (nos. 12–13), but the ground and the voice part preserve an almost perfectly symmetrical relationship.[29] Against the background of that symmetry the ground's shift to the dominant becomes more meaningful. If the fixed level of the ground in her last aria may symbolize Dido's resolution, then this shift in the ground, as she sings of her unlawful love, must symbolize the weakness of her resolve to resist that love. Significantly, over those transposed ("weak") statements of the ground she sings the words of line 4, "I languish till my grief is known."

Even as Dido sings her first notes, the structure of the ground betrays her restlessness and instability to the listener. This first ground, like the last, is written in triple time, and by coincidence both contain ten notes, but there the resemblance ends. This one is an amazing amalgam of duple and triple meter (Example 6).

Example 6. Purcell, *Dido and Aeneas*, "Ah, Belinda," ground.

---

[29]The first two phrases enter on notes 5 and 2, and then repeat. All subsequent phrases enter on note 10.

Twenty-one times, like one of those flickering optical illusions, it promises the ear duple meter, only to lapse into triple meter at every cadence. The structure of this ground, like Dido's emotional state, is inherently unstable and thus agrees with the musical portrait deduced here. One phrase in the aria even seems to hint at the flaw in Dido's character: the setting of line 3. She sings the words, "Peace and I . . . " by imitating that metrically irresolute ground; but her version of those notes moves in blunt triple time against the wavering bass (Example 7)—as if to say that, despite her conflicting feelings, her choice is made. Purcell concludes this aria, too, with a postlude over further statements of the ground, and here, again, the three upper strings enter imitatively with music related to the ground, but their subject is still Dido's willful version of "Peace and I."[30]

Example 7. Purcell, *Dido and Aeneas*, "Ah, Belinda."
a. Mm. 48–54.

---

[30]Although the readings of the three pieces offered here tend to support each other, one point remains unaccounted for. The opera includes yet another song over a ground—"Oft she visits this lone mountain" (no. 25), sung by "Second Woman" in Act 2. Aligning this ground with the other two in the opera, while not essential to our conclusions, would make the argument neater; in fact, this does seem possible. Second Woman sings to seven statements of a running ground, after which six statements in the ritornello presumably accompany a dance of some sort. The song tells of Diana's revenge against Acteon, whom she caused to be pursued and slain by his own hounds. The scurrying motion of the ground's running eighth notes—another *perpetuum mobile*—depicts that pursuit. Although the ground never sounds in any key

Example 7, continued
   b. Postlude.

The portrait of Dido that has emerged from Purcell's score condemns her by
the standards of the age as a headstrong woman who, placing her feelings
above her duty and opposing a destiny of which she is completely aware (Dido:
"Fate forbids what you pursue," Act 1, no. 8), accepts her inevitable penalty.
In his Prologue to the opera, Tate seeks to excuse Dido's conduct by casting the
blame on Venus, but he shows only that he has failed to understand the
complexity of Virgil's argument and motives. Neither Tate's libretto nor

---

other than D minor, three times it does attempt to lead elsewhere, as if it (and Acteon) were trying vainly to
escape from D minor. (Statement 5 cadences on A; statement 10 [ritornello] cadences on F and is heard
again as statement 12 when that strain is repeated.) None of the digressions, however, manages to pull the
next statement of the ground out of its original key. At this point in the opera, a double meaning attaches to
the presence of a ground as a symbol of inevitability. It signifies the inevitability of Diana's revenge against
Acteon, and, at the same time, the inevitability of Aeneas' betrayal of Dido at what he takes to be Jove's
command. This fourth reading cannot prove the validity of the others, but it shows that a consistent
symbolic reading can account for the presence of all the grounds in the opera. However, this last
interpretation is not critical to our portrait of Dido.

Purcell's music will support that excuse. Dido lives and dies nobly and heroically, but with a passionate flaw.

At this point, a word of caution is in order. Were performers or producers to attempt to realize this portrait, at best they would succeed only in gilding a lily. Intelligent productions of Baroque opera must shun the excesses of Romantic theater. Purcell's Dido dwarfs the character conceived by Tate. To burden his slight libretto with so dark a reading would simply transform it from a deeply moving puppet-tragedy into commonplace soap opera. Tate's simple two-dimensional stick figures have the virtue of allowing the music to speak for itself. That, after all, is where the true drama resides.

Tom D'Urfey's epilogue seems to dissociate the girls of Mr. Priest's school from Dido's behavior.[31] It praises them as "Protestants and English nuns" who spurn the wanton behavior of the playhouse and those wits who would charm them to it. They may pity Dido's fate, but they are not to countenance her irresponsible conduct. Nevertheless, the beauty of Purcell's music and his neglect of Aeneas seem to temper such condemnation of her. In his sympathetic orchestral postlude to her final aria, Purcell seems to say of her, as Chaucer said of another unfortunate lady:

> Iwis, I would excuse hire yet for routhe.[32]

[31]Spoken by Lady Dorothy Burk, who, I assume, was a pupil at the school; vocal score, no. 40, p. 100.

[32]*Troilus and Criseyde*, 5.1099, in *The Works of Geoffrey Chaucer*, ed. F. N. Robinson, 2d ed. (Boston, 1957), p. 471.

Appendix
Madrigalism in Purcell's *Dido and Aeneas*

Many of the examples offered here may seem, *in themselves*, so elementary or so insignificant as scarcely to be worth notice. Nevertheless, their cumulative weight and their remarkable mutual corroboration give them a significance far above their individual values. An exhaustive commentary on the text influences in the whole opera would require a separate monograph, but the analyses below should provide a useful key to the rest of the opera. I have indexed the comments to the lines of the libretto, which I have numbered; the measure numbers are those of Laurie's edition.

A Reading of No. 2, "Shake the Cloud From Off Your Brow"

Belinda: (1) Shake the cloud from off your brow,
            (2) Fate your wishes does allow;
            (3)   Empire growing,
            (4)   Pleasures flowing,
            (5) Fortune smiles and so should you.[33]
Chorus: (6) Banish sorrow, banish care,
            (7) Grief should ne'er approach the fair.

Example 8. Purcell, *Dido and Aeneas*, "Shake the Cloud From Off Your Brow."

---

[33] In Purcell's day "allow" and "brow" would have rhymed with the modern "slow," to which the seventeenth-century "you" would have been closer.

Example 8, continued

sor- row, ban- ish_ care, Grief _____ should ne'er ap- proach, should ne'er ap-

proach the fair, Grief _____ should ne'er, should ne'er ap- proach the fair.

Line 1, m. 3: A fairly literal shaking, a dotted melisma on the word "shake." The reverse dotting of the first beat is an important detail missing from some sources.

Line 1, mm. 4–5: Although "cloud" is set on a note that is a local high-point, and it is conveniently higher than "brow," it is uncertain whether this represents a deliberate exercise of what I term the altitude convention.[34] The doubt arises from the fact that the "high point" is also the opening note of the preceding measure. The two are simply too close to allow a clear decision.

Line 3, mm. 7–9: "Empire," "Growing": The major-triadic shape of this melody signifies "empire" (for which trumpets, and hence triads, were time-tested symbols by Purcell's day). The upward trend of the passage represents growth, in what I have called the directional convention (see above, note 27).

Line 4, mm. 9–10: "Flowing": Melismas, dotted or otherwise, had long served as conventional representations for flow (or for things that flow: streams, tears, wind).

Line 5, m. 11: The dip D–G–D, subdividing the word "smiles," is intriguing, but of uncertain significance. It may mean no more than the melismatic emphasis of "wishes" in measure 6.

Lines 6–7, m. 18 [recte 20]:[35] It is significant that the words "care" and "grief" occur for the first time in a measure with chromatic harmony.

Line 7, mm. 19–20 [21–22]: The major cadence accords with the line's rejection of grief.

Line 7, mm. 22–23 [24–25], 26 [28]: "Grief" now occurs as a subject of imitation (soprano and bass) in a generally downward direction. When it returns in stretto a few measures later, the "painful" drop of a diminished fourth, a *saltus duriusculus*, adds another conventional detail.

The word "fate" (line 2) occurs on a weak local high point (m. 3, the E-flat having been heard three times in three measures). It obviously represents a pivotal word in the story of Dido, and possibly also in Tate's libretto, where it appears in nos. 2, 4, 5, 8, 18 (by circumlocution), 25, 35, and 38—where it is Dido's last mortal word. Purcell is curiously reticent in his handling of the word. He never gives it any melismatic

---

[34]The association of references to height, high places ("heaven," etc.), greatness, great size, and often to generally positive feelings and ideas, with melodic high points.

[35]Laurie's edition numbers the printed measures and ignores repeats.

emphasis, and he never marks it with a striking rhythm, immediate repetition, or unusual harmony. Only once (in no. 8) does he mark the word with a significant melodic leap—and there it implies denial. I take this musical conduct as evidence of Purcell's decision to emphasize the human elements in the story at the expense of the superhuman—which Tate bungles, anyway. This observation tends to confirm our readings of the overture and of Dido's arias.

A Reading of No. 6, "Whence Could So Much Virtue Spring?"

Dido:	(1)	Whence could so much virtue spring?
	(2)	What storms! what battles did he sing!
	(3)	Anchises' valour mix'd with Venus' charms!
	(4)	How soft in peace and yet how fierce in arms!
Belinda:	(5)	A tale so strong and full of woe[36]
	(6)	Might melt the rocks as well as you.
	(7)	What stubborn heart unmoved could see
	(8)	Such distress, such piety?
Dido:	(9)	Mine with storms of care oppress'd
	(10)	Is taught to pity the distress'd;
	(11)	Mean wretches' grief can touch,
	(12)	So soft, so sensible my breast,
	(13)	But ah! I fear I pity his too much.[37]

Example 9. Purcell, *Dido and Aeneas*, "Whence Could So Much Virtue Spring?"

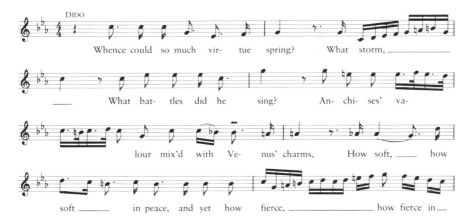

---

[36] Note again the rhyme for "you."

[37] Tate evidently means to say: "Since my so tender heart is touched by the grief of even lowly-born wretches, how can I close it to the claims on my sympathy of this noble Trojan?" Tate's polished syntax surpasses only that of this footnote—if that.

Example 9, continued

BELINDA

arms! A tale so strong and full of woe_ Might melt ____ the

rocks, as well as _ you. What stub-born heart un- mov'd ____ could

DIDO

see Such dis-tress, such pi- e- ty? Mine with storms ____ of

care ____ op-press'd Is taught to pi- ty the dis-tress'd; Mean wret-ches'

grief can touch, So soft, so sen-si-ble my breast, But ah! but

ah! ___ I fear I pi- ty his too_ much.

Line 2, mm. 2–3: Purcell decorates every occurrence of "storm" in the opera (twice here, and in nos. 20, 27, and 32) with melismatic emphasis. A typical madrigalism.

Line 2, mm. 3–4: "Battles" sounds the usual triadic trumpet.

Line 3, mm. 4–5: The melismatic emphasis of "valour" might not have been worth noting, were it not for the change from C minor to C major which Purcell introduces not only because of the positive associations with that word, but because of the needs he perceives in the next clause.

Line 3, mm. 5–6: For the words "with Venus' charms" the editors properly insert a flat, which merely restores the b-flat of the key signature after the accidental naturals of the melisma. The poetic usages of the time usually applied the adjective "soft" to Venus' charms (how did Tate miss that one!), and while hard and soft hexachords no longer had much influence on music theory in Purcell's day, the conventional association of softness with flats (or shifts in the flat direction along our circle of fifths), or with semitone movement, seems to have remained in force long after Purcell. The shift from the "hardness" of "valour" to the "softness" of "Venus" are probably to be regarded as a single musical gesture which receives confirmation in Purcell's setting of the next words.

Line 4, mm. 6–7: Purcell further "softens" the line for "how soft" by flatting the a-natural. Note that both occurrences of this word are set here with semitone motions.

Line 4, mm. 8–9: "Fierce" once again "hardens" the line by canceling all the flats.

Lines 5–6, mm. 10–11: Purcell characterizes Belinda's sympathy by decorating the word "strong" with its semitone neighbor. Confirmation of this intent appears in his use of the semitone more conventionally with upward chromaticism on "woe" (passus duriusculus) and with downward chromaticism on "melt." The magnitude convention[38] may account for the large leap away from "strong."

Line 7, m. 13: "Unmoved" receives durational emphasis and the semitone movement appropriate to the sense of the phrase rather than the meaning of the word itself. Is the reverse dotting of "stubborn" in fact a "stubborn" rhythm, and is the octave leap away from the word significant?

Line 8, m. 14: "Distress" receives the chromatic ornament of another passus duriusculus.

Line 9, m. 16: "Storms": melismatic emphasis.

Line 10, mm. 18–19: "Distress'd" is consistently ornamented with semitone movement.

Line 11, mm. 19–20: "Mean wretches" are socially low, and therefore invoke the altitude and directional conventions, while "grief" is approached by the appropriate chromatic semitone.

Line 12, mm. 21–22: "Soft," "so sensible my breast," and "ah" exhibit the continued consistent application of semitones to softer emotions.

Lines 8, 10, and 13; mm. 15, 18, and 24: The obviously expressive downward leaps on "piety" and "pity" derive from the traditional association of downward motions with humility, piety, etc.

A Reading of No. 8, "See Your Royal Guest Appears"

Belinda:	(1)	See your royal guest appears;
	(2)	How godlike is the form he bears!
Aeneas:	(3)	When, royal fair, shall I be blessed
	(4)	With cares of love and state distress'd?[39]
Dido:	(5)	Fate forbids what you pursue.[40]
Aeneas:	(6)	Aeneas has no fate but you!
	(7)	Let Dido smile and I'll defy[41]
	(8)	The feeble stroke of Destiny.

[38]The association of large or small intervals with allusions to the magnitude of objects, distances, powers, etc.

[39]Tate's only reference to Carthage in crisis.

[40]This vitally important speech establishes Dido's guilty knowledge of Aeneas' destiny. Tate fails to elaborate the point; instead, he obscures it with his unnecessary witches.

[41]Tate follows his first strong speech with this unforgettable jangle!

Example 10. Purcell, *Dido and Aeneas*, "See Your Royal Guest Appears."

Line 1, mm. 1–2: "Royal guest" (like "empire") evokes a triadic response.

Line 2, m. 3: "Godlike" is set on an absolute high point.

Line 3, mm. 4–8: Had Purcell wanted them, the line offered him plenty of opportunities to express its content: "royal," "fair," "bless'd," "cares," "state," "distress'd." The absence of word painting in Aeneas' first speech suggests that Purcell treats Aeneas as a hypocrite.

Line 5, mm. 8–9: The negation of Dido's "forbids" prompts a harmonic negation: the shift from the major to the minor triad—as well as the melodic leap down.

Line 6, mm. 9–10: Aeneas' first musically represented words, "no fate," are set to a downward *saltus duriusculus* (the largest in the opera thus far), suggesting denial and hence again implying insincerity.

Line 7, mm. 11–12: "Smile" and "defy" participate, appropriately, in upward melody, but the upward chromaticism (*passus duriusculus*) suggests a feeble, and hence an insincere, defiance.

Line 8, mm. 13–14: "Feeble" gets downward movement (directional convention) and the weak step of semitone ornamentation.

Opera Seria Borrowings in Le nozze di Figaro: The Count's "Vedrò, mentr'io"

Wye J. Allanbrook

"Vedrò, mentr'io," the *opera seria* set-piece which Count Almaviva delivers early in the third act of Mozart's *Le nozze di Figaro*, is an impassioned *aria di bravura* in the high style. Yet to me there has always seemed to be an intrusive element in the aria—an imbalance in the style—which, pushing against the limits of the *seria* convention, alters this convention in a subtle fashion. These alterations in fact suggest a comparison of "Vedrò, mentr'io" with arias sung by two other male characters in the opera, the bombastic old rogue Bartolo and, surprisingly, Figaro himself. That there could be any important similarity in the music of these three characters is puzzling and poses a challenge to received ideas about the opera.

Mozart's *Le nozze di Figaro* has traditionally been viewed as a straight-forward adaptation of the play from which its libretto was drawn, Caron de Beaumarchais' *Le Mariage de Figaro*. In Beaumarchais' play, Figaro, the ingenious and sympathetic protagonist, overcomes a variety of obstacles to his wedding, exposing in the process some of the social ills of the *ancien régime*. The Figaro of Mozart and da Ponte has, quite naturally, been viewed in much the same terms. There is, however, no reason to assume that in adapting Beaumarchais' play, da Ponte and Mozart should have set about to capture and convey the vision which underlay it. Indeed, if we study the opera carefully, we can see that its themes and characters are subtly but significantly different from those of the play. The play is concerned with specific social problems, the opera with more general ethical questions—particularly with the true nature of nobility. In the opera, the friendship of the gentle-born Countess and the base-born Susanna is a central concern, and the focus is on the women rather than the men. Figaro, although still an admirable character, is no longer the hero of the piece; he is seen to fall short of the women's grace of character and to require redemption by this grace.

The treatment of the aria types which each man sings is certainly one of the musical means by which Mozart shapes our responses to the male characters in *Figaro*. Bartolo, the Count, and Figaro all have set pieces which are essentially of the *aria di bravura* type. The aim of this essay is ultimately to demonstrate that Mozart, by introducing elements of *buffa* style into these arias, adapted the conventions of *opera seria* to serve his and da Ponte's particular vision of the story of Figaro's wedding. That discussion must, however, be prefaced by some general reflections on the use of the *seria* style in *Don Giovanni* and *Le nozze di Figaro*.

The significance of Mozart's treatment of the *aria di bravura* in *Figaro* is best understood in the context of the tradition to which it belongs. Donna Anna's splendid "Or sai chi l'onore" in *Don Giovanni* (Act 1, no. 10) can be considered a paradigm of what to Mozart was the heroic *seria* style.[1] Termed variously *aria di bravura, aria parlante, aria di strepito*,[2] the style has in Mozart's operas one important hallmark: it is written in duple meter, *alla breve* in scansion if not in actual time signature. The rhythmic style appropriate to high passion is not a triple-meter dance but a march, with a dignified yet resolute pace. Under the slow steady beat of the half-note pulse the quicker decorative figures give the aria its fire. The melody may simply move in half notes and in the dotted quarter figures (♩.   ♪) also typical of *alla breve*, or the singer may break into fervent coloratura passages, as long as the steady half-note tread remains the measure. I have termed this rhythmic type the "exalted march."[3] Donna Anna's *alla breve* tends to the purer end of the spectrum; her opening measures consist of a simple, eloquent sequential motive hung on a long-breathed rising line. Were it not for the pain and anger expressed in the text, "Or sai chi l'onore" would verge on the type of the *aria di portamento*, a more sedate and magisterial style which John Brown described as appropriate to "the Queen of gods and men."[4] But the urgency of

---

[1]One might equally well consider Konstanze's "Martern aller Arten" from *Die Entführung aus dem Serail* (Act 2, no. 11), or the Queen of the Night's "Der hölle Rache" from *Die Zauberflöte* (Act 2, no. 14), or the first phrases of Donna Anna's and Don Ottavio's duet "Fuggi, crudele, fuggi" (*Don Giovanni*, Act 1, no. 2).

[2]One of the best-known late eighteenth-century classifications of aria types is by the Englishman John Brown, in his *Letters on the Italian Opera* (London, 1791), pp. 28–141. In the class of arias depicting strong but noble passions he places the *aria di portamento* ("sentiments of dignity"); the *aria parlante* ("violent emotions of all kinds"—it may also be termed *aria agitata, aria infuriata, aria di strepito*); and the *aria di bravura (aria di agilità)*, which Brown regards as a debased form of the *aria parlante*, "composed *chiefly . . . merely* to indulge the singer in the display of certain powers in the execution, particularly extraordinary agility or compass of voice" (p. 39). Brown does not, however, consider coloratura ornaments to be wholly out of place in the expression of true passion ("as violent passion has a tendency to choak [*sic*] the voice, so in the expression of it by musical sounds, a *roulade . . .* has often a more powerful effect than distinct articulation" [pp. 86–87]), and indeed Mozart, in imitating the *seria* style, almost always includes some vocal passagework. Hence, I have used the term *aria di bravura*, the more familiar designation, in discussions of the *aria parlante*.

[3]For a more extensive discussion of this characteristic style, see my *Rhythmic Gesture in Mozart:* Le nozze di Figaro *and* Don Giovanni (Chicago, 1984), pp. 17–22.

[4]*Letters on the Italian Opera*, p. 60.

Donna Anna's passion is unmistakable, and it is reflected in the orchestra's highly decorated upbeats and string tremolos, which give the rhythm its compelling forward motion.

The high tragic *alla breve* aria is usually introduced by a *recitativo accompagnato*, thus unequivocally announcing itself as a troped aria convention from an old-fashioned style—an *opera seria scena*. The use of the convention, with its recognizable edges, is meant to be suggestive: by bringing into prominence the provenance of the singer's song, it gives its exalted formality a special resonance—a connection with all the tragic figures, historical, mythical, and imagined, who have appeared on the *opera seria* stage. It also connects such characters within the opera. Donna Anna and Donna Elvira, for example, are coupled as well by their aria styles as by their shared roles as victims of the Don.

Yet when such noble music must share the stage with arias in the comic mode, the juxtaposition cannot be without its effects. Comedy is not merely less serious than tragedy (or high melodrama, as the case may be); it can also be more supple, and at its best—in Leporello's "Notte e giorno faticar," for example, or his famous "catalogue" aria[5]—it subtly undercuts the monolithic intensity of the heroic style. Donna Anna is one of *buffa*'s victims: in the writings about Mozart's *Don Giovanni* which have accumulated since the opera was first performed, there is a persistent undercurrent of uneasiness about her moral integrity.[6] The source of many of these suspicions is the famous dialogue in which Donna Anna tells Don Ottavio the tale of the seducer who stole into her bedroom at nightfall and whom she took at first for her fiancé (Act 1, no. 10). But only the most disingenuous reading between the lines can indict Donna Anna for hypocrisy there; her character read in isolation, in both her words and her music, must remain unimpeachably what it seems. It is the satirical perspective of the *buffa* style which gives rise to questions about seemingly innocent conduct on Anna's part—her persistent postponement of her marriage to Ottavio, or her unswerving pursuit of Don Giovanni. Mockery is more persuasive than passion; it easily makes cynics of us all.

The music of Donna Anna's fiancé, Don Ottavio, belongs to a second general class of *seria* borrowings—the *aria cantabile*.[7] These arias are often set

---

[5]*Don Giovanni*, Act 1, nos. 1 and 4. (All citations to Mozart operas are to the editions of the *Neue Mozart Ausgabe* [Kassel, 1956–].)

[6]E. T. A. Hoffmann was, of course, certain that Anna was passionately in love with Giovanni, and the tradition has persisted in one form or another up to the present day; see, for example, Robert Moberly, *Three Mozart Operas* (New York, 1968), p. 148.

[7]"The subject proper for this air is the expression of tenderness. Though this be an expression which always tends to sadness, yet the sadness is of that pleasing kind which the mind loves to indulge . . . The *aria cantabile*, whilst it is susceptible of great pathos, admits, without prejudice to the expression, of being

in 2/4, a meter which admits of a slower, more reflective style, whether march[8] or song, than does *alla breve*. Ottavio's "Dalla sua pace" (Act 1, no. 10b) is an example of 2/4 set as a simple song, and like other such arias it sustains a lyric, frequently pathetic vein. Ottavio's other solo aria is also a *cantabile* piece, even though it is set *alla breve*: the double levels of the compound meter lend it first the strumming rhythms of a serenade, but then allow later, in the middle section, a brief excursion into the exalted march style, permitting Ottavio the only moment at which he could be said to appear heroic. Ottavio is often ridiculed,[9] but there is nothing in his music which should make him an object of derision, nothing which would not have been admired in another opera; his gentler moral virtues would figure better in a tale of constancy, renunciation, and elegiac grief. But in *Don Giovanni* the tender virtues all are savaged; outdistanced by wit and the sharper, swifter passions, mere decency appears effete. If we laugh at Ottavio, it is only because we are embarrassed that the seductive conventions of *buffa* have prevented our sympathizing with a character who is at once so decent and so defenseless.

Le nozze di Figaro also mixes the conventions of *opera buffa* and *opera seria*. But since it is less dark a work than *Don Giovanni* (it could be termed a romantic comedy, although not a Romantic one), the mixture is different, with more concentration on the center and less starkly etched extremes. The only woman of noble rank in the opera, the gentle Countess, has two solo arias, neither in the heroic mold: "Porgi, amor" (Act 2, no. 10) is an *aria cantabile* in 2/4 (see note 8), and "Dove sono" (Act 3, no. 19) a double aria composed of a *cantabile* section (in 2/4) followed by a more animated second half (in 4/4).[10] Her music—and her character—resemble Don Ottavio's.

---

highly ornamented; for this plain reason, that, though the sentiments it expresses are affecting, they are, at the same time, such as the mind dwells on with pleasure; and it is likewise for this reason that the subject of the *cantabile* must never border on deep distress, nor approach to violent agitation, both of which are evidently inconsistent with ornament" (*Letters on the Italian Opera*, pp. 44–45).

[8] The Countess' "Porgi, amor" (*Le nozze di Figaro*, Act 2, no. 10) is an example of the 2/4 meter treated as a slow march. The noble military topic alternates in the introduction to the aria with passages in a more lyrical style (the military occurs in mm. 1–2, 7–10, and 13–17).

[9] E. T. A. Hoffmann was also one of Ottavio's first detractors, and many others agree with him. See, for example, Edward Dent, in his *Mozart's Operas: A Critical Study* (2nd ed. [London, 1947], pp. 160–61), or Janos Liebner, who, in his *Mozart on the Stage* (New York, 1972), calls Ottavio's arias "so beautiful as to be almost unmanly" (p. 159), among other derogatory comments.

[10] "Dove sono" has some of the hallmarks of the high tragic style, namely its dramatic *recitativo accompagnato* introduction and the exalted march style of the *Allegro* (mm. 77–end). But the tone of the opening *Andantino* is elegiac—the Countess sings in alternation with a *concertante* band of *amoroso* winds—and the exalted march of the second half gives way at times to pathetic accents (mm. 80–81, 99) or to more passages in *amoroso* style (mm. 89–90, 94–95). The *alla breve* is invoked as it is in Ottavio's "Il mio tesoro," in order to depict a momentary flicker of passion as the Countess struggles against her gentle nature to turn pain into anger.

There are three *arie di bravura* in *Figaro*, all sung by male characters, and put to very different use from the heroic arias in *Don Giovanni*: Bartolo's "La vendetta" (Act 1, no. 4), Figaro's "Aprite un po' quegli occhi" (Act 4, no. 26), and the Count's "Vedrò, mentr'io" (Act 3, no. 17). Whereas Donna Anna's "Or sai chi l'onore" was composed as a pure example of its kind and is undermined only by *buffa*'s quickness and wit, in these three arias the very convention of the *aria di bravura* is degraded, with the result that high passion appears mere choler, at best simply comic but at worst unhinged.

In the case of Bartolo's aria, which by occurring earliest of the three helps to shape perceptions of the other two, Mozart's modifications of the *seria* style seem fairly obvious. "La vendetta" is an *opera seria* borrowing which had itself almost begun to seem a native convention of *opera buffa*. In D major, *alla breve*, scored with trumpets and timpani (a special effect Mozart usually reserved for the marching bands and *finalissimos* of the operas), it begins in all pomp and high passion with a triadic fanfare motive. But Bartolo seems most comfortable when his music dissolves into patter and a list:

> Con l'astuzia, con l'arguzia,
> Col giudizio, col criterio . . .[11]

The augmented sixths which follow this passage have a bathetic ring (on the text "Il fatto è serio,"[12] repeated three times), and upon the return to the tonic the aria lapses into a torrent of patter, again setting a list (mm. 58–66). The entire "recapitulation" consists of fifteen measures of patter answered by a pompous cadential epigram:[13]

> Tutta Siviglia
> Conosce Bartolo:
> Il birbo Figaro
> Vinto sarà![14]

This epigram is relentlessly repeated over thirty-two measures, supplying a firm D major cadence in *alla breve*. Bartolo is by nature a buffoonish character; the distance between his pretensions and his person makes his version of

---

[11] "With cunning, with wit, with prudence, with judgment . . . " (mm. 40–43).

[12] "The matter is serious" (mm. 46–48).

[13] Unlike the recapitulation in an instrumental movement, in Mozart's operatic "sonata forms" the return to the tonic is rarely marked by a return to the opening material. Since the emphasis is not on a re-hearing of that material in a new context, but on dramatic movement and characterization, new material will usually be far more effective. This freedom to alter the return also allows for condensation and simplification (fewer motives, more tonic harmony), and thus for greater cadential muscle: in "La vendetta" there are six different kinds of material involved in the move to the dominant and only two in the "recapitulation," but the two sections are about equal in number of measures. Liberation from the static form of the *da capo* aria was one of *buffa*'s innovations.

[14] "All Seville knows Bartolo; that rascal Figaro will get his comeuppance."

seria convention effectively a parody of the convention. The late eighteenth-century theorist Heinrich Christoph Koch in his *Journal der Tonkunst* (1795) complained of the debasement which the comic style had effected on the conventions of *opera seria*:

> Ever since they began to dress up buffoon ariettes in the form of extended arias, the serious arias have necessarily declined more and more in value; for as soon as the humorous masters the form of the serious, the serious itself thereby takes on certain features of the humorous.[15]

While Koch was certainly correct in assuming that the serious style (at least in eighteenth-century Italian opera) would never wholly recover from this devaluation, he was apparently unaware that he had described precisely the birth of a fertile new convention. The role of the *vecchio prepotente* is as old as comedy, and the flexible rules of the new comic opera permitted the introduction of a hybrid aria which borrowed from *seria* idiom in order to capture in music the fulminations of this stock character. Bartolo's style—this unlikely fusion of patter with the exalted—was already well on its way to becoming a comic cliché.

Figaro's aria is a less conventional and more spirited version of Bartolo's. "Aprite un po' quegli occhi," although set in 4/4, begins as a proud exalted march with an *alla breve* scansion, which is effected by the dotted rhythms of the vocal line and by strong punctuation on the first and third beats. But Figaro's obsessive jealousy breaks through in his long-spun-out list of paradoxical epithets for women:

> Son streghe che incantano
> Per farci penar,
> Sirene che cantano
> Per farci affogar,
>
> Civette che allettano
> Per trarci le piume,
> Comete che brillano
> Per toglierci il lume;
>
> Son rose spinose,
> Son volpi vezzose,
> Son orse benigne,
> Colombe maligne.[16]

---

[15] "Seitdem man aber angefangen hat, die Arietten der Spaßmacher in die Form des ausgeführten Arie einzukleiden, seitdem verliert die ernsthafte Arie nothwendig je länger je mehr von ihrer Würde; denn sobald sich einmal das Lächerliche der Form des Ernsthaften bemeistert, so bekömmt alsdenn das Ernsthafte selbst dadurch gewisse lächerliche Züge." (Heinrich Christoph Koch, ed., *Journal der Tonkunst*, 2 vols. [Erfurt, 1795], 2:102.)

[16] "They are witches who enchant us so to make us suffer, sirens who sing so to make us drown, screech

Here the march dissolves into patter (m. 49)[17]—lists are obviously endemic to the patter style—and the last two-thirds of the aria consist of the list, its almost literal repetition (mm. 70–102), and nine measures of additional cadence. This coda brings back the march style with horn fanfares, at which Figaro makes rather blatant jokes about being cuckolded:

> Il resto nol dico,
> Già ognuno lo sa.[18]

"Aprite un po' quegli occhi" is brilliant and sardonic, but its anger is not heroic. The obsessive character of the list, with its patter, the crude and repetitive pun on *corno* and *cornuto*,[19] are hardly exalted. Indeed, the similarities of style between this aria and "La vendetta" imply an underlying similarity in the characters of Figaro and Bartolo. Such a connection can hardly be complimentary to the opera's titular hero, for it suggests that in a moment of crisis the quick-witted and manly Figaro is guilty of the same blind and excessive anger as is the old *roué*.

"Vedrò, mentr'io" seems at first to sit more comfortably in the class of the *opera seria aria di bravura* than do the arias of Bartolo and Figaro. It belongs to the *primo uomo*, it is prefaced by a *recitativo accompagnato*, and it begins *Allegro maestoso* and *alla breve* with full orchestra. We must remember, nevertheless, that "Aprite un po' quegli occhi" also opens with a *recitativo accompagnato*, and that "La vendetta" shares not only its key (D major) with "Vedrò, mentr'io," but also the special orchestration of trumpets and timpani. As these similarities of detail suggest, there is to be no unalloyed expression of exalted wrath in *Le nozze di Figaro*. Da Ponte and Mozart manage to rob even the Count's anger of its nobility, although they do so more subtly than in the cases of Bartolo and Figaro. In the process, they expose not mere arrogance, but a near-manic vein in Almaviva's character.

We can look first to the text of the aria for a clue to the source of Almaviva's preoccupations. He has just received a cruel blow (cosseted by Susanna, who was forced momentarily to lead him on, he has overheard a conversation which has undeceived him about her motives), and any show of dignity on his

---

owls who allure us so to pluck out our feathers, comets who shine so to deprive us of light; they are thorny roses, charming vixens, kindly she-bears, spiteful doves" (mm. 49–61).

[17]Measure numbers in "Aprite un po' quegli occhi" and in "Vedrò, mentr'io" begin with the *recitative accompagnato* which precedes the aria.

[18]"I won't say the rest; everyone already knows it." In performance Figaro should cock his ear and point at each entry of the horns, accompanying the tedious joke with an exaggerated dumbshow.

[19]Figaro makes the same pun on "horn" and "horned" in "Se vuol ballare" (Act 1, no. 3), but, like all else he does in that witty aria, with considerably more elegance.

part would play on our sympathies. But his response fails of nobility; the text of his aria reveals him in all the arrogance of his limitations:

> Vedrò, mentr'io sospiro,
> Felice un servo mio?
> E un ben che invan desio
> Ei posseder dovrà?
>
> Vedrò per man d'amore
> Unita a un vile oggetto
> Chi in me destò un affetto
> Che per me poi non ha?[20]

The Count is a man in whom loss stirs not sadness or despair, but grim envy: it merely wounds his vanity. He mentions the object of his desires only impersonally, as "un ben," who has moved him while remaining herself unmoved. First on his mind is his "rival," who as a mere servant has no rights except those of punishment and deprivation. The vision of this "vile oggetto" besting and mocking him torments the Count, as he reveals in words which become the centerpiece of the aria:

> Tu non nascesti, audace!
> Per dare a me tormento,
> E forse ancor per ridere
> Di mia infelicità.[21]

Generations of arrogant assumptions about the absolute privilege of rank lie behind the verb "nascesti," and explain the Count's edgy tone as he envisions the derision of his energetic and clever challenger.

At the opening of "Vedrò, mentr'io," the prevalent style is more declamation than exalted march: the Count's first music, although cast in four-measure phrases, joins its motives in a loose and unperiodic relation while the orchestra actually organizes the energies of the period. In the vocal line two measures of a dotted and descending motive yield to two measures without dots, which ascend to a snapped-off octave leap (mm. 47–48). Measures 52–55 begin as a repetition of the phrase, but a sudden influx of bile at the thought of Figaro's possessing Susanna causes the Count to substitute for the original measures 3 and 4 a typical question cadence from accompanied recitative (an augmented sixth moving to the dominant for a half cadence). These fits and starts of declamation persist until measure 66 and the arrival in A major, when the customary exalted march finally takes wing.

---

[20] "Shall I, while myself sighing, see a servant of mine happy? And is he to possess a good which I desire in vain? Shall I see joined by the bond of love to a worthless object a woman who has aroused in me a feeling which she does not return?"

[21] "You were not born, O bold one!—to torment me, and perhaps even to laugh at my unhappiness."

Even that firm rhythmic footing is, however, short-lived. The new line of action which began in measure 66 is not developed, but peters out into uneasy exclamations of "Vedrò?" "Vedrò?" over a V–i oscillation in D (through m. 87). The *Allegro assai* and return to the tonic (mm. 88 ff.) provide a new and vigorous beginning, but after four measures the stride of the march is broken again by a series of five three-measure phrases, which set the important stanza "Tu non nascesti, audace!" This stunningly extended phrase, which in closer conformity to periodic norms would amount to ten or eleven measures, not fifteen (see Ex. 1 for both the "normal" and the "abnormal"—

Example 1. "Vedrò, mentr'io," mm. 92–106.

actual—version), is the critical moment of the aria. Afterward it makes its cadential drive, ending in a *bravura* mini-cadenza in measures 145–55.

The extensions of the "Tu non nascesti" phrase must be examined more carefully, for they reveal the near-dementia of Almaviva's jealousy and its source deep in his *amour-propre*. The first ones lay bare the extent of the Count's malice toward Figaro. The exclamation "Tu non nascesti, audace!" receives a vengeful caress, its first three words lasting two measures rather than one (the proper duration if the sentence were to fit into a four-measure period). The snapped-off "audace!", forced now out of rhythmic proportion with the first part of the phrase, makes the utterance all the more arresting and peremptory:

The words "Per dare a me tormento" receive the same caressing attention, to form a three-measure phrase (the "nascesti" phrase is repeated), rising a menacing chromatic third where the "paradigm" would have two measures and a more forthright diatonic ascent.

The treatment of the next words, "E forse ancor per ridere," reveals Mozart's sense of the Count's present state of mind. They could have been set in two measures—the pace of the normalized version and an effective angry quickening after the previous three-measure phrase—and then have been followed directly by the reach up to the high D for the broad "operatic" cadence figure.[22] But Mozart chose instead, by unexpectedly repeating the word "ridere," to fashion another triplet—an actual two-measure unit, but with the rhythm of measure 2 repeated (1-2-2 rather than 1-2-3, if the numbers are taken to represent entire measures). The three previous triplets were duplets stretched out of shape: quarter notes become half notes, dotted quarters become dotted halves. This fourth triplet, however, has a true extra measure: at the mere thought of Figaro's derision the Count gives an involuntary *frisson* of horror, adding two beats to the phrase. The dominant harmony initiated on the last quarter note of measure 8 (11) of Example 1 lasts one full measure more, emphatically darkened by a B-flat chromatic appoggiatura

[22]This cadential figure is itself an extension: maintaining duple measure groups exclusively would have entailed an even more banal, and anticlimactic, final cadence, not ascending the octave to D but moving from the subdominant G of "ridere" directly to the dominant and then the tonic (the third variant in Example 1). The cliché of the extended cadence is already necessary even in the normalized version in order to balance the long-breathed eight measures of the rise.

postponing the dominant in the bass line[23] and by the orchestra's *sforzando* (in the "paradigm" the dominant harmony would resolve to I♭ in measure 9 and return for the final cadence in measure 10). All this attention focussed on the one measure lends it a strong thetic accent, beside which the high D of the cadence pales. The word "ridere," surfacing the second time in this moment of insuppressible panicked anger, almost overwhelms the conventional musical climax of the phrase. Figaro the dancing master stalks the Count's nightmares, even though Almaviva has not actually been present to witness the mocking challenge Figaro delivered to him in "Se vuol ballare." A repetition of the long phrase (without the first of the two "nascesti" groupings) makes plain the obsessive quality of his vision. But this moment of inadvertent self-revelation is fleeting; the Count recovers himself, and the aria closes in the normal accents of *opera seria* with a Handelian cadenza on the word "giubilar."

"Vedrò, mentr'io" is not, as first it seems to be, a typical old-fashioned *scena* in which a well-born character in an *opera buffa* vents his noble wrath. Edgy and bellicose, the Count's *alla breve* music lacks the superb and natural haughtiness, the classical purity of Donna Anna's "Or sai chi l'onore." Moreover, before the Count enters to utter the clichés which are proper to his rank, the exalted style has already been given a dangerously comic critique by a minor character; thus the nobleman cannot escape being tarred with the same brush as the buffoon. Unlike the disreputable old lawyer Bartolo, however, the Count cannot be dismissed with a laugh; he is a man to be reckoned with, someone who has the power to harm decent people. The anomalies in his stance—the declamatory bombast, the vengefully distorted march, the edge of rising panic—have the effect of cartoon, but not of comedy. When the exalted and noble show an hysterical underside, disturbing cracks appear in things which are usually considered to be worthy of respect. The Count is a nobleman somehow dislocated from the limits which define noblemen as good men. He displays a capacity for excessive and erratic behavior which is not a part of the noble code of conduct. His *alla breve* stance, undermined by Bartolo's fulminating and by its own air of manic decay, becomes a flawed and unsettling gesture.

Clearly, Mozart's *opera seria* borrowings in *Le nozze di Figaro* are of a different order from those in *Don Giovanni*. In *Don Giovanni, alla breve*— the "exalted march"—is a noble style, and any doubts we may have about the characters who assume it are raised by the collision of the high noble style with the satiric wit of *opera buffa*. In *Figaro*, however, the high noble style is itself flawed, and reveals the excessive and intemperate passions of the three men

---

[23] It could be also read as a diminished seventh chord, if you will.

who affect it, Bartolo, the Count, and Figaro himself. In "Vedrò, mentr'io," the transformations effected by Mozart in the *seria* style are especially artful, the psychology particularly penetrating. Nevertheless, to a greater or lesser extent Mozart worked such transformations in all three arias, and the juxtaposition of *seria* and *buffa* elements in each identifies the three men, at least momentarily, as a trio.

This suggestion of a "family resemblance" among the hero, the rival, and the panderer challenges the widely accepted account of the opera as a covert manual for revolution with the quick-witted and iconoclastic Figaro as spokesman.[24] In Beaumarchais' *Mariage*, the outcry against social injustice is overt, and a central theme. Critics usually share Edward Dent's assumption that da Ponte sought to eliminate Beaumarchais' "new social point of view" from the libretto, but that Mozart put it back in the music.[25] But if one compares the play with the libretto, it is clear that, contrary to this view, da Ponte's *Figaro* is no mere translation into singable Italian of the spirited dialogue of *Le Mariage*.[26] Careful carpentry work, especially on the fourth and fifth acts of the play, brought about a decided shift of emphasis in the opera's themes. The changes were worked primarily on the scenes involving Figaro and Marcellina, and on Figaro's eloquent *tirade* against the ills of society. At the moment when Figaro rushes off in angry jealousy to spy on Susanna, the libretto stresses the beaming Marcellina's conversion; she declares true affection for Susanna and solidarity with her sex in a fusty but heartfelt aria on a pastoral text (Act 4, no. 24).[27] Figaro's targets in his soliloquy are no longer censorship and the arrant abuse of authority; instead, jealous and obsessed with thoughts of

[24] This view is well represented by Siegmund Levarie in *Mozart's Le nozze di Figaro: A Critical Analysis* (Chicago, 1952).

[25] For Edward Dent's notion of the collaboration between da Ponte and Mozart, see, for example, *Mozart's Operas*, p. 95.

[26] That the alterations imposed on *Le Mariage de Figaro* had a consistent intent is, it seems to me, clear. We are more in the dark about who actually made them. In the cases of others of his operas, namely *Idomeneo* and *Die Entführung aus dem Serail*, Mozart's letters have made us privy to the intelligence of his thoughts about the drama and his insistence on collaborating with his librettists. Letters written by Mozart to his father in the period between November 1780 and January 1781 report on his efforts to have the Abbate Varesco improve the libretto for *Idomeneo*. Letters to his father from Vienna, August to October 1781, detail similar struggles with Stephanie, the *Entführung* librettist. Unfortunately, no similar source of information exists for the composition of the libretto of *Figaro*. But it is hardly to be supposed that Mozart held himself aloof from the proceedings. And whether we judge that a collaboration did in fact take place, or decide that Mozart merely responded to da Ponte's idiosyncratic vision of the story, that vision is carried out in—indeed, crowned by—Mozart's music.

[27] "Il capro e la capretta/Son sempre in amistà;/L'agnello all'agnelletta/La guerra mai non fa;/Le più feroci belve/Per selve e per campagne/Lascian le lor compagne/In pace e libertà." ("The he-goat and the little she-goat are always friendly; the lamb never makes war with his little ewe. The most ferocious beasts in the forests and in the fields leave their companions in peace and freedom.")

cuckoldry, he denounces women, whom he styles "roses with thorns."[28] In the light of the heroines' obvious grace and uprightness (which even Marcellina has come to appreciate), this denunciation must be held against him. As a result of these changes, and of a constellation of similar smaller ones throughout the work,[29] the emphasis of the opera is shifted away from social matters to a consideration of true nobility, a quality which, of all the characters in *Figaro*, only the noblewoman and the servant girl can be said fully to possess. The treatment of the three male characters is obviously of great moment to the transformation of the play. The line between rectitude and base behavior must be drawn more clearly than it is in *Le Mariage*: the youthful and attractive Count of the play must in the opera seem more of a bully, his hypocrisy and philandering more vicious than they appeared in Beaumarchais' play (where the Countess, herself more youthful-seeming, was on the verge of a serious flirtation with Cherubino; she keeps herself far more aloof from him in the opera). Figaro, his stature diminished, can no longer stand at the center of the work. Instead, the center is occupied by the friendship of the two women, and the transforming power of their good and gentle eros—its nature passive and receptive, in short "feminine"—becomes the opera's theme.

The prevalent musical style of *Le nozze di Figaro* might be designated as *di mezzo carattere* (or *halbe Charakter*—I invoke the categories set forth by the article in Sulzer's *Allgemeine Theorie der schönen Künste* on theatrical dance).[30] I have already mentioned the Countess' two *cantabile* arias, which resemble Don Ottavio's music in *Don Giovanni*. But in *Figaro* the *mezzo carattere* gesture is canonical, and *buffa*, no longer black and mocking, plays an ancillary role. In addition to the *cantabile* arias, another frequently invoked style of the middle ground is the pastorale: the slow 6/8 of the famous "letter duet" between the Countess and Susanna (Act 3, no. 20) is one example,[31]

[28] See p. 88 and n. 16 for the entire quotation.

[29] For a more extensive discussion of the changes which da Ponte made in the Beaumarchais play, see my *Rhythmic Gesture in Mozart*, pp. 167–71.

[30] "The third class includes the dances called in technical language *halbe Charaktere (demi-caractères)*. Their content is an everyday action in the character of the comic stage—a love affair, or any intrigue in which people from a not wholly ordinary kind of life are involved. The dances require elegance, pleasant manners, and fine taste." ("Die dritte Classe begreift die Tänze, die man in der Kunstsprache *halbe Charaktere* [*demi Caractères*] nennt. Ihr Inhalt ist eine Handlung aus dem gemeinen Leben, in dem Charakter der comischen Schaubühne, ein Liebeshandel, oder irgend eine Intrigue, darin schon Personen von nicht ganz gemeiner Lebensart verwickelt sind. Die Tänze erfodern schon Zierlichkeit, angenehme Manieren und feinen Geschmack." Johann Georg Sulzer, ed., *Allgemeine Theorie der schönen Künste*, 2nd ed., 4 vols. [Leipzig, 1786–87], s.v. "Tanz.")

[31] Koch defined the pastorale as "a piece of rustically simple but also tender character, in which the song of the idealized world of shepherds is to be expressed" ("ein Tonstück von ländlich einfachem, aber dabei zärtlichem Charakter, wodurch der Gesang der idealischen Hirtenwelt ausgedrückt werden soll"— *Musikalisches Lexikon* [Frankfurt am Main, 1802], s.v. "Pastorale"). It is to be written in 6/8, legato, and

and several times the pastorale is suggested by the more sophisticated gavotte.[32] Servant girl and mistress, they nevertheless find a meeting place, in the Arcadian never-never land, which provides a refuge beyond class and time where the two women can meet temporarily as equals.

In *Don Giovanni*, the music of the high tragic style delineates nobility pure and simple, set in stark relief by the supple counterpoint of *buffa*. The music of *Le nozze di Figaro* figures a luminous middle ground in the gentle light of which the styles of the extremes—patter and *alla breve*—show up as flawed and excessive. *Alla breve* was considered by many eighteenth century musicians to be a meter which was most appropriate for music for worship, and which had only recently (to some, improperly) been appropriated for music in the theater style.[33] This link between the grandest passions and the ecclesiastical style seems to imply that to be noble is to be the closest of humans to divinity, while the mode of expression which is *di mezzo carattere* lays its emphasis on the human side of nobility rather than on the divine. In *Figaro* the exalted accents of the *seria* style—the music of "divine inspiration"— seem at best empty posturing, and at worst the perversion of true passion, while the truer nobility resides in the humane and reflective gestures of the lyric mode.

---

dottings characteristic of its sister, the siciliano. Other pastorale movements in *Figaro* are the peasant choruses in Acts 1 and 3 (nos. 8 and 21), Barbarina's "L'ho perduta" (Act 4, no. 23), Susanna's "Deh, vieni" (Act 4, no. 27), and Susanna and Figaro's reconciliation scene in the fourth act finale (no. 28, mm. 275–334).

[32]Notably in the central moment of the second act finale, when the conspirators, seemingly having bested the Count, join in a prayer that their wedding take place immediately (no. 15, *Andante*, mm. 398–466). The gavotte is typically connected with pastoral texts in the late eighteenth century.

These pastorale and gavotte arias would probably come under Brown's category of *aria di mezzo carattere* ("neither the pathetic, the grand, nor the passionate, but the pleasing" [*Letters on the Italian Opera*, p. 69]). This aria type is not to be confused with Sulzer's designation of *halbe Charakter* for certain theatrical actions, for his is obviously a broader category, which embraces both the *aria cantabile* and the *aria di mezzo carattere*.

[33]"Its proper seat is in truth the church, where it was meant to be used in choruses, fugues, and polyphonic pieces, but since the meter is now also used for other pieces, one must get used to it." ("Es ist wahr, ihr eigentlicher Sitz ist die Kirche, wo sie vorzüglich in Chören, Fugen und gearbeiteten Sachen zu gebrauchen wäre; allein da sie nun auch zu andern Sachen gebrauchet wird; so muss man sich darein finden." Johann Adolf Scheibe, *Über die musikalische Komposition, Band 2: Die Theorie der Melodie und Harmonie* [Leipzig, 1773], pp. 203–4.) See also J. P. Kirnberger, *Anleitung zur Singcomposition* (Berlin, 1782), p. 12.

Cartesian Principles in Mozart's *La clemenza di Tito*
Don Neville

Mozart's *La clemenza di Tito* was composed for the coronation of Emperor Leopold II, an event that took place in Prague in the autumn of 1791. Based on a 1734 libretto by Pietro Metastasio, revised by Caterino Mazzolà, the opera was the outcome of a commission dated 8 July 1791 and was premiered in Prague on 6 September at the National Theater. The final performance of the initial run was given on 30 September and coincided with the opening of *Die Zauberflöte* at the Freihaus Theater in Vienna.

La clemenza di Tito fared well neither with the opening night audience nor with generations of subsequent critics. The premiere must have been a disaster: the light-hearted aristocratic audience enjoyed neither the relatively austere action of Mazzolà's libretto nor Mozart's musical setting; the ceremony's organizing body felt that its wishes had not been met; the court was prejudiced against the composition; the work was regarded by the performers as difficult and was under-rehearsed; and the singers, particularly the "fleshy mass" who sang the role of Sesto, were unconvincing.[1] The opera gained in

---

[1] The Mozart-Mazzolà *Tito* did not comply with the requirements of the Bohemian Estates for "una grand' Opera Seria" or with the suggestion of the Vorbereitungs-Kommission for an opera followed by a grand ballet. See the contract drawn up between Domenico Guardasoni and the Bohemian Estates, cited in Tomislav Volek, "Über den Ursprung von Mozarts Oper *La clemenza di Tito*," *Mozart-Jahrbuch 1959* (Salzburg, 1960), p. 281. See also Volek's comments on p. 280 and his citation of a contemporary comment, p. 285, n. 33.

In the same note, Volek also cites a statement that indicates the existence of court feelings against Mozart's compositions. With regard to this question, it may be noted that Mozart was overlooked for all other festivities surrounding the accession of Leopold II, and that neither Mozart nor Mazzolà was mentioned by Guardasoni when the contract was being drawn up. Mazzolà, at this point, had recently been dismissed as imperial court poet; see Helga Lühning, "Zur Entstehungsgeschichte von Mozarts *Titus*," *Die Musikforschung* 27 (1974): 308, and Joseph Eibl, "Zur Entstehungsgeschichte von Mozarts *Titus*: Bemerkungen zu dem Beitrag von Helga Lühning in Heft 3/1974," *Die Musikforschung* 28 (1975): 77–80.

A contemporary commentator reports that in an all-Mozart concert given in Prague on 7 February 1794, the works were difficult to perform. Vitellia's "Non più di fiori" (*La clemenza di Tito*, no. 23) was included on this program. See the *Prager neue Zeitung*, [9] February 1794, cited in Otto Erich Deutsch, *Mozart: A Documentary Biography*, 2nd ed., trans. Eric Blom, Peter Branscombe, and Jeremy Noble (London, 1965), p. 469. For the "fleshy mass," see the quotation from the *Allgemeine europäische Journal* (October–December 1794), p. 564, in Erik Smith's "Descriptive Notes" to a recording of *La clemenza di Tito* (Decca SET 357–59, 1968), p. 8.

popularity at the beginning of the nineteenth century, but later critics were harsh. Otto Jahn used the terms "obsolete," "superficial," and "repulsive"; Wagner described it as "stiff and dry"; and Edward Dent classified it as a "museum piece."[2] Various reasons were proposed to explain the failure. Since Mozart's first biographer, Franz Niemetschek, had imagined that the opera was composed in only eighteen days, some dismissed the work as "written in haste."[3] Others cast blame on the libretto, assuming that Mozart, who had composed the enormously successful *Die Zauberflöte* in the same year, could not be at fault.

Recent scholarship, however, has led to a reevaluation of *La clemenza di Tito*. Analysis has revealed masterly craftsmanship in the dramatic structuring of the opera and in its musical presentation of character, situation, and dramatic progression.[4] Although a considerable part of the score was probably written down in August 1791, no one now seriously believes that the opera was composed in eighteen days.[5] Since the late 1960s, the work has begun to be included in the repertoires of major opera houses and to be recorded for commercial sale. Today *La clemenza di Tito* is recognized as one of Mozart's *Meisteropern*.

Fundamental to the impact of the opera is the system of moral philosophy, derived from Descartes, which Metastasio's libretto "demonstrates" and which Mazzolà and Mozart embody in their opera. It is the operation of this moral system in Metastasio's libretto and its treatment by Mazzolà-Mozart that the following pages will discuss.

I

For a serious work intended for the coronation of a Hapsburg emperor, a libretto dealing with the qualities of moral virtue and statesmanship appro-

[2]Otto Jahn, *The Life of Mozart*, 2nd ed., trans. Pauline D. Townsend, 3 vols. (1882; repr. New York, n.d.), 3:290–93; Richard Wagner, "Über die Anwendung der Musik auf das Drama," *Gesammelte Schriften und Dichtungen von Richard Wagner*, 10 vols. (Leipzig, 1871–73), 10:235; and Edward Dent, *Mozart's Operas*, 2nd ed. (1947; repr. London, 1973), p. 212.

[3]Franz Niemetschek, *W. A. Mozarts Leben nach Originalquellen* (1798; new ed. by Ernst Rychnovsky [Prague, 1950]), pp. 32 and 56.

[4]See Daniel Heartz, "Mozart's Overture to *Titus* as Dramatic Argument," *The Musical Quarterly* 64 (1978): 29–49; and his "Mozart and His Italian Contemporaries," *Mozart-Jahrbuch 1978–79* (Salzburg, 1980), pp. 275–93. See also my own articles in *Studies in Music from the University of Western Ontario*, vols. 1–3, 5–7 (1976–78, 1980–82).

[5]For a list of articles that discuss the genesis of the Mozart-Mazzolà *Tito*, see Alan Tyson, "*La clemenza di Tito* and its Chronology," *The Musical Times* 106 (March 1975): 221, n. 3. To this list could be added Tyson's own article; Eibl, "Entstehungsgeschichte," pp. 75–81; and Andrew Porter, "Musical Events: *Imperial*," *The New Yorker*, 12 November 1979, pp. 206–16.

priate for a ruler was a suitable choice. Like any Metastasian libretto intended for the imperial court, the 1734 libretto chosen by Mozart and Mazzolà had the two-fold function of placing a vision of the ideal ruler before the emperor's eyes and equating that ideal with the person of the present emperor in the minds of the audience. In the case of *Tito*, the incidents and characters illustrating moral and political virtues are drawn from events in the reign of the Roman emperor Titus Vespasian, as recounted by such historians as Suetonius and Dio Cassius (Mestastasio cites his sources at the end of his *argomento*).[6] The historical events and characters, however, have been interpreted in accordance with moral principles current among the Italian academies that formed the Arcadian movement at the end of the seventeenth and the beginning of the eighteenth centuries. An important influence on the Arcadians at this time was the philosophy of René Descartes, and it is in the light of Cartesian ideals of virtue that Metastasio's *Tito* must be understood.[7]

The influence of Descartes had always been strong among Arcadians ever since the founding of the Accademia degli Arcadi by members of the coterie of Christina of Sweden, whom Descartes had served as tutor during the last months of his life, from October 1649 to February 1650.[8] Metastasio could

[6]The story of Titus Vespasian's pardon granted to two young patricians who led an attempt on his life, his dismissal of Berenice from Rome, his aid to the victims of an eruption of Vesuvius, and other smaller references are taken from Suetonius, Dio Cassius, and others. However, the characters have been heightened in a manner inspired by selected models from the works of Pierre Corneille and Jean Racine. On this process, see Robert Moberly, "The Influence of French Classical Drama on Mozart's *La clemenza di Tito*," *Music and Letters* 55/3 (July 1974): 286–98.

[7]The Arcadian interest in Descartes is evident in the writings of the Arcadians themselves. Compare, for example, the discussion of true and false judgments in Gianvincenzo Gravina, *Della ragion poetica, libri due* in *Gianvincenzo Gravina scritti critici e teorici*, ed. Amadeo Quondam, Scrittori d'Italia, no. 255 (Rome, 1973), bk. 1, chaps. 1–11, pp. 200–18 (*Ragion Poetica* was first published in 1708), and René Descartes, "Meditations IV and VI," *Meditations on First Philosophy*, in *The Philosophical Works of Descartes*, trans. Elizabeth S. Haldane and G. R. T. Ross, 2 vols. (1931; reprint ed., Cambridge, 1979), 1:173, 189. (The *Meditationes de prima philosophia* were first published in 1641; the Haldane and Ross translation of the works of Descartes was first published in 1911.)

The standard edition of the works of René Descartes is *Œuvres de Descartes*, ed. Charles Adam and Paul Tannery, 13 vols., reissued in association with the Centre national de la recherche scientifique (Paris, 1971–75). All subsequent references to Descartes' works will first cite the standard edition as AT, followed by the reference(s) to the English translation as HR. The present citation would thus be: "Meditations IV and VI," AT, 7:54–55, 76–77 (Latin); 9/1: 43–44 (French); HR, 1:173, 189.

Compare also the physiological explanation of the relationship between imagination and intellect in Lodovico Antonio Muratori, *Della perfetta poesia italiana*, ed. Ada Ruschioni, Scrittori italiani, 3 bks. in 2 vols. (Milan, 1971), bk. 1, 1:82 [first published, 1706], and Descartes, "Meditation VI," AT, 7:86–88; 9/1:69–70; HR, 1:196–98.

[8]On Descartes' association with Christina of Sweden, see Descartes' letter to Pierre Chanut, 20 November 1647, AT, 5:87–88, cited in John J. Blom, *Descartes: His Moral Philosophy and Psychology* (New York, 1978), p. 231. See also Bernard Williams, *Descartes: The Project of Pure Enquiry* (London, 1978), pp. 23–24.

have encountered Arcadian principles as early as 1708, when, at the age of ten, he entered the household of Gianvincenzo Gravina, a founding member of the Accademia degli Arcadi in Rome. Gravina had studied in Naples with the Cartesian philospher Gregorio Caloprese—with whom Metastasio himself was to stay for some months in 1712.[9] Ten years later Metastasio was admitted to the Arcadian Accademia Aletina in Naples.[10] When, in 1730, he became Caesarian Court Poet in Vienna, he assumed a post that had traditionally been held by Arcadians. Indeed, Mestastasio's predecessors in Vienna had been Silvio Stampiglia and Apostolo Zeno, Arcadians whose libretti reflect familiarity with the works of Descartes and with French tragedy of the seventeenth century, replete with its own Cartesian leanings.[11]

The Arcadian ideal was an ethical-aesthetic blend: it sought to embrace moral instruction while delighting the senses. Exegeses of the means of creating this kind of aesthetic experience abound in Arcadian writings, but no definitive moral code is provided on which to base the ethical features of such an experience. Clearly, such a code already existed, and the single source that stands out as directly relevant to the activities of Arcadian librettists is Descartes' *Les Passions de l'âme*, first published in 1649. Whether or not Metastasio had a copy of this treatise on hand, *Tito*, as we shall see, demonstrates a fundamental dependence on the principles enunciated by Descartes in this extremely popular and influential work.

Descartes held that emotions arise "from all kinds of perceptions and all kinds of knowledge." Even where understanding is erroneous because of what he regarded as the deceptive possibilities of the imagination and sense perception, any passion aroused is real, since "we cannot be . . . deceived regarding the passions, inasmuch as they are so close to, and entirely within our soul, that it is impossible for it to feel them without their being actually such as it feels them to be."[12] Thus the passions are all registered within the soul or the thinking self. Their continuance, however, depends upon the body by means

[9]On Metastasio's associations with Gravina, see Bruno Brunelli, "Cronologia della vita e delle opere di Pietro Metastasio," in *Tutti le opere di Pietro Metastasio*, ed. Bruno Brunelli, I classici Mondadori fondazione Borletti, 5 vols. (Verona, 1951–65), 1:[XLV], and Michele Maylender, *Storia delle accademie d'Italia*, 5 vols. (Bologna, 1926), 1:247.

[10]Maylender, *Storia delle accademie*, 1:135.

[11]Silvio Stampiglia, Zeno's predecessor as Caesarian Court Poet, was, like Gravina, a founding member of the Roman Accademia degli Arcadi; see ibid., 1:247. Zeno was a member of the Venetian Accademia degli Animosi; see ibid., 1:207. Further on the channels by which Cartesian philosophy could have reached Metastasio, see my "Moral Philosophy in the Metastasian Dramas," Proceedings of the Symposium "Crosscurrents and the Mainstream of Italian Serious Opera, 1730–1790," 11–13 February 1982, published as *Studies in Music from the University of Western Ontario*, 7/1 (1982): 189–90.

[12]*Les Passions de l'âme*, I, 26; AT, 11:348; HR, 1:343.

of a complex system involving the circulation of the blood and forces within the nervous system which Descartes identifies as the "animal spirits." The passions, Descartes claims,

> are nearly all accompanied by some commotion which takes place in the heart, and in consequence also in the whole of the blood and the animal spirits, so that until the commotion has subsided, they remain present to our thought in the same manner as sensible objects are present while they act upon the organs of our senses.[13]

Passions arouse desire, and Descartes sees most desires as terminating in some form of bodily action. It is therefore with forms of desire that the soul must reckon. Descartes reasons that

> because the passions can only bring us to any kind of action by the intervention of desire which they excite, it is this desire particularly which we should be careful to regulate, and it is in this that the principal use of morality consists.[14]

He cautions that the soul may

> easily get the better of the lesser passions but not the most violent and strongest, excepting after the commotion of the blood and spirits is appeased. The most that the will can do while this commotion is in its full strength is not to yield to its effects and to restrain many of the movements to which it disposes the body.[15]

Although the passions cannot be prevented, their duration or strength can be controlled indirectly, through reasonings that can produce counter-passions and consequently restrain bodily actions.[16]

To harness the passions, Descartes advocates a knowledge of the manner in which they function, the pursuit of truth (so that passions do not arise through misunderstanding or ignorance), and the acquisition of certain virtues or "attitudes of mind" which are conducive to the advantageous use of the passions. Descartes names "devotion" and "generosity" as the foremost attitudes of mind which, if steadfastly maintained, will provide the strength of will to withstand the onslaughts of destructive desires.

Devotion differs from affection and mere friendship:

> When we esteem the object of love less than ourselves, we have only a simple affection for it; when we esteem it equally with ourselves, that is called friendship; and when we esteem it more, the passion which we have

---

[13]*Passions*, I, 46; AT, 11:363; HR, 1:352.

[14]*Passions*, II, 144; AT, 11:436; HR, 1:395.

[15]*Passions*, I, 46; AT, 11:364; HR, 1:352.

[16]*Passions* I, 41, 45–46; AT, 11:359, 362–64; HR, 1:350–52.

may be called devotion. . . . In simple affection we always prefer ourselves
to the object loved; and, on the other hand, in devotion the thing loved is
so much preferred to the self, that we do not fear death in order to preserve
it.[17]

Objects of devotion, Descartes explains, may be a prince, country, town, or
even a particular man, when we esteem him much more than ourselves.[18]

For Descartes, fatherly love may be a particular case of the larger concept of
devotion:

> The love which a good father has for his children is so pure that he desires
> to have nothing from them, and does not wish to possess them otherwise
> than he does, nor to be united with them more closely than he already is.
> For, considering them as replicas of himself, he seeks their good as his
> own, or even with greater care, because, in setting before himself that he
> or they form a whole of which he is not the best part, he often prefers their
> interests to his, and does not fear losing himself in order to save them.[19]

Generosity, in Descartes' system, is composed of several qualities: the
determination to act according to the highest principles; the belief that others
are capable of doing the same; the willingness to excuse the weak; the ability
to subjugate anger; and a concern for the welfare of others. The generous man
knows that all that is rightfully his is his own free will, and that the only thing
for which he can be either praised or blamed is for the manner in which he
exercises that will. He therefore makes a firm resolution to use it well, "that is
to say, never to fail of his own will to undertake and execute all the things
which he judges to be best—which is to follow perfectly after virtue."[20] Those
who feel this way about themselves believe that all others are capable of the
same generosity. "That is why they never despise anyone; and, although
they often see that others commit faults which make their feebleness apparent, they are at the same time more inclined to excuse than to blame them. . . .
although they hate vices, they do not for all that hate those whom they see
subject to them, but only pity them."[21] For Descartes, generosity is "the key
to all other virtues, and a general remedy for all the disorders of the
passions."[22]

Understanding and knowledge may be important in controlling the passions, but the will must be helped towards positive action by a determined

---

[17]*Passions*, II, 83; AT, 11:390; HR, 1:368.

[18]Ibid.

[19]*Passions*, II, 82; AT, 11:389; HR, 1:367.

[20]*Passions*, III, 153; AT, 11:446; HR, 1:402.

[21]*Passions*, III, 187; AT, 11:469–70; HR, 1:416.

[22]*Passions*, III, 161; AT, 11:454; HR, 1:406.

cultivation of the desire for virtue.[23] Descartes concludes the second part of the *Passions*:

> Whoever has lived in such a way that his conscience cannot reproach him for ever having failed to perform those things which he has judged to be the best (which is what I here call following after virtue) receives from this a satisfaction which is so powerful in rendering him happy that the most violent efforts of the passions never have sufficient power to disturb the tranquillity of his soul.[24]

Just as there are attitudes of mind that for Descartes predispose a man toward virtuous behavior, so there are attitudes that tend to lead to wrong-doing and consequent shame, remorse, or despair. Such an attitude is that of unbridled desire, against which Descartes counsels specifically:

> As for the things which in nowise depend on us, good as they may be, we should never desire them with passion . . .[25]

"Burning ambition," in the modern sense, exemplifies such desire; if thwarted, such ambition leads to an anger described as

> a species of hatred or aversion which we have toward those who have done some evil to . . . not any chance person, but more particularly ourselves. . . . And for this we desire to avenge ourselves, for this desire almost always accompanies it.[26]

Descartes warns not only against this passion but also against envy and the unhappiness which is its consequence:

> There are few who are sufficiently generous and just not to bear hatred to those who get the better of them in the acquisition of a good which is not communicable to many, and which they had desired for themselves, although those who acquired it are as worthy or even more so.[27]

> There is no vice which so detracts from the happiness of men as that of envy; for, in addition to the fact that those who are tainted with it distress themselves, they also disturb to the utmost of their power the pleasures of others . . .[28]

Failure to control the passions may lead people to commit acts that they know to be morally reprehensible. For such people, the problem is not that they actively pursue vice but that they are insufficiently resolute in avoiding vice and pursuing virtue:

[23] *Passions*, II, 144; AT, 11:436–37; HR, 1:395.
[24] *Passions*, II, 168; AT, 11:422; HR, 1:399.
[25] *Passions*, II, 145; AT, 11:437; HR, 1:396.
[26] *Passions*, III, 199; AT, 11:477; HR, 1:420.
[27] *Passions*, III, 183; AT, 11:467–68; HR, 1:414.
[28] *Passions*, III, 184; AT, 11:468; HR, 1:415.

The most feeble souls of all are those whose will does not thus determine itself to follow certain judgements, but allows itself continually to be carried away by present passions, which, being frequently contrary to one another, draw the will first to one side, then to the other, and, by employing it in striving against itself, place the soul in the most deplorable possible condition.[29]

Descartes warns against a "vicious humility," which

consists principally in the fact that men are feeble or have a lack of resolution, and that, as though they had not the entire use of their free-will, they cannot prevent themselves doing things of which they know that they will afterwards repent.[30]

Failure of the will sufficiently to control the passions results in other unpleasant and disturbing passions: repentance, shame, despair, and regret— all of which Descartes describes as species of "sadness." Repentance Descartes attributes to "our believing ourselves to have committed some evil action . . . it is very bitter because its cause proceeds from ourselves alone."[31] Shame "proceeds from the apprehension or the fear which we have of being blamed."[32] Regret Descartes defines as

a kind of sadness which has a particular bitterness inasmuch as it is always united to a certain despair and to the memory of the pleasure which gave us joy, for we regret nothing but the good things regarding which we rejoiced and which are so lost that we have no hope of recovering them at the time and in the same guise in which we regret them.[33]

However, Descartes believes that even the weakest man can learn to control his passions and avoid their undesirable consequences:

Even those who have the feeblest souls can acquire a very absolute dominion over all their passions if sufficient industry is applied in training and guiding them.[34]

II

These principles, outlined in *Les passions de l'âme* and echoed and elaborated in countless subsequent works, form the basis of the moral system which is embodied in Metastasio's 1734 *La clemenza di Tito*. Metastasio's plot is

---

[29]*Passions*, I, 48; AT, 11:367; HR, 1:354.

[30]*Passions*, III, 159; AT, 11:450; HR, 1:404.

[31]*Passions*, III, 191; AT, 11:472; HR, 1:417.

[32]*Passions*, III, 205; AT, 11:482; HR, 1:423.

[33]*Passions*, III, 209; AT, 11:484–85; HR, 1:425.

[34]*Passions*, I, 50; AT, 11:370; HR, 1:356.

simple: Vitellia, daughter of the deposed and now deceased emperor Vitellio, views Tito as a usurper, since he occupies the throne taken from Vitellio by Tito's father, Vespasiano. Vitellia is ambitious to regain the throne, but her desires are complicated by her secret love for Tito and her jealousy at his having overlooked her as his empress-elect. Driven by rage, envy, and thwarted ambition, Vitellia goads Sesto, her infatuated admirer and Tito's closest friend, into leading an attempt on the emperor's life. This attempt fails, and Sesto is arrested, but only after Annio, the fiancé of Sesto's sister Servilia, has been falsely accused. Tito asks Sesto the reason for his rash behavior, but Sesto remains silent in order to protect Vitellia. Assuming Sesto to have been condemned on her account, Vitellia confesses her guilt to Tito, who generously forgives all.

Each of Metastasio's three main characters (Tito, Vitellia, and Sesto) embodies particular Cartesian virtues or vices. Tito, a model of devotion and generosity, is the Cartesian hero; secure in his commitment to the general good, he can be at peace with himself. Vitellia, plagued by ambition and rage, suffers the inevitable consequences: repentance, shame, and regret. Sesto is a vacillating weakling who, lacking control of his passions, falls victim to remorse and despair.

Let us consider Tito in some detail. As emperor, Tito is devoted to the good of Rome; throughout the action his devotion and generosity are continually tested. Even before he appears onstage, an example is provided of his civic-minded self-abnegation. Although he loves the Judaean princess Berenice, he has relinquished her because he believes that Rome would prefer "one of her own daughters" as empress. Annio describes the conflict between Tito's personal desires and the good of Rome:

> Eh! si conobbe
> Che bisognava a Tito
> Tutto l'eroe per superare l'amante.
> Vinse, ma combatté. Non era oppresso,
> Ma tranquillo non era; ed in quel volto,
> Dicasi per sua gloria,
> Si vedea la battaglia e la vittoria.[35]

[35] "Ah! It was clear that Tito needed all the hero in order to subdue the lover. He conquered, but he fought. He was not oppressed, nor was he undisturbed; and in that countenance (to his glory, it may be said) was seen the battle and the victory." Pietro Metastastio, *La clemenza di Tito*, Act I, sc. 2, in *Tutte le opere di Pietro Metastasio*, ed. Bruno Brunelli, I classici Mondadori, fondazione Borletti, 5 vols. (Verona, 1951–65), 1:700–701; Wolfgang Amadeus Mozart and Caterino Mazzolà, *La clemenza di Tito*, Act I, sc. 2, in *Wolfgang Amadeus Mozart: Neue Ausgabe sämtlicher Werke*, ser. II, workgroup 5, vol. 20, ed. Franz Giegling (Kassel, 1970), pp. 33–34. Further references to Metastasio's libretto are to the Brunelli edition; further references to Mozart's opera are to Giegling's edition. In both cases, only act, scene, and page numbers will be given. All translations are my own.

Like Descartes' devoted father, Tito stands ready, if necessary, to give up his life for Rome. Still stunned by the assassination attempt, Tito says to Vitellia,

> Il perder, principessa,
> E la vita e l'impero
> Affligermi non può. Già miei non sono
> Che per usarne a benefizio altrui.
> . . . Ma, quando a Roma
> Giovi ch'io versi il sangue,
> Perché insidiarmi?[36]

Not surprisingly, Tito is introduced as "father of his country," both by Sesto before Tito appears on stage and by Publio (captain of the Praetorian guard) at the emperor's first entrance:

> Te 'della patria il padrè'
> Oggi appella il Senato.[37]

Like a good father, Tito desires nothing more from the citizens of Rome than the respect due him. As Sesto puts it,

> Ei [Tito] regna, è ver; ma vuol da noi
> Sol tanta servitù quanto impedisca
> Di parir la licenza.[38]

Just as Tito embodies the Cartesian virtue of devotion, so he also demonstrates Cartesian generosity. During the first act, we see several examples of Tito's generosity. Offered riches and a temple in his honor, Tito redirects the funds in support of the victims of an eruption of Vesuvius (sc. 4). Read a proscription list, he pardons those named (sc. 6). When Servilia requests not to be considered as consort, he responds not with anger at being rejected, but with enthusiasm and delight at her honesty and fidelity (sc. 7).

The events of the first act prepare us for the extreme test to which Tito's generosity is put in the second. Faced with Sesto's evident betrayal, Tito reacts first with anger. But even in the grip of that passion, the emperor retains sufficent self-control to delay acting until he has interviewed Sesto:

> Ah! sì, lo scellerato mora.
> Mora? . . . Ma senza udirlo
> Mando Sesto a morir? . . . Sì, già l'intese

---

[36] "Princess, the loss of either life or empire cannot distress me. Indeed they are mine only so long as they are used for the benefit of others. . . . but, why lay snares for me when for Rome I would gladly shed my blood?" Metastasio, Act 1, sc. 10, 1:727.

[37] "Today the senate names you 'Father of your country.'" Metastasio, Act 1, sc. 5, 1:703; Mozart, Act 1, sc. 4, p. 62.

[38] "He [Tito] reigns, it is true; but he requires from us only as much subjection as will prevent the violation of liberty." Metastasio, Act 1, sc. 1, 1:698.

Abbastanza il Senato. E s'egli avesse
Qualche arcano a svelarmi? . . . S'ascolti . . . [39]

So Tito seeks an explanation:

Cerchiamo insieme una via di scusarti. [40]

But Sesto remains silent. Although the emperor realizes that justice demands Sesto's execution, he questions the moral virtue of putting to death a Roman citizen and a friend, however unfaithful. Tito knows that whatever he decides, some will consider it wrong; he concludes that an error of clemency would be preferable to one of cruelty.

Tito's generosity has its final test when Vitellia's complicity in the crime is revealed. When Vitellia finally confesses, Tito responds:

Congiuran gli astri,
Cred'io, per obbligarmi, a mio dispetto,
A diventar crudel. No! non avranno
Questo trionfo. A sostener la gara
Già s'impegnò la mia virtù. [41]

It is the Cartesian quality of generosity that makes "la clemenza di Tito"—the final pardon—possible. Tito's behavior illustrates step-by-step the Cartesian process of subduing base passions by applying the will to higher virtue. As Annio remarks, "Tito ha l'impero / E del mondo e di sé." [42]

If Tito represents the Cartesian "hero," Vitellia and Sesto represent Cartesian "miscreants." Ambitious both for the throne and for Tito's hand, Vitellia yields completely to her anger and envy when she is passed over as Tito seeks a consort:

S'aspetta forse
Che Tito a Berenice in faccia mia
Offra, d'amore insano,
L'usurpato mio soglio e la sua mano? [43]

A little later, she demonstrates the same lack of self-control:

---

[39] "Ah yes, the villain shall die. He shall die! But do I condemn Sesto to death without giving him a hearing? Yes, the Senate has already heard enough. But if he had some secret to reveal to me? Let him be heard." Metastasio, Act 3, sc. 4, 1:737.

[40] "Let us seek together a way to excuse you." Metastasio, Act 3, sc. 6, 1:740; Mozart, Act 2, sc. 10, p. 222.

[41] "The stars conspire, I believe, to compel me, in spite of myself, to become cruel. No: they shall not have this triumph. I have already pledged my virtue in support of this contest." Metastasio, Act 3, sc. 12, 1:748–49; Mozart, Act 2, sc. 17, pp. 294–95.

[42] "Tito holds the empire of both the world and himself." Metastasio, Act 1, sc. 2, 1:700.

[43] "You wait, perhaps, until Tito, in my presence, offers her [Berenice], through his foolish affection, his hand and the throne he has usurped from me?" Metastasio, Act 1, sc. 1, 1:697; Mozart, Act 1, sc. 1, pp. 21–22.

> E più non pensi
> Che questo eroe clemente un soglio usurpa
> Dal suo tolto al mio padre?
> Che m'ingannò, che mi ridusse (e questo
> È il suo fallo maggior) quasi ad amarlo?[44]

Early in the action, these uncontrolled passions succeed in generating malevolent demands:

> Prima che il sol tramante,
> Estinto io vò l'indegno.[45]

Ironically, no sooner does Vitellia succeed in inspiring Sesto to lead an attempt on Tito's life than she is summoned as Tito's consort. Only at this point does she begin to understand the consequences of her fury and to repent of her rage:

> O sdegno mio funesto!
> O insano mio furor![46]

By the end of the first act finale, believing that Tito is dead, she is reduced to such despair that she can only join the general utterances of dismay and lamentation.

News that Tito has survived the assassination attempt alleviates Vitellia's initial despair but inspires new concerns. Fearful that her role in the conspiracy will become known and that her reputation will be destroyed, she urges Sesto to flee:

> Tu sei perduto,
> Se alcun ti scopre, e se scoperto sei,
> Pubblico è il mio segreto.[47]

After Sesto's arrest, Vitellia's fears increase:

> Per me vien tratto a morte:
> Ah, dove mai m'ascondo!
> Fra poco noto al mondo
> Il fallo mio sarà.[48]

---

[44] "And do you no longer recall that this merciful hero usurps a throne stolen from my father by his [father]? That he deceived me, that he charmed me (and this is his greatest fault) almost into loving him?" Metastasio, Act 1, sc. 1, 1:699; Mozart, Act 1, sc. 1, pp. 23–24.

[45] "Before sunset, I want the worthless [creature] dead." Mozart, ACT 1, sc. 1, p. 27, based on Metastasio, Act 1, sc. 1, 1:700.

[46] "O my fatal anger! Oh my demented fury!" Mozart, Act 1, sc. 10, p. 119, based on Metastasio, Act 1, sc. 12, 1:715.

[47] "You are lost if anyone finds you out, and if you are found out, my secret will become public." Metastasio, Act 2, sc. 14, 1:732; Mozart, Act 2, sc. 2, p. 167.

[48] "Through me he goes to his death; ah, where shall I hide? My crime will soon be known to the world." Mozart, Act 2, sc. 2, pp. 170–71, altered from Metastasio, Act 2, sc. 16, 1:733.

To the fear Vitellia now experiences are added shame and regret. Although she finally does succeed in subjugating her ambition and, of her own free will, confessing her guilt, she is left with the bitter knowledge that her own behavior has removed any possibility of marriage to Tito.

Vitellia's career follows in all particulars the Cartesian model; her sufferings are a direct consequence of her failure to restrain her ambition, envy, and anger.

Like Vitellia, Sesto is a victim of uncontrolled desires. His problems stem not from ambition and anger but from his passion for Vitellia. Unlike Vitellia, he is not blind—or, rather, indifferent—to the moral implications of his actions: he is perfectly well aware of the iniquity of betraying Tito, but he lacks the firmness and commitment to morality necessary to keep him to the strait and narrow. Sesto's actions illustrate the natural process of what Descartes calls "vicious humility": Sesto does not actively pursue vice; rather, he is insufficiently resolute in avoiding vice and pursuing virtue. Unlike Tito, who can sacrifice his personal desires in the best interests of Rome, Sesto allows his infatuation with Vitellia to drive him to betray his friend. Torn between loyalty to Tito and desire to please his beloved Vitellia, he vacillates:

> Tu vendetta mi chiedi;
> Tito vuol fedeltà. Tu di tua mano
> Con l'offerta mi sproni; et mi raffrena
> Co' benefizi suoi. Per te l'amore,
> Per lui parla il dover.[49]

Sesto pays for his failure to control his emotions. He regrets his rash participation in the conspiracy even before the assassination is attempted, but finds himself unable to stop what he has set in motion. Unmasked before Tito, he is driven by remorse and shame to a state of despair. Forgiven by the Emperor, he is left with memories of Tito's generosity and of his own meanness and duplicity.

III

The libretto provided by Mazzolà for Mozart preserved the moral perspectives of Metastasio's text, but "streamlined" the plot and placed greater emphasis on Tito. The first scenes of Metastasio's second act became the new Act 1 finale; the remainder of that act was suppressed, so that a series of events centering around Sesto and Annio was removed. The roles of Annio and Servilia, who in Metastasio's version had served as foils to Sesto and Vitellia, were greatly reduced, and several passages of moral exhortation were deleted.

---

[49] "You require vengeance of me; Tito claims fidelity. You incite me by the offer of your hand; he restrains me by his beneficence. For you speaks love—for him, duty." Metastasio, Act 1, sc. 1, 1:698.

On the other hand, in scenes where moral issues were the very substance of the dramatic action, the more economical presentation in Mazzolà's new libretto heightened their effect.

Mozart's music underscores the moral processes so fundamental to the Metastasio-Mazzolà libretto. Mozart has given to the three principal characters music that conveys their several emotional states and underlines the stress they experience as they grapple with moral conflicts.

One of the means by which Mozart most effectively depicts the struggles undergone by his three principal characters is clever manipulation of aria forms. All three of Tito's arias are tightly structured on simple tonic-dominant tonal relationships. The first two share the equally simple ABA form, and the last is cast in a concise sonata form. The more adventurous two-tempo arias and rondò structures, with their tonal digressions, are reserved for Vitellia's and Sesto's arias and for ensembles and scenes in which the "miscreants" are involved. Tito's mental state is clear and uncomplicated before each of his arias begins, and the aria serves to magnify and uphold this mental state, not to advance psychological or physical action. (This practice recalls the old operatic structure, with its da capo aria.) Quite the contrary is true of most of the numbers involving Vitellia and Sesto, where emotional complexities, far from being resolved prior to the musical numbers, are carried into them. Here, the individual's unrest prompts dramatic action—either direct confrontation with others or personal conflict.

The first opportunity afforded Mozart for the depiction of Tito in musical terms is no. 6, the aria "Del più sublime soglio." To Sesto's wonder at Tito's generosity the emperor responds that generous actions afford the ruler his only reward; all else is torment and servitude. "Reward" and "virtue" serve as key words to the mood inflections depicted in the central section of the aria, which contains the principal climax; "torment" and "servitude" are the key words of the outer sections.

The limpid simplicity of the aria reflects Tito's emotional composure and lack of complexity at the time. The aria has no instrumental introduction and a postlude of only three measures, and is in a simple ABA form, involving only a single dominant modulation and return. Except for some occasional harmonic reinforcement from the wind instruments, the orchestration is for strings throughout, and the dynamic range lies between just piano and forte, with a general leaning toward the former. The first measures of the vocal line set the tone of the aria (see Example 1). In mm. 1–3, the range does not exceed a fifth, the line undulates gently, and at the andante tempo the dotted half-notes placed on the first beats of mm. 1 and 2 prevent any sense of unsteady rhythmic activity. The orchestral accompaniment is light and is marked piano. Measures 10 and 11 display a similar steadiness. Measures 4–9

Example 1. Mozart, *La clemenza di Tito*, no. 6 (Act I, sc. 4), mm. 1–11.

provide some degree of contrast to the surrounding phrases. A crescendo to forte coincides with a strongly-marked dotted rhythm which appears in the voice part in mm. 4, 6, and 8, but which has already been heard in the strings. The melodic line, instead of undulating, now rises and falls directly, and the range is expanded to a tenth in mm. 7–8. The anacrusic movement from the dotted rhythm upwards to the strong third beat in m. 8 marks the climax of the entire line. The directness of the melodic motion is complemented by the marked clarity of the two-bar phrasing.

In keeping with the general character of the aria, its central climax in the B section is distinctly marked but dramatically restrained. The regular two-bar phrasing of the B section is broken at m. 30, at the beginning of the approach to the climax; by this time the note g'' has been sounded five times as the apex of the B section's first phrases. As the irregular phrases begin, the emphasis on f'' prepares for a new approach back through g'' to a'', the highest peak of the aria, which coincides, of course, with the word "merto" at m. 35 and resolves upon the word "virtù" in mm. 36–37. Without destroying his portrayal of Tito's geniality and composure, Mozart has done service to his strength of soul, his potential capacity for strong feeling, and even to his clarity of mind.

Tito's second aria (no. 8) is prompted by Servilia's candid refusal to accept the royal proposal of marriage; it expresses his delight in Servilia's honesty. The aria begins with a seven-measure orchestral introduction in an allegro tempo. An eighth-note quasi-ostinato figure enforces the solidity of a firmly anchored home key with a clearly audible I–IV–V⁷–I progression. The gentle undulation of mm. 11–13 and 17–19 contrasts sharply with the more forth-right activity of mm. 8–10 and 13–16 (see Example 2a), and the musical techniques employed are similar to those utilized in the first aria. In the concluding measures of no. 8 (Example 2b), more florid writing expresses Tito's enthusiasm for virtue. The motive which occurs on the key word "felicità" (motive a) ends forcefully with a wide ascending leap to a long note on the first beat of the following bar, in sharp contrast to the quick, unaccented, florid descent immediately preceding. The motive, clearly set apart by rests, gains power through repetition. In fact, Mozart has again built into the vocal line a slowly mounting intensity, which accumulates over five measures (mm. 53–58) and resolves in one (mm. 58–59). If we extract the notes of longer duration, beginning with the last note of m. 53, we find a melodic line that follows the outline D–E–F-sharp, D–E–F-sharp–G–A; from this climax follows a rapid descent to the final tonic. Rising and climaxing with this melodic line is, of course, Tito's expression of "felicità." Tito's exaltation ends in a well articulated I_4^6–V^7–I cadence which affirms the solidity of the home key as did the introduction. Tito's delight in true virtue is strong and secure.

Example 2. Mozart, *La clemenza di Tito*, no. 8 (Act 1, sc. 7).
   a. mm. 8–18.

   b. mm. 51–59.

Tito's third and final aria (no. 20) occurs on the occasion of his decision to pardon Sesto. Tito, having fought off the base desire for vengeance and having allowed his generosity to triumph, expresses his sense of victory. In some sense, this aria begins where aria no. 8 left off. The "felicità" motive of the second aria (Example 2a) recurs literally in m. 20 of the third aria, transposed up a half-step (Example 3a). In no. 8, Mozart used the florid writing of the "felicità" motive to express Tito's enthusiasm for virtue; here the motive becomes a point of departure. The first motive marked in Example 3b (motive a') seems to be derived from the "felicità" motive; it forms but a part of the ensuing fioritura section. The descending arpeggio (shown in Example 3c) in which the entire florid section terminates echoes Tito's first aria, no. 6, but now its range is extended, its starting point is both the climax of the aria and

Tito's highest note in the opera, and its impact has been heightened by the rhythmic tension of syncopation. As in aria no. 8, the tonal boundaries have been purposefully articulated, and the emotional content of this earlier aria has here found an even greater exuberance of expression.

Example 3. Mozart, *La clemenza di Tito*, no. 20 (Act 2, sc. 12).
   a. mm. 11–22.

   b. mm. 94–100.

   c. mm. 105–7.

Taken as a group, Tito's three arias increase in formal complexity, melodic interest, and scope. No. 6 has no introduction. The introduction to no. 8 is seven measures long and is scored for strings and partial winds; that to no. 20 is ten measures long, is scored for full winds including horns, and strings, and gains impetus from orchestral syncopation, detached articulation, marked accents, and sixteenth-note movement, all of which continue into the aria and are thrown into relief by its contrasting central section. This increase in musical density across the three arias reflects the intensification of Tito's strength of will to champion his noble convictions in the face of opposing base desires.

Mozart reserves for recitative the depiction of Tito's chief moments of inner conflict and indecision. Tito's first moment of extreme trial occurs just prior to his interview with Sesto, when, alone and feeling the full weight of Sesto's treachery, he expresses his horror and then chides himself for hesitating over the death sentence ("Che orror! che tradimento," Act 2, sc. 7). For this scene

Mozart employs *recitativo obbligato*, beginning with a single measure for strings in rapid tempo and syncopated rhythm, and a diminished seventh chord on F-sharp which does not resolve to G minor until the fourth measure. Tito asks rhetorically why he should hesitate to sign the warrant (m. 13); a pause and a two-measure orchestral passage follow this question. Now, in the key of D-flat major, Tito prepares to sign (m. 16). This is the moment when both Tito's thinking and the tonality of the recitative are at their furthest distance from the place of final resolution. Tito then begins to reconsider; he needs to hear Sesto's viewpoint. The tonality works back from D-flat major, touching A-flat major and E-flat major, reaching B-flat major (the relative major of the original key), and finally G minor (m. 31) as Tito's mind wanders from the painful central issue to the contemplation of a rustic life. Simultaneously, the forte interjections of the string accompaniment settle back to soft, sustained chords, and the entire scene finally resolves to the quiet calm of *recitativo semplice*. In this passage the libretto illustrates a process explicitly recommended by Descartes—subduing passions by turning one's thoughts to matters that arouse feelings of a contrary nature.[50] This is what Tito does, and this is what Mozart portrays in musical terms in a most effective manner.

The final test of Tito's moral commitment occurs in the finale, during which the greatness of Tito's character is made manifest by his forgiveness of Vitellia and Sesto. With the full ensemble and chorus assembled, this *scena* begins in *recitativo semplice* with various pleas for Sesto's life, culminating in Vitellia's confession. An increase in dramatic intensity follows, demanding a *recitativo obbligato* setting (no. 25—"Ma che giorno mai è questo?"), in which Tito fights with himself for the cause of his higher beliefs. Dotted rhythms, unstable harmony, and the opposition of voice and strings portray Tito's internal struggle as he wonders whether betrayal or mercy will win the day (mm. 21–23 and following). The tutti that follows serves both to end the opera and to celebrate the final victory of the hero, whose voice, the only one missing from the Act 1 finale, now rises independently above the multitude, begging the gods to end his life on the day when the good of Rome is not his greatest care. Indeed, "Tito ha l'impero / E del mondo e di sé," and the qualities of "devotion" and "generosity," fundamental to the attainment of Descartes' ideal of virtue, are here honored in the exalted musical setting.

The progress of Sesto's and Vitellia's careers and their resultant repentance, despair, and regret is as effectively represented in their arias as is Tito's constancy in his.

---

[50] *Passions*, III, 211; AT, 11:487; HR, 1:426.

The opening duet (no. 1, "Come ti piace imponi") establishes both Sesto's weakness and Vitellia's force of character. The text consists of four strophes—one for Sesto, one for Vitellia, one in which the two speak alternately, and one for both together. Mozart creates a two-tempo structure to set this: Sesto and Vitellia each sing a strophe alone at a moderate tempo; the third strophe is set as a transitional passage, and the final one, for both together, is sung twice at an allegro tempo—once in a homorhythmic setting and then in imitation. Here again, Mozart's manipulation of the musical details serves clearly to depict the characters of the two participants.

As Sesto begins, the dynamic level is piano, and the texture has been reduced from the opening winds and strings to sparse string chords. In the last line of his strophe, a semblance of motion is created by eighth notes in the vocal line. Yet the shape and rhythm of this passage, with its two-note slurs softening the strength of the natural pulse, hardly depicts the audacity of one bent on vengeance (Ex. 4a). The goal implied by the word "tutto" here is the assassination of a Roman emperor; the musical setting suggests that we are justified in doubting whether this character is likely to achieve that goal.

Now it is Vitellia's turn. Using the eighth-note pattern as a logical rhythmic transition, Mozart accelerates the rhythm to sixteenth notes in second violins and violas and adds a restless dotted pattern between bass and first violins. Vitellia's agitation and the urgency of her demand for vengeance are immediately apparent both from the rhythmic agitation and from the sweeping descent of her melodic line, which spans a tenth within the first four measures, creating a sense of determination absent in Sesto's strophe (Ex. 4b). Her forcefulness becomes even more manifest as she completes her strophe: the sweeping downward arpeggio of m. 22, which now spans a fourteenth, is followed immediately by an upward leap of a thirteenth, and two bars later, after again covering an octave, the melody returns unshaken to the note from which its wide-ranging excursions began (Ex. 4c). Vitellia's drive, unrest, and fixed determination are as sharply portrayed as was Sesto's irresolution.

Mozart also uses the tonality and its movement in the service of character delineation. Sesto's opening strophe is completely bound to F major. Vitellia's, which begins in this key, modulates immediately to the dominant, in which contrasting key her strophe remains. Sesto's lines in the third strophe

Example 4. Mozart, *La clemenza di Tito*, no. 1 (Act 1, sc. 1).
    a. mm. 10–13.

tut- to fa- rò per te,   tut- to,_   tut- to fa- rò_ per_ te.

Example 4, continued
b. mm. 13–17.

c. mm. 22–25.

d. mm. 29–34.

are uttered in Vitellia's key ; so much is he now under her sway that although he leads back to the very edge of F major, the modulatory cadence is completed not by Sesto but by the orchestra (Ex. 4d).

Sesto and Vitellia finally sing together in the fourth strophe, which Mozart sets twice in an allegro tempo to conclude the number. The first time the strophe is sung, Sesto moves in tandem with Vitellia, always a third or sixth below her. The increased tempo, the ornamented melody in the strings, the syncopated rhythm, and the constant eighth-note activity in the last two lines all serve to drive the rhythm forward. When the strophe is repeated, Vitellia begins and Sesto follows her lead in strict imitation a measure later. Only at the end of the strophe, as the lines draw together for a cadence, does Sesto have a flourish of his own (mm. 64–65)—but Vitellia, unable to let him have the last word, soars well above her companion's line when she takes up the flourish herself (mm. 67–68). Musically, the two "miscreants" are clearly set apart—both from Tito and from each other; Sesto is completely under Vitellia's domination.

The key moments in Sesto's decline and fall are marked by his two arias, nos. 9 and 19. In no. 9, Sesto is roused into action against Tito. In no. 19, his part in the plot having been revealed, Sesto gives voice to his despair and shame. Each of Sesto's arias is juxtaposed to one of Tito's—no. 9 to Tito's no. 8, and no. 19 to Tito's no. 20. Sesto's weakness and meanness of character are contrasted to Tito's strength and magnanimity: by means of both text and music, the emotional turbulence and moral weakness of Sesto are made to stand out in dramatic contrast to the determination and probity of the Emperor.

Sesto's "Parto, parto" (no. 9) reveals Vitellia's success in goading him to assassinate Tito. It is a three-tempo aria. In most of the initial adagio, as in the opera's opening duet between Sesto and Vitellia, soft dynamics, feminine cadences, sparse texture, and lack of rhythmic drive depict Sesto's weakness of character (Ex. 5a). The last three vocal phrases (mm. 37–43), however, end in masculine cadences, as Sesto's words describe not what he is, but what he would be in order to gain Vitellia's admiration (Ex. 5b); this gesture has been anticipated in mm. 19–21. Both of the remaining sections of the aria open with the words "Guardami, e tutto oblio, / E a vendicarti io volo" (Look at me, and I forget all, / and fly to avenge you). As Sesto becomes determined to act, the tempos of these sections quicken, dotted rhythm and syllabic text setting become predominant, and leaps to notes on strong beats, of longer duration, or of higher pitch increase (Ex. 5c and 5d). The aria reaches its climax with the lines "Ah qual poter, o Dei! / Donaste alla beltà" (Ah, what power, o gods, / have you given to beauty). The fioritura on the word "beltà" provides ample evidence of beauty's power to instigate action; there is no doubt at the end of the aria: the assassination will be attempted.

This aria also derives force from an increase in orchestral activity; the chief contributor is the solo clarinet, which acts throughout as a lyrical partner to

Example 5. Mozart, *La clemenza di Tito*, no. 9 (Act 1, sc. 9).
    a. mm. 4–13.

Example 5, continued
    b. mm. 37–43.

    c. mm. 50–56.

    d. mm. 99–104.

the voice. The solo instrument enters the adagio section some measures after the singer and answers the vocal phrases with melodic arabesques. At the first tempo change, it precedes the voice, which enters on the last note of the solo instrument's rapid, deeply descending flourish. By the allegro assai, the clarinet anticipates the triplets of the vocal fioritura, and in mm. 117–18 it accommodates them in its triplet motion. The voice, having taken a tentative lead at the beginning of the aria, becomes part of the action established and continued by the solo instrument. In this sense, the concertato instrument has become symbolic of the intangible force that drives Sesto into action.

Sesto's final aria (no. 19) shows him in a state of despair: racked with shame, Sesto is all but incapable of any action. The aria, a two-tempo rondò, has an opening adagio in ABA form and an allegro in quasi-rondo form. The refrain of the rondo (Ex. 6a) has no sense of forward movement; its widest contour does no more than outline the tonic triad in even eighth notes, and the harmony moves, one chord per measure, V–I–I–V. The refrain is thus as fixed as Sesto's mental state; its constant recurrence conveys Sesto's inability to escape the shame and remorse he feels. His emotional outbursts become the property of the episodes. The text of the first and third episodes, "Disperato vado a morte" (mm. 38 and 104), describes Sesto's despair, and this passion motivates a sudden increase in rhythmic activity (ascending sixteenth notes in the strings) and in dynamic level, and, in the first episode, a modulation to the lowered mediant. The third episode, which retains the tonic key, is followed by a coda in which a sighing motive and syncopated accompaniment reflect Sesto's despair and inner turmoil (Ex. 6b). The text of the rondo's second episode communicates Sesto's remorse and self-pity, and the music corresponds (m. 72), with a soft dynamic level, modulation to the lowered submediant, and broken descending lines. The aria leaves us with a sense of the suffering and impotence to which Sesto's weakness has brought him.

Example 6. Mozart, *La clemenza di Tito*, no. 19 (Act 2, sc. 10).
    a. mm. 53–57.

    b. mm. 133–36.

Like so many villains, Vitellia is in many ways the most interesting character on stage, and the music that depicts her is the most complex. Her "big scene" occurs at her moment of reckoning, Act 2, sc. 15. This *scena* consists of the *recitativo obbligato* "Ecco il punto, o Vitellia" (no. 22) and the two-tempo rondò "Non più di fiori" (no. 23). During the course of this scene Vitellia struggles with her conflicting desires: to save her reputation by keeping her role in the conspiracy secret, or to attempt to save Sesto and acknowledge his love for her by confessing her guilt. By the end of the recitative, Vitellia is resigned to the loss of empire and marriage that confession will bring.

In the ensuing rondò, Mozart uses the two-tempo form to convey in musical terms the progressive unsettling of Vitellia's noble resignation and her struggle to regain control over the anguish expressed at the beginning of the allegro section. The conflicting emotional states merge in a single sentiment of nervous agitation, which Vitellia finally masters with her familiar strength of character and determination.

The theme of the opening larghetto (which, like the opening adagio section of Sesto's rondò, no. 19, is in a simple ABA form) conveys the state of resignation that Vitellia has reached by the end of the preceding recitative: she will confess to Tito (Ex. 7a). The flowing, almost pastoral melody is given first to the solo basset horn and then to the voice; both times, it is supported by second violins and violas in parallel thirds and doubled by first violins an octave higher. Increasing rhythmic activity (sixteenth-note triplets) and the change to wind accompaniment signal the onset of Vitellia's unrest (m. 29).

In the allegro section (like the fast section of no. 19, a quasi-rondo form), we see the further collapse of Vitellia's resignation run parallel with her attempt to control more unruly anguished emotions. The section opens with a passage of extreme emotional disquietude: the tempo increases, the meter shifts from 3/8 to common time, and the basset horn leads a harmonic progression from F major through F minor to A-flat major, as Vitellia describes her fear for her reputation:

> Infelice! qual orrore!
> Ah di me che si dirà?[51]

The A-flat tonic chord is stressed by the dynamic marking *subito forte* and by a syncopated, descending arpeggio in the violins at the climactic word "orrore." The allegro thus begins with a sudden and intense outburst, which, in its leap out of the established key, takes with it Vitellia's emotional control.

The recurring theme of the rondo is introduced by the basset horn (mm. 56–60) and is then taken up by Vitellia in mm. 60–64 (Ex. 7b). The key has returned to F major, the theme gently undulates in stepwise movement over the basic harmonic foundation of I–V–V–I, and the voice is given simple string support with first violins doubling at the octave. In the context, this is the music of resolution—of an arrival point. Yet the resolution is disturbed by the half-step chromatic motion that occurs in the second and fourth measures of the theme and by the way the theme closes on the mediant rather than the tonic. The text soon reveals Mozart's subtlety in bringing about the state of troubled self-pity whence Vitellia can derive her only solace: "Whoever could see my suffering would have pity on me."

Vitellia's thoughts now stray back to the beginning of the larghetto, but the rhythm of the opening melody has been disrupted by the shift to common time. The distorted larghetto theme is followed by another marked contrast: in low register, Vitellia repeats the ominous statement, "Veggo la morte ver me avanzar" (I see death approaching me); the episode ends on a C major

---

[51] "How wretched! What dread! Ah! What will be said of me?" Mozart, Act 2, sc. 15, p. 269, based on Metastasio, Act 2, sc. 16, 1:733.

Example 7. Mozart, *La clemenza di Tito*, no. 23 (Act 2, sc. 15).
  a. mm. 9–16.

  b. mm. 60–64.

chord approached by lowered submediant and augmented-sixth harmony in
the preceding two measures (mm. 103–5). Both the harmony and Vitellia's
emotions are completely discordant.

The solo basset horn again points the way back to the rondo theme, but in
the "wrong" key—the lowered mediant anticipated at the outset of the allegro
section; thus, like the main theme of the larghetto, this theme has been
dislodged from its proper place, just as Vitellia's resignation has been disturbed by her conflicting emotions.

Only a brief episode (mm. 121–26) separates this appearance of the theme
from its return in the tonic key and the concluding coda. In these six measures,
thoughts of wretchedness and dread return. Yet the words "Infelice! qual
orrore!" cause no tonal shift, and the augmented-sixth harmony that had
previously marked the ends of the episodes is replaced by a less dissonant
dominant seventh, which leads back to the recurring theme, now restored to F
major. Vitellia's "troubled self-pity," thus prepared and reasserted, is followed by a return to the opening larghetto text. So calmly enunciated at the
beginning of the aria, these words are now heard in short broken utterances, in
the rhythm

to an accompaniment of sparse, staccato chords in the strings. A state of
disquietude continues as the remainder of the larghetto text is set as a single
rising phrase over string tremolos and sforzando accents. Vitellia's noble
resignation has so disintegrated since the beginning of the aria that it now
combines with her self-pity to produce this single expression of unrest. Now,
at m. 142, where the text reaches its climax and the word "infelice" might have
been expected, Vitellia masters herself and regains her self-control: four bars

of woodwinds in unison softly usher in the coda and its theme. From here the text never deviates from the introspective lines associated with the recurring theme, and the tonality remains firmly in F major as Vitellia's passionate energy is progressively channeled toward a determined acceptance of her pitiable state. As she reaches the last measures of the aria, there is no doubt that here is the old Vitellia in a new frame of mind.

To what extent did Mozart understand the Cartesian philosophy which underlay the libretto he was setting? Was his music a response to questions that he had consciously considered in philosophical terms, or was he simply responding in a general way to philosophical commonplaces some of which Cartesian thought shares with other philosophical systems? Did the Cartesian content strike familiar chords with Masonic ideals, or was Mozart merely performing his function as a composer responding to the possibilities afforded by a libretto? It is, of course, impossible to answer these questions. Metastasio's moral instruction, like that of many before and after him, was aimed both at the mind and at the heart; it taught both by making favorable impressions upon the mind and by moving the emotions in favor of the moral issue.[52] Descartes' writings—embodying a philosophy in which moral reason rules supreme and the handling of the passions is of the essence—offered a perfect complement to the ethical and aesthetic aims of Metastasio and his fellow Arcadians. Mozart's first extant arias are childhood studies in translating into music the passions revealed in Metastasian texts.[53] They were followed by his efforts to discover moral process as laid out by Metastasio, in settings of the oratorio *La Betulia liberata* (1771), the serenata created from *Il rè pastore* (1775), and above all, the *azione teatrale Il sogno di Scipione* (1772), in which the question of moral choice forms the single action throughout.

Certainly, the use of a Metastasian libretto, even in 1791, implies a conscious concern with moral philosophy. The traditional purpose of a "coronation opera"—to consider by means of examples the qualities that make for good and bad rulers—may also be adduced as evidence that Mozart could not have been indifferent to the moral implications of his text. It is, then, difficult to argue that Mozart and Mazzolà, both of them aware of the importance of

[52] "I piaceri che non giungono a far impressioni su la mente et sul cuore sono di corta durata" (pleasures which do not succeed in making impressions on the mind and on the heart are of short duration)— Metastasio's letter to François-Jean *marquis* de Chastellux, 15 July 1765; *Lettere in Opere*, no. 1433, 4:399.

[53] A discussion and listing of all Mozart's compositions based on Metastasian texts is provided in Rudolph Angermüller, "Mozart and Metastasio," *Mitteilungen der Internationalen Stiftung Mozarteum*, 26 (February 1978): 12–36.

moral philosophy to their endeavor, would have been altogether ignorant of the philosophy with which they were dealing. Awareness, however, does not necessarily imply full understanding of the philosophical system being employed—or the desire to present that system in any but very simple terms.

There should be no question, however, that Mozart must have found in the Metastasio-Mazzolà libretto moral tenets to which he could respond positively—even if he did not necessarily understand the full Cartesian implications. Many of the premises of Descartes' thought are similar to the Masonic ideals which played so important a part in *Die Zauberflöte*, composed in the same year. In a sense, Tito may be viewed as a Sarastro figure. He is, however, more human than the High Priest, for he is permitted to fall into error and to show a capacity for the baser human passions against which he must do battle in order to gain personal victory. Like Sarastro, Tito has his strength of soul from the outset. The desire for virtue and devotion even unto death demanded in Sarastro's kingdom is among Tito's qualities. Reason, wisdom, and truth are as vital to the emperor as to the priest. Tito and Sarastro share the same attitude towards both vengeance and pardon, and Tito could well speak of an empire just as Sarastro speaks of a kingdom in which "Kann kein Verräter lauern, / Weil man dem Feind vergibt" ("No traitor can lurk, because men forgive their enemies").

Parody and Melodic Style
in Bellini's *I Capuleti e i Montecchi*

Charles S. Brauner

Observers have long been reluctant to regard the bel canto opera of Bellini and his Italian contemporaries seriously as drama.[1] The formal conventions that governed the dramatic structure of bel canto operas produced scenes that often reveal familiar patterns; larger structural units are also often annoyingly predictable and leave the impression that the plot has been shaped by the dictates of convention rather than by the dramatic requirements of the *fable*. Typically, the plot of a bel canto opera unfolds in bursts of activity punctuated by the long lyrical episodes in which the musical interest principally lies. Bel canto musical style emphasizes melody, to which it subordinates all other aspects of music. The characteristic bel canto melody is long, formal, and symmetrical, with accompaniment that tends to be simple and repetitive in rhythm, predictable in harmony, and thin in texture.

Bel canto style lacks the rhythmic flexibility of Mozart, the textural richness of Wagner or the late Verdi. Consequently, the musical portrayal of characters' emotions seems relatively simple, with little sense of psychological complexity. The conventionality of dramatic structure and the limitations of the musical style combine to give bel canto operas a stiffness and artificiality of dramatic rhythm that listeners accustomed to the greater flexibility of other operatic traditions often find difficult to accept.

These factors notwithstanding, there were composers working in the bel canto tradition who were concerned with the dramatic aspects of the operas they wrote. Among them was Vincenzo Bellini. Although he had some tolerance for singers' temperaments—as, indeed, did all Italian composers who wished to be successful—Bellini insisted on their performing in character, and he praised their dramatic abilities to encourage them to do so. He insisted on working with Felice Romani, in his opinion the best librettist available. Although he wrote within the formal and stylistic conventions of his day, he endeavored to make those conventions work dramatically.

---

[1] See, for example, Joseph Kerman, *Opera as Drama* (New York, 1959), pp. 137, 144–45. For a recent serious consideration of an opera of this period, see Philip Gossett, *Anna Bolena and the Artistic Maturity of Gaetano Donizetti* (Oxford, 1985).

Since all other features of drama in bel canto opera were subordinated to the requirement of providing a vehicle for the performance of beautiful melodies, an important task for Bellini was the creation of a melodic style that would carry emotional conviction. A curious set of circumstances enables us to gain some insight into how he sought to solve this problem at a critical point in his career.

When Bellini began composing, the dominant figure of the Italian stage was Rossini, and it is not surprising to see the influence of Rossini in Bellini's earliest operas—in the brilliant, highly florid melodic style in particular. In these same early works, however, we also find Bellini trying out a much simpler, declamatory style of melody.[2] The work in which this declamatory style is used most is his fourth opera, *La straniera* (Milan, 1829). *La straniera* was a great success at its premiere at La Scala. The attraction seems to have been the novel melodic style, something different from what one critic called the "genere brilliantissimo di Rossini."[3] But not everyone shared the general enthusiasm for the work; one critic, who dismissed Bellini's new melodic style by observing that "we hardly know whether to call it sung declamation or declaimed song,"[4] gets to the heart of the issue:

> The fact remains that what pleases in the opera of Bellini, and what should please, as it likewise pleases us, consists of arias, trios, quartets, all the pieces in which there is true shaped and expressive song [*canto figurato e sensibile*], etc., and all these pieces are of the same build as always, they are music, beautiful music, as it is always made, music that is well understood, that agrees with or resounds in the soul, that stays in the mind, etc.[5]

The "declamazione cantata o canto declamato" did not, for this critic, resound in the soul, stay in the mind.

Perhaps Bellini himself was not entirely satisfied with the results of the experiment in *La straniera*, despite its popular success. His next opera, *Zaira*

---

[2] For a discussion of Bellini's declamatory style, see Friedrich Lippmann, "Vincenzo Bellini und die italienische Opera Seria seiner Zeit," *Analecta musicologica* 6 (1969): 238 ff.

[3] Anonymous review in *I teatri*, Milan, 16 February 1829, reprinted in Vincenzo Bellini, *Epistolario*, ed. Luisa Cambi (n.p., 1943), p. 191. The consistency of Rossini's style is sometimes exaggerated. While much of his music is quite florid, he occasionally wrote in a simpler, less brilliant style. It was the brilliant style, however, that Bellini's contemporaries had in mind when they commented on Bellini's independence from Rossini.

[4] "... non ben sappiamo se debba dirsi declamazione cantata, o canto declamato." Anonymous review in *L'eco*, Milan, 16 February 1829, reprinted in Bellini, *Epistolario*, p. 196.

[5] "Il fatto sta che quello che nell'Opera del Bellini piace, e deve piacere, come piace a noi pure, consiste in arie, in terzetti, e quartetti, in tutti i pezzi dove vi è vero canto figurato, e sensibile, ecc. e tutti questi pezzi sono della fattura sempre usata, sono musica, bella musica, come si è sempre fatta, che ben s'intende, che risponde, o risuona nell'anima, che si tiene a mente, ecc." *L'eco*, 23 February 1829, reprinted in Bellini, *Epistolario*, p. 202.

(Parma, 1829), returned to a more balanced mixture of the severe and the brilliant styles. However, *Zaira* was Bellini's most complete failure, and this failure must have worried him, even though it had as much to do with external circumstances—Bellini's undiplomatic handling of a local Parmese poet and his prediction of success, among others—as with the quality of the opera itself.[6]

At this crucial moment in his career, Bellini was unexpectedly called to produce on short notice an opera for La Fenice. This commission came during the carnival season of 1829–30, when the composer was in Venice supervising a revival of his third opera, *Il pirata*. The management of the Teatro la Fenice asked him to be available in case Giovanni Pacini should prove unable to provide an opera for the season—the likely result of Pacini's overcommitments. When Pacini did in fact default, Bellini had scarcely two months to compose and rehearse a new opera.[7]

In part responding to the need for haste, both Bellini and Romani turned to material which each had written and used before. Romani recycled his *Giulietta e Romeo*, a libretto written originally for Nicola Vaccai in 1825. Bellini plundered the ample supply of melodies with which the failure of *Zaira* had left him, and which, unless reused in another opera, were unlikely to be heard again.[8] He also lifted a melody from his first opera, *Adelson e Salvini*, and even took over, with modifications, important structural elements from Vaccai's earlier setting of Romani's libretto. The result was *I Capuleti e i Montecchi*, begun in January 1830 and first performed on March 11. By comparing the pre-existent material and Bellini's use of it in *I Capuleti* we can derive insight into the development of Bellini's style and can infer something about the dramatic effectiveness for which Bellini was aiming.

The table below lists the parodies from *Zaira* and *Adelson* interspersed through *I Capuleti*.

[6]On the circumstances surrounding the failure of *Zaira*, see Herbert Weinstock, *Vincenzo Bellini: His Life and Operas* (New York, 1971), pp. 72–78.

[7]Bellini's letters make it clear that he felt severely pressured in composing *I Capuleti* (see Bellini, *Epistolario*, pp. 235–36). However, he had scarcely more time to compose this opera than he had to compose *Zaira* and *La sonnambula*. It seems likely to me that Bellini's sense of pressure and his decision to reuse many melodies from *Zaira* had more to do with his stylistic crisis, discussed below, than with the amount of time available.

[8]Most of the facts about the parodies—which pieces from *Zaira* were used for which pieces in *I Capuleti*—have long been available; see Lippmann, "Vincenzo Bellini," pp. 380–81, for example. However, the parodies have been studied in detail only in two Ph.D. dissertations: my own ("Vincenzo Bellini and the Aesthetics of Opera Seria in the First Third of the Nineteenth Century," Yale University, 1972, ch. 8), and Charlotte Greenspan's ("The Operas of Vincenzo Bellini," University of California at Berkeley, 1977, ch. IIB).

	Parody in *I Capuleti*	Source (in *Zaira*, except as noted)
1.	"È serbata a questo acciaro" Tebaldo, aria, Act 1, *primo tempo* Poetic form: eight lines of *ottonari*	"Per chi mai, per chi pugnasti?" Act 1, *primo tempo* Poetic form: eight lines of *ottonari*

2.	"Se Romeo t'uccise un figlio"
	Romeo, aria, Act 1,
	  primo tempo
	Poetic form: six lines of *ottonari*
		"O Zaira! in quel momento"
		Nerestano, aria, Act 2,
		  primo tempo[9]
		Poetic form: ten lines of *ottonari*

3.	"La tremenda ultrice spada"
	Romeo, aria, Act 1, *cabaletta*
	Poetic form: eight lines of
	  ottonari
		"Ah! crudeli, chiarmarmi alla vita"
		Zaira, aria, Act 2, *cabaletta*
		Poetic form: eight lines of
		  decasillabi

4.	"Oh! quante volte,
	  oh! quante"
	Giulietta, *romanza*, Act 1
	Poetic form: two strophes of four
	  lines each in *settenari*
		"Dopo l'oscuro nembo"
		  (from *Adelson e Salvini*)
		Nelly, *romanza*, Act 1
		Poetic form: three strophes of four
		  lines each in *settenari* with some
		  lines of *quinari*

5.	"Sì, fuggire! A noi non resta"
	Giulietta-Romeo duet,
	  Act 1, *primo tempo*
	Poetic form: two strophes of six
	  lines each in *ottonari*
		"Oh! qual vibrasti orribile"
		Zaira-Nerestano duet from finale,
		  Act 1, *primo tempo*[10]
		Poetic form: two strophes of eight
		  lines each in *settenari*

6.	"Ah! crudel, d'onor ragioni"
	Giuliette-Romeo duet,
	  Act 1, *secondo tempo*
	Poetic form: two strophes of eight
	  lines each in *ottonari*
		"Segui, deh! segui a piangere"
		Zaira-Nerestano duet from finale,
		  Act 1, *secondo tempo*
		Poetic form: two strophes of eight
		  lines each in *settenari*

7.	"Se ogni speme è a noi rapita"
	Romeo-Giulietta-chorus, finale,
	  Act 1, *cabaletta*
	Poetic form: four lines of *ottonari*
		"Non si pianga si nasconda"
		Zaira-Nerestano-Lusignano trio,
		  Act 1, *cabaletta*
		Poetic form: four lines of *ottonari*

[9]The melody of parody no. 2 was also used in the sixth of Bellini's *Sei ariette* (reprinted in the *15 Composizioni da camera*), "Ma rendi pur contento." According to plate numbers furnished by Lippmann ("Vincenzo Bellini," p. 382), the *ariette* were published by Ricordi between the excerpts from *Zaira* and the complete score of *I Capuleti*; of course, this does not necessarily indicate when they were written.

[10]Greenspan, p. 175, points out that, while most of the melody of "Sì, fuggire!" is taken from "O qual vibrasti," the opening is derived from Zaira's Act 1 aria, *primo tempo*, "Amo ed amata io sono." Greenspan is, I believe, the first to notice this derivation. Lippmann ("Vincenzo Bellini," p. 381) notes that the violin figures here also come from "Amo ed amata."

	Parody in *I Capuleti*	Source (in *Zaira*, except as noted)
8.	"Morte io non temo, il sai" Giulietta, aria, Act 2, *primo tempo* Poetic form: fourteen lines of *settenari* with some lines of *quinari*	"Che non tentai per vincere" Zaira, aria, Act 2, *primo tempo* Poetic form: ten lines of *settenari*
9.	"Ah! non poss'io partire" Giulietta, aria, Act 2, *cabaletta* Poetic form: eight lines of *settenari*	"Sì, mi vedrà la barbara" Nerestano, aria, Act 2, *cabaletta* Poetic form: eight lines of *settenari*
10.	"Pace alla tua bell'anima" Romeo-Tebaldo duet, Act 2, funeral chorus Poetic form: two strophes of four lines each in *settenari*[11]	"Poni il fedel tuo martire" Zaira, aria, Act 2, funeral chorus Poetic form: two strophes of four lines each in *settenari*
11.	"Deh! tu, bell'anima" Romeo, aria, Act 2 Poetic form: ten lines of *quinari*	"Non è, non è tormento" Zaira, aria, Act 1 Poetic form: eight lines of *settenari*

All in all, there are thirteen numbers in which we may identify substantial debts to pre-existent material: ten come from *Zaira*, one from *Adelson e Salvini*, and two from Vaccai's earlier setting of the libretto. The relationships between the parodies and their models are surprisingly diverse. In some cases we are dealing only with melody, while in others we are dealing with structures of entire scenes. In some cases the parodies are virtually identical with the models, while in others there is substantial revision, to the point where, occasionally, only vestiges of the model are still to be found.

In principle, the parodies involving melody only are easiest to deal with, and we shall consider them first. The dramatic factor that we might expect most to influence Bellini in his selection of a melody to parody at a particular moment in *I Capuleti* is the ability of the melody to convey the character's state of mind. We might also expect that the scene from which the model is taken would be to some extent emotionally similar to the one into which the parody is to be inserted. Also important are such factors as poetic form and melodic range.

However, in deciding what melody to borrow for a particular scene in *I Capuleti*, Bellini seems to have cared little about how closely the original dramatic context or poetic form agreed with the new one. Evidently, the factors in his decision were type of piece and vocal range: arias were parodied

---

[11] Both strophes appear in the original libretto, but Bellini cut the first in the autograph score.

for arias, duets for duets, female melodies for female singers. As the table shows, of the eleven parodies only five numbers in *I Capuleti* have the same poetic form as their models (parodies 1, 4, 7, 9, and 10). Four differ in meter (nos. 3, 5, 6, and 11, even if we count nos. 4 [parody] and 8 [source] as essentially in *settenario*),[12] and four in the number of lines of text they set (nos. 2, 5, 8, and 11).[13] In addition, four parodies occur in dramatic contexts that differ substantially from those of their models (nos. 1, 3, 9, and 11). In fact, only three parodies (nos. 4, 7, and 10) agree pretty much with their models in both poetic form and emotional content.

Adapting a borrowed melody to a new poetic form did not seem to present many problems for Bellini. For example, transforming a melody for a *settenario* into one for an *ottonario* might be accomplished merely by the addition of one or two notes of upbeat (see parody no. 6, Example 3a below, for example). However, even metric adjustments that necessitated awkward deformation of the text did not deter Bellini: thus, in parody no. 11 (Romeo's "Deh! tu, bell'anima" from Act 2) the composer was obliged to repeat the opening of each line (in effect expanding *quinario* into *settenario*)[14] and to drop two lines of text (see Example 1).[15]

[12]Although in parody no. 2 the texts in both *Zaira* and *I Capuleti* are in *ottonari*, the text of the arietta that also uses this melody (see note 9) is in *settenari*.

[13]As it appears in the original libretto, the text of parody no. 8 in *I Capuleti*, Giulietta's "Morte io non temo il sai," is in two five-line strophes for Giulietta, after each of which are two lines for Lorenzo. If we ignore Lorenzo's lines, then the number of lines is the same as in the model, Zaira's "Che non tentai per vincere." However, in *Zaira* the ten lines are divided 4 + 6, not 5 + 5.

[14]Greenspan (pp. 152–53) believes—plausibly—that the repetition in the opening line of the model suggested this procedure to Bellini.

[15]Musical examples have been based on the following sources:

I Capuleti: score—autograph score in the Museo belliniano, Catania; libretto—libretto of original production:

> I CAPULETI | E | I MONTECCHI | TRAGEDIA LIRICA | DA RAPPRESENTARSI | NEL GRAN TEATRO | LA FENICE | Il carnovale dell' Anno 1830. | IN VENEZIA | DALLA TIPOGRAFIA CASALI.

Although the libretto is divided into four "parti," the autograph score, followed here, is in the more traditional two acts.

Zaira: score—autograph score: Naples, Conservatorio di San Pietro a Maiella, Rari 4.2.10/11; libretto—libretto of original production:

> ZAIRA | TRAGEDIA LIRICA | DA RAPPRESENTARSI | IN OCCASIONE DELLA GRANDE APERATURA | DEL | NUOVO DUCAL TEATRO | DI PARMA | LA PRIMAVERA | DEL M. DCCC. XXIX. | PARMA | DALLA STAMPERIA CARMIGNANI.

Vaccai, *Giulietta e Romeo*: score—piano-vocal score (Milan and Florence: Ricordi, no date [probably 1820s]; plate numbers 2473–85, 2487–91); libretto—published libretto:

> GIULIETTA E ROMEO | DRAMMA SERIO PER MUSICA | DA RAPPRESENTARSI NELL' IMP. E R. TEATRO | DEGL'INTREPIDI | L'AUTUNNO DEL 1828 | SOTTO LA

Example 1. Parody no. 11.

a. *Zaira*: Zaira, "Non è, non è tormento."

b. *I Capuleti*: Romeo, "Deh! tu, bell'anima."

To adapt a melody to a new dramatic context, Bellini would alter the tempo (as in Ex. 1, where Zaira's joy at her forthcoming marriage becomes Romeo's lamenting Giulietta's supposed death), the mode, or the nature of the accompaniment. However, none of these changes requires altering the melody itself—i.e., the sequence of pitches—and as a corollary, we may conclude that the appropriateness of many bel canto melodies for their dramatic and emotional contexts is determined much more by such considerations as tempo, mode, and the texture of the accompaniment than by the configuration of the melody.

The parodies in *I Capuleti* are not, however, simply mechanical re-renderings of the models. Notwithstanding the pressure under which he was working, Bellini made substantial modifications in the melodies he adapted. Where the text permitted, Bellini modified the melodies in *I Capuleti* so that the new versions reveal the flowing, moderately ornamented melodic style that we associate with the mature works to follow, *La sonnambula* and *Norma*. Since, as we have seen, Bellini could have gotten by with minimal

PROTEZIONE DI S. A. E R. | LEOPOLDO II. | GRAN-DUCA DI TOSCANA | ec. ec. ec. | FIRENZE | Nella Stamperia Fantosini.

Reductions of the accompaniments are my own, except for those of Vaccai's opera, for which only a piano-vocal score was available. I have tried to show as much of the orchestral texture as possible, without regard for pianistic considerations. Some octave doublings have been omitted.

changes in the melodies he was reusing, and since, as his letters attest, he was under severe time pressure, why did he make so many changes? The answer seems to be that the composer was experiencing a stylistic crisis. The consistency with which the adapted melodies were changed suggests that his primary concern was not with flaws in individual melodies but with the basic style itself. Remembering the failure of *Zaira* and dissatisfied with both the ornate style of Rossini and his own austere style that had developed in reaction, Bellini seems to have been searching for a new melodic style; in reworking his melodies, he was seeking to improve them.

A representative example of such stylistic transformations is found in parody no. 2. For Romeo's Act 1 aria "Se Romeo t'uccise un figlio" Bellini changes the meter from 3/4 to 9/8 and therefore uses the lilting triplet more consistently in the new version (see Example 2):

Example 2. Parody no. 2.
   a. *Zaira*: Nerestano, "O Zaira! in quel momento."

   b. *I Capuleti*: Romeo, "Se Romeo t'uccise un figlio."

The parody is also more ornate than the model, but Bellini does not retain the turn figures in m. 3 of the model, which have a rather jerky effect; the change produces a more graceful line. The ambitus is doubled from one octave to two. This expansion was no doubt due in part to the different singers involved: Nerestano is a rather small part, originally sung by one Teresa Cecconi, and most of his (her) melodies are restricted in range. Romeo, on the other hand, is the star of the opera, and the part was sung by the star of the cast, Giuditta Grisi. But the change cannot be completely explained by the singer's ability; *La straniera* had starred the equally renowned soprano Henriette Méric-Lalande, and in that work Bellini had adhered to the sparer style.

Two sections of the Act 1 duet between Romeo and Giulietta are parodies (nos. 5 and 6). In parody no. 6, the slow section of the duet, Romeo's "Ah! crudel, d'onor ragioni," the added upbeats are necessary, as we have already noted, to accommodate the change in poetic meter from *settenario* to *ottonario* (see Example 3). However, they also serve to soften the melody. The upbeats, the use of triplets instead of two eighth notes in mm. 1 and 5, the filling in of the third in m. 3, all contribute to making the version of the melody in *I Capuleti* more graceful, less austere, than its model in *Zaira*. Moving the leap of a tenth from the third beat to the second (m. 6) relieves some of the squareness of the original and helps to propel the line forward. There is nothing especially wrong with Nerestano's melody; indeed, it is rather touching in its simplicity. But the changes give the melody a vitality, especially a rhythmic vitality, that it had lacked. The result of these changes is to make Romeo's plea to Giulietta (and her subsequent reply) seem more heartfelt, more resonant in the soul, if you will, and therefore more convincing dramatically, than Nerestano's to Zaira.

Example 3. Parody no. 6.
    a. *Zaira*: Nerestano, "Segui, deh! segui a piangere."

Example 3, continued
  b. *I Capuleti*: Romeo, "Ah! crudel, d'onor ragioni."

In parody no. 5, "Sì, fuggire! A noi non resta" (see Example 4, p. 134), we can actually see Bellini wrestling with the new style. In most numbers, the autograph of *I Capuleti* suggests that the parody procedure was relatively effortless; there are few erasures or second thoughts. However, parody no. 5 is one of two exceptions to this rule. The erasures evident in the autograph (see Plates 1 and 2) show uncertainty about where to have the voices enter: Bellini originally had the vocal entrances coincide with the second phrase of the instrumental accompaniment, and then changed the entrances to coincide with the third phrase. But more than this, the erasures reveal a complete reworking of the melody. Example 4b gives the final version.

It is customary to begin the closed section of a duet with a brief instrumental introduction that anticipates the vocal melody. Here the introduction uses the first two phrases (four measures) of the vocal melody. The introduction in *I Capuleti* is the same as that in *Zaira*; once Bellini decided to have the voice enter after four measures (instead of two), he apparently decided to use the melody from *Zaira* pretty much intact. The autograph (p. 120, mm. 2–4; see Plate 2) clearly shows that the second phrase was originally very similar to that in *Zaira*, and that Bellini then erased this phrase and substituted his original opening phrase. By the time he had finished revising the melody, only the first phrase (and its repetition in the third) showed a close correspondence between parody and model.

The two melodies also differ greatly in character. The original in *Zaira* was in declamatory style: not only was it mostly syllabic, but it also tended to center around single pitches—G at first, then E-flat, and then a series of monotone phrases in rising sequence. In *I Capuleti*, the new second phrase and the other modifications of the melody (beginning with the addition of an upbeat, necessitated by the meter of the text, to the opening) substitute the new flowing style for the declamatory intensity of the original.

Example 4. Parody no. 5.
  a. *Zaira*: Nerestano, "Oh! qual vibrasti orribile."

  b. *I Capuleti*: Romeo, "Sì, fuggire! A noi non resta."

The changes may in part be attributed to the different dramatic situations in the two operas. Both characters are agitated, but Nerestano's agitation (in *Zaira*) is the result of anger (he has discovered that his sister Zaira is in love with a Moslem who has imprisoned their father), while Romeo is fearful (lest he be prevented from escaping with Giulietta from her father's house). It might well be argued that the melody as modified for Romeo would not have

Plate 1. Bellini, *I Capuleti*, autograph score, p. 119. (Reproduced with the kind permission of the Museo belliniano, Catania.)

Plate 2. Bellini, *I Capuleti,* autograph score, p. 120. (Reproduced with the kind permission of the Museo belliniano, Catania.)

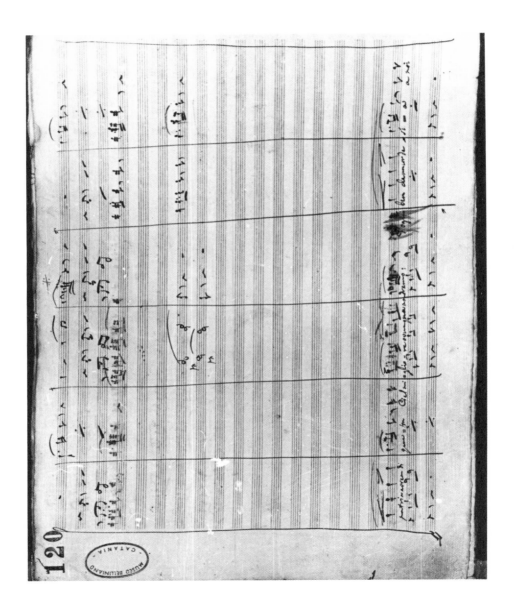

been suitable for Nerestano, and on the other hand that the rising monotone phrases give Nerestano's anger an appropriate tone of menace. The converse, however, is not true: Nerestano's melody would have worked, after a fashion, for Romeo. But Bellini, under the impetus of his stylistic crisis, could not leave the melody as it was.

Let us now examine this duet in detail, to see how the conventions of bel canto opera work and how they are affected by the revisions Bellini made in the melodies. The text of the duet is as follows:[16]

Rom.	Sì, fuggire: a noi non resta
	Altro scampo in danno estremo.
	Miglior patria avrem di questa,
	Ciel migliore ovunque andremo:
	D'ogni ben che un cor desia
	A noi luogo amor terrà.
Giu.	Ah! Romeo! Per me la terra
	E ristretta in queste porte:
	Quì mi annoda, quì mi serra
	Un poter d'amor più forte.
	Solo, ahi! solo all'alma mia
	Venir teco il ciel darà.
Rom.	Che mai sento? E qual potere
	È maggior per te d'amore?
Giu.	Quello ah! quello del dovere,
	Della legge e dell'onore.

a 2

Rom.	Ah! crudel, d'onor ragioni
	Quando a me tu sei rapita?
	Questa legge che mi opponi
	È smentita dal tuo cor.
	Deh! t'arrendi a preghi miei,
	Se ti cal della mia vita:
	Se fedele ancor mi sei,
	Non udir che il nostro amor.
Giu.	Ah! da me che più richiedi,
	S'io t'immolo e core e vita?
	Lascia almeno, almen concedi
	Un sol dritto al genitor.
	Io morrò se mio non sei,
	Se ogni speme è a me rapita:
	Ma tu pure alcun mi dei
	Sacrifizio del tuo cor.

---

[16] Texts are given as they appear in the original libretto of *I Capuleti* (Venice: Casali, 1830), with a few obvious misprints silently corrected. There are minor differences among the sources.

> *(Odesi festiva musica da lontano)*
>
> Rom.   Odi tu? L'altar funesto
>   Già s'infiora, già t'attende.
> Giu.   Fuggi, ah! fuggi.
> Rom.   Teco io resto.
> Giu.   Guai se il padre ti sorprende!
> Rom.   Ei mi sveni, o di mia mano
>   Cada spento innanzi a te.
> Giu.   Ah! Romeo! *(supplichevole)*
> Rom.   Mi preghi invano.
> Giu.   Ah! pietà, di te . . . di me.
>
>   *a 2*
>
> Rom.   Vieni, ah! vieni, e in me riposa:
>   Sei mio bene, sei mia sposa;
>   Questo istante che perdiamo
>   Più per noi non tornerà.
>   In tua mano è la mia sorte,
>   La mia vita, la mia morte . . .
>   Ah! non m'ami come io t'amo . . .
>   Ah! non hai di me pietà.
> Giu.   Cedi, ah! cedi un sol momento
>   Al mio duolo, al mio spavento:
>   Siam perduti, estinti siamo,
>   Se più cieco amor ti fa.
>   Deh! risparmia a questo core
>   Maggior pena, orror maggiore . . .
>   Ah! se vivo è perchè io t'amo . . .
>   Ah! l'amor con me morrà!
>   *(Vinto dalle preghiere di Giulietta, Romeo si parte per l'uscio*
>   *segreto. Ella si allontana tremante.)*[17]

---

[17] *Rom.*: Yes, flee. There is no other safety for us in our extreme danger. We will have a better country than this one, a better sky anywhere we go. For us, love will be every good a heart could desire.

    Giu.: Ah! Romeo! For me the earth is restricted to these doors. Here a power greater than love binds me, closes me in. Heaven will offer only my soul to come with you.

    Rom.: What do I hear? And what power is stronger for you than love?

    Giu.: That of duty, of law, and of honor.

    Rom.: Ah! cruel one, do you reason about honor when you are being stolen from me? This law with which you oppose me is rejected by your heart. Oh! surrender to my prayers, if you care about my life. If you are still faithful to me, listen only to our love.

    Giu.: Ah! what more can you ask of me, when I sacrifice to you both my heart and my life? At least leave, at least concede, one sole right to my father. I will die if you are not mine, if every hope is taken from me. But you also owe me some sacrifice of your heart.

    (Festive music is heard from a distance).

    Rom.: Do you hear? The deadly altar is already adorned with flowers, already awaits you.

    Giu.: Flee, ah! flee.

A duet normally consists of four sections, and here the poet has already divided the scene for the composer: the first section (conventionally fast) consists of the first two six-line strophes and the following pairs of couplets; the second (conventionally slow) begins at "Ah! crudel, d'onor ragioni" and consists of two eight-line strophes; the *tempo di mezzo* comes when the off-stage music is heard ("Odi tu?"); and the *cabaletta* consists of the final two eight-line strophes ("Vieni, ah! vieni"). There is not a great deal of action in this scene. It consists solely of Romeo's urging Giulietta to flee with him and Giulietta's resistance. It cannot be said that Romani was very inspired in applying the standard duet structure to this particular situation. Nevertheless, there is emotional movement: Romeo's pleas become more plaintive at "Ah! crudel"; the festive music creates a heightened sense of urgency for the *cabaletta*.

It is conceivable that the composer could have done something else with this text, and on other occasions Bellini did form his scenes in less stereotyped ways. However, here he followed the conventions to the letter, going beyond the large-scale formal conventions to those that govern the smaller musical units as well. This high degree of conventionality makes this number particularly useful for study, since its very success as a dramatic scene derives from the dramatic potential of the conventions themselves.

In addition to organizing the scene into the four sections described above, Bellini gave the strophic poetry strophic musical settings, despite the characters' very different emotions.[18] The *primo tempo* of a conventional duet often begins with *parlante* or some other "open" melodic writing and turns to closed melody only after a few lines of text. Here the first two lines are treated in open style, the remainder in closed form. The result is that Romeo's initial

---

Rom.: I am staying with you.

Giu.: Woe if my father should surprise you here!

Rom.: Either he will kill me or by my hand he will fall dead before you.

Giu.: Ah! Romeo! *(beseeching)*

Rom.: You implore me in vain.

Giu.: Ah! pity, for you . . . for me.

Rom.: Come, ah! come, and repose in me. You are my dear, you are my wife. This instant we are losing will never return for us. In your hand is my fate, my life, my death . . . Ah! you don't love me as I love you . . . Ah! you have no pity for me.

Giu.: Yield, ah! yield for only one moment to my sorrow, to my fear. We are lost, we are dead, if love makes you still more blind. Oh! spare this heart greater pain, greater horror. Ah! if I live it is because I love you. Ah! my love will die with me.

(Defeated by Giulietta's pleas, Romeo leaves by the secret passage.)

[18]Unlike Bellini, Donizetti frequently gives characters different melodies under such circumstances. See Gossett, *Anna Bolena*, passim.

plea, reiterating his previously announced plan for the lovers to elope ("Sì, fuggire") is given special urgency by the typical *parlante* texture of vocal line over a repeated orchestral figure, as well as by the open style itself, which carries with it a sense of instability, the need for resolution into closed melody. In this melody (shown in Ex. 4b above), Romeo tries to persuade Giulietta that he will replace her father and home ("Miglior patria avrem di questa"). The repetition of the final couplet ("D'ogni ben") is the passage that replaced Nerestano's monotone phrases described above. Romeo has short, rhythmically free phrases (performed *colla parte*) with chromatic lower neighbors and ending with an upward appoggiatura into a surprising diminished seventh (m. 31) before the final cadential passage. This passage has a cajoling effect; Romeo is using all his powers of persuasion. It has become the most distinctive and dramatically convincing place in the melody.

Giulietta's rejection ("Ah! Romeo!"), set to the same music, has the same effect. The parallelism of Romani's text strongly urges a strophic setting; the result of this strophic treatment is that the characters are felt to be sharing the same degree of agitation, and using the same powers of persuasion, even though Romeo's desire is to flee while Giulietta's is to remain loyal to her father. The use of *parlante* at the beginning of each strophe gives both musical and dramatic logic to its resumption for the closing couplets of each section; the dramatic logic is that the dispute ("Che mai sento?") is a continuation of the characters' previously articulated positions and previously stated emotions.

Romeo's pleading proves unable to convince Giulietta, and so the characters reach a stand-off, expressed by the orchestral transition to the next (slow) section of the duet. The text of this section is similar to the first: Romeo continues his attempts at persuasion, and Giulietta continues to resist. The music, however, is very different (see above, Ex.3b). Romeo, no longer agitated or cajoling, instead pours out his heart in a long, slow melody. A few individual places in the text are given special emphasis. Twice the melody leaps from low F to high A-flat ("È smentita dal tuo cor" and "Non udir che il nostro amor"). There are also the strikingly low range on "dal tuo cor," the interpolated "ah" before "non udir," and the fermata on "nostro amor," all ways of underlining the importance of these moments. The differences between parody and model here are subtler, less far-reaching than those in the opening section; nevertheless, the changes—particularly the move of the tenth leap from the third beat to the second, the descent on "dal tuo cor," and the ascent to the leading tone in m. 11—once again give Romeo's emotions greater force than Nerestano's had. Giulietta, of course, has virtually the same melody, hence the same outpouring of emotion, and also almost the same emphases (since there is no low phrase on "genitor" comparable to "dal tuo cor," there is no special emphasis on that word). The intensity of emotion both are feeling at this point is sustained in the following coda, largely in parallel thirds. Once again, a conventional device works to dramatic ends: despite their differences over the proper course of action, the lovers' hearts are clearly united.

The sound of off-stage music, the celebration of Giulietta's forthcoming wedding, recalls them to the dangers of the moment. They argue furiously (*parlante:* "Fuggi, va." "No, teco io resto."), and once more Romeo tries urgent persuasion. This is the *cabaletta* ("Vieni, ah! vieni"), in typical form for a duet—that is, a strophe for Romeo, a second strophe for Giulietta (joined at the end by Romeo), a brief middle section, a concluding strophe combining the first two, and a rapid *stretta*. As all through the duet, Romeo initiates the exchange, but the characters are equal. And here the concluding strophe is begun by Giulietta ("Cedi, ah! cedi"), to indicate the triumph of her position: she will not run away with Romeo.

Although careful analysis of the duet reveals the craftsmanship with which it has been assembled, the principal strength of this duet is not in its details but in the power of its melodies. Indeed, the strophic form tends to militate against our concentration on detail as opposed to the overall effect. The details of the relationship between text and music in these melodies are far less crucial to the dramatic power of the scene than is the beauty of the melodies as a whole and the appropriateness of their expressivity to the dramatic situation. The details become significant only after we accept this overall effect, and at best they are of relatively minor importance. For an artist working in the bel canto tradition a fundamental task was to create a melodic style that would carry emotional conviction, and *I Capuleti* represents a change in what Bellini believed emotionally convincing melody should be.

The degree to which Bellini's melodic style has evolved from the style he inherited from Rossini—the style imitated by most opera composers of the time—can be seen by comparing two scenes from his *I Capuleti* with the scenes in Vaccai's *Giulietta e Romeo* from which they are derived. Romani reused several sections of his earlier libretto for Bellini, notably the two finales (except for the *cabaletta* of Finale 1), and here Bellini turned for inspiration to Vaccai's earlier setting. The structures of these finales are less conventional than those of other numbers; nevertheless, Bellini adhered closely to the structural models Vaccai had provided. The differences, once again, lie in the melodic styles; thus, we have the opportunity to compare the effects of the different styles in identical dramatic situations.

At the beginning of the Act 1 finale, the Montecchi invade the palace of the Capulets. In the following section, Giulietta enters as the tumult dies down. She beseeches heaven to aid Romeo. He then joins her and renews his entreaties to flee.

(Scena 3)

Giu.   Tace il fragor . . . silenzio
            Regna fra queste porte . . .
            Grazie ti rendo, o sorte:
            Libera io sono ancor.
        Ma de' congiunti il sangue
            Per me versato or viene . . .
            Forse trafitto, esangue,
            Giace l'amato bene . . .
            Forse . . . Oh! qual gel! qual foco
            Scorrer mi sento in cor!
        Ah! per Romeo v'invoco,
            Cielo, Destino, Amor.

(Scena 4)

Rom.   Giulietta!
Giu.   Ahimè! . . . chi vedo?
Rom.   Il tuo Romeo: t'acqueta.
Giu.   Ahi lassa! . . . e ardisci?
Rom.   Io riedo
        A farti salva e lieta.
            Seguimi.
Giu.   Ahi! dove? ahi! come?
        Te perderesti e me.
Rom.   Io te lo chiedo in nome
        Della giurata fè.
Coro (di dentro)
        Morte ai Montecchi!
Giu.   Ah! lasciami;
        Gente ver noi s'avvia.
Rom.   Io t'aprirò fra i barbari
        Con questo acciar la via.
        [at which point Tebaldo, Capellio, Lorenzo, and the Capulets
        enter.][19]

---

[19]*Giu.*: The noise has stopped. Silence reigns within these doors. I thank you, o fate. I am still free. But the blood of my relatives is now being spilled for me. Perhaps my beloved lies wounded, drained of blood. Perhaps . . . oh! what a chill, what fire I feel running through my heart. Ah! for Romeo I invoke you, Heaven, Destiny, Love.

Rom.: Giulietta!

Giu.: Ah, me! Whom do I see?

Rom.: Your Romeo. Calm yourself.

Giu.: Ah, alas! . . . And you dare?

Rom.: I return to save you and make you happy. Follow me.

Giu.: Ah! where? Ah! how? You will lose yourself and me.

Rom.: I ask it of you in the name of our sworn faith.

This text could be set in several ways, or so we might assume. Its form seems most obviously to suggest a one-tempo aria for Giulietta, followed by *parlante*. However, Vaccai took a different approach, and Bellini followed his lead. Both composers noticed the presence in Romani's text of two prayers or invocations: Giulietta's "Ah, per Romeo v'invoco, / Cielo, Destino, Amor," and Romeo's "Io te lo chiedo in nome / Della giurata fè" (Vaccai gives the latter to both Romeo and Giulietta). Both composers elected to build their scenes around these prayers, suppressing the lyric potential in the surrounding text. Eschewing a full-scale aria for Giulietta, they allowed the lyricism to blossom forth only at these moments. The opening section of each composer's finale is shown in Example 5.

Example 5
    a. Vaccai, *Giulietta e Romeo*, from Act 1 finale.

Chorus (within): Death to the Montecchi!

Giu.: Ah! leave me. People are coming this way.

Rom.: I will open the way through the savages with my sword.

Example 5, continued
  b. Bellini, *I Capuleti*, from Act 1 finale.

In comparing the two settings, we find both composers state the text of "Ah
per Romeo" twice, intensifying the emotional power by taking the melody
higher and adding ornaments the second time the words are sung. Vaccai,
however, dissipates the emotional force in a shower of embellishments, while
Bellini proceeds more simply, giving the line a single expressive center—the
high A-flat and the syncopation that follows (mm. 14–15). Bellini also makes
much more of "Io te lo chiedo . . . ": instead of placing it within a continuous
dialogue, he separates the request from the preceding material by a pause and
broadens the tempo, so that it becomes the undisputed emotional climax of the
scene. The basic design of the scene, however, is Vaccai's.

   The duet in the second act finale, in which the dying Romeo says farewell to
Giulietta, is probably the most highly praised number in Bellini's opera. It is
similar in many respects to Vaccai's earlier setting of the same scene. Again
the text might have been set in several ways:

Giu.   Ah! crudel! che mai facesti?
Rom.   Morte io volli a te vicino.
Giu.   Deh! che scampo alcun t'appresti! . . .
Rom.   Ferma, è vano . . .
Giu.   Oh rio destino!
Rom.   Cruda morte io chiudo in seno . . .
Giu.   Ch'io con te l'incontro almeno . . .
              Dammi un ferro . . .

Rom.   Ah! no . . . giammai.
Giu.   Un veleno . . .
Rom.   Il consumai.
              Vivi . . . vivi . . . e vien talora
              Sul mio sasso a lagrimar.
Giu.   Ciel crudele! ah! pria ch'ei mora,
              I miei dì tu dei troncar.
Rom.   Giulietta! . . . al seno stringimi:
              Io ti discerno appena
Giu.   Ed io ritorno a vivere
              Quando tu dei morir!!
Rom.   Cessa . . . il vederti in pena
              Accresce il mio martir.

                    a 2
              Più non ti veggo . . . ah! parlami . . .
              Un solo accento ancor . . .
              Rammenta il nostro amor . . .
              Io manco . . . addio! . . .
Giu.   Oh! sfortunato! attendimi . . .
              Non mi lasciare ancor . . .
              Posati sul mio cor . . .
              Ei muore . . . oh! . . . Dio![20]

The sense of the words, however, suggests that the final strophic section be slow and that, after the intense opening dialogue, there be some melodic expansion at the pair of couplets beginning "Vivi, vivi, e vien talora," after which the poetic meter changes. Both composers follow this plan; in both

---

[20]*Giu.*: Ah! cruel one! What have you done?

Rom.: I wanted death near you.

Giu.: Oh! if only you prepared some escape! . . .

Rom.: Stop, it is useless . . .

Giu.: Oh cruel destiny!

Rom.: I enclose cruel death in my breast . . .

Giu.: Would that at least I could meet it with you. Give me a sword . . .

Rom.: Ah! no . . . never.

Giu.: Poison.

Rom.: I consumed it all. Live, live and come sometimes to weep on my tombstone.

Giu.: Cruel heaven! ah! before he dies you must cut short my days.

Rom.: Giulietta! . . . Press me to your breast. I can hardly see you.

Giu.: And I return to life when you must die!!

Rom.: Cease . . . To see you in pain increases my suffering. I can no longer see you. Ah! speak to me . . . yet one more word . . . Remember our love . . . I am failing . . . Farewell! . . .

Giu.: Oh! unfortunate one! wait for me . . . Do not leave me again . . . Rest on my heart . . . He dies . . . oh! . . . God!

settings, the final strophes are sung in alternation, and there are some motivic resemblances, as well (see Example 6). Each composer introduces Romeo's final death agony with a striking harmonic event (Vaccai, m. 15: a deceptive cadence; Bellini, m. 13: a change to tonic minor). The lovers repeat their final cries to each other at the same pitch level, and Romeo expires in the middle of Giulietta's name, having begun it with an upward leap: "Giuliet-." (This last feature, common to both composers, is not suggested by the libretto.)

However, Bellini makes some significant changes in emphasis. Both composers slow the tempo at "Vivi, vivi . . . ," but Bellini's lyrical episode is much shorter (nine measures compared to Vaccai's 28), and his ensuing dialogue is not separated from the lyric section. Bellini has the vocal phrases leading to the denouement rise in sequence (mm. 5–10), creating a greater sense of climax than in Vaccai's setting. Bellini's duet culminates in a lyric outburst a 2 (mm. 10–13), a moment of intense beauty before the final cries, which gives added poignancy to the lovers' impending separation. Yet even with this addition, Bellini's version is considerably shorter and more concentrated.

If these resemblances are more than coincidences, then we must regard these scenes in Bellini's opera as, in a sense, parodies of those in Vaccai's. These parodies sometimes involve motivic material but more often formal organization. In the first finale, Bellini's expansiveness and the separation of "Io te lo chiedo" from the preceding material distinguishes his version from Vaccai's; in the second finale, the opposite techniques, Bellini's conciseness and continuity, set his version apart from its predecessor. It could be argued that the former is dramatically more appropriate for the former scene and the latter for the latter, but it may not matter very much. Although we have observed differences—some of them significant—in detail between Vaccai's settings and Bellini's, the success of Bellini's scenes really depends more upon their melodies than upon the details of how they are joined to the surrounding material.

What makes Bellini's melodies distinctive is that ultimately unanalyzable quality, their beauty. The declamatory style of La straniera, effective in special situations, lacks the intense lyricism of the style Bellini began developing in I Capuleti. His task in the parodies was to make the melodies more beautiful by expanding their ranges, smoothing their lines, and adding a modest amount of ornamentation while avoiding the Rossinian encrustation of ornament that gives the impression of ornament for the sake of virtuosic display. The changes in Bellini's melodic style, revealed on the one hand by comparing the new versions of his own melodies taken over from Zaira with their predecessors and on the other by comparing Bellini's treatment of the finales with Vaccai's previous setting, led to a considerable increase in expressive power.

Example 6

a. Vaccai, *Giulietta e Romeo*, from Act 3 finale.

Example 6a, continued

Example 6, continued
   b. Bellini, *I Capuleti*, from Act 2 finale.

Example 6b, continued

A few final points: Bellini's ability to create compelling melodies did not begin with *I Capuleti*. One of the most beautiful melodies in the entire score, Giulietta's "Oh! quante volte," (Act 1, *romanza*) is, after all, a parody, changed rather little, of an aria ("Dopo l'oscuro nembo") in Bellini's student opera *Adelson e Salvini* (1825).[21] In other words, despite some improvements over the years, the core of Bellini's melodic style was present from the beginning of his career.

Furthermore, the pervasion of *I Capuleti* with melody goes beyond the arias and duets discussed here. One of the great advantages of Giulietta's "Oh! quante volte" over the corresponding number in *Adelson* is that the scene in which Giulietta's aria occurs begins with a haunting melody for solo horn that sets the melancholy tone of Giulietta's character and situation. The use of beautiful melodies in the orchestral introductions to scenes (there is another for Giulietta's aria in Act 2, "Morte io non temo, il sai") and during the recitatives (rare in *I Capuleti*, but see Romeo's "Sorgi, mio bene . . . " in the final scene; such melodies are among the most compelling moments in *Norma* [1831]) became conventional in bel canto opera.

Finally, not all the changes Bellini made when he revised his melodies for *I Capuleti* are dramatically persuasive, and we must be careful not to oversell the successes here. Romeo's version of the melody given in Example 2 may be an improvement over Nerestano's, but I do not find it particularly convincing. In parody no. 11 (see Ex. 1), Romeo's farewell to Giulietta at the tomb (before she revives), what should have been a deeply moving piece, crucial to the success of the drama, is rather bland. Bellini failed to turn what was originally a happy melody into a convincingly melancholy one, and the repetitions of text necessitated by the different poetic meter become irritating in their obsessive regularity.

But these failures serve to reinforce the conclusion that in bel canto opera melody is the primary dramatic vehicle. The essence of drama, after all, is not so much in the characters' actions as in the ways in which those actions affect their inner emotional lives. It is these inner lives that the arias reveal, and the more powerful and expressive the melodies, the deeper and more whole the characters seem, and, therefore, the more compelling is their drama. The conventionality of form and the stiffness of dramatic rhythm typical of bel canto style are still present in *I Capuleti* and Bellini's mature operas, but they are also the very means through which the composer creates convincing drama.

---

[21] To be more precise, the first strophe is changed rather little. Strophes 2 and 3 in *Adelson* and strophe 2 in *I Capuleti* all present different ornamented versions of the melody. The coda is also changed.

Musical-Dramatic Parallels in the Operas of Hector Berlioz
Jeffrey A. Langford

The operas of Hector Berlioz contain many scenes of particular beauty and dramatic effectiveness. One of the most powerfully evocative of these occurs at the end of Act 4 of *Les Troyens*: the love duet between Dido and Aeneas. The setting is Carthage on a warm, fragrant, summer night, with the calm waters of the Mediterranean Sea lapping gently on the shore. A luminous moon casts a spell over the two lovers as "la nuit étend son voile et la mer endormie murmure en sommeillant les accords les plus doux."[1] In this scene Berlioz celebrates not so much the love of a queen and her hero as the serenity and enchantment of the night that envelops the lovers. The duet begins:

Dido and	Nuit d'ivresse et d'extase infinie!
Aeneas	Blonde Phoebé, grands astres de sa cour,
	Versez sur nous votre lueur bénie;
	Fleurs des cieux, souriez à l'immortel amour!
Dido	Par une telle nuit, le front cient de cytise,
	Votre mère Vénus suivit le bel Anchise
	Aux bosquets de l'Ida.
Aeneas	Par une telle nuit, fou d'amour et de joie,
	Troïlus vint attendre aux pieds des murs de Troie
	La belle Cressida.[2]

This lovely text, laden with vivid imagery, helps to convey the emotional ambience of this special—almost magical—moment in the developing romance of Dido and Aeneas.

What a surprise, then, to discover in Berlioz's next—and last—opera,

---

[1] "Night extends its veil, and the sleeping sea murmurs the sweetest harmonies" (last two lines of text from the septet that precedes this duet). Quotations—both textual and musical—from *Les Troyens* are from the New Berlioz Edition, vol. 2a, b, and c, ed. Hugh Macdonald (Kassel, 1969–70). The present quotation is from Act 4, no. 36 (vol. 2b, pp. 570–73).

[2] *Dido and Aeneas:* Night of rapture and infinite ecstasy! Fair Phoebe, and great stars of her court, pour on us your blessed light. Flowers of heaven, smile on our immortal love.

Dido: On such a night, her brow wreathed in blossoms, your mother, Venus, followed the handsome Anchises to Ida's groves.

Aeneas: On such a night, mad with love and joy, Troilus came to wait, under the walls of Troy, for the lovely Cressida. (Act 4, no. 37; vol. 2b, pp. 575–88.)

Béatrice et Bénédict, the very same "magical moment" transported, so to speak, from Carthage to Sicily. In *Béatrice* (Act 1, no. 8), Hero, accompanied by her confidante Ursula, muses on her forthcoming marriage to Claudio. As in *Les Troyens*, the scene is built around a duet—here for the two women—and, as in the earlier opera, the setting is a moonlit night: "La lune se lève et éclair la scène de ses rayons qui se reflètent dans l'eau."[3] Like its counterpart in *Les Troyens*, this duet is not a love duet *per se*, but rather a duet *about* love (if such a subtle distinction is possible)—specifically, love under a moonlit Mediterranean summer sky. The text here reads in part:

> Nuit paisible et sereine!
> La lune, douce reine,
> Qui plane, en souriant . . .
> Harmonies infinies,
> Que vous avez d'attraits
> Et de charmes secrets
> Pour les âmes attendries![4]

Night, serenity, the warm fragrant Mediterranean atmosphere, and even a reference to sweet "harmonies" are all primary elements in both scenes.

These two moonlit love duets share not only their settings and mood but also various musical elements. Immediately recognizable are certain surface similarities in style. Each duet is written in 6/8 meter with an indicated tempo of eighth note equals 126. In each duet the orchestra, with a continuous and rhythmically unvaried accompaniment, seems metaphorically to assume the role of the sea. In each duet the solo voices move on a different rhythmic plane from the orchestra; they use rhythmic unison and longer note values to create the effect of floating over the accompaniment at a slow and unhurried pace.

Beyond these immediately recognizable connections between the music of the scenes in question lie two less obvious but equally important similarities. Berlioz orchestrates both in nearly identical ways. In each he relies almost exclusively on the color of the full string section playing with mutes. To the violins and violas he relegates the motor rhythm which so aptly symbolizes the gentle undulation of the sea, while to the celli and basses he assigns the

---

[3] "The moon rises illuminating the scene with a light that reflects in the water." These stage directions appear in the full score from the Berlioz *Werke*, ed. Charles Malherbe and Felix Weingartner (Leipzig, 1907; reprinted Kalmus, [1969]). Hugh Macdonald's edition of this work for the New Berlioz Edition, vol. 3 (Kassel, 1980), does not contain these and many other stage directions because they do not appear in Berlioz's autograph manuscript. However, these particular stage directions originated with the German production of *Béatrice et Bénédict* at Weimar in 1863 and probably had Berlioz's approval. See Macdonald's foreword and critical notes in NBE, vol. 3, for details. All citations of *Béatrice et Bénédict* are to this edition.

[4] "O night peaceful and serene! The moon, gentle queen hovering above, smiling . . . Endless harmonies, what attractions and secret charms you have for tender souls." (Act 1, no. 8; vol. 3, pp. 174–78.)

Example 1. *Les Troyens*, Act 4, no. 37, "Nuit d'ivresse et d'extase infinie,"
mm. 1–6.

Example 2. *Béatrice et Bénédict*, Act 1, no. 8, "Nuit paisible et sereine,"
mm. 12–17.

function of percussively punctuating the strong beats of the 6/8 meter. (See Examples 1 and 2, pp. 154 and 155.)

Another—even less obvious—musical connection between these scenes lies in their harmonic structure: the subtle vacillation of key center between tonic major and relative minor. In *Les Troyens* Berlioz begins in G-flat major, but after only nine measures he slips into E-flat minor for a short time. (See Example 3.) In *Béatrice et Bénédict*, by comparison, the shift of mode is more subtle. The measure in which the voices enter contains a C-sharp in the bass followed by a G-sharp. The harmony that accompanies this descending perfect fourth is not, however, the expected tonic-to-dominant progression in C-sharp minor, but rather a progression from i to III^6 in C-sharp minor or, depending on how one hears the passage, from vi to I^6 in E major. (See Example 4.) Regardless of how we analyze these passages, the major-minor fluctuation is an important aspect of the sound of each: it is yet another, albeit a subliminal, element in the composer's remarkably similar conceptions of these two scenes.

Admittedly, dramatic parallels are not always significant. Such parallels can occur in "stock" situations—tavern scenes, love duets, mad scenes, to mention just a few—that reappear in opera after opera throughout the nineteenth century, and that are often treated musically in much the same way by composers of quite different backgrounds and temperaments; the similarities among such stock scenes do not tell us much. However, dramatic parallels such as those in the moonlit night scenes in *Les Troyens* and *Béatrice et Bénédict*, involving repeated constellations of music and dramatic situation, are of a different sort from such stock scenes; recurring in the few operas of a composer of the stature of Berlioz,[5] they call attention to themselves. Nor are we dealing here with the literal melodic borrowings that Hugh Macdonald has shown to occur so often in Berlioz's works.[6] The particular technique of self-borrowing identified by Macdonald involves the use of literal quotations quite different from the recurrent pairing of dramatic situation and music that concerns us here.

What do such musical-dramatic parallels mean? Are they the result of some sub- or semi-conscious process, or are they deliberate applications of the composer's views of the relationship between music and drama?

Notwithstanding the considerable body of writings on music that Berlioz

---

[5]*Benvenuto Cellini* (1838), *Les Troyens* (1858), and *Béatrice et Bénédict* (1862). For the purposes of this study I also include the dramatic legend *La Damnation de Faust* (1846) in this list because of its overtly operatic qualities.

[6]Hugh Macdonald, "Berlioz's Self-Borrowings," *Proceedings of the Royal Musical Association* 92 (1965–66): 27–44.

Example 3. *Les Troyens*, "Nuit d'ivresse"—harmonic analysis.

Example 4. *Béatrice et Bénédict*, "Nuit paisible"—harmonic analysis.

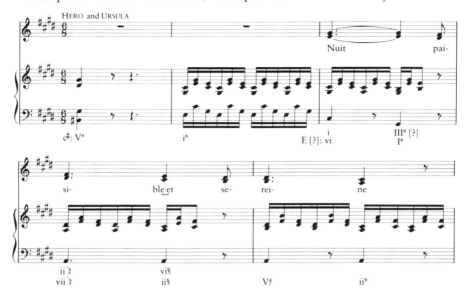

has left, we find relatively little that will enable us to answer these questions. It is clear, however, that Berlioz believed that there are certain emotions that can be conveyed effectively by music and others that cannot. In an article for *La Revue et gazette musicale* (1837) in which he dealt with what he called imitation in music, Berlioz explained that "music will easily express blissful love, jealousy, carefree gaiety, anxious modesty, violent threats, suffering, and fear."[7] In the *Journal des débats* (also 1837), he used his review of Onslow's opera *Guisa, ou les états de Blois* to reiterate this view of the expressive potential of music:

> Love, enthusiasm, melancholy, joy, terror, jealousy, calm of the soul— these are the sentiments and passions that are proper for musical development. Ambition and political intrigues, on the contrary, do not lend themselves to such development.[8]

Thus, we can see that for Berlioz there were certain emotions or moods which he thought appropriate for musical presentation, and to which he might be expected to return in his own compositions.

[7] "La musique exprimera bien l'amour heureux, la jalousie, la gaîté active et insouciante, l'agitation pudique, la force menaçante, la souffrance, et la peur." "De l'imitation musicale," *Revue et gazette musicale de Paris*, Année 4, no. 2 (8 January 1837), p. 16; translated and reprinted as "The Limits of Music" in *Pleasures of Music*, ed. Jacques Barzun (Chicago, 1951), p. 74.

[8] "L'amour, l'enthousiasme, la mélancolie, la joie, la terreur, la jalousie, le calme de l'âme sont des sentiments et des passions propres au développement des forces musicales; l'ambition, les intrigues politiques, au contraire, ne s'y prêtent en aucune façon." Quoted in Katherine Kolb Reeve, "The Poetics of the Orchestra in the Writings of Hector Berlioz" (Ph.D. dissertation, Yale University, 1978), p. 26.

Curiously, Berlioz is almost silent on the matter of plot—i.e., on the sorts of *fables* suitable for opera and on the ways in which suitable *fables* should be presented on stage. What seems to have interested him more is the emotional content of an opera, and from this we may infer that considerations of emotional color were more important to this particular music-dramatist than were the selection and arrangement of the incidents that make up a plot. Indeed, if we examine the structure of the works for which Berlioz himself created the librettos, we find that such works as *Les Troyens* and *Béatrice et Bénédict* are not carefully plotted in accordance with the principles to which Berlioz's contemporaries in the Paris theater gave such attention (i.e., *le livret bien fait*), but are, instead, series of scenes each dominated by a particular mood.

Given the contemporary concern with dramatic structure, Berlioz's preference for successions of emotion-oriented vignettes takes on special significance. If we conclude that his indifference to accepted dramatic structure derived from the view that the success of an opera libretto depended more upon the underlying mood of the individual scene than upon clever or intricate plotting, then we can at least partially explain the recurrence of scenes of similar dramatic and musical content as the result of the composer's returning to situations that he had found dramatically effective and for which he believed he had found effective means of musical expression. Thus we should not be surprised to discover that Berlioz's handful of operas, which are all based on dissimilar subjects, nonetheless share many similar dramatic situations.

Although these recurring scene-types are consistently realized in similar musical fashions, Berlioz never directly confronted the question of the relationship between music and drama in his writings on opera. This fact forces us to make some educated guesses about the significance of these musical-dramatic parallels. To do this, we must turn to the works themselves.

As we have seen in the duets from *Les Troyens* and *Béatrice*, Berlioz's use of the orchestra is important in creating dramatic mood. The exact nature of his technique deserves further elaboration. Perhaps the simplest example of this technique lies in Berlioz's consistent use of specific instruments to convey specific dramatic moods. The atmosphere of terror or horror was one in which Berlioz seems to have been particularly interested. In the nineteenth century scenes of this type were usually described as *fantastique*.[9] They offered the opportunity for some very passionate and colorful musical renderings, and may have sparked Berlioz's interest for just that reason. The responsibility for establishing a musical ambiance appropriate to this dramatic type rested, as far

---

[9]See Berlioz's own description of Weber's *Der Freischütz* as a drama of the "fantastique sombre, violent, diabolique" in *A travers chant* (Paris, 1862; reprint, Paris, 1971), pp. 258–59.

as Berlioz was concerned, on only a few special instruments of the orchestra.
In his *Traité de l'instrumentation* Berlioz mentions one of these specifically:
"If, particularly, the chords be brief, and broken by rests . . . [the trombone]
has the effect of strange monsters giving utterance, in dim shadow, to howls of
ill-suppressed rage."[10] In several dramatically parallel scenes of terror Berlioz
uses the trombones in just this manner. A fine example is the curious scene in
the first act of *Les Troyens* in which Aeneas reports the death of Laocoön:

> . . . gonflés de rage,
> Deux serpents monstrueux s'avancent vers la plage,
> S'élancent sur le prêtre, en leurs terribles nœuds
> L'enlacent, le brûlant de leur haleine ardente,
> Et le couvrant d'une bave sanglante,
> Le dévorent à nos yeux.[11]

At exactly the point where the text reads "swollen with rage" Berlioz interjects
the grotesque sound of three trombones playing a contra A in unison while
literally swelling from piano to fortissimo in just two measures—a most
unmusical but dramatically appropriate gesture.

Similar to Aeneas' narrative is Cellini's description of his own narrow
escape from the authorities after having killed Pompeo in a sword fight: he
explains to Teresa:

> . . . je fuis . . . mais on me suit!
> Les cris de mort de cette populace,
> Cet habit blanc qui la met sur ma trace,
> Tout dans ma course et m'arrête et me glace!
> Une seconde encor, ô désespoir![12]

While this particular narration does not include the supernatural element of
Aeneas' story, it does contain the same kind of hair-raising terror—sufficient
reason for Berlioz to apply to it his "fantastic" orchestration, featuring
trombones playing low pedal tones in ugly crescendos.

Perhaps the most prominent example of this dramatic type appears at the
end of *La Damnation de Faust*. In the diabolical "Ride to the Abyss," Faust,

[10]". . . Où les accords sont bref et entrecoupés de silences, on coirt entendre des monstres étranges
éxhaler dans l'ombre les gémissements d'une rage mal contenue." Berlioz, *Grand traité d'instrumentation
et d'orchestration modernes* (Paris, 1844), p. 222; translated by Mary Cowden Clarke as *A Treatise on
Modern Instrumentation and Orchestration* (London, 1856), p. 171.

[11]". . . Swollen with rage, two monstrous serpents advanced toward the shore, rushed toward the
priest, entwined him in their terrible coils, scorched him with their fiery breath, covered him with a bloody
slaver, and devoured him before our eyes." (Act 1, no. 7; vol. 2a, pp. 125–28.)

[12]"I fled . . . but I was chased. The crowd yelling for my death, this white habit that I wore, all worked
against me. I stopped, I froze! Another moment and—oh, desperation!" Quotations from *Benvenuto
Cellini* are from the Kalmus reprint of the Berlioz *Werke*, vol. 17; the present quotation is from Act 3, no.
12, pp. 358–59.

accompanied by Mephistopheles, charges off on horseback in what he thinks is a mission to rescue Marguerite from prison. In fact he rides only to his own destruction. Along the way he is pursued (or imagines he is) by various monsters, birds of the night, and skeletons. "Un monstre hideux / En hurlant / Nous poursuit,"[13] he yells, and at this very point in the scene we again hear the low pedal tones of the trombones. The fact that Berlioz reserves the trombones for such a limited and specific use in these scenes of the *fantastique* underscores the systematic nature of his orchestrational technique in dramatic music.

Another constellation of music-cum-dramatic situation that consistently received similar orchestration was that involving ghosts, tombs, or the underworld. Common to such scenes was an orchestration featuring a continuous rhythm in low pizzicato strings supporting a slowly moving chordal melody in low brass (often including stopped horns) and low woodwinds. It was with this combination of timbres, rhythms, and textures that Berlioz first established this dramatic situation in his Prix de Rome cantata of 1829, *La Mort de Cléopâtre*. In that libretto (a prescribed text by P. A. Vieillard), the queen of Egypt prays to the spirits of the pharaohs that she may be allowed to rest with them in the tomb of the pyramids:

> Grands Pharaons, nobles Lagides,
> Verrez-vous entrer sans courroux,
> Pour dormir dans vos pyramides,
> Une reine indigne de vous?
> Non! de vos demeures funèbres
> Je profanerais le splendeur.
> Rois, encor au sein des ténèbres,
> Vous me fuiriez avec horreur.[14]

Two years later, the music for this scene, including most of the orchestration, was taken over almost literally as "Chœur d'ombres" for use in Berlioz's monologue *Le Retour à la vie*. There a new text with completely different words was fitted to the old music:

> Froid de la mort, nuit de la tombe,
> Bruit éternel des pas du temps,
> Noir chaos où l'espoir succombe, . . . [15]

---

[13] "A hideous beast shrieks in pursuit of us." *Le Damnation de Faust*, New Berlioz Edition, vol. 8a, ed. Julian Rushton (Kassel, 1979), Part 4, sc. 18, pp. 406–7.

[14] "Great Pharaohs, noble Lagides, will you without wrath watch her enter, to sleep in your pyramids, a queen unworthy of you? No! I would profane the splendor of your funereal home. O Kings, even in the bosom of darkness and gloom, you would fly from me in horror." Quoted from the Kalmus reprint of the Berlioz *Werke*, vol. 14, *Meditation*, pp. 18–29.

[15] "Coldness of death, night of the tomb, eternal sound of the march of time, black chaos where hope expires, . . . " Quoted from the Kalmus reprint of the Berlioz *Werke*, vol. 12, pp. 11–13.

The text of "Chœur d'ombres" evokes the same dramatic mood as the text it replaces in *Cléopâtre*. That Berlioz could use interchangeably with the same music two different texts which shared the same mood suggests how important he must have felt the relationship of mood and music to be.

Berlioz returned to this dramatic situation much later in his career, and here again he used the special orchestration described above. Cassandra's opening recitative in Act 1 of *Les Troyens* features the sound of Berlioz's "ghost music" at the point where she sings, "J'ai vu l'ombre d'Hector parcourir nos remparts / Comme un veilleur de nuit."[16] And a similar orchestration accompanies the opening scene of Act 2, in which the ghost of Hector visits Aeneas to warn him to flee Troy for Italy, there to establish a new empire.

Harmonic formulae also play an important if somewhat more limited role in Berlioz's musical depiction of mood. One particularly effective and simple device is the melodic alternation of the fifth and flatted sixth scale degrees over a tonic pedal point, which Berlioz uses in connection with the concept of wedded bliss. In the septet from Act 4 of *Les Troyens*, it is carried through the entire number until it emerges from its accompanimental obscurity after the vocal ensemble sings its last words, "La mer endormie murmure en sommeillant les accords les plus doux."[17] (See Example 5.) After the septet in *Les Troyens* Dido and Aeneas disappear into the night, embracing as they walk off, presumably to partake of the joys of love. The same harmonic device recurs with only slight variation in *Béatrice et Bénédict* near the end of the opera, where Beatrice sits alone in pensive thought after Hero and Ursula have just told her that she needs a husband. Suddenly she hears in the distance a chorus singing to Hero, "Viens! de l'hyménée victime fortunée! . . . l'heureux époux attend."[18] At these words Berlioz finishes the number with one melodic line oscillating between the fifth and lowered sixth degrees on a tonic triad. (See Example 6.) After this wedding chorus both pairs of lovers are united in blissful wedded happiness. The similarity of sound, mood, and dramatic positioning between these two scenes is immediately recognizable. In each case the chorus of which this harmonic device is a part is casting the spell of marriage over two lovers.

Once we are prepared to accept the premise that Berlioz pairs particular musical motives with passages of particular dramatic import, we may then be able to make inferences about passages of uncertain dramatic significance by

---

[16] "I saw the ghost of Hector traversing our ramparts like a night watchman." (Act 1, no. 2; vol. 2a, p. 37.)

[17] "The sea murmurs in its sleep the sweetest harmonies." (Act 4, no. 36; vol. 2b, pp. 570–73.)

[18] "Come to marriage, happy victim. . . . The blissful bridegroom awaits." (Act 2; vol. 3, pp. 253–54.)

Example 5. *Les Troyens*, Act 4, no. 36, end of septet, mm. 41–44, 53–56.

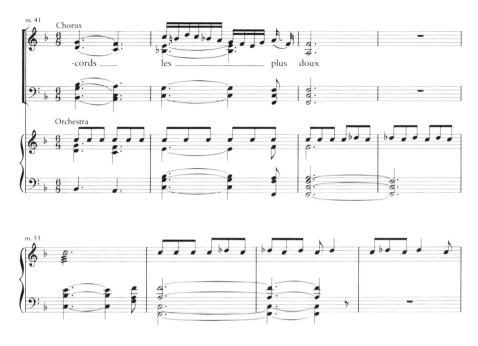

Example 6. *Béatrice et Bénédict*, Act 2, offstage wedding chorus, mm. 41–45.

comparing these passages to others with similar music and more certain dramatic meaning. As an illustration of this approach let us consider three soprano arias: Hero's "Je vais le voir" and Béatrice's "Il m'en souvient" (both from *Béatrice et Bénédict*), and Teresa's "Entre l'amour et le devoir" (from *Benvenuto Cellini*). Regarding the two arias from *Béatrice*, there seems little doubt as to their significance. "Il m'en souvient" is the aria in which Béatrice first accepts the notion that she might actually love the very object of her greatest disdain. She sings:

> Il m'en souvient
> Le jour du départ de l'armée,
> Je ne pus m'expliquer
> L'étrange sentiment de tristesse alarmée
> Qui de mon cœur vint s'emparer.
> Il part, disais-je, il part, je reste.[19]

In the same opera Hero, like Béatrice, has been separated from her love, and like Béatrice, she feels the pangs of longing as she sings:

> Je vais le voir, je vais le voir,
> Son noble front rayonne
> De l'auréole du vainqueur.
> Cher Claudio, que n'ai-je une couronne,
> Je te la donnerais, je t'ai donné mon cœur.[20]

Both these arias are representative of emotions which Berlioz himself identified as appropriately musical—a combination of "blissful love" and "anxious modesty." Each text presents a woman in the act of timidly expressing love for someone she greatly admires.

Berlioz uses similar musical devices to portray this state of mind in both arias. Both arias share details of form, tempo, meter, rhythm, and melody. Specifically, the structure of each aria involves an overall division into two large parts (corresponding to a shift of mood in the texts); the first part of each aria is also subdivided into a simple ABA form. In addition, the tempo and meter of each aria also mirror the overall bipartite form. The opening section of each is in slow triple meter, while the second half of each changes to a contrasting meter and faster tempo.[21] In addition to these structural paral-

---

[19] "I remember the day the army left, I could not explain the strange feeling of anxious sadness that seized my heart. He is leaving, I said, while I remain behind." (Act 2, no. 10; pp. 213–14.)

[20] "I am going to see him, his noble brow shining with the victor's wreath. Dear Claudio, had I a crown I would give it to you as I have given you my heart." (Act 1, no. 3; pp. 76–81.)

[21] Except for the tripartite division of its first half, this two-part form imitates the general pattern of the cavatina-cabaletta so popular in nineteenth-century Italian opera. But throughout Berlioz's operas the use of this form is exceptional; it is limited exclusively to these three arias.

lels, both arias display some remarkable melodic similarities. The opening measures of each aria are marked by a simplicity of melodic construction based on the use of regular two- or four-bar motivic modules (see Example 7). Such tunefulness and regularity of phrase structure are far from normal in Berlioz's operas. In the second halves of these arias we find additional similarities, including the use of an all-pervasive dotted rhythm, melodic anticipations, and syncopations. (See Example 8.)

Example 7
   a. *Béatrice et Bénédict*, Act 1, no. 3, "Je vais le voir," mm. 11–20.

   b. *Béatrice et Bénédict*, Act 2, no. 10, "Il m'en souvient," mm. 54–61.

Example 7b, continued

jour ____ du ____ de- part ____ de l'ar- mé- e

Example 8

a. *Béatrice et Bénédict*, Act 1, no. 3, "Je vais le voir," mm. 84–96.

Il me re- vient fi- dè- le   Plus d'an-

gois- se mor- tel- le   Nos tour- ments, ____ nos -

tour- ments sont fi- nis ____ Nous al- lons ê- tre u- nis

b. *Béatrice et Bénédict*, Act 2, no. 10, "Il m'en souvient," mm. 162–74.

Je ne m'ap- par- tiens plus, ____ je ne suis plus moi-

mê- me   je ne suis plus moi- mê- me Sois ____

____ mon vain- queur ____ Domp- te mon coeur ____

The state of mind presented in Teresa's aria, however, is somewhat more complex. The text reads:

> Entre l'amour et le devoir
> Une jeune cœur est bien à plaindre.
> Ce qu'il désire il doit le craindre,
> Et repousser même l'espoir.
> Se condamner à toujours feindre,
> Avoir des yeux et ne point voir,
> Comment, comment le pouvoir?[22]

The significance of these lines is somewhat obscure. Do they suggest bitterness and frustration? Pessimistic resignation? A key to their interpretation lies in the music to which they are set. Berlioz uses in Teresa's aria many of the same musical devices he employed in the two arias in *Béatrice and Bénédict*. We find here many of the same details of form, tempo, meter, and rhythm enumerated above. Even the melody shares many of the characteristics of Hero's and Béatrice's arias (see Example 9). These musical parallels suggest that the state of mind that Berlioz meant to convey in Teresa's aria was neither frustration nor resignation, but the same mixture of "blissful love" and "anxious modesty" as he did in the arias of Hero and Béatrice. At least, that is the conclusion we can reach if we are prepared to accept this constellation of musical characteristics as Berlioz's personal musical shorthand for a compound of "blissful love" and "anxious modesty."

These musical parallels suggest that Berlioz probably thought of all three scenes as representing dramatic situations of much the same emotional content. True, how Berlioz thought of these scenes may not be decisive in how they are experienced by audiences, but the intentional fallacy aside, such a procedure as we have just undertaken does give us some useful and unexpected insight into a passage that is an important part of Berlioz's delineation of Teresa's character.

We may infer that the recurrent pairing of musical features and dramatic situations in the operas of Berlioz stems at least in part from the composer's belief that there is a limited number of human emotions that can be successfully translated into dramatic music. Such a belief must necessarily have consequences for the composer's approach to librettos. Berlioz's selective list of appropriate dramatic situations must surely have limited the kinds of librettos he was willing and able to accept—and the librettists with whom he was prepared to work. Unlike other opera composers—Verdi, for one—who

---

[22] "Torn between love and duty, a young heart might well complain. That which it most desires, it must fear. Even hope must be rejected. Condemned always to pretend, to have eyes but not to see; how is this possible?" (*Benvenuto Cellini*, Act 1, no. 2; pp. 15–18.)

Example 9

a. *Benvenuto Cellini*, Act 1, no. 2, "Entre l'amour et le devoir," p. 15.

b. *Benvenuto Cellini*, Act 1, no. 2, "Entre l'amour et le devoir," p. 20.

were equally particular about the kinds of librettos they set, Berlioz preferred not to waste his energy wrestling and negotiating with unsympathetic librettists. Although he began his career collaborating with "professional" writers (e.g., Léon de Wailly and Auguste Barbier on *Benvenuto Cellini*), Berlioz eventually resorted in his last two operas to writing his own librettos. By taking control of the entire creative process he was able to create librettos built around the limited number of dramatic situations that he thought contained musical potential. The result of such complete artistic control was the creation of librettos with dramatic priorities far different from those of contemporary nineteenth-century French standards. In the finished product we see not a play set to music, but a series of discrete vignettes each of which encapsulates an important moment in the drama. Berlioz's dramatic "theories" must thus have necessitated a selective process much like the one described by Gary Schmidgall:

> The composer and his librettist must search for moments in literature . . . which permit them to rise to an operatic occasion. They must . . . seek moments of expressive crisis—nuclear moments in which potential musical and dramatic energy is locked.[23]

The recurring dramatic situations we find in the operas of Berlioz are just such "nuclear moments"—points of highest emotional expressivity—used and reused because Berlioz was satisfied with their inherent musical-emotional potential. He seems to have searched for them in those *fables* which he chose to set to music. But frequently Berlioz was not satisfied with merely searching for the right dramatic moments. Sometimes we find him actually *making* the right dramatic moments, augmenting the dramatic potential of his subjects by working into the libretto appropriate scenes not otherwise indicated in his literary source. The two moonlit love duets discussed at the outset of this essay are, in fact, excellent examples of how Berlioz manipulated his subject matter to produce the kinds of dramatic situations he liked best. Neither of these scenes is essential to the plot of the opera in which it appears. The duet in *Les Troyens* is not, like most of the rest of that opera, based on Virgil's *Aeneid*, but rather is an interpolation which owes much to a scene in Shakespeare's *Merchant of Venice*. In a passage not at all central to the action of Shakespeare's play, Lorenzo, a minor character, says:

> In such a night
> Stood Dido with a willow in her hand
> Upon the wild sea banks, and waft her love
> To come again to Carthage.[24]

Evidently, Berlioz thought the mood conveyed by these lines so appropriate for his Trojan opera that he built a scene around it, making of it one of the nuclear moments by which he was to recount the story of Dido and Aeneas. The inclusion of the same moonlit scene in *Béatrice et Bénédict* is even more remarkable because the scene is even more irrelevant. *Béatrice et Bénédict* is based on Shakespeare's *Much Ado About Nothing*. The point in Shakespeare's play which corresponds to the scene in which Berlioz's Hero-Ursula duet occurs is Act 3, sc. 1, and the Shakespearean text gives not the slightest hint of any moonlit reveries by the sea. Here again Berlioz seems to have included a scene simply because he liked and wanted the musical-dramatic effect that it promised to produce.

Ultimately, we are tempted to ask whether or not Berlioz's musical-

---

[23] *Literature as Opera* (New York, 1977), p. 11.

[24] *The Merchant of Venice*, New Arden edition, ed. John Russell Brown (Cambridge, 1959), 5.1.9–12.

dramatic parallels are part of a consciously worked out operatic theory. Although the composer must surely have been aware of what he was doing when he recreated effective dramatic situations and reused specific musical elements from one opera in another, the possibility that this practice reflects an elaborate "theory" for the writing of opera seems unlikely for two reasons. First, notwithstanding the considerable quantity of his writings, Berlioz has not left very much discussion on this subject. Second, musical-dramatic pairings such as those we have discussed do not occur consistently throughout his operas—even though scenes of similar dramatic content often receive similar musical treatment, this is not always the case: scenes of similar dramatic content are sometimes treated very differently in music. I think it safer to describe what we have been examining here as a system—probably "informal" in its application—of a sort of "musical-dramatic rhetoric" in which certain musical qualities were thought—and therefore used—to convey certain "dramatic affects." We may identify two general principles underlying this practice:

(1) From the composer's own writings we may extrapolate the idea that music is capable of expressing only a limited variety of very general human passions or emotions, and that, therefore, only specific kinds of dramatic situations will offer potential for musical development.

(2) From the composer's practice we may infer that for each type of dramatic situation there exists a musical realization which best captures and distills the essential mood of that scene.

Examining both Berlioz's writings and his dramatic music, we can see that these principles governed Berlioz's entire approach, both as a composer and as a critic, to opera. They shed light, perhaps for the first time, on some of the idiosyncrasies of his operatic attitudes and practices. Now we can begin to understand what compelled him to write his own librettos, why those librettos deviate from the accepted structural norms of nineteenth-century French opera, and why he was so preoccupied with the principles of what he called "dramatic truthfulness" (i.e., the appropriateness of the relationship between text and music) in all his journalistic writing about opera. Finally, the identification of such a system of "musical-dramatic rhetoric," whether used consciously or unconsciously, focuses our attention on and clarifies the unique position that Berlioz occupies in the world of great composers of opera.

Opera and *Drame*: Hugo, Donizetti, and Verdi*

Gary Tomlinson

Abramo Basevi, shrewd nineteenth-century student of Verdi's operas, began the chapter on *Ernani* in his *Studio sulle opere di Giuseppe Verdi* with some provocative general observations; they may serve as our beginning as well. Basevi perceived in *Ernani* a reorientation of Verdi's style, a lessening of his dependence on the methods of Rossini and an increased understanding of those of Donizetti. Specifically, according to Basevi, Donizetti's *Lucrezia Borgia* offered Verdi the model for a new type of music-drama.

> With *Lucrezia Borgia* Donizetti began a revolution on the Italian stage—one that he did not want to complete, or could not complete, or perhaps one whose importance he did not recognize. In this opera music is associated with the most vivid, comprehensive, and universal passions, thus initiating a new *realism* in music which had not before been so perfectly or completely achieved.[1]

The new realism of *Lucrezia* was, in Basevi's view, taken up again in *Ernani*. And the connection of these two works is not unexpected, since both take their start from dramas by Victor Hugo, romantic polemicist and luminary of French theater throughout the 1830s. His *Lucrèce Borgia*, says Basevi,

> belongs to a group of dramas in which Hugo set out on a new path in dramatic art, a path that joined with that of dramatic music, since both aimed to free themselves from the old, limiting rules of art, and above all to strike the listeners in the most forceful way.[2]

An earlier version of this paper was read at a joint meeting of the American Institute for Verdi Studies and the Greater New York Chapter of the American Musicological Society, New York University, 7 March 1981.

[1] "Il *Donizzetti*, colla sua *Lucrezia Borgia*, aveva iniziata sulla scena italiana una rivoluzione, che non volle poi, o non seppe compire, o piuttosto non reputò di quel momento che era. Colla predetta Opera la musica drammatica venne associata alle passioni le più vive, le più comprese e partecipate dall'universale; iniziando così un *realismo* di cui la musica non aveva prima un modello più perfetto e completo." Abramo Basevi, *Studio sulle opere di Giuseppe Verdi* (Florence, 1859), p. 40. Unless otherwise indicated, all translations are my own.

[2] "La *Lucrezia* appartiene a quel mazzo di drammi, con i quali volle *Hugo* segnare un nuovo passo nell'arte drammatica; passo che coincide con quello della musica drammatica; perchè ambidue mirano soprattutto a percuotere gli animi nel modo il più forte, emancipandosi dalle strette, ed antiche regole dell'arte." Ibid., p. 41.

And Basevi, following Hugo, did not hesitate to specify the ideological context of these artistic goals:

> In a preface that Hugo wrote to . . . [*Hernani*], he tells us that he aimed to bring about in the theater the revolution that was already in men's minds in the political and social spheres. . . . *Liberalism* in art—this is what Victor Hugo proposed.[3]

Basevi's assertions—the connections he pointed out between Verdi and Donizetti and between both composers and Hugo—do not, to be sure, come as a surprise. What is surprising is that only fleeting attention has been paid by more recent writers on Italian opera to the principles behind Hugo's dramaturgical program, and to the general attraction they exercised on Italian composers from the 1830s almost until the rise of *verismo* near the end of the century. In this essay I should like to pass quickly over the much-traveled ground of Hugo's romantic drama and suggest how this soil could nurture a new and vigorous strain of Italian music-drama.[4]

[3] "In una prefazione, che il predetto *Hugo* scrisse a schiarimento di quel suo dramma, ci avverte, che egli intese di effettuare nell'arte drammatica quella rivoluzione, che già era nell'animo dell'universale, rispetto alle cose politiche e sociali; e che poco appresso, nel 1830, vedemmo manifestarsi in atto sulle pubbliche vie di Parigi. Il *Liberalismo* nell'arte; ecco cio che si propose *Vittore Hugo*." Ibid., p. 41.

[4] Both Julian Budden (*The Operas of Verdi*, 3 vols. [New York and London, 1973–81]) and David R. B. Kimbell (*Verdi in the Age of Italian Romanticism* [Cambridge, 1981]) are much aware of the resonance of Hugo's dramaturgy in Verdi's operas (see the chapters on *Ernani* and *Rigoletto* in Budden's first volume and Kimbell's ch. 21, "Verdi and French Romanticism—*Ernani*"); but the opera-by-opera approach each adopts keeps them from exploring its wider ramifications. These ramifications amount to a definable tradition, stemming from *Lucrezia Borgia*, of Italian operas on Hugo's dramas, a tradition whose musical and dramatic means intersect at crucial points with operatic adaptations of plays by Schiller, Byron, other romantic authors, and Shakespeare. For a listing of operas on Hugo's dramas see Arnaud Laster, "Hugo, Victor," *The New Grove Dictionary of Music and Musicians*, 20 vols. (London, 1980), 8:769–70. The tradition of Hugolian opera is the subject of Giancarlo Franceschetti's "La fortuna di Hugo nel melodramma italiano dell'ottocento," in Milan, Università cattolica del Sacro Cuore, Seminario di Filologia Moderna (now Istituto di Filologia Moderna), *Contributi: serie francese*, 2 (1961): 168–251; Franceschetti concerns himself more with the censors' and critics' responses to these operas than with the operas themselves.

For Hugo's dramas and dramaturgy, aside from his own writings (especially *Œuvres dramatiques complètes* [Paris, 1963], vol. 4 of his *Œuvres critiques complètes*, ed. Francis Bouvet, 4 vols. [Paris, 1961–64]), I have followed in particular W. D. Howarth, *Sublime and Grotesque: A Study of French Romantic Drama* (London, 1975); also Charles Affron, *A Stage for Poets: Studies in the Theatre of Hugo & Musset* (Princeton, 1971); Michel Butor, "Le Théâtre de Victor Hugo," *La Nouvelle Revue Française* 12 (1964): 862–78 and 1073–81, 13 (1965): 105–13; Samia Chahine, *La Dramaturgie de Victor Hugo, 1816–1843* (Paris, 1971); N. H. Clement, *Romanticism in France* (New York, 1939); David-Owen Evans, *Le Théâtre pendant la période romantique, 1827–1848* (Paris, 1925); Maurice Souriau, *Le Préface de Cromwell: Introduction, Texte et Notes* (Paris, 1897; rpt. Geneva, 1973); and René Wellek, *A History of Modern Criticism, 1750–1950* (New Haven, 1955), vol. 2, pp. 252–58.

I

Hugo's artistic and political intentions were manifested, in different ways and with varying success, in the group of dramas to which Basevi alluded—works like *Cromwell*, *Hernani*, *Le Roi s'amuse*, *Lucrèce Borgia*, and *Angelo*. And they were detailed, in more or less developed form, in the prefaces he wrote to these dramas, starting with the lengthy and important *Préface de Cromwell* of 1827. Hugo's prescriptions in this manifesto—the alterations in the structure, content, and technique of French drama that he envisaged—were for the most part not new. They continued a long tradition of complaints against the stringent Aristotelian rules of classical French tragedy, a tradition in which François Guizot, Stendahl and Manzoni were only the most recent participants.[5] Many of these prescriptions had already been realized in such anti-classical dramatic genres as the *drame bourgeois* and *comédie larmoyante* of the eighteenth century, or the popular *mélodrame*, with its striking scenic effects, humble personages, and sentimental plots, of the early nineteenth.[6] But the flamboyant, prepossessing rhetoric of Hugo's argument and the novel conception of literary history that served as its starting point lent his position a decisive authority. Many years later Théophile Gautier would recall that "the preface of *Cromwell* shone in our eyes like the tables of law on Mt. Sinai, and its arguments seemed irrefutable."[7]

Hugo's preoccupation in the *Préface* was the dramatist's search for reality and truth—*réalité* and *vérité*. The necessity for and nature of this truth originated in Christian religion, he argued, with its recognition of the two-sided nature of mankind, at once spiritual and bestial. In history this recognition led away from the monolithic view of reality implicit in ancient paganism, which tended to identify gods and men, to a broadened view that perceived "an abyss between soul and body, an abyss between man and God."[8] Such a view necessarily encompassed not only the beautiful, graceful, good and sublime, but also the ugly, deformed, evil and grotesque as well. All of

[5] François Guizot, *Shakespeare et son temps* (1821), Stendahl, *Racine et Shakespeare* (two parts, 1823 and 1825), and Alessandro Manzoni, *Lettre à M. Chauvet sur l'unité de temps et de lieu dans la tragédie* (1823). On these predecessors and others see Souriau, *Le Préface*, pp. 1–43; Howarth, *Sublime and Grotesque*, ch. 1, passim, and pp. 74–85; Clement, *Romanticism*, pp. 265–92; and Wellek, *A History*, 2:241–52.

[6] See Howarth, *Sublime and Grotesque*, ch. 1, passim, and pp. 51–73; Evans, *Le Théâtre*, pp. 49–54; and Clement, *Romanticism*, pp. 265–92.

[7] "La préface de *Cromwell* rayonnait à nos yeux comme les Tables de la Loi sur le Sinaï, et ses arguments nous semblaient sans réplique." Théophile Gautier, *Histoire du Romantisme* (Paris, 1884), reprinted as vol. 11 of Gautier's *Œuvres complètes* (Geneva, 1978), p. 5.

[8] " . . . un abîme entre l'âme et le corps, un abîme entre l'homme et Dieu." Hugo, *Œuvres dramatiques*, p. 141.

these had to be reflected in a dramatic art that would be true to the Christian view of reality. One of the main goals of Hugo's new romantic genre, *le drame*, was then to mirror the rich variety of life through the joining of the grotesque and the sublime. It was a hybrid, along Shakespearean lines, of the classical genres of tragedy and comedy. (A decade later, in the preface to *Ruy Blas* of 1838, Hugo would reluctantly acknowledge the important traits of his *drame* taken over from the *mélodrame*, as well.[9]) It did not admit of conventional rules limiting the inspired artistic representation of reality, rules like the pseudo-Aristotelian unities of time and place. "The cage of the unities," wrote Hugo, "holds nothing but a skeleton."[10]

For Hugo *vérité* had to arise also from an accurate representation of the time and locale depicted in the play. This search for what Hugo called *le caractéristique* entailed not just superficial effects of local color, but a pervasive fidelity to the inner spirit of the period and people on stage. It reflects Hugo's participation in the widespread interest of Romantic artists in earlier historical periods. And, on a deeper level, it manifests the growing cultural relativism—the sense "that the past differed from the present in a great deal more than the clothes people wore and the buildings they inhabited"—that Hugh Honour has singled out as a distinctive feature of Romantic historical perceptions.[11]

At the same time as it projected characteristic thoughts and actions of the period and locale it depicted, Hugo's *drame* sought to create characters of a rounded, true-to-life complexity. This new, subtle characterization was an essential element of Hugo's search for *vérité*. It called for characters who showed the contradictory impulses of real men and women, characters who united within themselves the grotesque and the sublime, the evil and noble instincts that Christianity revealed in us all. If historians could not supply such a full portrait of a character, as in the case of Cromwell, so much the better: the poet, guided by his inspired conception of the historical moment Cromwell inhabited and by his understanding of human nature, could provide the missing dimensions.[12]

---

[9]Ibid., p. 627. Hugo's reluctance here is revealed in inconsistency: after enumerating the features united in the *drame* from the three genres tragedy, comedy, and *mélodrame*, he ignored the latter in calling his new genre "la troisième grande forme de l'art, comprenant, enserrant, et fécondant les deux premières [tragedy and comedy]." On the *mélodrame* and Hugo's debt to it see Howarth, *Sublime and Grotesque*, pp. 61–73, 182–83, and ch. 7, passim, and Clement, *Romanticism*, pp. 285–86.

[10]" . . . la cage des unités ne renferme qu'un squelette." Hugo, *Œuvres dramatiques*, p. 145.

[11]Hugh Honour, *Romanticism* (New York, 1979), p. 192 and ch. 5, passim. On the development of Hugo's view of the Middle Ages, see Patricia A. Ward, *The Medievalism of Victor Hugo* (University Park, Pennsylvania, 1975); for a tabulation of his opinions on sixteenth-century writers, see Robert E. Turner, *The Sixteenth Century in Victor Hugo's Inspiration* (New York, 1934).

[12]The rich and seemingly paradoxical juxtaposition here of cultural relativism and the belief in a universality of the human condition is typically Romantic; see Honour, *Romanticism*, p. 201. On Hugo's characterization see Howarth, *Sublime and Grotesque*, pp. 163–64.

The dramatic poet achieved *vérité*, finally, by means of a new poetic style. Hugo insisted in the preface to *Cromwell* that dramas should be written in rhymed verse, but he proposed a more natural poetic style than earlier dramatists had employed. This style would give an idealized impression of the varied cadence of real speech through a loosening of the rigid rules of the French Alexandrine—a blurring of the caesura and a freer, more frequent use of *enjambement*. It would avoid studied and complex syntax, and pass easily and naturally from comedy to tragedy, from the grotesque to the sublime.[13]

In all these features, then, Hugo's *drame* offered a more true-to-life depiction of character and action than the classical dramaturgy it was meant to supersede. But we should not confuse Hugo's search for *réalité* and *vérité* with the later realism of Flaubert and Zola.[14] Hugo did not turn away, in his writings on drama or in his dramas themselves, from the conventional view of art as an ennobling, magnifying lens turned upon its subject.[15] Verse was necessary in drama, he said, because, "made in a certain way, it enhances things that would be insignificant and ordinary without it."[16] And indeed a supple, varied, and by no means naturalistic lyricism unknown to earlier French drama is the paramount novelty of *Hernani*. This static, anti-dramatic lyricism manifests itself most clearly in the *tirades* of Hernani, Don Carlos, and Don Ruy Gomez de Silva—lengthy, grandiloquent soliloquies of a sort Stendahl and, ironically, even Hugo himself had admonished modern dramatists to avoid.[17]

Just as Hugo's new poetic style did not intend slavishly to reproduce real speech, so the enriched characterization that he sought was not meant to yield a mundane reflection of everyday personalities. Rather it sought to project and enlarge the outstanding features of his protagonists: "each figure should be

[13] Hugo, *Œuvres dramatiques*, pp. 148–49. Hugo applied these recommendations inconsistently: three of his mature dramas, *Lucrèce Borgia, Marie Tudor*, and *Angelo* (1833–35), are in prose. For some explanation of this inconsistency see Howarth, *Sublime and Grotesque*, pp. 239–41.

[14] On the renunciation of traditional, idealizing rhetorical formulas entailed in this later realism—a renunciation precisely contrary to Hugo's practice—see Charles Rosen and Henri Zerner, "What Is, and Is Not, Realism?," *New York Review of Books*, 18 February 1982, pp. 21–26, esp. pp. 24–25.

[15] Hugo's own simile compared dramatic art to a mirror—but no ordinary mirror: "Il faut donc que le drame soit un miroir de concentration qui, loin de les affaiblir, ramasse et condense les rayons colorants, qui fasse d'une lueur une lumière, d'une lumière une flamme." Quoted by Howarth, *Sublime and Grotesque*, p. 131.

[16] "Fait d'une certaine façon, il communique son relief à des choses qui, sans lui, passeraient insignifiantes et vulgaires." Hugo, *Œuvres dramatiques*, p. 149.

[17] See Hugo, *Œuvres dramatiques*, p. 149 (*Préface de Cromwell*) on the need for modern dramatic verse to avoid *tirades*; also Stendahl: "The *tirade* is perhaps the most anti-romantic thing in the system of Racine. If it were absolutely necessary to choose, I would rather see the two unities preserved than the *tirade*." *Racine and Shakespeare*, trans. Guy Daniels (n.p., 1962), p. 135.

revealed in his most salient, individual, and typical trait."[18] Even Hugo's doctrine of *le caractéristique*, finally, was not a simple search for historical veracity. The careful study it demanded of the poet—and, presumably, the stylized "atmosphere" it lent the drama—would "guard the drama against a fatal vice—the *commonplace*."[19] Hugo's projection in his plays of a new, truer-to-life characterization and a more authentic, broadened range of situation and scenic effect by means of rhetorical, non-naturalistic expressive means brings to mind the idealized realism of some contemporary French painting; one thinks of Géricault's *Raft of the Medusa*.[20] It would soon serve, in the hands of Donizetti and Verdi, as a potent stimulus to new developments in operatic dramaturgy, where realism is necessarily attenuated.

Hugo's later, shorter prefaces, especially those to *Hernani*, *Lucrèce Borgia*, and *Angelo*, added a final, distinctive ingredient to his program for Romantic dramaturgy, one rarely suggested in the preface of *Cromwell*. In these writings, under the influence of current political events and burgeoning movements of social reform (especially Saint-Simonism), Hugo stressed the political, moral, and didactic ends of the *drame*.[21] The preface to *Hernani* proclaimed the identity of Romanticism and liberalism:

> Romanticism, so often ill-defined, is on the whole . . . nothing but *liberalism* in literature. . . . Literary liberalism will not be less popular [—or is Hugo's *populaire* better translated as "populist"?—] than political liberalism. Liberty in art and liberty in society: this is the double goal to which all right-thinking spirits must, as one, aspire.[22]

Hugo's linking of art to political ideology suggested a new role for drama, one that he outlined in the preface to *Lucréce Borgia*:

> . . . every work of art is a [political] act. . . . The theater, it cannot be said too often, has an immense importance in our times, an importance that grows with civilization itself. The stage is a rostrum. The stage is a pulpit. The stage speaks strongly and loudly . . . drama . . . has a national mission, a social mission, a human mission. . . . The poet has charge of

[18] " . . . toute figure soit ramenée à son trait le plus saillant, le plus individuel, le plus précis." Hugo, *Œuvres dramatiques*, p. 148.

[19] " . . . garantira le drame d'un vice qui le tue, le *commun*." Ibid.

[20] Honour, *Romanticism*, pp. 40–41; Rosen and Zerner, "Realism," p. 25.

[21] For a description of Saint-Simonism and similar movements and their influence on Hugo and French Romanticism in general, see Clement, *Romanticism*, pp. 222–64.

[22] "Le romantisme, tant de fois mal défini, n'est, à tout prendre, . . . que le *libéralisme* en littérature. . . . le libéralisme littéraire ne sera pas moins populaire que le libéralisme politique. La liberté dans l'art, la liberté dans la société, voilà le double but auquel doivent tendre d'un même pas tous les esprits conséquents et logiques. . . ." Hugo, *Œuvres dramatiques*, p. 347.

souls. He must not let the multitudes leave the theater without carrying away a deep and austere moral.[23]

These two passages give eloquent voice to what Charles Rosen has called "the magnificent and fatuous optimism of Hugo."[24] We can well imagine the profound sympathy such humanitarian, Romantic populism must have aroused in the young Verdi and other free-thinking Italians of the 1830s and 40s.

II

It is easy to see why Basevi considered Donizetti's *Lucrezia Borgia* a revolutionary work. The opera is altogether unprecedented in its self-conscious application of Hugo's ideals to music-drama. Felice Romani's fidelity to Hugo's drama—his unwillingness to mutilate the action so as to fit it to the straightjacket of operatic convention—demanded a new formal freedom from the composer. And Donizetti was equal to the task. First, he abandoned the double aria as a dominant musical building block. There is only one in the opera as he originally conceived it, though two others resulted from the addition of *cabalette* demanded by his sopranos for the 1833 premiere at La Scala and the 1840 Parisian premiere.[25] Orsini's two solos are both strophic songs—one a *racconto*, therefore with some claim to realism as a sung piece ("Nella fatal di Rimini / e memorabil guerra"), and the other a *ballata* replacing Gubetta's stage song in the last act of the play ("Il segreto per esser felici"). Most strikingly, there is only one solo movement, another strophic *racconto*, for Gennaro, the leading tenor ("Di pescatore ignobile"). It is not even an independent number, but serves as the slow movement of his duet with Lucrezia in the Prologue.

Throughout the opera Donizetti achieved a novel continuity of musical

---

[23]" . . . toute œuvre est une action. . . . Le théâtre, on ne saurait trop le répéter, a de nos jours une importance immense, et qui tend à s'accroître sans cesse avec la civilisation même. Le théâtre est une tribune. Le théâtre est une chaire. Le théâtre parle fort et parle haut . . . le drame . . . a une mission nationale, une mission sociale, une mission humaine. . . . Le poëte aussi a charge d'âmes. Il ne faut pas que la multitude sorte du théâtre sans emporter avec elle quelque moralité austère et profonde." Ibid., p. 458.

[24]Rosen, "Isn't It Romantic?" *New York Review of Books*, 14 June 1973, pp. 12–18; see p. 18.

[25]Henriette Méric-Lalande, the first Lucrezia, insisted upon the addition of the *cabaletta* "Era desso il figlio mio" to the final scene of the opera. Letters from Donizetti concerning a Roman revival in 1841 reveal his dislike of the piece; it was cut, and the finale as a whole revised, for the Milanese revival of the work in 1840. See Guido Zavadini, *Donizetti: Vita–Musiche–Epistolario* (Bergamo, 1948), pp. 49–50, 547–48, 558, 561; and William Ashbrook, *Donizetti and his Operas* (Cambridge, 1982), pp. 81, 349. Donizetti appended the *cabaletta* "Si voli il primo a cogliere" to Lucrezia's *romanza* "Com'è bello quale incanto" (and in the process cut the repeat of the *romanza*) for Giulia Grisi, who sang the role in the premiere at the *Théâtre-Italien*. See Guglielmo Barblan, *L'opera di Donizetti nell'età romantica* (Bergamo, 1948), p. 97.

texture, and hence a greater musico-dramatic realism, by blurring the boundaries between numbers and movements. The Largo of Duke Alfonso's aria "Vieni la mia vendetta," for example, emerges with no clear orchestral introduction out of the party music that dominates the *scena*. Orsini's two songs are each skillfully embedded in lengthy and varied party scenes. His duet with Gennaro in Act 2 proceeds smoothly out of the *pianissimo* finish of the chorus of Duke Alfonso's thugs before it. The fade-out of the ruffians' music mirrors the action: they move backstage and hide there during the duet, plotting quietly at one point in its opening *parlante* movement. They whisper among themselves again during the hushed peroration after Gennaro and Orsini's *cabaletta*—extraordinarily, there is no stop for applause here—and then they quickly begin a final, restrained chorus of gloating. This chorus too ends softly, with a varied reprise of the music that had closed the *cabaletta*, as the thugs wander off. (Its final tonic, D, is contradicted awkwardly by a sustained G^7 chord, the dominant of the key of the following *pezzo concertato*. Not all of Donizetti's attempts to enhance musical continuity in *Lucrezia* are successful.)

Even when Donizetti retained conventional structures in *Lucrezia*, he and Romani strove to invest them with uncommon dramatic significance. Only in the last lines of the Prologue, for example, do Gennaro's companions reveal to him that the unknown woman he has wooed is the dreaded Lucrezia Borgia. This ordering follows Hugo's drama closely, and renders the brief *stretta* of the finale a vivid dramatic crescendo up to the revelation, instead of the usual prolonged and, as it were, after-the-fact venting of emotions. A similar transfiguration of a conventional musical form occurs in Lucrezia's *romanza* in the Prologue ("Com'è bello quale incanto"). Its two strophes are separated by a quick exchange between Duke Alfonso and his henchman Rustighello, masked and hiding in the background. Only at this moment are the Duke's suspicions of Lucrezia's infidelity apparently confirmed, because only now does Lucrezia remove her domino to dry her tears. This, by the way, is the first we have seen of the Duke, the *primo basso* of the opera. His introduction here as a masked eavesdropper, delivering a few *parlante* lines and skulking off stage not to be seen again until Act 1, is the most striking novelty of all in this passage.

All of these innovative operatic formulations—and others, such as the off-stage chanting of monks in the finale of Act 2—reflect the wide diversity of situation and effect in Hugo's drama, a diversity he had adopted especially from the *mélodrame*. Such effects characterize Hugo's dramatic output as a whole, and their appearance in Donizetti's *Lucrezia* anticipates in a general way the most vivid *coups de théâtre* of *Rigoletto* (based on *Le Roi s'amuse*): the two entrances of Monterone, the kidnapping of Gilda, and the final reprise of "La donna è mobile." Even the complex divided stagings of Acts 2, 4, and 5 of *Le Roi s'amuse* (Act 1, scene 2, and Act 3 of *Rigoletto*) recall the elaborate, spectacular scenography of the *mélodrame*.[26]

It will have become clear by now that eavesdropping and hired bravos play a large part in *Lucrezia*. In this Donizetti and Romani adhered to Hugo's doctrine of *le caractéristique* (in the preface to his libretto Romani spoke of the "tinta dei tempi" that he had attempted to preserve in reworking Hugo's play).[27] Hugo, like Byron before him, viewed Renaissance Italy as a land of political repression, ruled cloak-and-dagger fashion by tyrannical princes through the intrigues of secret police and spies. For these writers exotic poisons and dead-of-night assassinations formed an ever-present fact of Renaissance life—especially in mysterious Venice, where disposing of the corpse presented no greater difficulty than lugging it off to the nearest canal. *Lucrezia Borgia* is to my knowledge the first Italian opera to reflect this view of the Renaissance. Sinister motives darken even its party scenes; and these scenes function, as in Hugo, to set off all the more starkly the Machiavellian manipulations around them. Donizetti's attempt in such scenes to mirror Hugo's tinselly hedonism depends, not in vain, on the raucous strains of the *banda*. Romani's search for characteristic elements led him so far as to echo Lorenzo de' Medici's "Quant'è bella giovinezza," a real Renaissance lyric famous in Romani's time as in ours, in the text of Orsini's *ballata*. In giving voice to this new, quintessentially Romantic view of Renaissance Italy, *Lucrezia* stands at the head of a long and rich tradition of Italian opera, including Donizetti's own *Marino Faliero*, Mercadante's *Il bravo*, Verdi's *I due Foscari* and *Simon Boccanegra*, and Ponchielli's *La Gioconda*.

Of course Hugo's thugs, and their leaders Rustighello and Astolfo, are not wholly serious characters. They also provide a contrasting element of grotesque comedy in the otherwise somber drama. Donizetti admirably captured the black humor of these characters in his music—both in the somewhat too jaunty choruses of Rustighello and his henchmen, which anticipate in mood and style the assassins' chorus of *Macbeth* and the kidnappers' chorus of *Rigoletto*; and in the well-known *parlante* confrontation of Rustighello and Astolfo in Act 1, with its scoring of clarinet and bassoon supported by pizzicato strings and punctuated by ominous timpani rolls (see Example 1, p. 180). Julian Budden and others have noted the dramatic and musical similarities of this passage to the *parlante* duet of Rigoletto and Sparafucile. And Budden, in characterizing the situation of both as one of "grotesque humour," reveals how effectively Donizetti's music served Hugo's expressive ends.[28]

---

[26] Howarth, *Sublime and Grotesque*, pp. 66–67, 182.

[27] Romani's preface is reproduced in *The Donizetti Society Journal* 2 (1975): 178.

[28] Budden, *The Operas*, 1:492.

Example 1. *Lucrezia Borgia*, Act 1, sc. 3.

Finally, and most impressively, Donizetti realized Hugo's dramatic ideals in *Lucrezia* through a new subtlety and breadth of musical characterization. Partly this arose from the novel theatrical situations described above—situations that Donizetti's formal flexibility allowed him to embrace. Duke Alfonso's introduction as a masked eavesdropper, for example, reveals his vicious jealousy in a moment, with a dramatic elan that few standard entrance arias could match. Romani included many such situations in the libretto—telling details from the play that other librettists probably would have avoided. Gennaro's whispering in Orsini's ear the treachery of Duke Alfonso during their duet in Act 2, so as not to be overheard, is another simple example. Librettists of Rossinian *opera seria* rarely asked for such trivial and down-to-earth actions from their overblown, almost Metastasian heroes.

Donizetti's deepened characterization springs also, simply, from the growth of his musical powers. The finale of Act 1 is a small masterpiece of musical character-portrayal, with its *parlante* depiction of the Duke's cruel dissimulation—he proposes to salute Gennaro in a toast, all the while planning to serve him poisoned wine—and its Verdian distinction in the trio of the characters' differing emotional stances. This deepening of Donizetti's interest in musical characterization may well have been stimulated by his reading of Hugo's play. In his preface to *Lucrèce Borgia*, Hugo had enunciated clearly and simply the problem of character he considered the crux of the drama: "moral deformity purified by maternal love."[29] In Lucrezia Borgia Hugo had found a historical figure he could imbue with the unambiguous mixture of contrasting instincts he had pronounced essential to modern drama in his preface to *Cromwell*. Romani, for his part, was sufficiently impressed by Hugo's phrase to repeat it in the published preface to his libretto.

So it is not surprising that Donizetti left us eloquent musical testimony, in the two recurring themes of his opera, that he too grasped the opposed components of Lucrezia's personality. The first of these themes, introduced at the climax of the brief, evocative orchestral prelude, is a melodic motive of a rising and falling minor third, often harmonized with a diminished chord (see Example 2); this motive represents Lucrezia's ruthless bloodlust and reappears most clearly in the opening scene, as Gennaro's companions rebuke Gubetta for mentioning the "cursed name" of Borgia, and at the end of the Prologue, at the crowd's climactic revelation to Gennaro of Lucrezia's identity. (See Examples 3a and 3b, p. 182; other related uses of this motive occur in the finale of

Example 2. *Lucrezia Borgia*, Prelude.

---

[29] "... la maternité purifiant la difformité morale, voilà *Lucrèce Borgia*." Hugo, *Œuvres dramatiques*, p. 457.

Example 3. *Lucrezia Borgia*, Prologue.
  a. Scene 1.

  b. Finale.

Act 1, as Gennaro drinks the Duke's poisoned wine; just before Lucrezia's entrance in Act 2, as the guests first realize they are trapped; and, altered to a major third but retaining the diminished harmony, in Orsini's *racconto* in the Prologue, at the words "dov'è Lucrezia è morte.") The second of Donizetti's recurring themes is associated with Lucrezia's maternal love for Gennaro. It is first heard as the orchestral introduction to her *romanza* in the prologue; the stage directions in the score instruct her to approach the sleeping Gennaro during this introduction, "gazing on him with pleasure and respect." This music returns only once, but with potent effect, as the orchestral basis of the *parlante* in Act 1 in which Lucrezia pleads with Duke Alfonso for Gennaro's life (see Examples 4a and 4b).

There is much to admire in *Lucrezia Borgia*, then; and much was it admired in the nineteenth and even at the beginning of the twentieth century. To be sure, the opera also has its conspicuous weaknesses. The duet of Lucrezia and Gennaro in the Prologue is as implausible as the corresponding scene in the play. The Duke's vengeance aria, the one double aria included in all versions of the score, is a lapse into the most inappropriate operatic convention, without even the meager saving grace of a significant dramatic stimulus for the *cabaletta*. The motivations of Lucrezia—the reason for her unwillingness to admit to the Duke that Gennaro is her son, for example—are generally less clear here than in the play.

But to appreciate Donizetti and Romani's success in this work, we have only to glance at another opera based on a drama of Hugo, one that triumphed at La Scala in 1837, less than four years after *Lucrezia*: Saverio Mercadante's *Il*

Example 4. *Lucrezia Borgia.*
   a. Prologue, scene 2.

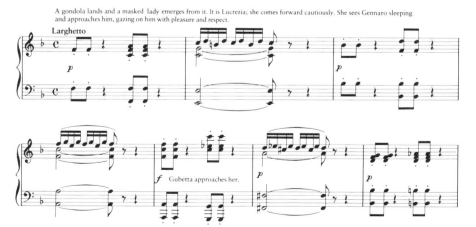

Example 4, continued
  b. Act 1, scene 6.

giuramento. Gaetano Rossi's libretto, based on Hugo's *Angelo*, is a shambles. Budden hardly exaggerates in pronouncing it "incomprehensible without a knowledge of [its] literary source."[30] But the choice itself of *Angelo* for an opera reveals either a blithe ignorance of the playwright's dramatic goals, or a grave miscalculation of their adaptability to a musical context. For *Angelo* is not, like *Lucrèce Borgia*, a character sketch in vivid primary colors. Instead it is a play enlivened mainly by ideas, as Hugo tacitly acknowledged in stressing the didactic function of drama in his preface. *Angelo* is, too transparently, a lectern from which Hugo delivered himself of teachings on women's equality to men, human rights, and the evils of political repression.

[30]Budden, *The Operas*, 2:67.

The conceptual monologues in which Hugo put across these ideas are not, of course, the stuff of *primo ottocento* opera. Catarina's outraged comparison of her chaste infidelity with her husband's open adultery, Tisbe's musings on the inhumane treatment accorded actors and actresses by the aristocracy, and Angelo's paranoid admission of the narrow limits of his power—all of this is purged from Rossi's libretto, leaving nothing but the complicated contrivances and unrequited loves by which Hugo patched together his plot. Not even Hugo's *caractéristique* elements are preserved: Homodei, the Byronesque representative of the police state of Renaissance Venice and the most vivid character in the play, is reduced in *Il giuramento* to a jilted second tenor out for revenge. (He would be more successfully transplanted to the operatic stage in a later opera based on *Angelo*, Ponchielli's *La Gioconda*; and through this work he would re-echo in Verdi's Iago.)

In such a sparse dramatic context, the much-touted reforms of Mercadante's music could hardly work to optimum effect. Many of these reforms seem to have been inspired by *Lucrezia Borgia*—especially Mercadante's attempts to achieve greater continuity through the binding of one piece to another and the *diminuendo* postludes to choruses. And Mercadante's opening party scene, with its strophic *racconto* for Elaìsa, recalls clearly the opening of Donizetti's opera. But Donizetti had forged his novel style in the hot fire of Hugo's romantic dramaturgy. Mercadante perceived the need only for the musical reforms themselves, not for their dramatic validation. Donizetti's reforms followed logically from Hugo's play, while Mercadante's drift aimlessly in the free-fall of a theatrical vacuum.

III

Hernani, like *Angelo* but for different reasons, was not the most suitable of Hugo's plays for operatic treatment. Its characters, with the exception of Don Carlos, are one-sided in thought and action, rendered vital only by the lyric beauty and rhetorical potency of their long speeches. But these *tirades* could hardly find straightforward expression in the Italian opera of the 1840s; they disappeared from Piave's libretto almost without a trace. The special interest of the character of Don Carlos remained, but this too was beyond Verdi's powers of musical portrayal at this time.

Carlos' characterization depends upon his mildly self-deprecating humor in Acts 1 and 2 of the play. The comic acknowledgment of fallibility entailed in this humor prepares us for Carlos' descent into true self-doubt in his great soliloquy before Charlemagne's tomb. We experience this passage and his subsequent pardon of the conspirators, then, as the deepening of an established personality, the full exposure of a richness of character already in partial view. In 1843–44 Verdi could not yet accommodate Carlos' humor in a serious opera, even if he could have prevailed upon the censors to allow it in the portrayal of a king. Without it, Carlo's soliloquy and pardon in Act 3 of the opera became an obscurely motivated peripety of character—a conversion looking back in its unfathomable religious quality to that of Nabucco two years earlier. Carlos' complex personality in the play was replaced in the opera by two distinct and as it were separate personalities, each as single-minded as Ernani or Silva. In this important regard Verdi was ill-equipped to project the particular richness of character he encountered in Hugo's *Hernani*. Without the profound portrayal of Don Carlo, and in spite of formal and expressive advances reminiscent of *Lucrezia*—like the evocative prelude with its important dramatic connotations, and the magnificent, continuous music of the final scene—Verdi's opera remains the province of larger-than-life, rigid characters.[31]

But Hugo's intent was nevertheless not altogether obscured here, as it had been in *Il giuramento*. Verdi was able to respond warmly to a different aspect of Hugo's program: the embodiment of liberalism in art. Verdi expressed this ideal of an art of the people through a new, popular musical style. I have argued elsewhere that the simple melodic forms of Verdi's early arias represent not a neutral continuation of the lyric regularity of Bellini and Donizetti, but a resounding reaffirmation of it in the face of the more studied aria styles of Mercadante and Pacini around 1840.[32] And certainly Verdi gave this energetic, straight-speaking melodic style a prominence in *Ernani* unmatched in his earlier works. It marks the extraordinarily rich series of solo numbers in the score, as well as the ensembles, in particular those of Acts 1 and 2. It extends even into the choruses, which are generally simpler in technique and effect than their counterparts in *Nabucco* and *I Lombardi*. And, of course, it is essential to "Si ridesti il Leon di Castiglia," the splendid example of the most popular device of Verdi's early operas, the unison patriotic chorus, that Verdi contrived to insert into Hugo's conspiracy scene.

Simplicity and directness—these are characteristics that led contemporary critics to label Verdi's early style *volgare*, an adjective with a greater connotation of "popular" than our "vulgar." Certainly these traits were present in Verdi's works before *Ernani*. But in his reading of Hugo's *Hernani*, and undoubtedly of its preface as well, Verdi stumbled upon an eloquent kindred soul.[33] The straightforward, forceful action of the play and the political views

---

[31] For a somewhat different view of Don Carlos' conversion and Verdi's treatment of it, see Joseph Kerman, "Notes on an Early Verdi Opera," *Soundings* 3 (1973): 56–65.

[32] Gary Tomlinson, "Verdi after Budden," *19th Century Music* 5 (1981): 170–82; see pp. 174–77.

[33] Verdi's letters to Piave during the writing of *Ernani* reveal clearly his close study of Hugo's drama. See Franco Abbiati, *Giuseppe Verdi*, 4 vols. (Milan, 1959), 1:473–86, and Budden, *The Operas*, 1:141–45.

of the preface must together have caused Verdi to focus the popular aspects of his style with a new self-consciousness and sense of mission. Verdi's *Ernani* is the first Italian declaration of Hugo's "liberalism in art."

It was left for Verdi to realize Hugo's more strictly artistic goals—those that Donizetti had previously addressed in *Lucrezia Borgia*—in *Rigoletto*. Verdi's choice of subject was, this time, astute, for *Le Roi s'amuse* is a straightforward incarnation of the dramatic program of the *Préface de Cromwell*. It unites the characteristic hedonism of Renaissance court life (as Hugo conceived it) with actions of both high gravity and grotesque humor and a complex, contradictory protagonist, all in an eventful plot that spins to its conclusion with wrenching inevitability.

Verdi's letters reveal his sensitivity to these aspects of the play.[34] Already in 1848 he had complained to Piave of the unbroken dreariness of many tragic subjects, citing the example of his own *I due Foscari*. And two years after the premiere of *Rigoletto*, writing to Antonio Somma, he held up this opera as the best example among his works of the new dramatic variety that he sought.[35] As to the inevitable progress of the plot, Verdi followed Hugo's statement in his preface that the whole drama devolves from the curse of Saint-Vallier in Act 1; he instructed Piave to substitute *La maledizione di Vallier* for Hugo's title if necessary to appease the censors.[36] And Verdi was in no doubt about the rich duality of the main character, either. When the whole project seemed doomed to rejection by the censors, he wrote to Carlo Marzari, president of La Fenice, "I find it truly wonderful to portray this character, ridiculous and deformed outside but passionate and full of love inside."[37]

By 1850 Verdi had developed the musical means to incorporate and transform all these features of *Le Roi s'amuse*. As David Lawton has shown, he activated tonal relations spanning the whole of the opera—specifically the juxtaposition of the keys D-flat and D in Acts 1 and 3—to underline the relation of the curse to the final catastrophe.[38] He laid bare the two sides of Rigoletto's personality again and again throughout the opera, and contrasted

---

[34]On the genesis of *Rigoletto* see Abbiati, *Verdi*, 1:59–72, 81–89, 91, and 96–108, and Budden, *The Operas*, 1:477–84. On the merging in it of comic and tragic elements see Piero Weiss, "Verdi and the Fusion of Genres," *Journal of the American Musicological Society* 35 (1982): 138–56.

[35]Letters to Piave of 22 July 1848 and Somma of 22 April 1853, in Giuseppe Verdi, *Autobiografia dalle lettere*, ed. Aldo Oberdorfer (Milan, 1951), pp. 195–96 and 243–44.

[36]Letter of 3 June 1850, in Abbiati, *Verdi*, 2:63–64.

[37]"Io trovo appunto bellissimo rappresentare questo personaggio estremamente deforme e ridicolo, ed internamente appassionato e pieno d'amore." Letter to Marzari of 14 December 1850, in Abbiati, *Verdi*, 2:87.

[38]David Lawton, "Tonality and Drama in Verdi's Early Operas" (Ph.D. dissertation, University of California, Berkeley, 1973), ch. 4.

them explicitly in Rigoletto's furious condemnation of the courtiers in Act 1, scene 2, and the famous transformation that follows.

Verdi's description of Rigoletto—"ridiculous and deformed outside but passionate and full of love inside"—reminds us of the preface to *Lucrèce Borgia*, where Hugo had asserted the essential dramatic similarities between Lucrèce and Triboulet, his Rigoletto. Whether or not Verdi knew this preface, he clearly recognized the close connection of these two subjects: consciously or not, he returned time and again to Donizetti's *Lucrezia Borgia* for guidance in composing his opera.[39] The evocative orchestral prelude of *Rigoletto*, dominated by a musical motive associated with Monterone's curse, looks back to *Lucrezia*, as does the following party scene, with its strophic *ballata* for the Duke and lively *banda*. Like Donizetti, Verdi abandoned the traditional double aria almost entirely—there is only one in *Rigoletto*, the Duke's "Parmi veder le lagrime"—and he realistically accommodated solos as stage songs in Acts 1 and 3 (the Duke's "Questa o quella" and "La donna è mobile"). He extended the formal freedoms of *Lucrezia* so that the music moved in time to the changing emotions of the drama, as in Rigoletto's three-movement aria "Cortigiani, vil razza dannata." In the forlorn *scena* preceding this aria, and in the sinister duet of Rigoletto and Sparafucile, which we have seen to emulate the confrontation of Rustighello and Astolfo in *Lucrezia*, Verdi expanded the expressive variety of Donizetti's *parlante* techniques to explore new realms of emotional subtlety. And the stunning diversity of melodic characterization united in the quartet of *Rigoletto* built upon the already notable disparities of the trio of *Lucrezia*. (Indeed Verdi borrowed from Donizetti's trio, in addition to its clear melodic distinction of different characters, the stirring harmonic progression beginning at Gennaro's "Madre! esser dee . . ." and leading sequentially through a tonicization of ♭III to a prolongation of V. Compare the six measures beginning at Rigoletto's "Taci, il piangere non vale.")

The spine-chilling coda of Gilda's "Caro nome," as the stage fills with courtiers gathering to kidnap her and the music becomes suffused with sinister chromaticism, and the coda of the Duke's first rendition of "La donna è mobile," with Rigoletto and Sparafucile quietly arranging his murder, took their cues from the *diminuendo* ending of Orsini and Gennaro's *cabaletta*, as Alfonso's thugs emerge from their hiding place. Through such dove-tailing of separate movements and dramatic events Verdi achieved, as Donizetti had, a musico-dramatic continuity extraordinary in Italian opera of the time. Verdi even borrowed from Donizetti the rising minor-third motive with diminished harmony introduced in the prelude to *Lucrezia*—the motive of Lucrezia's

---

[39]Budden (*The Operas*, 1:482) perceptively characterizes *Lucrezia* as "the nearest opera to *Rigoletto* in form and dramatic content."

bloodlust. It is an important component of the distinctive musical *tinta* of *Rigoletto* (to which Verdi referred in a letter of August 1850), and it is associated, as Martin Chusid has pointed out, with Monterone and his curse (see Example 5).[40]

Verdi employed all of these techniques, as Donizetti had before him, in the musical transformation of Hugo's theatrical conception. He derived from them an expressive flexibility that allowed him to capture Hugo's essential dramatic variety in his music. And even in the one dramatic misfire of the opera, the Duke's "Parmi veder le lagrime," we may suggest that Verdi kept Hugo's ideals in mind. Here Verdi realized that the censors would force him to depart from Hugo's Act 2, scene 2, with its overly explicit insinuation of the off-stage rape of Blanche, Hugo's Gilda. "It will be necessary for us to find something better," Verdi confidently wrote to Piave.[41] The conventional

Example 5. *Rigoletto*, Act 1, scene 6.

[40]Letter to Marzari of 24 August 1850, in Abbiati, *Verdi*, 2:68–69. Martin Chusid, "Rigoletto and Monterone: A Study in Musical Dramaturgy," in *International Musicological Society: Report of the Eleventh Congress, Copenhagen, 1972* (Copenhagen, 1974), pp. 325–36.

[41]" . . . converrà per noi trovare qualche cosa di meglio. . . . " Letter [of November 1850], in Abbiati, *Verdi*, 2:84.

Example 5, continued

double-aria-with-chorus that stands in place of this scene, in which the Duke laments Gilda's disappearance in decidedly uncharacteristic terms, is not better. But it may in fact represent Verdi and Piave's misguided attempt to enrich the Duke's portrayal with ambivalences and contradictory impulses like those of Rigoletto himself.

IV

So Basevi was only half right. The revolution that Donizetti began but did not complete was carried out in *Ernani*, with, however, the emphasis on an ideological stance inherent in Hugo's play but extrinsic to its deeper levels of lyric and dramatic expression. The true fulfillment of the new music-drama adumbrated in *Lucrezia* came only in *Rigoletto*, where Verdi penetrated beyond Hugo's populist politics to capture and project the central dramatic traits of his play. This, however, Basevi was not able to see. He pronounced both *Rigoletto* and its source immoral, and judged impossible what he saw as Verdi's attempt to make physical deformity attractive through music.[42] But we know this was not Verdi's goal. His drama, like Hugo's, depended on the

---

[42]Basevi, *Studio*, pp. 183–85, 200.

richness gained from the emphasis of deformity, not a bland homogeneity sought in its neutralization. The ultimate irony of Basevi's analysis is that the budding revolution he welcomed in *Lucrezia* blossomed in *Rigoletto* into an impassioned music-drama of a stylized realism overpowering to his orthodox tastes. The revolution was then complete. And its completion left us the most enduring testament of all to Hugo's romantic drama.

Perhaps it is fitting that this testament should have taken operatic form, for numerous writers have called attention, with varying degrees of literalism, to the operatic qualities of Hugo's plays. Charles Affron and W. D. Howarth, for example, have each argued that the lyric emphasis and idealized rhetoric of Hugo's verse dramas loosened the conventional dramatic constraints of plot structure and character development, much as in opera musical utterance suspends dramatic time and audience disbelief with it.[43] In this central feature, then, Hugo created a spoken drama that aspired to the condition of opera: the tension in it between realistic subject and idealized, lyrical expression is analogous to the rich opposition of song and drama intrinsic to opera. It is appealing to suppose that Donizetti and Verdi sensed the affinity of these two stylized dramatic genres, at least dimly, when they seized eagerly upon Hugo's *drame* for operatic treatment.

But to demonstrate that Verdi and Donizetti were attracted to Hugo's dramas for their more specifically dramatic qualities as well, it is enough to recall that *Lucrezia Borgia* was not based on a verse drama at all, but on a drama in prose, and that both *Lucrezia* and *Rigoletto* took as their starting points dramas in which the lyricism of *Hernani* was subordinated to self-conscious character study and a welter of melodramatic effects. The composers found in Hugo's joining of comic and serious elements the opportunity for a broadened expressive variety in Italian serious opera. In the aspects of his stagecraft that derive most clearly from the *mélodrame*—*coups de théâtre* such as the chanting monks of *Lucrèce Borgia* or the divided stage settings of *Le Roi s'amuse*—they sought the means to an expanded range of scenic effect. They discovered in his *caractéristiques* elements of historical veracity the possibility of an atmospheric musical *tinta*, an over-arching expressive coloration that could lend their works a deep-seated coherence. His guileless, black-and-white embodiment of contradictory impulses in Lucrèce and Triboulet—too simplistic, ultimately, to hold the spoken stage—led them, within their more narrowly circumscribed musico-dramatic tradition, to a new richness of musical characterization.

Such practical dramatic concerns point up the wide disparity of perspective between Hugo on the one hand and the Italian composers on the other. Hugo's

---

[43]Affron, *A Stage*, pp. 6–11; Howarth, *Sublime and Grotesque*, pp. 164–69.

attempt to revivify French spoken theater depended only secondarily on the numerous precepts of characterization and plot structure and content advanced in the *Préface de Cromwell*—precepts recommended and even put into practice, after all, already before 1827. It depended crucially, instead, on the liberated, lyrical poetic language he advocated in the *Préface* and realized fully in *Hernani*. And in pursuing this language Hugo evolved an opera-like poetic theater, a spoken *drame lyrique*. In contrast, Donizetti and Verdi both grew up in a native dramatic tradition suffocated, so to speak, by its own excessive lyricism: the tradition of Rossinian *opera seria*. Of Hugo's lyricism they had no need. But the characteristics that were of secondary importance to Hugo were lacking in their tradition, and hence essential to their attempts to resuscitate it. No doubt the enriching effect of incorporating these traits in their Hugolian operas encouraged them to explore other playwrights, good and bad, who displayed similar qualities—Byron, Schiller, Zacharias Werner, Antonio García Gutiérrez, and of course Shakespeare. In this way Hugo's impact on Italian opera extended far beyond the works actually based on his plays, to operas as varied as *I due Foscari*, *Macbeth*, and *La forza del destino* (to speak only of Verdi's works). Hugo's Romantic *drame* set criteria and standards for operatic dramaturgy that would endure in Italy almost until the close of the nineteenth century.

When Hugo wrote proudly in 1834, "Je fis souffler un vent révolutionnaire," he surely had neither opera nor Italy in mind. But the winds of change he set in motion blew loud and long on the Italian operatic stage.

Satire and Sentiment in *The Yeomen of the Guard**
Ronald Broude

Although *The Yeomen of the Guard* was once the most admired of the Savoy operas, it has not proven one of the most durable. Introduced as an "entirely new departure" from Gilbert and Sullivan's previous collaborations,[1] *Yeomen* was cheered by audience and reviewers alike; the *Daily Telegraph*'s critic hailed the work as "a genuine English opera, forerunner of many others, let us hope, and possibly significant of an advance towards a national lyric stage."[2] Its favorable reception nothwithstanding, however, *Yeomen* has never held the stage in opera houses, and even among Gilbert and Sullivan enthusiasts it has not achieved the popularity of such perennial favorites as *H. M. S. Pinafore*, *The Pirates of Penzance*, or *The Mikado*. In part, *Yeomen*'s blighted promise may be attributed to its unsettling mixture of tragedy and farce, of grand opera and comic operetta. Audiences from the first night to the present day have been baffled by this ambiguity of genre; even the original cast, creating their parts under the direction of the composer and librettist, seem to have been disoriented. *Punch* reported of the premiere that "none of the actors play with conviction. They seem uncertain as to the character of the piece—is it serious, or isn't it?"[3] But such criticism as *Yeomen* received during its first run was directed principally at Gilbert's libretto; reviewers seem to have been charmed by Sullivan's music. Wrote the critic for the *Times*:

> Sir Arthur Sullivan's score is fully equal to his previous achievements, and the success of the piece will no doubt be largely due to it.[4]

*My thanks go to Fredric W. Wilson of the Gilbert and Sullivan Collection of the Pierpont Morgan Library, New York, both for reading and commenting upon this paper and for his kind assistance during my visits to the Collection. And thanks from all who use the Collection must go to Reginald Allen, who was so instrumental in assembling it.

[1] The phrase first occurs in Sullivan's diary entry for 31 October 1887: "Gilbert told me that he had . . . found another [plot] about the Tower of London, an entirely new departure." (New Haven, Yale University, Beinecke Rare Book and Manuscript Library.) Presumably, D'Oyly Carte circulated the phrase, for we find references to a "departure" in opening night reviews, e.g., *The Standard* (4 October 1888). For excerpts from reviews expressing similar sentiments, see Reginald Allen, *The First Night Gilbert and Sullivan* (New York, 1958), pp. 308–10. For later criticism using the phrase, see, for example, François Cellier and Cunningham Bridgeman, *Gilbert, Sullivan, and D'Oyly Carte* (2nd ed., London, 1927), p. 257.

[2] 4 October 1888.

[3] 13 October 1888.

[4] 4 October 1888.

Today, with the perspective of historical criticism, we are not much bothered by *Yeomen*'s mingling of comic and serious elements. We are familiar with the Romantic practice of juxtaposing the sublime and the grotesque,[5] and if we must assign *Yeomen* to a specific dramatic genre, we can invoke John Fletcher's definition of tragicomedy—a definition with which Gilbert was probably familiar, since J. St. Lo Strachey's Mermaid edition of Beaumont and Fletcher's best known plays had been published (with some fanfare) while Gilbert was writing *Yeomen*:

> A tragi-comedy is not so called in respect of mirth and killing, but in respect it wants deaths, which is enough to make it no tragedy, yet brings some near it, which is enough to make it no comedy. . . .[6]

What puzzles us today is that *Yeomen*'s music, while clearly more complex than the scores Sullivan wrote for Gilbert's other Savoy libretti, seems, somehow, also more naive.

Gilbert and Sullivan were at the height of their creative powers when they wrote *Yeomen*, and both considered it their best collaboration.[7] This fact, together with the admiration that *Yeomen* once enjoyed, suggests that we may be overlooking qualities that its original audience saw and appreciated. To recover these qualities, we should, ideally, be able to propose a reading of *Yeomen* that will demonstrate the existence of a unified artistic purpose

---

[5]For the classic statement of this esthetic, see Victor Hugo's preface to *Cromwell* (1830), in *Œuvres complètes*, vol. 12 *(Critique)*, ed. Jean-Pierre Reynaud (Paris, 1985), pp. 3–33.

[6]*The Faithful Shepherdess*, "To the Reader" (London, 1887), vol. 2, p. 321.

[7]That Gilbert and Sullivan both considered *Yeomen* the best of their collaborations is a belief frequently encountered among Savoyards, although, like so much else in Savoy mythology, it is difficult to trace farther back than secondary sources. On the collaborators' satisfaction with *Yeomen*, see Arthur Lawrence, *Sir Arthur Sullivan* (Chicago and New York, 1900), p. 177; Sidney Dark and Rowland Grey, *W. S. Gilbert, His Life and Letters* (London, [1923]), p. 106; and Hesketh Pearson, *Gilbert and Sullivan* (New York, 1935), who writes (p. 189):

> Both Gilbert and Sullivan thought that *The Yeomen of the Guard* was their finest work together. The general public did not agree with them, and the general public was right. It is a serious opera, and owing to the restrained nature of their relationship, seriousness did not agree with them.

Harold Watkins Shaw's Grove 3 article on Sullivan (London, 1932–34, vol. 5, p. 189) reminds us that *Yeomen* "is understood to have been regarded by its composer and author as the best and most meritorious of the great series." In retrospect, "meritorious" has an ominous ring. Notwithstanding their satisfaction with *Yeomen*, Gilbert and Sullivan must have realized that their eleventh collaboration would not be as successful as they had hoped, for in their next joint effort, *The Gondoliers*, they returned to the familiar mixture of sense and nonsense to which the previous Savoy operas had owed their popularity.

Cellier and Bridgeman, obviously *Yeomen* fans, recall the initial euphoria (p. 258):

> By a select number of true cognoscenti, it [*Yeomen*] has been pronounced the best English light opera ever given to the stage. In the early days of its production it was universally predicted that "The Yeomen" would be living long after the more frivolous pieces of the Savoy répertoire were forgotten.

behind the combination of disparate elements. In the absence of such a reading—and, perhaps, as a means to arriving at one—Gilbert and Sullivan scholarship has sensibly sought insight into the considerations that induced composer and librettist to depart from what Reginald Allen has called "the tried and true formulas of topsy-turvydom."[8] There is general agreement that the mixed reception of *Yeomen*'s immediate predecessor, *Ruddigore*, may have convinced the collaborators that these formulas were becoming stale. Moreover, Sullivan had for some time been asking for a libretto that would provide more scope for his music. Five years and two operas before *Yeomen*, Sullivan had written to Gilbert explaining his position:

> I should like to set a story of human interest and probability, where the humorous words would come in a humorous (not serious) situation, and where, if the situation were a tender or dramatic one the words would be of a similar character. There would then be a feeling of reality about it which would give me fresh interest in writing, and fresh vitality to our joint work.[9]

Some indication of the qualities Gilbert and Sullivan may have sought to avoid in *Yeomen* may be provided by reviewing the criticism of earlier Savoy operas. We can identify several themes in such criticism. Perhaps the most recurrent objection—an objection voiced on occasion by Sullivan himself— was to the "topsy-turvydom" that was so essential an ingredient of Gilbert's libretti. In the Savoyard's lexicon, "topsy-turvydom" denotes the workings of the self-contained world in which Gilbert's libretti are set. Critics complained that Gilbert's topsy-turvydom produced "puppet shows" in which the characters are mere dolls put through mechanical demonstrations.[10] The artificiality of language and delivery upon which Gilbert, as director, insisted no doubt contributed to this effect. A second theme, related to the first, is that Gilbert's characters are unreal and inhuman. In fact, Gilbert's characters are probably no further removed from reality than those of any other Victorian playwright; what this objection means is simply that Gilbert does not employ any of the conventions that governed the delineation of characters in the "realistic" drama of his day.[11] A third theme is that Gilbert's humor is cruel, and

---

[8]*The First Night Gilbert and Sullivan*, p. 308.

[9]Letter of 2 April 1884, written from the Hotel Continental, Paris. New York, Pierpont Morgan Library, Gilbert and Sullivan Collection, MA 4106.096.01.

[10]In 1895, Bernard Shaw can be found describing a scene in Oscar Wilde's *The Importance of Being Earnest* as "quite in the literary style of Mr. Gilbert, and almost inhuman enough to have been conceived by him." (*Our Theatres in the '90s*, in the Standard Edition of Shaw's works [London, 1932], vol. 1, p. 42.) See also Sullivan's diary, 4 September 1887, where, dismissing a new plot proposed by Gilbert, he writes: "It is a 'puppet show,' and not human. It is impossible to feel sympathy with a single personage."

[11]On the conventions governing "realistic" portrayals of characters in Victorian drama—and on the "lines" that reduced such "realistic" characters to stock types—see Martin Meisel, *Shaw and the*

that, to use the description of an anonymous contemporary, Gilbert's work shows "coldness of temper, lack of sympathy, want of heart."[12] This objection amounts to the accusation that Gilbert not only fails to provide characters with attractive qualities that might enable us to identify with them, but that he includes in each of his *dramatis personae* a selection of repulsive or grotesque figures at whom we are invited to laugh. Most of the criticism of Sullivan can be reduced to the complaint that by providing music for Gilbert's libretti he was wasting energy and gifts that might better have been spent on more respectable music.[13]

Most of these objections have, of course, some basis in truth. Gilbert's libretti make no attempt to imitate the reality of everyday life, and his humor can without doubt be cruel. But these qualities form the basis of Gilbert's comic style. And that Gilbert's comic style, however cruel it may be, is nevertheless a valid comic style is demonstrated by the persistence with which his works have held the stage for more than a hundred years. As for Sullivan: it is, after all, one of the great ironies of Sir Arthur's career that his reputation today rests principally upon the comic operettas he grew to feel so uncomfortable writing.

But after the mixed reception of *Ruddigore*, we can understand that Gilbert might have decided to answer his critics by showing that he could also write a Savoy libretto that was set in a "real" world, and that was peopled with attractive characters whose predicaments he treated sympathetically. Although Gilbert is remembered primarily as a comic writer, he had had several serious plays produced, and we can understand his wishing to remind playgoers that he was not only a humorist but also a dramatist capable of appealing to his audience's sentiments. And we can see why Sullivan would have found in *Yeomen*'s story, which he described as "very human, and funny also,"[14] just the sort of libretto for which he had been asking.

To approach *Yeomen* from this point of view—to suggest the ways in which composer and librettist departed from the techniques they had employed in the other Savoy operas—should afford us insight not only into *Yeomen* but

---

Nineteenth-Century Theater (Princeton, 1963), pp. 18–37. The D'Oyly Carte company had actors some of whose lines differed from the usual ones, but there can be no question that "types" recur in one Savoy opera after another.

[12] "Mr. Gilbert as a Dramatist," an unsigned article in *The Theatre*, 26 June 1877. Reprinted in John Bush Jones, ed., *W. S. Gilbert: A Century of Scholarship* (New York, 1970), pp. 7–16, where the passage quoted occurs on p. 13.

[13] Such complaints became particularly frequent after Sullivan was knighted in 1883; for a sampling of the advice Sullivan received, see Christopher Hibbert, *Gilbert and Sullivan and Their Victorian World*, (New York, [1976]), pp. 166–68.

[14] Sullivan's diary, 25 December 1887.

also into the unique combination of qualities that have enabled the best of the other Savoy operas to entertain English-speaking audiences (and even non-English-speaking ones) for more than a century.

In the comic strategy of both Gilbert and Sullivan, parody plays an important part. Held up to genial ridicule are the themes and conventions of melodrama, verse tragedy, comic opera, and grand opera—as well as the exotic settings, occult effects, extravagant plots, and synthetic sentiments that were the stuff from which so many Victorian stage works were woven. Such dramatic and musico-dramatic types depend upon conventions of action, character, language, and music that are capable of inducing an emotionally heightened state but that, viewed in the cold light of reason, are often so artificial as to seem ludicrous. We can accept such conventions if we are prepared to enter into the state of mind described by Coleridge as "that willing suspension of disbelief for the moment, that constitutes poetic faith."[15] But this state of mind—and the heightened emotional state it may produce—can be sustained only as long as we are not reminded of the absurdity of the conventions. The technique employed by Gilbert and Sullivan is to call attention to these conventions, jarring us into awareness of their extravagance and causing us to laugh not only at the conventions themselves but at the social and moral values that works employing these conventions usually affirm. To accomplish their ends, composer and librettist keep us "detached" from both action and characters, appealing to our intellect rather than our emotions. Gilbert's contributions to this technique include the artificiality of his language, the outrageousness of his characters, and the improbability of his plots. And, just as Gilbert's libretti keep us at a distance, so does Sullivan's music, which either innocuously supports Gilbert's mischievous lyrics or comments ironically on the characters, events, and conventions that Gilbert so adroitly manipulates. Thus, instead of drawing us emotionally into the action, Sullivan's music—sometimes slightly inapposite, sometimes manifestly unsuitable, but usually self-conscious and witty—constantly reminds us that we are watching parody—and invites us to laugh at the conventions of which he is making fun. Our experience of the Savoy operas employing this technique is complex and intellectual: we simultaneously accept and laugh at the operations of the conventions parodied. We understand—in its own terms—what is happening onstage, but instead of becoming involved emotionally we remain intellectually alert, sensitive to the artificiality—and the silliness—of what we are seeing.

---

[15]*Biographia Literaria* (London, 1817), ch. 14. For a modern edition, see Samuel Taylor Coleridge, *Collected Works*, vol. 14, ed. James Engell and W. J. Bate (London and Princeton, [1983]), p. 6.

Perhaps the most important way that the libretto of *Yeomen* differs from the libretti of earlier Savoy operas is that it does not make use of parody. Although today *Yeomen*'s plot and characters may seem sufficiently strained to invite ridicule, it is clear that Gilbert intended the action of *Yeomen* to be taken seriously. (We know, for example, that on opening night there was concern that the audience would laugh at Phoebe's melancholy opening number, "When Maiden Loves," thereby compromising irreparably the serious tone so essential to the opera.[16]) Another respect in which *Yeomen* differs from earlier Savoy operas is that its plot is neither an invention of Gilbert's nor a parody of a familiar piece; it is, instead, an adaptation of another playwright's work, Adolphe-Philippe d'Ennery's *Don César de Bazan*.[17] It is tempting to speculate that what attracted Gilbert to this fable are the grotesque complications inherent in the predicament of a condemned man who marries a stranger in order to thwart his heirs and who then escapes execution. But even though there are grotesque possibilities in this situation, Gilbert is concerned with its emotional rather than its comic potential. Nevertheless, *Yeomen*'s claim to being an "entirely new departure" notwithstanding, its libretto shares many qualities of character and plot with Gilbert's other Savoy creations, and it conveys no less effectively the cynicism that marks almost all of Gilbert's dramatic output.

The characters with which Gilbert peoples the Savoy operas are on the whole a rather unappealing lot. They are, in the Aristotelian sense, "worse"[18] than we are: they are intended not to engage our sympathies but to keep us at a distance from which we may safely laugh at their failings without endangering our own self-esteem. Gilbert's comic characters are usually outlandish or grotesque; his heroes tend to be pompous and prissy, while most of his heroines are frankly self-centered. With few exceptions, Gilbert's characters display a limited range of motivation. Desire for wealth, for admiration, for social position—or, in moments of crisis, for personal safety—are the factors that usually move these figures; the frankness with which they admit their motives—or the transparency with which they seek to hide them—is an important element of Gilbert's comedy.

[16]*The Standard* (4 October 1888) observed that "it was not certain that spectators so used to finding fantastic drolleries hidden beneath apparently grave speeches would accept seriously what was meant to be serious, that, in fact, they would not laugh in the wrong place."

[17]Vincent Wallace had composed an opera, *Maritana*, produced in London in 1845, based on d'Ennery's play. David Eden observes that Gilbert also drew upon Harrison Ainsworth's 1840 novel, *The Tower of London*, (*Gilbert and Sullivan: the Creative Conflict* [Rutherford, NJ, (1986)], p. 113.)

[18]*Poetics*, [2], i.e., 1448[a] ff. in W. D. Lucas' edition (Oxford, 1968). Interpretation of the idea expressed in this chapter is controversial, but it seems likely that Aristotle distinguishes between tragedy, which depicts subjects morally better than we are, and comedy, which depicts people who are morally inferior.

In *Yeomen*, however, Gilbert gives us *dramatis personae* collectively more diverse and individually more complex than those of any other Savoy opera. To be sure, there are characters familiar from Gilbert's farce. We recognize in Wilfred Shadbolt, who boasts the typically Gilbertian title of "chief jailer and assistant tormentor," the unprincipled rogue with a frank interest in pain and suffering. The "mature" and somewhat forbidding Dame Carruthers is another character whom we have met elsewhere in the Savoy operas; she combines a morbid attachment to the Tower with an incongruous need to be loved. Like Wilfred, she is not above using blackmail to coerce affection.

But in *Yeomen*, such characters co-exist with others drawn straight from the romantic drama and the grand opera of the day. Even a secondary character such as the Lieutenant of the Tower is more complex than we would normally expect a Gilbertian character to be. Bound by duty to manage the execution of a brother officer whom he respects and likes, the Lieutenant moves through the action with a suitable mixture of military efficiency and gentlemanly regret.

The Merylls—father, daughter, and son—are also intended to be appealing. Sergeant Meryll is a soldier whose life has been saved in battle and who stands ready not only to acknowledge his gratitude but also—and, at considerable risk—to repay his debt. Phoebe, who loves Fairfax secretly and from afar, is prepared to help the Colonel escape—also at some risk to herself. And Leonard, a hero returning from the wars, offers his services to help his father and sister in their dangerous project.

Also unusual for a Savoy opera is Elsie Maynard, whom Gilbert has made suitably virtuous without being unattractively prudish. Gilbert has been careful to show that Elsie agrees to marry Fairfax because she needs money to help her mother, who is ill. Once married to Fairfax, Elsie honors her vows—even though she believes she has made a bad bargain.

Fairfax himself is a character who would be out of place in any other Savoy opera. He is almost unique among Gilbertian protagonists in being a military man who has demonstrated bravery in battle and who is sincerely admired by the men he has led. Bravery is a rare commodity in the Savoy operas, where commanders lead their regiments from behind, where privateers flee from the enemy at the first shot, and where major generals, learned in all branches of knowledge save military strategy, shamefully deny their parentage in order to save their lives. But Fairfax, atypically for a Gilbertian military man, displays a cavalier attitude towards death (cf. "Is Life a Boon?" Act 1, no. 4[19]).

---

[19]Quotations from and citations to the Savoy operas are taken from the respective first editions of the vocal scores—*Yeomen* (1887), *Pinafore* (1878), *Iolanthe* (1882), *Ruddigore* (1886)—all published in

The Lieutenant, the Merylls, Elsie, and Fairfax: these are characters with whom we can identify—whose emotions we are invited to share rather than to laugh at. Their function is quite different from that of the characters in the other Savoy Operas.

In Jack Point, the sad jester, Gilbert seems to have compressed into a single character the contradictions that create the tensions of genre in *Yeomen*.[20] On the one hand, Point is a figure straight from Gilbert's farce: a facile schemer, an unscrupulous fibber, a rascal with his eye perpetually on the main chance. He is neither professionally competent nor personally attractive. For all his pretensions, he is not an amusing jester nor is he an instructive philosopher. Moreover, he is callous and indelicate enough to make capital of the colonel's misfortune, and even though he "loves" Elsie, he does not object to her marrying Fairfax—provided that the fee be promptly paid. Normally, such a character would be an object of derision, a figure with whom we would certainly not wish to identify. But Gilbert asks us to sympathize with Point. He reminds us that even jesters can have personal tragedies and that even scoundrels, when disappointed in love, can suffer. True, such observations are not especially profound, but within the conventions of the relevant genres Gilbert's Point is unusual, and he evokes an uncharacteristically complex response, since neither in farce nor in romance do we expect to be asked to view the action from a rascal's point of view.

Although the plots Gilbert provided for the Savoy operas before *Yeomen* make no pretense of imitating "reality," we understand and accept them because they have an internal consistency that depends in part upon the conventions of plot and character they parody and in part upon the mechanical qualities that were both the delight and despair of Gilbert's audiences. Gilbert's plots presuppose a world in which self-interest is the principal moving force—and in which society functions smoothly (if not always equitably) as long as the operation of self-interest remains undisturbed. But if greed and vanity are the lodestars by which Gilbert's characters navigate, they can navigate intelligently only as long as every one acts strictly—and therefore

---

London. The plates of these vocal scores seem for the most part to reflect changes made during the first run; they were used for several issues each.

[20] Point is clearly one of the tragic clowns so popular in the nineteenth century; Rigoletto (1851) and Canio/Pagliaccio (1892) are perhaps the best known members of this tradition. A character who in a similar situation elicits a similar ambivalent response is Arnolphe in Molière's *L'École des femmes*; like Point, Arnolphe loses the young lady on whom he has set his heart to a young man who would make a more appropriate husband for her. Savoy folklore holds that Gilbert identified with Point (see, for example, Pearson, p. 181); Molière (who played Arnolphe himself) had actually married the young actress who played the girl he lost.

predictably—in accordance with his own best interests. When characters are distracted from the rational pursuit of self-interest, the complications that arise inevitably create difficulties that must be resolved if the world is to return to normal. Altruism—usually in the form of misguided but well-meant "reform"—is clearly a phenomenon capable of creating serious disruption in Gilbert's world. Thus, Alexis' use of the Sorcerer's love potion, Ida's retreat to the college of women, the Mikado's law against flirting, and King Paramount's plan to reform Utopia by importing British institutions bring chaos to communities that had previously been functioning without evidence of strain. Only when the schemes of such reformers have been defeated can normality return. But the rational pursuit of self-interest can also be subverted by the inexplicable emotion that Gilbert's characters imagine to be love. Sir Joseph's desire to marry Josephine upsets the otherwise efficient functioning of the Royal Navy; Iolanthe's marriage to the Lord Chancellor threatens to have dire consequences for the institution of Parliament. Fortunately, love rarely triumphs more than temporarily over self-interest. Yum-Yum may love Nanki-Poo, but she is not prepared to be buried alive with him; Sir Joseph reminds the quondam Captain Corcoran-Rackstraw that love levels ranks only to a certain extent; Ko-Ko may adore Yum-Yum with passion tender, but he adores himself with passion tenderer still.

In Gilbert's plots, the complications presented by such departures from rational behavior create obstacles to the marriage of one or more couples. The action of each opera is concerned with the ways in which the characters seek to overcome these obstacles, thereby making possible the marriages with which all comic operas should properly conclude. In the end, however, these obstacles can be overcome only by the application of the curious sort of logic that obtains in Gilbert's topsy-turvy world. Gilbert usually manages his denouements by extending to their literal and logical—albeit ludicrous—conclusions the premises which have caused the complications in the first place. Thus, although the denouements in Gilbert may seem slap-dash—achieved through theatrical devices such as misplaced babies (*Pinafore, Gondoliers*), by the application of sophistry (*Mikado, Ruddigore*), or by the invocation of social privilege (*Pirates, Iolanthe*), these endings are nevertheless logical, given the initial premises from which the action proceeds. If the Mikado's power is such that he can put an end to flirting simply by decree, then his mere order to arrange an execution must be of such force and effect that one might as well consider the execution accomplished. If adopting British institutions has brought such prosperity to Utopia that it is on the brink of ruin, then the country can be saved by adopting yet one more British institution—the two-party system. If society really places as much importance on who one's parents are as creates the complications in *Pinafore* and *Gondoliers*, then it follows that when the true facts of parentage are discovered, all other considerations can be thrown aside. Denouements effected on pretexts such as these may not be what we expect to find in traditional drama; they would certainly leave us angry and frustrated were the conventions invoked "realistic" ones or were we emotionally involved in the action. But Gilbert's comedy has nothing to do with either emotional involvement or realism, and so within its unique set of conventions such endings seem perfectly appropriate.

In *Yeomen*, however, Gilbert's plot is intended to obtain another sort of effect. *Yeomen* is unique among the Savoy operas in having a plot structured along the lines of the *pièce bien faite*.[21] In accordance with the formula developed by Eugène Scribe and refined by such playwrights as Alexandre Dumas, *fils* and Émile Augier, there is a secret known to the audience but withheld from some of the characters: in *Yeomen*, the secret is that Sergeant Meryll and his daughter have helped Fairfax to escape and have disguised him as Leonard Meryll. The action proceeds by a series of reversals—Fairfax's last-minute escape, its discovery, and the tale of cock-and-bull—to the *scène à faire*—here the finale (Act 2, no. 10), in which the truth about the Colonel's escape and disguise is revealed, to the discomfiture of Point and the joy of Elsie.

Gilbert invests this boulevard-comedy structure with content rather more serious than that of his other Savoy libretti. The action of *Yeomen* proceeds from the greed of the Colonel's kinsman, who has caused Fairfax to be condemned to death. When we move from a premise in which well-meaning or lovesick characters create comic obstacles to one in which greed is being satisfied at the cost of human life, we have left the domain of farce. Moreover, the plot of *Yeomen* is moved along not only by the self-interested machinations of Wilfred and Point, but also by the generosity of the Merylls—father, daughter, and son. And the "happy ending"—at least for Elsie and Fairfax—is made possible not by a sophistic quibble or an *infans ex machina* but by the sacrifices of Phoebe and Sergeant Meryll, who must marry to buy silence.

Notwithstanding their manifest absurdity and their polished humor, the vision conveyed by Gilbert's libretti is one of uncompromising cynicism. To be sure, Gilbert provides "happy" endings: obstacles are overcome, and couples are married. But the improbable means by which these obstacles are overcome and the careless manner in which many of the marriages are arranged—although outrageous and delightful—prevent our accepting them at face value. We can, of course, regard such endings as satiric thrusts at the conventions of the drama and opera that the Savoy operas parody; we can read Gilbert's endings as ironic reminders of how infrequently such happy endings occur in real life. Or, we may go a step further: Gilbert shows us the comical

---

[21]On the *pièce bien faite*, see Stephen S. Stanton, "Eugène Scribe and Victorien Sardou: The Technique of the Well-Made Play," *Camille and Other Plays* (New York, 1957), pp. xi–xxv.

results of taking literally the ideals that society professes. Ought we therefore to infer that society as we know it survives only because in real life its members pay these ideals not the slightest regard?

In *Yeomen* Gilbert qualifies his cynicism by showing us unselfishness that is not absurd. But if there are in *Yeomen* characters who are loyal, generous, and honorable, they, like other Gilbertian characters, inhabit a world in which self-interest remains the controlling force. In such a world, the happiness of attractive characters must be purchased at the cost of suffering: in this case, the marriage of Fairfax and Elsie is made possible by the sacrifice of the Merylls. The bittersweet finale of *Yeomen*, so disquieting in its refusal to adhere to the tenets of poetic justice, underlines this fact. Fairfax and Elsie are properly united; through a variety of testing procedures, they have shown that, notwithstanding the accidents that have brought them together, they are in fact well suited to each other. And the rejection of the selfish Point, the schemer who is singularly unfit to be Elsie's husband, is likewise appropriate. Such a ringing affirmation of traditional values should close the play on a positive note. But the Merylls, father and daughter, are also to marry, and their marriages will be unions of form only. Both will take their vows under duress; both will be wed to spouses for whom they have entertained understandable loathing and whose attentions they have long sought to escape; and both have employed the same phrase to point up the difference between giving one's heart and giving one's hand. If the marriage of Fairfax and Elsie promises to be all that a marriage should be, the Merylls' marriages promise to be considerably less.

In the end, then, Gilbert's *Yeomen* libretto is no less satirical than his other Savoy libretti, and the world of *Yeomen* is really no different from the world of the other Savoy operas. It is a world peopled by such self-centered rogues as Wilfred, Point, and the Colonel's greedy kinsman. In *Yeomen*, however, we also encounter bravery, generosity, and fidelity. But so rare are these qualities—or so much influence do the self-interested wield over the workings of this world—that only through a combination of accident and sacrifice can the brave, the generous, and the honorable ever hope to enjoy the happiness that comic literature keeps insisting should be their reward. This is rather a dark view, and, in its balance, in its considered qualification, it may well be a more unsettling view than the cynical vision that sees life in uncompromisingly—and therefore unrealistically—bleak terms.

Like Gilbert's libretto, the music Sullivan provided for *Yeomen* is both similar to and different from the music of earlier Savoy Operas. In *Yeomen*, we find the same charming melodies, the same interest in harmony and counterpoint, and the same musical intelligence that we have encountered in Sullivan's other Savoy scores. In *Yeomen*, however, Sullivan is concerned with sentiment rather than satire, and this involves a fundamental redefinition of the relationship between music and libretto that had obtained in previous Savoy operas.

In the Savoy operas before *Yeomen*, Sullivan had provided a musical complement for Gilbert's literary parody, inverting the relationship between music and libretto that is normally understood to obtain in musico-dramatic works. Traditionally, of course, the function of music in such works is to intensify the expression of the emotions felt by the characters and implied by the situations dramatized. Music's ability to do this depends in large part upon conventions, e.g., the association of "minor" with sadness, of increasing tempo with agitation, of modulation with change of mind or emotional state. The humor in Sullivan's music lies in the discrepancy between what these conventions lead us to consider musically appropriate in any particular situation and what Sullivan offers us instead. When music satisfies our expectations, we accept it almost without thinking, allowing it to induce the state of mind that the relevant convention dictates; in such cases, our response is naive—i.e., unself-conscious—and we experience the music as music. But when music does not seem appropriate, we are jarred into awareness of these conventions, and we compare what we hear to what we were expecting to hear; in such cases, our response is intellectual, and we respond to the music not simply as music but as commentary on conventions that upon reflection may strike us as stale or silly. Not all of the music that Sullivan wrote for the earlier Savoy operas is satirical in this sense: there are charming solos and delightful ensembles with musical interest sufficient to hold our attention and command our respect; there are also comic songs in which music is perfectly suited to text. But in most Savoy operas, musical satire occurs with sufficient frequency and at sufficiently important moments to influence our perception of entire works—to keep us intellectually alert and to inhibit that "willing suspension of disbelief" that is necessary for us to become emotionally involved in the action of the opera.

The contribution of Sullivan's musical satire to the impact of the Savoy operas had been recognized quite early in his collaboration with Gilbert: reviewing *Pinafore*, the *Times* critic had remarked that the composer "loses no opportunity to emphasize comic points or to indicate hidden irony by a slight touch of exaggeration. A very sophisticated audience might accept, for instance, Ralph's ballad, 'A Maiden Fair to See,' as the real sentiment of which it is an admirable caricature."[22] But the same critic was also aware that writing such musical satire for Gilbertian puppet shows deprived Sullivan of the opportunity to write the more serious—i.e., emotion-enhancing—music expected of a composer of his stature; reviewing *Pirates*, he argued:

[22] 27 May 1878.

Music is fully able to deal with broadly comic phases of human life, but Mr. Gilbert's characters are not comic in themselves, but only in reference to other characters chiefly of the operatic type, whose exaggerated attitude and parlance they mimic. He writes, in fact, not comedies but parodies, and the music has accordingly to follow him to the sphere of all others most uncongenial to it—the mock-heroic. The skill and ingenuity evinced by Mr. Sullivan in such disadvantageous circumstances cannot be sufficiently admired. His tunes are always fresh and lively, and the few opportunities of genuine sentimental utterance offered to him are turned to excellent account.[23]

For some time before Gilbert proposed the *Yeomen* libretto, Sullivan had been asking that his collaborator provide him with just such opportunities. After the production of *Princess Ida*, he wrote to Gilbert:

With "Princess Ida" I have come to . . . the end of my capability in that class of piece. . . . I am continually keeping the music down. . . . And this very suppression is most difficult, most fatiguing, and I may say most disheartening, for the music is never allowed to rise and speak for itself. I want a chance for the music to act in its own proper sphere. To intensify the emotional element not only of the actual words, but of the situation.[24]

Gilbert's *Yeomen* libretto clearly promised the opportunity of genuine sentimental utterance for which Sullivan had been asking. In preparing the *Yeomen* score, the composer abandoned the musical satire that was so essential an element of his previous Savoy operas, since such satire would undercut the sentimental potential of the libretto. Beyond this, however, Sullivan's transition from the satirical to the sentimental seems in many respects mechanical: in *Yeomen* he is often content to adapt for sentimental affects many of the devices he had used for comic ones in previous Savoy operas, playing for pathos at moments when he would formerly have played for laughs. We can observe this strategy in operation in Sullivan's handling of brief phrases, in his treatment of entire numbers, and in his management of larger dramatic units.

In the earlier Savoy operas, Sullivan had usually found the clichés of word-painting good for a laugh. A bit of comic exaggeration or an overly obvious suiting of music to words: such touches called attention to themselves—and brought smiles to the faces of knowledgeable audiences. But in *Yeomen* Sullivan "plays it straight" with the very conventions he had formerly satirized. The "Tower Song" ("When Our Gallant Norman Foes," Act 1, no. 3) provides an example of the care with which Sullivan tries to convey the emotional content of Gilbert's text. In this number, Gilbert is

---

[23] 5 April 1880.
[24] Letter of 2 April 1884, cited in fn. 9 above.

concerned with the thesis that in order to serve England, the Tower—and its warders—must be indifferent to human suffering. Gilbert sums up this idea in the refrain:

> The screw may twist and the rack may turn,
> And men may bleed and men may burn,
> O'er London town and its golden hoard
> I keep my silent watch and ward!
> (mm. 26 ff.)

For an opera, this is a grotesque passage, a sort of librettist's sick joke. Music is normally not required to deal in the abstract with instruments of torture. In earlier Savoy operas, Sullivan might have set the words "screw" and "rack" with exaggerated dissonance, undercutting by comic means any visceral response the reference to these instruments might elicit. In *Yeomen*, however, Sullivan catches the emotional potential of the refain by setting not the individual words but rather the idea underlying the refrain—the indifference of the Tower and warders to the pain of the men and women committed to them. Sullivan sets the first two lines almost as monotone, with a relentless beat over a pedal point accompaniment (he breaks this pattern for the last two lines). The dull, insensible, relentless quality of Sullivan's music conveys effectively the idea that no matter how much people may suffer, the Tower of London continues unmoved.

Another satiric device that Sullivan adapts in *Yeomen* for sentimental purposes is his burlesque use of familiar musical types and styles. In previous Savoy operas, Sullivan had often employed musical types and styles having specific associations to set texts that undercut the values with which these types and styles were usually associated. The lively sea-ballad usually tells a tale of daring seamanship and bravery in battle, but in *Ruddigore* Sullivan uses Richard Dauntless' ballad "I Shipped, D'ye See, in a Revenue Sloop" (Act 1, no. [6]) for a narrative of cowardice and hypocrisy. Music of pomp and patriotism, at which Sullivan excels, often serves in Savoy operas to set trivial or degrading texts. The entrance march of the Peers in *Iolanthe* ("Bow, Bow, Ye Lower Middle Classes," Act 1, no. 6) satirizes the British preoccupation with birth and titles. And in the same opera the grand, patriotic roll of the chorus "When Britain Really Ruled the Waves" (Act 2, no. 3) promises that the glory of England will continue if not forever then at least as long as

> the House of Peers withholds
> Its legislative hand,
> And noble statesmen do not itch
> To interfere with matters which
> They do not understand. . . .

In *Yeomen*, however, there is no such discrepancy; quite the reverse, text and music are invariably appropriate to each other, and Sullivan loses no opportunity to emphasize sentimental qualities in the text. The entrance march of the Yeomen ("Tower Warders," Act 1, no. 2) is typical of Sullivan's martial music—in this case a brisk "cut time" meter; a strong, regular beat; a melody in which arpeggios figure prominently; and a simple harmony. But there is nothing tongue-in-cheek about this number: we are meant to accept these guardsmen as worthy soldiers. Indeed, there is a heroically pathetic quality in these aging warders who look back to their bygone days of daring while serving in the relatively undemanding post of yeomen of the Tower guard. Sullivan sets the lines "In the evening of our day / With the sun of life declining" (mm. 36–40) to diatonically descending phrases, and there does not seem anything comically self-conscious in Sullivan's use of this device. Sullivan even gives a sentimental setting to the Yeomen's nostalgic boast:

> But our year is not so spent,
> And our days are not so faded,
> But that we with one consent,
> Were our loved land invaded,
> Still would face a foreign foe. . . .
>   (mm. 78 ff.)

This is one of those passages that hover between the pathetic and the ludicrous. It is essential to the opera that the yeomen be perceived as sentimental figures, and Sullivan's music rescues these lines from the laughter that would destroy the delicate mood.

As early as the Judge's Song in *Trial by Jury* (no. 4), Sullivan had devised techniques for setting Gilbert's patter-song texts, and in *Yeomen* these techniques are used in the service of sentiment. The texts of Gilbert's patter-songs are formally quite simple: they depend upon their strophic structure, their regular (if sometimes intricate) meter, and their simple rhyme schemes to prepare the malicious couplet with which each stanza concludes. Sullivan's settings, declamatory in style, with basic harmonies and strong impulse towards final cadences, set up Gilbert's punch-lines: the combination of rhyme, meter, and harmony, all driving towards closure, fixes our attention on formal elements, so that the malicious content of the concluding couplet sneaks up on us, surprising but inevitable. In Point's patter-song "A Private Buffoon" (Act 2, no. 2), Sullivan uses the same techniques to set up punch-lines that are pathetic rather than satirical. In the Judge's Song or Sir Joseph's "When I Was a Lad" (*Pinafore*, Act 1, no. 9), the singers are comic figures at whom we laugh because they tell us outrageous things about themselves without betraying the slightest embarrassment. Point, however, asks for our pity; his song combines bitterness and pathos, and we are meant to sympathize with him. "A Private Buffoon" is a series of complaints about Point's employers, who insist that he amuse them, regardless of how wretched he may feel at the moment or how deficient their senses of humor may be. Each stanza is a variation on this theme, and each concludes with a punch-line that stresses the difficulty of Point's situation, e.g.:

> Tho' your wife ran away with a soldier that day,
> And took with her your trifle of money;
> Bless your heart, they don't mind—they're exceedingly kind—
> They don't blame you—as long as you're funny!
> (mm. 18 ff.)

In the comic strophic ensembles Sullivan had written for earlier Savoy operas, musical settings of successive stanzas are not normally differentiated. "Here's a How-de-do" (*Mikado*, Act 2, no. 4), for example, offers three parallel comic responses to a single situation. In *Yeomen*, however, Sullivan uses strophic structure to emphasize parallelisms that heighten the contrast of opposing emotional states. "When a Wooer Goes a-Wooing" (*Yeomen*, Act 2, no. 8) is a quartet consisting of three verses that are structurally parallel but dissimilar in textual content, melody, and harmony. The first verse, sung by Elsie and Fairfax, expresses the joy of happy lovers: it is written in D-flat major, and its melody is a sequence of ascending scales (expressive of happiness). After the refrain (sung by all four characters), the signature changes to four sharps, and the second verse, sung by Phoebe, is set as a series of descending diatonic passages. The third verse, sung by Point, repeats the first two phrases of the first verse (but a fifth lower, in G-flat major), and then sets the next two lines, "Food for fishes only fitted, / Jester wishes he was dead," to a descending chromatic scale. The chorus is then sung twice, the first time in D-flat major, the second time shifted for the first three phrases to G-flat major and for the last phrase to G-flat minor (with a B-double-flat, used in the pivot chord by which Sullivan regains D-flat major) to emphasize Point's pain. Clearly, Sullivan is intent upon extracting every bit of pathos that the plights of Phoebe and Point are capable of generating.

In the Savoy operas before *Yeomen*, Sullivan's large-scale planning had been concerned primarily with comic matters—with the pacing and arrangement of numbers, and with devices such as running gags (e.g., the bridesmaids in *Ruddigore*). In *Yeomen*, where Sullivan wants a sentimental affect, he manages larger units so as to create and sustain tension or to heighten the emotional impact of sudden reversals of fortune.

In the earlier Savoy operas, much depends upon the relationship between the first and second act finales. Normally, the first act finale brings the curtain down on a comic crisis that will be resolved by the time the final curtain descends. In works such as *Iolanthe* and *The Mikado*, the first act finales consist of series of mildly contrasted numbers ending in ensembles of comic frenzy. In *Yeomen*, however, a more serious first act finale is needed, and Sullivan creates one by compressing into a few minutes pieces alternating between sharply opposed emotional states. The finale (no. 12) begins with the introduction of Fairfax (disguised as Leonard) to the warders; it proceeds through the comic song (laced with dramatic irony) in which Wilfred confides Phoebe to Fairfax's care; then comes the solemn march as preparations are made for the prisoner's execution. Comic confusion attends the discovery that Fairfax has escaped, but the comic mood is dissipated by the Lieutenant's ominous proclamation:

> A thousand marks to him I hand
> Who brings him here alive or dead.

The curtain descends on the Lieutenant, Point, and Elsie each responding to Fairfax's escape in a different way, but the last word that each sings—the word into which the confusion resolves and the word upon which the curtain falls—is "dead."[25]

The grand finale of *Yeomen* marks an important departure from Sullivan's usual Savoy practice. In pieces such as *Iolanthe*, *Mikado*, and *Ruddigore*, where the happy ending is effected by a bit of sophistry, the reversals that avert impending disaster are given in prose dialogue, and the celebratory finales whip up afterwards to bring the curtain down. These finales are sometimes so obviously nothing but matters of formal closure that they must be taken ironically. In *Yeomen*, however, the finale is entirely without dialogue, so that the emotional content of the whole unit is traced by the music.

Yeomen's grand finale (Act 2, no. 10) is structured upon a series of reversals culminating in the *scène à faire*, in which Elsie realizes that Fairfax is not only the man to whom she is married, but, happily, the man with whom she has fallen in love. In Aristotelian terms, this is a scene in which emotion is generated by the reversal of Elsie's fortune (*peripeteia*) as she realizes in a scene of recognition (*anagnorisis*) that Fairfax and her Leonard are in fact one. The emotional progress of the scene is marked by changes in key signature that divide the finale into units; each signature represents not necessarily the tonality in which most of the unit is written, or even the tonality in which it ends, but rather the tonality that Sullivan evidently considered the most important for that unit.

[25] Printed libretti in the Gilbert and Sullivan Collection of the Pierpont Morgan Library indicate that no earlier than 1911 the final verse was changed, so that instead of responding each in his own way, the three characters—the Lieutenant, Point, and Elsie—all sing the lines originally sung by the Lieutenant only.

As the finale opens, Elsie, believing Fairfax dead, is about to marry the man she knows as Leonard Meryll. The scene begins with a passage in F major as the bridesmaids discourse on wifely duties; there follows Elsie's song, also in F, three-quarter time, "With Happiness My Soul Is Cloyed." The first reversal is signaled by a change of signature to C major, as the Lieutenant enters to announce that Fairfax is alive. The surprise and consternation of all concerned are expressed by a series of unstable harmonies over a bass that conveys increasing tension as it moves upwards chromatically from C to E-flat. The signature darkens to C-minor, as Fairfax steps forward to claim his bride. Elsie pleads; Fairfax professes himself unmoved. Now the signature changes to five flats; Elsie affirms her undying love for Leonard; impending hysteria is suggested as a pedal-point A-flat gives way to a chomatically ascending accompaniment, which eventually arrives at D-flat. The final reversal of fortune is signaled by a change of signature to the distant (and brighter) key of A major; this unit, eight measures long, is the shortest unit in the finale. Summoning her courage, Elsie resolves to accept Fairfax ("Sir, I obey! I am thy bride!") The signature now changes to D, as a diminished seventh chord on B-sharp holds us in suspense until Elsie recognizes Fairfax ("Leonard! My own!"). The diminished fifth B-sharp–F-sharp resolves to the third and fifth of an A major triad, and Elsie repeats (this time in A Major and in common time) "With happiness my soul is cloyed."

This second statement of the lines "With happiness my soul is cloyed" should announce the happy ending of the opera. But in *Yeomen*, since pathos is desired, the happy ending is qualified, and at this critical moment attention is directed to the disappointment of Point. Plaintively, he repeats the first verse of "I Have a Song to Sing, O," the piece that he and Elsie had performed in the first act as "The Singing Farce of the Merryman and His Maid" (no. 7). The song tells the story of a merryman who loves a maid, even though the maid loves a noble lord. When the lord rejects her, the maid accepts the merryman, and the two presumably live happily ever after. The narrative is conveyed by four strophes, which are built up by the process of incremental repetition. Each strophe (except the first) repeats the preceding one, and adds a new line recounting a new development in the story. Each new line is set to a new phrase of music, so that each event in the narrative is associated with a specific musical phrase. This is the final strophe (which incorporates the events recounted in the three preceding strophes):

> It's the song of a merrymaid, once so gay,
> Who turned on her heel and tripp'd away
> From the peacock popinjay, bravely born,
> Who turned up his noble nose with scorn
> At the humble heart that he did not prize;
> So she begged on her knees, with downcast eyes,

For the love of the merryman, moping mum,
Whose soul was sad and whose glance was glum,
Who sipped no sup, and who craved no crumb,
As he sighed for the love of a ladye [i.e, the maid].

In the finale, however, when Elsie rejects Point, she does so with the same phrase of music that had previously been associated with the noble lord's rejection of the maid. By this means, Sullivan applies to the jester's disappointment the pathos evoked by the noble lord's callous indifference. As Gilbert originally conceived it, there is a heartless quality in Elsie's treatment of Point, and Sullivan's juggling of musical phrases catches this.[26]

In *Yeomen*, Sullivan's concern with realizing the emotional potential of Gilbert's libretto produced a score more varied and richer than any he had written for a previous Savoy opera. Nor should this be surprising: the comic music he had composed for the satirical Savoy operas did not allow him the variety of pace or the complexity of harmony and orchestral texture that Gilbert's *Yeomen* libretto permitted. The unique qualities of *Yeomen*'s score, however, are probably to be found not in Sullivan's skillful handling of conventional devices but rather in the way his music reflects *Yeomen*'s ambiguous tone ("is it comedy or tragedy?"). Sullivan casts most of the music of *Yeomen* in major keys, but nevertheless contrives to convey the sense of melancholy we associate with minor. "I Have a Song to Sing, O," no doubt the best known piece in *Yeomen*, is remarkable for its ambivalence of mood, for the same music is made to set both a happy farce (in the first act) and a painful rejection (in the finale). The words "I have a song to sing, O" are sung to a D major triad, and the refrain "Heigh-dy! Heigh-dy! Misery me" is set to a descending D major scale, yet this piece, so firmly anchored in D major, has a sad and haunting quality.[27] Sullivan undercuts the "major" feeling by slowing the tempo, by employing a drone accompaniment, and by stressing the

---

[26]Originally, Gilbert had Elsie sing:

It's the song of a merrymaid, peerly proud,
Who loved a lord, and who laughed aloud
At the moan of the merryman. . . .

These lines are now performed:

It's the song of a merrymaid, nestling near,
Who lov'd her lord, but who dropped a tear
At the moan of the merryman. . . .

This alteration was effected during the confusion that had begun to surround Point's character—does he die, or has he only fainted?—during the 1897 revival. The change makes Elsie less heartless, but it gives Point less cause to be sorrowful; Point's position is far more pathetic if Elsie rejects him—as she does in the original version—without a second thought.

[27]We should recall that the melody of "I Have a Song to Sing, O" is not altogether Sullivan's invention.

depressingly repetitive structure imposed by incremental repetition. By such means Sullivan keeps his music hovering between the comic and the melancholy in a way quite different from what he has done in other Savoy scores.

But even though *Yeomen*'s music is richer, its harmonies fuller, and its emotional range broader, we somehow experience Sullivan's score as more naive, less complex than those of other Savoy operas. In part, this is because the music lacks the satirical element that is so much a part of the other Savoy operas. Our response to *Ruddigore* and its predecessors is complex, intellectual, and self-conscious; in *Yeomen*, however, Sullivan asks that our participation be naive, that we accept and respond to conventions for arousing our emotions. This is a fundamental departure from previous Savoy practice, and its novelty within the Gilbert and Sullivan canon explains why audiences approaching *Yeomen* with expectations formed by other Savoy operas have often found themselves confused. But in order to compensate for the absence of the complex intellectual response that we have come to expect from Savoy scores, Sullivan would have had to create for *Yeomen* a score of considerable emotional power. We do not know whether Sullivan was capable of creating such a score, but in *Yeomen* he does not dwell at any length upon strong emotions. *Yeomen* is punctuated by occasional emotional outbursts—e.g., Point's realization in the first-act finale that he has lost Elsie, or Elsie's anguish in the grand finale when she learns that Fairfax is alive—but such passages are of short duration. Sullivan seems unwilling to develop in depth such emotional crises; instead, he gives us "serious" numbers such as Fairfax's formal meditation on death, "Is Life a Boon?" (Act 1, no. 5); Phoebe's conventional expression of lover's melancholy, "When Maiden Loves" (Act 1, no. 1); or Fairfax's paradoxical ballad, "Free From His Fetters Grim" (Act 2, no. 4). Sullivan clearly understood that the display of strong emotion—as opposed to sentiment—would have been singularly unsuitable for the sort of work that he was trying to compose in *Yeomen*. The English comic opera towards which Sullivan was striving—and which he and his admirers believed he had succeeded in creating—was a comfortable entertainment that dealt in neither grand passion nor tragic agony but in sentiment—conventional emotion called forth by conventional dramatic situations. If we seek in *Yeomen* musical qualities such as we find in the grand opera then being written in Germany and Italy, we will be disappointed. Sullivan was not aiming for such emotion, and, truth to tell, even those Victorian audiences able to accept the

---

When Gilbert composed the words, he had in mind a a sea-chanty he had heard sung by the sailors aboard his yacht; when Sullivan had difficulty setting Gilbert's words, he asked Gilbert if he had had any melody in mind when he wrote them, and Gilbert provided the chanty. The chanty is in turn derived from a Welsh melody. The story of how Sullivan set this piece is told by Dark and Grey, pp. 107–8, and Pearson, pp. 185–86, among others.

works of Verdi or Wagner would probably have been embarrassed should an English composer have offered them the same fare.

Today, we see *Yeomen* in the context of the dozen other Savoy operas for which both words and music have survived. But we are likely to forget that *Yeomen*'s original audience would have seen it in terms not only of other Gilbert and Sullivan collaborations but of scores of Victorian musico-dramatic works the titles of which figure only in dusty archives and ambitious histories of the nineteenth-century English stage. When it was first produced, *Yeomen* must have seemed a refreshing change not only from Gilbert and Sullivan's previous collaborations but also from the works offered by other purveyors of comic opera. If *Yeomen* is not among the most popular of the Savoy operas today, it is probably because it does not make the best of those talents that have endeared Gilbert and Sullivan to admirers of such works as *Mikado*, *Pinafore*, *Pirates*, and *Gondoliers*.

Gilbert's genius was for satire rather than sentiment, and the attraction of his libretti lies not only in the cleverness of his language and the ingenuity of his plots but also in the truly malicious humor that these convey. In *Yeomen*, however, Gilbert makes his points not with satiric humor but by inducing us to make an emotional investment in his characters and their fortunes. We can rejoice at the happiness of Fairfax and Elsie, but we must then sympathize with what awaits Sergeant Meryll and Phoebe. We understand that the comic form of *Yeomen*—the marriage of its "hero" and "heroine"—is telling us that the ending is a happy one, but our emotions belie this impression. This tension between comic form and melancholic content is one of the disquieting—and effective—ways in which *Yeomen* conveys Gilbert's cynical vision. On the other hand, *Yeomen* was for its day an ideal comic opera libretto: it has enough sentiment mixed with enough humor to qualify as comic opera, yet it has a darkness of vision that sets it apart from other specimens of its genre. If *Yeomen* is not the masterful blend of sense and nonsense for which the other Savoy operas are so admired, it nevertheless depends upon a delicate balance of sentiment and cynicism that is no less difficult to achieve.

Like Gilbert, Sullivan displayed in *Yeomen* gifts that were more valued in his own day than in ours. There is a characteristically Victorian quality in Sullivan's restraint; we are assured that he will do nothing indecorous, that his music will be as suitable—perhaps even more suitable—for the drawing room as for the Savoy stage. It is also likely that *Yeomen*, with its Tudor setting and its passages in what passed for Elizabethan style, pleased critics who were looking for a distinctly English musico-dramatic form—something that was refined (i.e., unemotional) and that drew on English musical traditions. We may recall that *The Daily Telegraph* praised *Yeomen* as "a genuine English opera." *The Daily News* called it "a work of which lovers of true

English music have good reason to be proud,"[28] and the *Era* announced that in *Yeomen* Gilbert and Sullivan "approached more closely than they have done before the old school of English opera."[29] In retrospect, it seems likely that such critics' enthusiasm owed as much to their hopes and expectations as to the merits of *Yeomen* or to the viability of a genre such as *Yeomen* seemed to prophesy. The limitations imposed by the sort of comic opera that Sullivan was hailed for attempting were simply too many and too restrictive. Sullivan was probably right in thinking that he had succeeded in what he set out to do, but to us today he seems to have been trapped by the very conventions of music, drama, and thought he had previously so successfully satirized.

If, by some quirk of fate, all the Savoy operas save *Yeomen* had been lost, it seems likely that we would see "The Merryman and His Maid" as merely another Victorian comic opera—with all the naive charm and all the short-comings of the type. No other example of the type has attracted the attention of modern audiences. Nor is this surprising, since Victorian comic opera neither in its music nor in its libretti sought to overcome the clichés of its day. Although trapped by the conventions of its type, *Yeomen*, in its way, comes as close as any Victorian comic opera to overcoming them. But the verdict of posterity seems to be that it has fallen short—perhaps because it asks us to respond emotionally to characters and situations that today seem superficial and irrelevant, and perhaps because its tragicomic form evades the serious and "timeless" issues that are supposed to arouse real emotions. Can we blame Gilbert and Sullivan for failing to transcend such limitations in *Yeomen*? After all, genius is expected to transcend or reshape the conventions of its day. But in the earlier Savoy operas, Gilbert and Sullivan *had* transcended these limitations—albeit in a comic way. It is no doubt unrealistic—and unfair—for us to expect them to find a second way to do so.

[28] 4 October 1888.

[29] 6 October 1888. On the English qualities of *Yeomen*, see Arthur Jacobs, *Arthur Sullivan, A Victorian Musician* (Oxford and New York, 1984), p. 275.

Tone, Style, and Form in Prokofiev's Soviet Operas: Some Preliminary Observations

Richard Taruskin

I

When Prokofiev returned to Russia, he never imagined that he was turning his back irrevocably on the West. A world-famous composer and pianist, he foresaw only the continuation of a brilliant international career. Although Soviet historiography dates his return to the year 1932, Prokofiev maintained an apartment in Paris until 1936. In 1938 he made a lengthy concert tour of Western Europe and the United States, and planned another for 1940.

Then, on 23 August 1939, the curtain fell. With the signing of the Ribbentrop pact, the Soviet Union and Nazi Germany became (in a popular phrase of the time) "sworn friends,"[1] and cultural intercourse between Russia and Western Europe came to a virtual standstill. The Pact gave way to the so-called "Great Patriotic War" in 1941, and the Patriotic War, in turn, to the Cold War. Prokofiev spent his last fifteen years in isolation.

The period of Prokofiev's residence in the Soviet Union was, moreover, a time of especially hard-line esthetic policy. In 1932, the very year Prokofiev first took up part-time residence in his Soviet homeland, a sweeping reorganization of the country's cultural life took place. All existing literary and artistic organizations were liquidated and replaced by the Writers', Artists', and Composers' Unions, bodies overseen by and directly answerable to the Communist Party.[2] Party controls were asserted gradually but inexorably, and finally clamped tight around music, and opera in particular, with the publication of the famous *Pravda* editorial of 28 January 1936—"Confusion in Place of Music," an attack on Shostakovich's *Lady Macbeth of the Mtsensk District*. In this diatribe against modernism, which dates from Prokofiev's first year of

---

[1] See Valentin Kataev's extraordinarily frank remarks to Ludmila Skorino on his collaboration with Prokofiev on *Semyon Kotko*, in L. Skorino, *Pisatel' i ego vremia* (Moscow, 1965), p. 307. Translations from Russian sources, unless otherwise attributed, are mine.

[2] For an excellent account of this period, see chapter 6 of Boris Schwarz, *Music and Musical Life in Soviet Russia, 1917–1970* (New York, 1972).

full-time residence in the USSR, the approved style for Soviet opera was for the first time identified with the "classical traditions" of nineteenth-century Russian music. Quasi-Tolstoyan ideals of simplicity and universal accessibility were asserted and held up as an enforceable requirement, and traditional Russian xenophobia was brought into play in condemnation of composers and operas that enjoyed favor with "bourgeois audiences" abroad.[3]

Well, at least Prokofiev had not been guilty of this last. In fact, with the exception only of *The Love for Three Oranges*—which enjoyed favor not only abroad but in the Soviet Union too during the NEP period—his operatic career had been one of unremitting failure. At the moment of his return he was reeling from the greatest setback of his career—the total fiasco of *The Flaming Angel*, on which he had labored for eight years, but which he had not been able to get produced though he had offered it to opera houses on both sides of the Atlantic. The only hearing Prokofiev had been able to secure for this most central of his works (and, indeed, the only performance of it he was ever to hear himself) had been a concert performance of the second act in Paris under Koussevitzky, who, as the opera's publisher, had a vested interest in its success. *The Gambler*, the work with which the 24-year-old Prokofiev had self-confidently set out to revitalize opera in 1916, waited thirteen years for its first production, and that had taken place neither in Russia nor in Russian, but in Brussels, of all places, in a French translation. There had been no further performances. *Maddalena* languished unperformed in a publisher's warehouse (where, for complicated legal reasons, it continued to languish until 1979).[4] Has an important composer—and one, moreover, who saw opera, above all, as his true vocation—ever had a more frustrating career? It hardly seems that Prokofiev would have needed guns pointed at his head for him to reconsider the stylistic and dramaturgical commitments that had brought him so little success.

And yet, given the pressures both internal and external, the wonder is how little he compromised in his early Soviet years. Throughout his life, in fact, Prokofiev remained true to the operatic ideal of his youth—the through-composed dialogue opera in prose. There was a tradition for this sort of thing in Russia, centering around two radical works of the late 1860's—Dargomyzhsky's *The Stone Guest* and Musorgsky's *Marriage*. These were not so much operas as "sung plays," to borrow Kerman's useful term,[5] that is,

[3]The full text of this editorial (*Sumbur vmesto muzyki*) is reprinted in *Sovetskaia opera: sbornik kritičeskix statei*, ed. M. Grinberg and N. Polyakova (Moscow, 1953), pp. 11–13.

[4]See Rita McAllister, "Prokofiev's Early Opera 'Maddalena,'" *Proceedings of the Royal Musical Association* 96 (1970): 137–48, and idem, "Prokofiev's 'Maddalena,' a Premiere," *The Musical Times*, vol. 120, no. 3 (March 1979): 205–6.

[5]Joseph Kerman, *Opera as Drama* (New York, 1956), ch. 6: "Opera as Sung Play" (the term is there applied primarily to *Pelléas et Mélisande*).

verbatim settings of pre-existent stage dramas, in which the whole idea of *dramma per musica* was scrapped in the interests of realism and "truth," and the problem of the structure of the libretto bypassed. *The Stone Guest* was a setting of one of four so-called "little tragedies" in verse which Pushkin had written in 1830. Musorgsky's *Marriage*, an even bolder break with operatic tradition, was a setting of a laconic prose comedy by Gogol, and deserved, far more than Dargomyzhsky's work, to be designated "recitative opera." In these works, virtually all shaping was done by the text and a few rather skimpily deployed leitmotives, but the musical interest was at all times centered in the voice parts, never the accompaniment.

This rather aberrant manifestation, which Musorgsky christened "*opéra dialogué*," came and went without leaving, it seemed, much of a trace on the development of Russian opera. And then, all at once around the turn of the century, composers everywhere began reopening the questions these strange Russian works had raised. The other three "little tragedies" of Pushkin were set between 1897 and 1903 by Rimsky-Korsakov, Rachmaninoff, and César Cui.[6] Abroad, Émile Zola was furnishing naturalistic prose texts of an unprecedented laconicism to Alfred Bruneau, who as critic, significantly enough, was one of Russian music's most active foreign propagandists.[7] A similar laconicism characterized the libretti of the Italian verismo school (though Italy was never willing to give up verse, however terse). Musorgsky's ideal of approximating the "intonations of the speaking voice" reached a rather doctrinaire apogee in the operas of Janáček and served Schoenberg's expressionistic purposes as well. Nor should we forget that some of the early twentieth century's most influential operas—*Pelléas* and *Salome* come instantly to mind, to say nothing of the somewhat later *Wozzeck*—were "sung plays."

It was in this atmosphere that Prokofiev came of age, and the influence of Musorgsky's *Marriage* on him was especially direct. He witnessed the work's incredibly belated premiere performances in 1909 and at the very same time composed an expressionistic recitative *scena* on the final pages of one of

[6]Nikolai Rimsky-Korsakov, *Mozart and Salieri* (1897); César Cui, *A Feast in Time of Plague* (*Pir vo vremja čumy*, 1901); Sergei Rachmaninov, *The Miserly Knight* (*Skupoj rycar'*, 1903).

[7]The Bruneau-Zola operas were *Messidor* (1897), *L'Ouragan* (1901), and *L'Enfant roi* (1905). *L'Ouragan* was given in Moscow in a Russian translation in 1905. Bruneau's *Musiques de Russie et musiciens de France* (Paris, 1903), heavily indebted to Cui's *La Musique en Russie* (Paris, 1880), reports of Dargomyzhsky's *Stone Guest* that it marks "une date importante dans l'histoire de la musique russe, car la déclamation lyrique y remplaça presque à chaque page l'air, le duo, le choeur, de forme traditionelle et conventionelle. . . . C'est une des partitions les plus nettement 'avancées,'—si l'on tient compte de l'époque à laquelle elle a été écrite,—les plus vigoureusement, les plus notablement pensées que je sache." If he truly knew it, and not just knew of it through Cui's book, this might suggest that Dargomyzhsky's work was not totally without influence outside of Russia. It is very likely that Bruneau did know the work at first hand, since he not only knew many Russian musicians but also made a quasi-official musical tour of Russia on behalf of the French government in 1901–2.

Pushkin's little tragedies, *A Feast in Time of Plague* (already set by Cui).[8] Interviews Prokofiev gave the press shortly after completing *The Gambler* fairly paraphrase the aggressive, militant letters Musorgsky wrote around the time of *Marriage* and the first version of *Boris*—letters which were given an important edition in 1916, the very year of Prokofiev's opera.[9] Along with Musorgsky, Prokofiev called for the complete renunciation of the set piece in favor of freely flowing dialogue, and contemptuously dismissed verse texts as "an utterly absurd convention." Not only was Prokofiev personally committed to the idea of prose recitative opera that made little or no departure from the dramaturgy of the spoken drama, he actually saw in it the only chance of salvation for an art form whose validity was being called into question by such trend-setters as Diaghilev and Stravinsky. But whereas Musorgsky's motivation had been a neo-Aristotelian conviction that mimesis of speech was the key to the portrayal of character and emotion—a conviction that seems to have come in large part through Georg Gervinus and his *Händel und Shakespeare* (1868)[10]—Prokofiev's concerns were more narrowly those of stage-craft, what he called the "scenic flow" in his interviews related to *The Gambler*.[11]

Perhaps because Prokofiev's philosophy of opera was not strongly tied to an overriding philosophy of art but only to considerations of effect, there were important differences in practice between his prose operas and Musorgsky's. These are hinted at in a letter with which Prokofiev's life-long friend and artistic confidant Nikolai Miaskovsky greeted the belated publication (1930) of *The Gambler* in piano-vocal score:

[8]The public premiere of *Marriage* (one act in piano-vocal score, as it was left by the composer) took place at one of the Karatygin-Krizhanovsky "Evenings of Contemporary Music," 19 March (1 April) 1909 (cf. Pavel Lamm's note to the published score of the work [Moscow, 1933]). Prokofiev, who had begun to appear himself on these programs at the end of the previous year (see Israel Nestyev, *Prokofiev*, trans. Florence Jones [Stanford, 1960], p. 34), undoubtedly attended not only the performance but the rehearsals as well. On his scene from *A Feast in Time of Plague*, see Prokofiev's *Autobiography* (Moscow, 1973), p. 575. As a child Profokiev had made a previous setting of the whole play (see his *Autobiography*, pp. 134–47, passim).

[9]M. P. Musorgsky, *Pis'ma k V. V. Stasovu*, ed. N. F. Findeisen (St. Petersburg, 1916). Letters to Rimsky-Korsakov and to the Purgold sisters had appeared in the *Russkaja muzykal'naja gazeta* between 1909 and 1911.

[10]See Musorgsky's autobiographical sketch, in Jan Leyda and Sergei Bertensson, *The Musorgsky Reader* (New York, 1947), p. 420. The matter is pursued in Boris Asafiev, "Muzykal'no-èstetičeskie vozzrenija Musorgskogo," in *M. P. Musorgsky: K piatidesiatiletiju so dnja smerti, 1881–1931. Stat'i i materialy*, ed. Yu. Keldysh (Moscow, 1932), pp. 33–49, and in my own "Handel, Shakespeare and Musorgsky: The Sources and Limits of Russian Musical Realism," in *Music and Language*, Studies in the History of Music 1 (New York, 1983), pp. 247–68.

[11]These interviews are reprinted in *S. S. Prokofiev: Materialy, dokumenty, vospominanija*, ed. S. I. Shlifshtein, 2nd ed. (Moscow, 1961; henceforth abbreviated Prok: MDV), pp. 205–6.

It pleases me extraordinarily—a real solution to the problem of declamational–intonational opera [N.B.: The influence of Soviet critical jargon is evident]. It is the same task as was set by *Marriage* and *The Stone Guest,* only now solved for the first time in a way that gives music its due.[12]

An examination of Prokofiev's operas through *The Flaming Angel,* along with his extended narrative song in prose, *The Ugly Duckling* after Anderson—which was conceived as a kind of operatic trial balloon right before *The Gambler,* and which exhibits all of the operas' salient musical and textual characteristics in a more neatly self-contained form—reveals a concern for declamation that matches Musorgsky's, but which is embodied in a musically far more varied way. At the naturalistic extreme there is a kind of Russian *Sprechgesang* in which rhythm, tempo, and contour are modeled fastidiously on the patterns of conversational speech, with particular care taken with that most endemic of Russian linguistic traits, the tonic accent. In quick spoken Russian, the accent is spaced evenly and creates something approaching a beat, around which unaccented syllables arrange themselves in freely varying *gruppetti.* Lines set in just this way are legion in Musorgsky, common in Prokofiev, and surprisingly rare in the work of other Russian composers. Prokofiev is also given to an inherently more "musical" recitative style that suggests knowledge of and affinity for the somewhat earlier example of *The Stone Guest.* In this style of writing, the text is carried by phrases of equal note values, usually introduced and terminated with one or two notes of greater duration. This method is not at all a naturalistic way of setting Russian speech, but it has obvious antecedents in Italian and particularly in French recitative. At climactic moments, Prokofiev is apt to slow the tempo of the voice part to a patently "singing" pace—something that Musorgsky never permitted in *Marriage,* and Dargomyzhsky only rarely in *The Stone Guest.* At such moments in Prokofiev, regular lyric phrase structure in parallel rhythmic periods often emerges.

The way Prokofiev was able to achieve this lyrical quality without departing either from the prose medium or from scrupulous adherence to correct declamation is perhaps his most original operatic technique, and the one by which he was most conspicuously able (recalling Miaskovsky) to "give music its due." Prokofiev often invents a melodic idea quite independently of his text. This phrase can then act either as a leitmotive or as an abstractly musical "theme." It furnishes a kind of mold into which just about any line of prose can be poured by observing the prosodic habits described above. Example 1 shows how the trick is done in *The Ugly Duckling.* The hypothetical model,

---

[12]Letter of 12 June 1931. Published in S. S. Prokofiev and N. Ya. Miaskovsky, *Perepiska* (Moscow, 1977), p. 357.

Example 1. *The Ugly Duckling*, op. 18 (1914)

V ze- lë- nom u- gol- ke,   sre- di   lo- pu- xov
(In a green nook among the burrs . . .)

Ej   by- lo   skuč- no
(she was bored . . .)

Po- šël u- ti- nyj vy- vo- dok na pti- čij dvor.
(The brood of ducklings went out into the courtyard.)

U- tja- ta niz- ko klan- ja- lis' i- span- skoj ut- ke
(The ducklings bowed low to the Spanish duck.)

Plo- xo   pri- šlos' tol' ko bed- no- mù ne- kra- si- vo (mu utën ku)
(Things went badly only for the poor ugly duckling.)

deduced from a comparison of all the variants, is given above the various rhythmic versions we actually hear in the course of the musical narrative. The most obvious instance of this technique in the early operas is the small part of the Innkeeper in the first act of *The Flaming Angel*. Her two appearances are framed by lines set to the same melodic model, which here acts as an identifying leitmotive (Example 2). The use of such "melodic molds," as we may choose to call them, gives Prokofiev a much greater versatility in his prose settings than Musorgsky enjoyed in *Marriage*. No longer bound to his text as sole shaper of every musical utterance, the composer is free to conceive his music more abstractly and thematically, confident that through his method practically any prose text can be made to fit it.

Attention to purely musical shape is felt on the larger levels of design, too. More sensitive than either Dargomyzhsky or Musorgsky to considerations of musical form—possibly because, unlike them, he was a conservatory graduate—Prokofiev was far more disposed than they to give his vocal compositions an easily comprehended overall shape. The use of melodic molds, for instance, ties *The Ugly Duckling* into a neat ABA package. And sometimes unifying devices do double duty, as much rhetorical as musical, as in the case of a textual refrain set invariably to the same musical idea—one of Prokofiev's

Example 2. *The Flaming Angel*, op. 37 (1919–27), Act 1, sc. 1, the Innkeeper's repliques.

favorite methods.[13] The composer also made considerable use of what may be called the "generalizing accompaniment," which unifies long spans, or returns in thematically significant or recapitulatory ways,[14] as well as of what might be termed the "underlying melody"—that is, a recurrent melody without dramatic associations which accompanies the voice part at formally strategic moments, but is itself never sung.[15]

In sum, then, Prokofiev took as his operatic point of departure what we may call the traditions of Russian operatic radicalism. For all his careful attention to form and proportion, he made sure that not one of his pre-Soviet operas sported so much as a single "closed" vocal number. The only "detachable" music in them, if one may put it so, is orchestral, and in the case of *The Gambler* and *The Flaming Angel*, even that much was detachable only by dint of considerable recasting.[16] Prokofiev sought, and in large part achieved, a

[13]Cf. the setting of the recurring line, "That's because I'm so ugly" (*Čto ot togo, čto ja takoj gadkij*) and its derivatives, in *The Ugly Duckling* (Moscow, 1962), at rehearsal numbers 21, 26, 42, 50.

[14]Cf. *The Ugly Duckling*, rehearsal numbers 1–3, 35–37, 38, 47–49.

[15]Cf. the middle section of *The Ugly Duckling* (rehearsal numbers 26–35).

[16]Music from *The Flaming Angel* was reshaped into the *Third Symphony*, op. 44 (1928). *Four Portraits and the Denouement from "The Gambler,"* op. 49, a symphonic suite put together in 1931, gave the composer trouble. He had to sort the pages of his piano score into piles on the floor corresponding to the four characters whose portraits he was trying to extract from the seamless "scenic flow" of his opera. See Nestyev, *Prokofiev*, p. 237.

truly on-going scenic action, supported by music that asserts perhaps a more conspicuous shaping role than in the works which provided him with his evident models, and yet where—in keeping with just about every Russian composer's anti-Wagnerian credo—at least as much melodic interest is concentrated in the voice part as in the orchestra. The latter is never permitted to preempt the musical content of the opera to the extent that it does in the operas of the Wagner-Strauss school, for this had always been the principal Russian objection to Wagnerian opera. Though leitmotive is employed, as it had been in Dargomyzhsky and Musorgsky, its use is restrained and rather primitive, compared with the Wagnerian prototype, lest it compromise the essential nature of the sung play by turning it—to cite the other member of Kerman's dichotomy—into a "symphonic poem."[17]

II

That Prokofiev did not at first regard his return to the Soviet Union as the stylistic watershed it now appears to be is evident from an essay he wrote describing his first Soviet opera, *Semyon Kotko* (1939), on a subject derived from Valentin Kataev's novella, *I, Son of the Working People*.[18] Despite Prokofiev's oft-quoted lip service to "a new people, new feelings, a new life [requiring] new means of expression," we realize on reading the essay that these new means—new, that is, to Soviet audiences—are in fact Prokofiev's accustomed style. No less than in his cocky *Gambler* interviews, Prokofiev expresses the conviction that operatic action must be dynamic and continuous, that the traditional numbers format prevents this, and that static musical moments on stage are to be avoided at all costs. Recognizing that this prescription was a bit radical for Soviet tastes, and recognizing, too, that Soviet arts policy was increasingly oriented toward the safest elements in the Russian "classical heritage," Prokofiev adopts a sly tactic in promulgating his operatic credo before his new audience: he paraphrases a well-known letter to von Meck in which Chaikovsky acknowledged his operatic failures and admitted that—in Prokofiev's words, now—"when a person goes to an opera he wants not only to *hear* but to *see*."[19] Prokofiev goes on to justify his operatic

---

[17]*Opera as Drama*, ch. 7: "Opera as Symphonic Poem" (on Wagner).

[18]"Semën Kotko," written in 1940 for a projected symposium on the production of the opera by the Stanislavsky Theater; published for the first time in Prok:MDV, pp. 235–38.

[19]Chaikovsky put it this way (27 Nov. [9 Dec.] 1878): "In composing an opera the stage should be the musician's first thought; he must not abuse the confidence of the theatergoer who comes to *see* as well as *hear*" (Modeste Tchaikovsky, *The Life and Letters of Peter Ilich Tchaikovsky*, trans. and ed. Rosa Newmarch [London, 1906], 1:358). Prokofiev's appropriation ignores a fundamental difference in context: Chaikovsky speaks not against the use of "numbers," but against the excessively "symphonic" style he had employed in *The Voyevoda* and in *Vakula the Smith*.

procedures by citing precedents not only from Chaikovsky's writings but from his operas as well. One remembers that 1940, the year in which Prokofiev wrote his essay, was Chaikovsky's centenary, and a kind of official canonization of the nineteenth-century master was taking place in line with the Party's new interest in resurrecting the classical Russian tradition. Prokofiev cites two kinds of aria, both of which can be found in *Eugene Onegin*: the "Lensky type," which paralyzes action, and the type exemplified by Tatiana's Letter Scene, which carries the action along. Prokofiev promises that "my opera will have this second type of aria," and goes on to advertise the fact that "this is, of course, far more difficult, and occasionally I have had to substitute vocal parts which, though not arias in the exact sense, offer no less opportunity to the singer."[20]

One has to admire the way in which Prokofiev, not usually credited with a great deal of musico-political adroitness, managed to describe Russian radical opera in terms of its cardinal antithesis. Prokofiev insisted on prose texts and unbroken action to an extent his librettist Kataev found "terribly pedantic."[21] Kataev had envisioned a musical setting for his novella along the lines of the "song opera," a genre hatched in the 1930s as a kind of answer to Shostakovich's *Lady Macbeth*, and classically represented by Ivan Dzerzhinsky's *Quiet Flows the Don* and Tikhon Khrennikov's *Into the Storm*. (The latter had its premiere the same year as *Semyon Kotko* and in the same theater—a circumstance which led inevitably to invidious comparisons.) The "song opera" took for its basic unit of construction such doggedly accessible forms as strophic couplets and patter songs, and employed them dramaturgically in blatantly "expository" fashion, in keeping with the didactic aims of Socialist Realism. Little wonder, then, that Prokofiev and Kataev did not get along. The composer, for example, considered absurd the librettist's proposal to have a character who happens to be a sailor identify himself as such by dancing the *yablochko* (the famous "Russian Sailor's Dance" familiar to all the world from Glière's *Red Poppy* ballet).[22] The librettist, for his part, was bemused by Prokofiev's penchant for complex, multileveled scenic action, where as many as three scenes are played simultaneously in a frantic effort to avoid stasis.[23]

But there are, in fact, important differences between *Semyon Kotko* and Prokofiev's earlier operas—differences which suggest that Prokofiev did gen-

---

[20] Prok:MDV, pp. 236–37.

[21] Skorino, *Pisatel' i ego vremja*, p. 301. One reason that Prokofiev may have been difficult to work with was that he had written his own librettos for *The Gambler, Love for Three Oranges,* and *The Flaming Angel*.

[22] See Marina Sabinina, *"Semën Kotko" i problemy opernoj dramaturgii Prokof'eva* (Moscow, 1963), p. 83.

[23] Skorino, p. 301.

uinely look to the classical Russian tradition for guidance. I would contend, though, that at this point he did so not directly in response to Soviet pressure, the brunt of which he was yet to feel, but because he was determined not to repeat the staggering failure of *The Flaming Angel*. Most fundamental is a return to certain basic principles of dramaturgy he had formerly eschewed as outmoded. In his 1940 essay, Prokofiev rationalized the choice of Kataev's novella as subject by noting "its many contrasting elements: the love of young people, the hatred of the representatives of the old world, the heroism of struggle, mourning for the dead, the rich humor characteristic of the Ukrainian people."[24] It was probably the Nazi-Soviet pact that caused Prokofiev to omit from his description what is obviously the opera's fundamental contrast: the German invaders with their twisted, dissonant march music, and the open-hearted diatonicism of the positive characters, full of melodic turns appropriated from Russian and Ukrainian folk music. Never before in his operatic career had Prokofiev paid the slightest attention to elements of genre or to national character, and his prior dramaturgical convictions had rejected contrast in favor of a more organic dramatic shape based on a sustained cumulative sweep, what Prokofiev had called in the case of *The Gambler* a "steady dramatic crescendo." The libretti of *Maddalena*, *The Gambler*, and *The Flaming Angel* are all without significant elements of contrast, and this above all had been the undoing of the last-named opera, which starts at much too high a level of dramatic intensity and is virtually lacking in development either of character or of theme. Determined, as I say, not to repeat this blunder, Prokofiev went so far the other way as actually to copy the plot of Glinka's *A Life for the Tsar*—the very fountainhead of the Russian classical tradition in opera. Glinka's work is a paradigm of contrast dramaturgy—the underlying contrast being again expressed in terms of nationalities[25]—and it shares with *Semyon Kotko* the high patriotic theme of defending the motherland against foreign invasion. Prokofiev's opera contains a scene not present in the original novella, in which the Germans intrude upon the hero and heroine's betrothal ceremony, exactly as the Poles interrupt a similar scene in Glinka's opera. The composer even—probably unconsciously—recalled at this moment the swinging *krakowiak* and *polonaise* rhythms Glinka had used in his not overly subtle characterization of the Polish soldiers. The effect in Prokofiev's work is a kind of announcement of kinship with the classical traditions of Russian opera.

Further "classicalizing" modifications in Prokofiev's style include the intro-

---

[24] Prok:MDV, p. 236.

[25] The contrast of Polish and Russian music lay at the very root of Glinka's conception of the opera, by his own oft-quoted declaration; cf. his autobiographical *Zapiski*, in M. I. Glinka, *Literaturnye proizvedenija i perepiska*, 1 (Moscow, 1973): 267.

duction of a limited number of vocal set pieces, the incorporation of elements of genre both in the form of "interpolated" numbers and as a more generalized stylistic influence, and a noticeable effort to "lyricalize" the opera—all, it should be emphasized, within a continuing reliance on through-composed prose declamation as basic dramatic medium and provider of continuity.

The effort to lyricalize was born of Prokofiev's new-found reliance on contrast. In *Semyon Kotko*, levels of lyricism are not only functions of dramatic situation and mood, as had formerly been the case in Prokofiev's operas and in *The Ugly Duckling*, but are now an element of characterization as well. To put it baldly, positive characters sing, villains declaim. Thus, to observe Prokofiev's new lyric style we should look first to the roles of the hero and heroine, to the "kid sister" Frosya, and to the Ukrainian revolutionary partisans. A couple of technical observations will help us to understand this new lyricism. First, canny craftsman that he was, Prokofiev tried to give his music a more lyrical aspect by casting some of the dialogue, which would ordinarily have been set as recitative, as actual rhythmic speech—the kind of thing one indicates with "x's" in place of note-heads. This increased the total range of vocal styles by adding another level at the unmusical end, and by contrast emphasized the lyricism at the opposite extreme without recourse to formal arias. It was therefore possible for Prokofiev to make the somewhat puzzling claim that in *Semyon Kotko* he had "avoided dry [secco?] recitative."[26] In fact, what he did was to take the musical prose of his earlier opera and resolve it, in effect, into two precipitates: one more melodious than before, the other less so. Recitative, as Prokofiev used the term in his essay, was what would have fallen between the two styles. In more common usage, of course, much of what Prokofiev not entirely ingenuously referred to as "aria of the second type" was in fact a variety of recitative—more precisely, "melodic recitative," to borrow a term from the critical vocabulary of César Cui.[27]

The reasons for Prokofiev's modification of approach can be deduced from a paragraph in which the composer attempted to meet an anticipated objection to the "unmelodiousness" of his style:

> Any melody is easy to memorize if its design is familiar. On the other hand, if the design is new the melody will not impress itself on the ear of the listener until he has heard it several times. And more: an opera may have few tunes, but if each tune is repeated several times the listener will

---

[26] Prok:MDV, p. 237.

[27] This was a "kuchkist" catchword, coined initially in connection with *The Stone Guest*. For an especially systematic explication of "melodic recitative," see Cui's 1889 article, "A Few Words on Contemporary Operatic Forms" (*Neskol'ko slov o sovremennyx opernyx formax*), in C. Cui, *Izbrannye stat'i* (Leningrad, 1952), pp. 405–16.

remember them. If there are too many tunes the listener will be unable to absorb them all at the first hearing and is apt to mistake abundance for poverty. . . . Although it would obviously have been more advantageous from the standpoint of immediate success to have filled the opera with melodies of familiar design I preferred to use new material and write new melodies of new design and as many as possible.[28]

These remarks can easily be seen as a protest against the facile folksiness and the constant tune-plugging of the "song operas" of the thirties, a genre it would be safe to assume Prokofiev despised. But there is another dimension here, as well. For when referring to "the listener," Prokofiev cannot have meant only Soviet listeners, who had as yet no opportunity to judge Prokofiev's operatic style. He must also have had in mind the Western listeners who had rejected *The Gambler* and *The Flaming Angel*. And despite the show of defiance, Prokofiev had in fact striven to limit and more fully develop his melodic material in *Semyon Kotko* than he had in his earlier, through-composed operas, where he had truly written "as many melodies as possible," meaning that except for a few leitmotives and melodic molds, practically every line of text took a new melodic phrase. Beginning with *Semyon Kotko* there is an effort to "give music its due" at even the prosiest moments. This aim noticeably influenced the structure of the libretti in the Soviet operas, for now repetitions of words and phrases, as pegs on which to hang repetitions of melodic phrases, were actively sought and exploited as formalizing agents. No longer were such repetitions merely the pretext for ostinati (as in Renata's ravings in *The Flaming Angel* or Lyubochka's ravings, obviously derived from Renata's, in Act 3 of *Semyon Kotko* itself), but rather they offered a way of giving memorable thematic structure to a scene without recourse either to formal aria or to the more obvious device of orchestral melody.

The best example of this can be found in Act 2, sc. 2, of *Semyon Kotko*, the very first scene to have been composed (in March 1939). In the dialogue of Semyon and his bride Sonia, Sonia tries rather coquettishly to cut the encounter short with the teasing phrase, "Well, with that let's say good-bye" (*Nu i s tem dosvidan'ička*), a phrase lifted directly out of Kataev's novella. In the original scene as Kataev wrote it, the line occurs twice—once uttered by Sonia and once by Frosya.[29] In the libretto, Sonia alone sings it, and she sings it no fewer than seven times.[30] Its melodic contour becomes a transitory leitmotive to which a few other lines of text are also set, according to the principle of melodic molds Prokofiev had pioneered in his earlier operas, and it

---

[28] Prok:MDV, p. 237.

[29] Valentin Kataev, *Ja, syn trudovogo naroda* (Moscow, 1937), ch. 13, pp. 58, 62.

[30] See the vocal score (Moscow, 1950), pp. 43–49.

is even occasionally echoed by the orchestra alone. The line shares the characteristic play on the major and minor third which reaches its apotheosis in the love music of Act 3, the so-called "Nocturne"—all in all, a most instructive instance of the limitation and "thematization" of recitative melody in the interests of overall unity and memorability. Example 3 shows the relationship of the line to others which share its major-minor motive.

Example 3. *Semyon Kotko*, op. 81 (1939).
   a. Act 1, sc. 2.

   b. Act 3, sc. 1, "Nocturne."

The use of folk genre in the opera requires comment by reason of its novelty in Prokofiev's operatic style. The only instance of actual quoted folk melody occurs in Frosya's song (also in the second scene of Act 1), the middle section of which is based on a Ukrainian melody that had already served Chaikovsky for Vakula's third-act aria in *Cherevichki*. Unlike Chaikovsky's, Prokofiev's use of the tune does not violate the tenets of "realism." Frosya, left alone on stage, actually sings herself the folk song in the course of the action. She does not express her own personal feelings "to" the melody the way Chaikovsky's character does, in a manner that already offended the nineteenth-century "kuchkists." But while Prokofiev's positive characters never sing their dialogue to folk melodies, their musical speech does contain melodic elements ("intonations," as Soviet critics would call them) abstracted from the general style of folk music. An example obvious enough not to require documentation comes from the Act 1 love duet (see Example 4). The cadential formula 5-4-1 is familiar from world-famous Russian melodies found in compositions ranging from *L'Histoire du soldat* to Soloviév-Sedoi's "Moscow Nights."

Prokofiev made no attempt to set to their authentic melodies the wedding song texts which Kataev had incorporated into his novella (much as Ostrovsky often worked similar material into his plays). Characteristically, Prokofiev preferred to invent his own tunes. In the second act these choral wedding songs form the background against which the betrothal scene is played—a

Example 4. *Semyon Kotko*, Act 1, sc. 2.

(I simply cannot let you go. —Don't worry, I'll be back for good.)

device with roots in Russian opera going all the way back to the eighteenth century. But when one of the wedding choruses is reprised at the opera's finale, sung to a new text rejoicing in the dawn of Soviet power, we cross the boundary into specifically Soviet esthetic terrain, as we do when a chorus accompanying the burial of a revolutionary martyr is sung to a theme that had been heard previously as one of the hero Semyon's leitmotives. To use Semyon's theme as the basis of a general expression of faith in the revolution is to tie the individual to the collective in a way that has obvious connections with the tenets of Socialist Realism and with the dramaturgy of the song opera. But such devices had been specifically opposed by the operatic radicals of the nineteenth century on the grounds that they excessively generalized the portrayal of character.

Despite these touches and others like them, Valentin Kataev predicted the failure of Prokofiev's opera drawn from his novella. He was right. A controversy, largely devoted to the fruitless sacrifice of Prokofiev's opera on the altar of Khrennikov's *Into the Storm*, or the other way around, raged for half a year in the Soviet musical press. But the verdict stood for decades. Here it is in the words of Israel Nestyev, whose biography of Prokofiev has been somewhat tarnished by the passage of time, particularly as regards once controversial works over which the pendulum of official opinion has swung since the late 1950s:

> The theme of heroism is poorly realized in the opera. The portrayal of the hero, Semyon Kotko, is kept too strictly within the bounds of everyday life; his ideological growth, his transformation into a conscious fighter for the Revolution, is reflected neither in the action nor in the music of the opera. The Bolsheviks Remenyuk and Tsarëv also lack heroic stature. There are no musical themes which expess the selfless struggle for Soviet power. Particularly disappointing in this respect is the finale, with its idyllic song, which in no way expresses the pathos of the Civil War.[31]

[31] Nestyev, *Prokofiev*, p. 318.

Prokofiev, in short, had made the common mistake of confusing Socialist Realism with realism. As a matter of fact, Nestyev's remarks are inaccurate. What else could have been the purpose of the patently interpolated scene of Tsarëv's funeral with its chorus in folk style to the words of the famous poem (*Zapoved'*) by the nineteenth-century Ukrainian poet Shevchenko? This monumental affair is immediately felt to be, its pre-revolutionary words notwithstanding, the opera's most authentically "Soviet" moment. And why else did Prokofiev quote Semyon's leitmotive precisely here (as we have already observed), if not to reflect "his transformation into a conscious fighter for the Revolution"?

But it is senseless, after all, to try to rebut a dogmatic position. During the forties, not only Prokofiev's stock, but that of his operatic forebears, plummeted precipitously. Yuri Keldysh's 1948 *History of Russian Music* emphasizes, in its treatment of *The Stone Guest*, "the stamp [it bears] of a somewhat hermetic and *raffiné* intellectualism,"[32] and underscores, to the point where it emerges as a kind of warning, that the work—and works like it—can never achieve popularity. Tolerable in a remote historical personage like Dargomyzhsky, hermetic intellectualism was, in the Soviet Union just before the war (and even more just after it), grounds for suspicion, to say the least.

III

Before turning to Prokofiev's response to this latest operatic failure, it might be well to recall briefly the way in which Musorgsky, Prokofiev's most kindred operatic spirit and his adopted mentor, had dealt with an esthetic cul-de-sac of his own. One of the enigmas of Musorgsky's career has always been the stylistic retrenchment he seems to have made around the time of his revisions of *Boris Godunov*. It is difficult indeed to explain why Musorgsky went so much further in reshaping his masterpiece than anything that much maligned body, the Imperial Theaters Directorate, had demanded of him. The new-old direction initiated by the second version of *Boris*, moreover, was confirmed and carried much further in the two unfinished operas that ensued. Without presuming to give here in passing a definitive answer to this substantial and complex question,[33] I would like to draw attention briefly to two documents. The first is a letter from Musorgsky to Rimsky-Korsakov written right after a private run-through of some scenes from the first version of *Boris* at Stasov's summer estate. There, a rather bemused Musorgsky found that

---

[32] Yuri Keldysh, *Istoria Russkoj muzyki* (Moscow, 1948), 1:465–66.

[33] For an attempt to do so, see my "Musorgsky vs. Musorgsky: The Versions of *Boris Godunov*," *19th Century Music*, vol. 8, no. 2 (Fall 1984): 91–118, and no. 3 (Spring 1985): 245–72.

some of his audience thought his peasants *"bouffe,"* as he put it, while "others saw tragedy."[34] The other document is a passage in the memoirs of Musorgsky's literary collaborator Arsenii Golenishchev-Kutusov, who recalled Musorgsky on his deathbed confiding his wish to "get away from all this *prose*, which . . . doesn't give one a chance to breathe."[35] It would seem that Musorgsky felt the need, toward the end of his career, to "give music its due" to a greater extent than prose would let him. The letter to Rimsky-Korsakov certainly suggests a stylistic crisis in the making: Musorgsky, perceiving that in the eyes—or rather, ears—of his audience prose recitative was ineluctably bound up with comedy, its traditional vehicle, begins to rethink his whole operatic technique with an eye toward elevating its tone to the level of true tragedy. This would help account for the kinds of changes he made in the second version of *Boris*—changes which involved the elimination of some of the crowd music and the unwonted introduction of a rather formal aria into the title role. A wish to elevate the tone of his work may also have prompted Musorgsky's puzzling decision to interpolate such a wealth of often trivial genre numbers—particularly into the second act, which also contains Boris' aria—that, ironically enough, at least one of them is almost invariably cut in performance. By making more decisive the contrast between what is *bouffe* and what is tragic, these genre interpolations helped define and focus the latter.

Prokofiev faced a similar dilemma and made a similar response. The criticisms levelled most consistently against his operas by Soviet critics and officials had mainly to do with tone—with Prokofiev's failure, due to his commitment to prose and to through-composed techniques of construction, to attain the tragic, heroically exalted tone his subjects, particularly his Soviet subjects, demanded. And some of the ways Prokofiev came to terms with his critics were very much like Musorgsky's ways: (1) the strengthening of the lyric element, both by permitting closed and detachable vocal numbers and further "musicalizing" his prose declamation, along lines—it should be emphasized—already implicit in his earlier work; (2) the incorporation, sometimes amounting to out-and-out interpolation, of genre elements he had formerly shunned; (3) the strengthening of the role of leitmotive and reminiscence to the point where they could assert their traditional form-governing properties. And in addition Prokofiev sought ways of strengthening the ties between his operas and those of the "classical," rather than the "radical," Russian operatic tradition. We have seen that all of these aspects are already present in *Semyon Kotko*. They continued, now definitely under Soviet

[34] 23 July (4 August) 1870. See Modest Musorgsky, *Literaturnoe nasledie*, 1 (Moscow, 1971): 117; also *The Musorgsky Reader*, p. 148.

[35] *The Musorgsky Reader*, p. 412.

pressure, to increase in prominence. Prokofiev's next opera, *The Duenna*, or *Betrothal in a Monastery*, after Sheridan, is usually looked upon as a kind of refuge in comedy—that is, a retreat to a dramatic medium for which Prokofiev's methods are unquestionably suitable, and in which there could be no requirement for heroism. This would certainly accord with our thesis about tone. But even in the case of *The Duenna*, there is evidence that Prokofiev consciously "Sovietized" his style. Although it is little remarked, little documented, and all but uninvestigated in the secondary literature, the work underwent a thorough revision in 1943 that produced what amounted to a second version, after the cancellation of its announced premiere in 1941. A single laconic sentence in a statement Prokofiev made shortly before embarking on the revisions indicates that the composer felt it necessary to enhance the melodic content of the opera's recitatives.[36] In a textual note at the end of the published vocal score, the editor, Evgenii Ratzer, specifies the extent of the revisions, which was indeed considerable.[37] There is obviously a story here that needs telling, and we need also an explanation of the original postponement. The reason usually given (the "outbreak of the war") is in itself insufficient, and we should recall that during the course of that same 1941 season the controversial *Semyon Kotko* was dropped from the repertoire under fire. In the absence of details, we will limit ourselves here to noting the huge esthetic gulf that separates *The Duenna* from Prokofiev's other comic opera, *Love for Three Oranges*. The earlier opera is pure farce, and virtually limited in its vocal style and forms to prose recitative in the composer's earlier manner. The later work is a lyrical romantic comedy, with a heavy reliance on rounded vocal numbers—albeit mainly of minuscule proportions in the manner of *Gianni Schicchi*, a work that had an indubitable influence on *The Duenna*—and an equal reliance on the device of reminiscence. Either opera could have been handled in either way; the differences cannot be attributed to the respective literary sources.

Fortunately, we are in possession of copious documentation for the creative history of Prokofiev's next opera, *War and Peace*,[38] so we may point with

---

[36] "The premiere of *Betrothal in a Monastery* was to have taken place in 1941, but the war prevented the production from opening. Since then two years have gone by and, leafing through the opera after this interval, I saw a whole series of places in it in a new light, and likewise found that several recitatives could be made more melodious." (Prok:MDV, p. 243.)

[37] "In all, more than a dozen places were redone, including several parts of scenes 1, 4, 5, and 7 that were rewritten entirely. Of the vocal parts, that of Don Jerome underwent the most substantial change." (S. Prokofiev, *Betrothal in a Monastery* [Moscow, 1964], editorial note on p. 361.) According to Mira Mendelson's memoirs, Don Jerome's part was at first written tiringly high for the singer, in the interests of giving the character a grotesque, "shrieking" characterization. (Prok:MDV, p. 381.)

[38] Much of this is excellently summarized in Malcolm H. Brown, "Prokofiev's *War and Peace*: A Chronicle," *The Musical Quarterly* 63, no. 3 (July 1977): 297–326. To Brown's sources should be added the recent study by A. Volkov, "*Vojna i mir*" *Prokof'eva: Opyt analyza variantov opery* (Moscow, 1976).

some certainty to striking parallels between this third of Prokofiev's Soviet operas and *Boris Godunov*—parallels which are indeed instructive in the light of our brief discussion above of Musorgsky's opera. Of particular interest is the recasting of the role of General Kutuzov in the second half of the opera, the Scenes of War. A glance at the creative history of his two arias (scene 8, before the battle of Borodino; scene 10, war council at Fili) will further illuminate the role of genre and of classical precedents in the transformation of Prokofiev's operatic style, along with some further stages in the process of imbuing his prose recitative with elements of traditional operatic lyricism.

The aria on the battlefield, originally a tiny arioso, was augmented around the beginning of 1945 with a second part in classical ternary form, the outer sections of which were based on Prokofiev's arrangement (unpublished until 1967) of a Russian lyrical folk song (*protiažnaia*) called "The Green Jug" (*Zelënaia kuvšina*). At first intended for the cycle of folksong arrangements published as op. 104, a cycle on which Prokofiev was to draw extensively for *The Story of a Real Man*, "The Green Jug" was not published with the rest, for it was, in the composer's opinion, not entirely appropriate to the original words, and the folklorist Evgenii Gippius, who had provided Prokofiev with the song, disapproved of the composer's proposal to substitute a contrafact text.[39] There was nothing, however, to prevent a contrafacture of a more radical kind, and the mood of the setting, if not the original song itself, seemed to express well the special combination of resolution, faith, and tranquillity that characterizes Kutuzov on the battlefield. In the opera, the original folk melody sounds forth in the trumpets, while Kutuzov follows its basic contour with a typical Prokofiev prose arioso of the period. While based in principle on the "melodic mold" technique, it embodies what for Prokofiev was a new kind of vocal lyricism, motivated perhaps in part by Miaskovsky's not altogether favorable reaction to the first draft of *War and Peace*. Reversing his former opinion, Prokofiev's closest friend now objected, in a letter to a third party, to the way the singers were made to "*speak*" against a background of marvelous music in the orchestra."[40] As if in answer to this kind of criticism, Prokofiev repeatedly teases the vocal line up to its highest register on unaccented syllables, in startling contrast to his former regard for the niceties of declamation, and most unnaturally of all, the highest note is reached in the midst of a short melisma—the kind of decorative touch one will seek in vain in any prior Prokofiev opera, Soviet or otherwise, save where the intention was clearly satiric. (See Example 5.)

[39] See V. Blok, "Neopublikovannye rukopisi Prokof'eva," *Sovetskaja muyzka* 31, no. 4 (April 1967): 94.

[40] To Vladimir Derzhanovsky, 21 February 1942. Cited after Brown, "A Chronicle," p. 302.

Example 5. *War and Peace*, op. 91 (1941–52), sc. 8, Kutuzov's aria (1945).

(The iron breast fears no storm; nor does it quail at the enemy's numberless hordes.)

Kutuzov's second aria, the famous hymn to Moscow, later reprised to form the opera's grand choral finale, was the most rewritten single item in the entire opera. The original conception, once again, was a short arioso linked to the scene 8 arioso (in *its* original conception) by shared leitmotivic material. It was conductor Samuel Samosud who goaded Prokofiev into expanding Kutusov's big moment into a full-fledged aria, one of the opera's central moments. For this aria, too, Prokofiev adapted a melody he had originally composed in an altogether different context, the film music for Sergei Eisenstein's *Ivan the Terrible*.[41] Samosud put his request to Prokofiev in the form of a comparison with the big arias of Ivan Susanin and of Prince Igor in the operas named for them. But what is almost uncanny is the way Prokofiev's solution to the problem recapitulated Musorgsky's process of revising Boris Godunov's Act 2 monologue, "I have attained the highest power." In both instances declamation over a texture of leitmotives was replaced by lyrical melody borrowed from a previously composed work (in Musorgsky's case from the unfinished opera *Salammbô*), and for the identical purpose: exaltation of tone and monumentalization of form.[42]

[41] I.e., the *Veličaln'aja* (chorus of celebration), *Kak na gorocke dubčiki stojat* ("The young oaks are standing on the hill").

[42] The two versions of Boris' monologue may be conveniently compared in the Oxford full score, edited by David Lloyd-Jones: Modest Musorgsky, *Boris Godunov* (London, 1975), 1:365–74 (1874 version); 2:976–78 (1869 version). The relevant passage of *Salammbô* is from the High Priest's part in the temple scene (Act 3, sc. 1, which also provided material for the close of the scene of Boris' death in the later opera). See M. P. Musorgsky, *Polnoe sobranie sočinenij*, ed. P. Lamm, 19 (Moscow, 1939): 108–9.

IV

The final stage of all these processes may be observed in *The Story of a Real Man*. This is the opera Prokofiev was working on at the time of the Communist Party's infamous Resolution on Music of 10 February 1948. Prokofiev wrote a widely publicized letter of response to the Central Committee in which, besides a certain amount of pro-forma recantation, he voiced with surprising courage the gist of the operatic credo he had formulated in connection with *Semyon Kotko* some eight years before. In fact it is evident that he had dusted off his old essay of 1940, which had not been published at the time, and paraphrased whole sections of it in those parts of his letter which touched on opera. About the work in progress he furnished little in the way of specific information beyond a somewhat hedged pledge that there would be "lucid melody, and as far as possible, a simple harmonic language," some "contrapuntally developed choruses" on Northern Russian folk songs, and new—for him—emphasis on ensembles, the worst of all operatic *bêtes noires* for adherents of the radical operatic realism of the nineteenth century and the early twentieth.[43]

In the event, *The Story of a Real Man* does give some evidence of a wish to placate, for it is in many ways a very faithful musical reflection of the Socialist Realist principles so notably embodied in the Boris Polevoi novel which furnished the composer and Mira Mendelson, his co-librettist and second wife, with their subject. The opera is a good example, to begin with, of the special Soviet brand of "conflictless" dramaturgy which was felt at the time to be the most suitable for the treatment of Soviet themes—the theory being that in Soviet classless society there were no conflicts, and so traditional conflict dramaturgy could not reflect Soviet reality. Accordingly, in Prokofiev's opera there are no negative characters for all that it is a war story, and the only struggle is the one waged by the wounded hero against his own despair. Then, too, a basic tenet of Socialist Realism is that art be optimistic ("life-affirming," in standard Soviet critical jargon), and so this opera about the agony of a legless aviator opens with the jolly music of Prokofiev's March for Wind Band, op. 99. Besides the March, no fewer than nine Prokofiev compositions of the 1930s and '40s—most of them examples of that most quintessentially Soviet of all musical genres, the *massovaia pesnja* ("mass song")[44]—along with a

---

[43] Prokofiev's letter is given in English translation in Nicolas Slonimsky, *Music Since 1900*, 4th ed. (New York, 1971), pp. 1373–74. It was originally published in *Sovetskaia muzyka*, 1948, no. 1, pp. 66–67.

[44] These are: *Anjutka*, op. 66/2 (1935; in 1936 awarded second prize in a mass-song contest organized by *Pravda*); *Pesnja o rodine* (Song of the Fatherland), op. 79/2 (1939); *Podruga bojca* (The Soldier's Girl) and *Ljubov' vojna* (Love Is War), op. 85/5, 7 (1942–42); *Zelënaja roščica* (The Green Grove), *Son* (A Dream), and *Sašenka*, all from op. 104 (1941); *Two Duets* for tenor and baritone, op. 106 (1945). For details on these pieces and the use to which Prokofiev put them, see S. Shlifshtein, *S. S. Prokof'ev:*

couple of previously published folk song arrangements and such other representatives of contemporary Soviet reality as a waltz and a rhumba, are
embedded in Prokofiev's opera, in most cases as patently, sometimes clumsily,
"interpolated" numbers, virtually unchanged. This raises the obvious and
tantalizing question: at what point was all of this Soviet genre music injected?
The hunch is inescapable that it was only after the Party Resolution that the
grafting took place, and that the version of the opera currently staged by the
Bolshoi, in which, among other changes and cuts, the overture is suppressed,
may in fact be closer to the original conception than the published score.
Confirmation of this hypothesis, of course, can only follow from an investigation of the source material now housed in the Central State Archives of
Literature and Art (*TsGALI*) in Moscow.

Some of the Soviet genre is incorporated into *The Story of a Real Man* in a
more subtle and sophisticated way, and at a profounder level of the drama.
Here we may observe a more genuine, and perhaps more sincere, response to
the demands of Socialist Realism. One of Prokofiev's mass songs of the 1940s,
"The Song of the Fatherland" (*Pesnja o rodine*), op. 79/1, runs through the
opera as a motto (sung to a new set of allegorical words about an oak tree that
weathered a storm) and also furnishes a leitmotive which is made to bear the
weight of the drama's turning point. As in the funeral scene of *Semyon Kotko*,
the fate of the individual is tied to the collective through the personalized use
of genre motifs.

The "story of a real man" is based on a novel which in turn was based on the
true story of a flyer shot down in the early days of World War II. He loses both
his legs but lives to fly again. In most respects Alexei Meresyov, the flyer, is a
typical "positive hero" of Soviet literature. But the relatively relaxed conditions of cultural policy during the war are reflected in the early stages of the
story, where the wounded man is portrayed in the throes of an understandable, if rather un-Soviet, despondency. He is brought round in the second act
by an old commissar he meets in the hospital. The commissar shows Alexei a
clipping about a Russian aviator of World War I who triumphed over a similar
handicap. When Alexei complains that his condition is worse than the other's,
the commissar imperturbably reminds him that he, after all, is a Soviet man,
and answers Alexei's protests by repeating this phrase like a hypnotic litany;
each repetition is sung to the theme of the "Song of the Fatherland," and each
is transposed a half step higher than the last. Finally, the commissar is wheeled

---

Notografičeskij spravočnik (Moscow, 1962), pp. 66–109, passim. A consideration of mass songs, that is,
songs for mass distribution and unison singing by organized amateur choruses (such as are published in
every issue of the mass-distribution Soviet music magazines), and their role in Prokofiev's operatic style
may be found in chapter 2 of M. Sabinina, *"Semën Kotko"* (see note 22 above).

out, but Alexei, left alone to reflect, takes up the refrain, and pushes it up yet another two half steps. The curtain falls on a new man.

In Example 6, the "Song of the Fatherland" is given first in its choral "motto" form, and then as it is used in the "conversion" scene. Alexei's protests are set in Prokofiev's older manner, with careful attention to the contour and rhythm of natural speech. The commissar's motto-derived refrain, however, obeys a "higher" reality, much as Socialist Realism was supposed to reveal a higher truth than what Soviet critics call naturalism. Judged by Musorgskian standards of declamation, the commissar's utterances reveal all the earmarks of clumsy contrafacture. The line, "After all, you are a Soviet man," would be given one single heavy accent, thus: *"A ved' ty že soVETskij čelovek!"* Its more emphatic repetitions would show an even more pronounced headlong dash to what Russian linguists call the "intonational center." But Prokofiev takes no steps to prevent the particle *"a"* and the conjunction *"no"* from falling on long notes, and on the downbeat at that. It would be easy to hypothesize the adjustments Prokofiev might have made in the prosody, according to the principles of melodic molds he had long since developed, and these, too, are given in the example.

Example 6. *The Story of a Real Man*, op. 117 (1947–48).
   a. Motto.

Vy- ros v Plav-njax du-bok mo- lo-   doj,   krep-kij du- bok ku- drja - vyj.

(In Plavny there grew a young oak, a strong, leafy young oak.)

   b. Act 2, sc. 6 (Alexei and the Commissar).

Example 6b, continued

vet- skij če- lo- vek. On le- tal na Far-ma-ne. Raz- ve è- to sa-mo- lët? Pro-sto è- ta-

žer- ka   No ved' ty že so- vet- skij če- lo-

Na něm če- go by ne le- tat'? ni by- stro- ty, ni lov-ko-sti ne

vek.   Od-

na- do.

na- ko ty vsë že so- vet- skij če- lo- vek!

(—Have you read it? Well, what do you say?)
—He only lost one leg.
—Only one . . . But then, you're a Soviet man.
—He flew a Farman. You call that an airplane? It's just a glider.
—But after all, you're a Soviet man.
—Anyone could fly it. You don't need speed, you don't need reflexes . . .
—But still, you're a Soviet man.)

c. Hypothetical "correction" of Commissar's declamation.

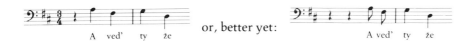

A ved' ty že   or, better yet: A ved' ty že

Removing the unaccented first syllable from the downbeat only minimally distorts the motto melody, and so the fact the Prokofiev chose *not* to take this simple step in the interest of declamation is a fair measure of what we may accordingly recognize to have been a genuine, rather than a forced, modification of his esthetic convictions. Here, too, we can find instructive analogues in Musorgsky, without benefit of Soviet esthetic dogma, in the folksong recitatives of *The Fair at Sorochintsy*. And before Musorgsky, Alexander Serov had tried to make urban folk song the bearer of drama at all levels from recitative through grand ensemble in his posthumously produced *Vrazhya sila* ("The Power of the Fiend"), a work given an epochal revival at the Bolshoi (in a revision by Asafiev) in 1947, the very year Prokofiev started work on *The Story of a Real Man*. Recalling the early critiques of Glinka's *A Life for the Tsar*, which saw the composer's highest achievement as consisting in "raising folk song to the level of tragedy," and expanding the concept of folk song to include all musical artifacts appropriated from the environment, we might suggest that Prokofiev tried through folk song to raise the tone of his work to a dramatic level comparable to that of the Russian classical tradition.

To regard *The Story of a Real Man* as nothing more than a concession to the rigors of totalitarian discipline and to the musical blatancy of the song opera would be a mistake, then. What is also often overlooked is the fact that of all Prokofiev's Soviet-period operas, this one is the only one which is truly innovative from the dramaturgical point of view. New ground is broken—it has since become, alas, a densely populated terrain in Soviet opera[45]—in adapting cinematic techniques to operatic purposes. These, of course, were techniques Prokofiev had ample opportunity to observe in his famous collaborations with Eisenstein and other Soviet film makers. The methods of flashback and montage are employed in *The Story of a Real Man* so as to permit characters present only in the hero's imagination—particularly his waiting bride, Olga—to appear on stage and even to sing. And what could be more appropriate—even necessary—in an opera wholly concerned with an internal struggle, in which the title character never leaves the stage? In the second scene of the opera, Alexei, crawling through a forest on his belly, takes out and gazes upon a photograph of his beloved. Olga then appears to the audience "as she appears in the photograph" and sings the first of the opera's interpolated songs—a diminutive ternary number in which she recalls their happy meetings in the past. The opening of Act 2 shows Alexei in the hospital,

---

[45]See, for example, my review of Kirill Molchanov's *The Dawns Are Quiet Here*, in "Current Chronicle," *The Musical Quarterly* 52, no. 1 (January, 1976): 105–15. For an interesting discussion of Prokofiev's dramaturgical innovations in *The Story of a Real Man*, see L. Aleksandrovsky, "Muzykal'naja dramaturgija opery S. Prokof'eva 'Povest' o nastojaščem čeloveke'," in *Iz istorii russkoj i sovetskoj muzyki*, ed. A. Kandinsky (Moscow, 1971), pp. 189–206.

delirious after his operation. The operation itself and consultations with the surgeons appear to him in flashbacks, as does Alexei's mother, along with Olga (who sings the same tune as in the preceding act), and Alexei's best friend, another flyer. The whole is "montaged" into one of the most strangely motivated yet convincing ensembles in all of opera.

In conclusion, a note of caution may be in order. In dealing with Prokofiev's Soviet period it is easy to fall into an accusing tone, to speak of coercion and capitulation. But most of the modifications Prokofiev's Soviet style displays are implicit in his earlier work, and ultimately it is possible to recognize the underlying continuity that links all phases of Prokofiev's career. It is possible, too, especially when contemplating a masterpiece like *War and Peace*, to see the modifications as introducing a new versatility into Prokofiev's operatic technique and therefore as constituting a legitimate enrichment of what had been a rather one-sided approach to musical drama. When we read in Mira Mendelson's reminiscences that it was precisely the scene of Andrei Bolkonsky's death—the present scene 12 of Prokofiev's *War and Peace*—that first suggested musical possibilities in Tolstoy's novel to the composer,[46] we have a fair measure of how far he had come from the days of his brash youth, when opera was to be seen only in terms of an irrepressible forward momentum with no time either to look back or to stand still. For this scene is a veritable object lesson in the use of reminiscence, a device the young Prokofiev had scorned. It would seem that Prokofiev discovered—as Musorgsky had discovered before him—that there are dramatic possibilities afforded by music which the spoken drama cannot match, and that herein lies the special virtue, indeed the *raison d'être*, of opera.

[46]M. Mendelson-Prokofieva, "O Sergee Sergeeviče Prokof'eve," Prok:MDV, p. 388.